WOMAN WAR CHIEF

The story of a Crow Warrior

by

Jerry A. Matney

with D. A. Gordon

ISBN: 1-4033-7846-0 (e-book)
ISBN: 1-4033-7847-9 (Paperback)
ISBN: 1-4033-7848-7 (Hardcover)

Library of Congress Control Number: 2002094651

This book is printed on acid free paper.

Printed in the United States of America
Bloomington, IN

Cover and Section illustrations
by Brent Naughton

1stBooks - rev. 12/30/02

Dedicated to my paternal great grandmother,
Sara Jane Stillwell Matney,
who was a member of the Cherokee tribe in
Haywood County, North Carolina

To my childhood pal,
John White. We
played some great
football against each
other and had some
great Saturday nights in
old Bridgeport.
Love always,
Jerry Matney

Woman Chief   Location Map 1

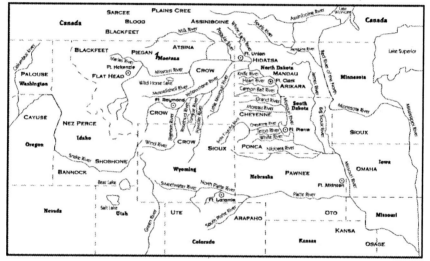

Fort Sites
State Names
NATIVE AMERICAN TRIBES
River/Lake Names
········ *State Borders*
~~~~~ *Rivers*

v

Woman Chief

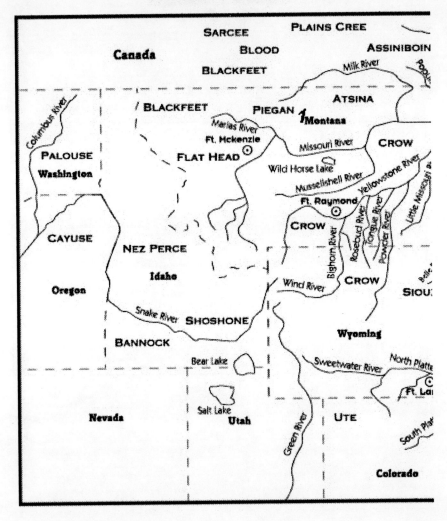

Location Map 1

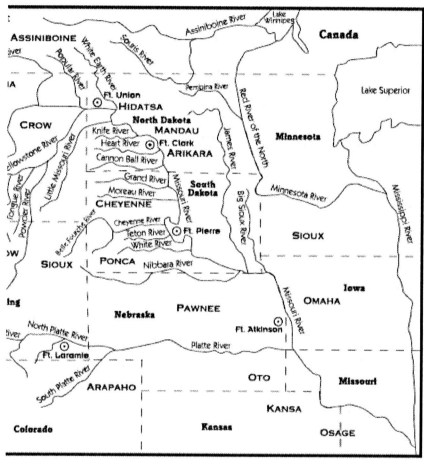

Assiniboine River
Lake Winnipeg
Canada

ASSINIBOINE
White Earth River
Souris River
Popular River
Pembina River
Red River of the North
Lake Superior

Ft. Union
HIDATSA

CROW
North Dakota
MANDAU
Knife River
Heart River · Ft. Clark
ARIKARA
Cannon Ball River

Yellowstone River
Little Missouri River
James River
Minnesota

Grand River
South Dakota
Missouri River
Minnesota River

Tongue River
Powder River
Moreau River
CHEYENNE
Big Sioux River

Belle Fourche River
Cheyenne River
Teton River · Ft. Pierre
White River
SIOUX

OW
SIOUX
PONCA
Niobara River

ng
North Platte River
PAWNEE
Nebraska
Ft. Atkinson
Missouri River
OMAHA
Iowa

iver
Ft. Laramie
Platte River

South Platte River
ARAPAHO
OTO
Missouri

Colorado
Kansas
KANSA
OSAGE

Fort Sites
State Names
NATIVE AMERICAN TRIBES
River/Lake Names
— · — *State Borders*
〜〜〜 Rivers

Woman Chief   Location Map 2

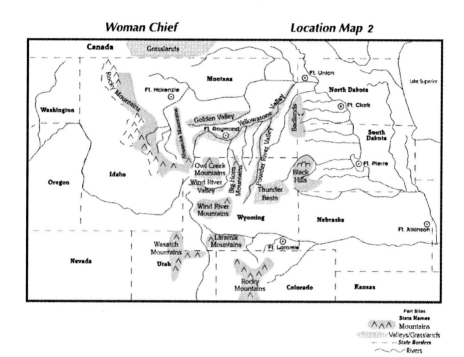

Canada

Grasslands

Lake Superior

Rocky Mountains

Montana

Ft. McKenzie

Ft. Union

North Dakota

Ft. Clark

Washington

Golden Valley

Yellowstone Valley

Ft. Raymond

Badlands

South Dakota

Powder River Valley

Oregon

Idaho

Owl Creek Mountains

Wind River Valley

Big Horn Mountains

Black Hills

Ft. Pierre

Thunder Basin

Wind River Mountains

Wyoming

Nebraska

Ft. Atkinson

Laramie Mountains

Wasatch Mountains

Ft. Laramie

Nevada

Utah

Rocky Mountains

Colorado

Kansas

Fort Sites
State Names
∧∧∧ Mountains
Valleys/Grasslands
------ State Borders
Rivers

Woman Chief

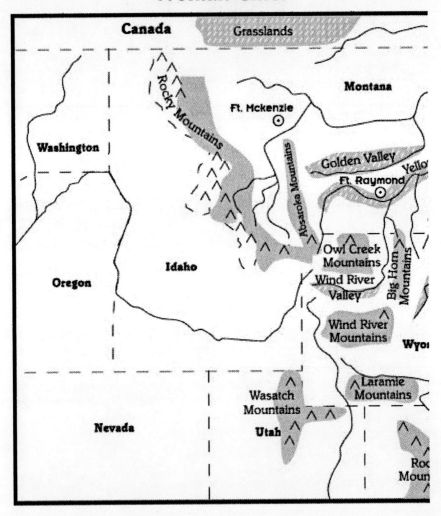

Location Map 2

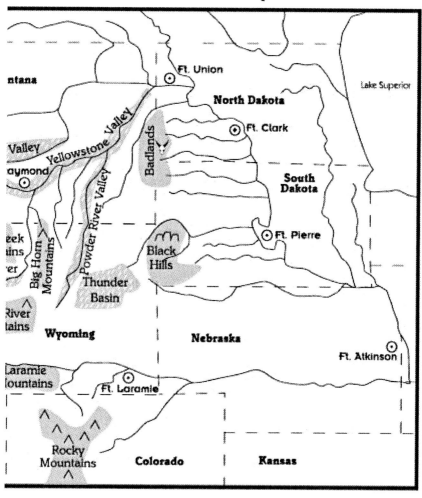

Ft. Union

North Dakota

Lake Superior

ntana

Valley

Ft. Clark

Yellowstone Valley

aymond

Badlands

South
Dakota

eek
ains
er

Big Horn Mountains

Powder River Valley

Ft. Pierre

Black
Hills

River
tains

Thunder
Basin

Wyoming

Nebraska

Ft. Atkinson

Laramie
ountains

Ft. Laramie

Rocky
Mountains

Colorado

Kansas

Fort Sites
State Names
Mountains
Valleys/Grasslands
State Borders
Rivers

ACKNOWLEDGMENTS

A big thanks to Thomas E. Mails for the encouragement and enthusiasm he shared with me regarding this project. Thank you Tom for the use of your great books on the Crow culture, including *The Mystic Warriors of the Plains*, *Dog Soldiers: Bear Men and Buffalo Women*, and *Fools Crow*.

Thank you to Nedra Matney and Bob Ridges for carefully reading the manuscript and offering thoughtful suggestions and editorial comments.

SECTION I

1805 - 1810

Jerry A. Matney with D. A. Gordon

CHAPTER 1

Shining Sun dipped the large gourd into the cool, sparkling water of the Milk River. Although the year was unknown to the small girl, it was the summer of the white man's year of 1805, a day clear and warm. Shining Sun had only seen five winters, and like most children her age, she became easily absorbed in everything about her. As the cool water washed into her container, she watched kingfishers diving in and out of the river, then glanced at the ravens cackling from their lofty perches.

When the girl pulled the dripping vessel out of the water, she smiled at the nervous, red-winged blackbirds flitting between thin reeds. Today was a good day; today she had finally gotten big enough to help her mother. With both arms, she hugged the full gourd against her short, chubby body and started back to the village. The youngster was only one of three thousand souls who made up the Indian tribe called the Atsina or White Clay People.

She walked up the well-worn path, bringing home the precious water as her ancestors had done before her. When she sighted her father standing before their lodge, she walked proudly to impress him at doing a woman's chore.

Like many young girls, Shining Sun worshipped her father—a strong warrior with a square jaw, sharp nose and high cheekbones—he was tall, handsome and proud.

As Shining Sun struggled up the path, White Flower came to take the gourd, praising her daughter's contribution; keeping a warrior's lodge could be an arduous task. Badger's chest warmed as he watched his wife hug their daughter—life had been good to him.

Badger's smile faded when he heard a scream. Thundering hooves and whooping war cries invaded the peace of the village. Yelling and shouting came from every direction. Dust rose from running feet and falling bodies as Badger dashed towards his lodge for his war weapons. To White Flower he yelled, "Take Shining Sun and run!" Badger and his warriors began firing arrows towards the invaders—the wildly painted riders were approaching fast, heading right into the heart of the village. As yet he could not identify the raiders' tribe, but obviously they were enemies of the White Clay People.

Badger watched volley after volley of arrows hit the attackers and their mounts. The horses whinnied in fear and pain—some collapsed while others ran into each other, sending their riders falling into a cloud of dust. He continued to encourage his troops: "Counter-attack! Go for their leaders! See their feathers? They are the big-bellied Hidatsa."

White Flower, the beautiful daughter of Elk's Heart, the former war chief, had run with Shining Sun into a plum thicket. After stuffing her daughter into the thicket, she stuck out her head in an attempt to spot her husband. A few attackers spotted her as she crouched just inside the thicket. Before she could crouch down by her daughter, she felt sharp pains in her side and back as enemy arrows pierced her body. With a final thrust of energy, she fled from the thicket to divert the attackers from her hidden child.

While Badger and his men fought the attackers, White Flower's body fluids drained from her as she fell on the beaten path leading to the river.

When Badger saw her fall, he rushed toward her. Crouching near her side, he turned and continued firing arrows with deadly accuracy. Several of the Hidatsa charged towards him, and though wounded, one warrior leapt from his horse to fall upon the devastated husband. As they rolled on the trail, the enemy's knife severed Badger's right ear from his head. Quickly he slashed out, furiously cutting his attacker again and again. While a mass of flesh, blood and war feathers littered the river path, Badger lay unconscious next to his lifeless wife and the mortally wounded Hidatsa.

When the fighting subsided, Badger shook his head, struggling against going into shock from the loss of blood. Then he remembered, and with a cry, he crawled over to White Flower. She lay crumpled with arrows protruding from her small frame, and he knew, even before lifting her that life had drained from her body and her soul had departed to the Great Spirit.

He held his wife in his bloody arms as he wailed loudly to the heavens. White Flower had been his spirit and his life. Whenever he completed a hunt or raid, he could think only of her until he was again safely in their lodge on the Milk River. But now he would never again see her smiling welcome, or feel her warm embrace.

Then he remembered his daughter. Laying his wife's body down, he ran into the brush, crying his daughter's name. "Shining Sun! Shining Sun!" he called, frantic that he may have lost both his wife and his daughter.

Out of a badger hole, deep in the thicket, crawled a small, dirty girl with mud-streaked tears on her round cheeks. When she saw the crumpled body of her mother, she wrapped her small arms around her father's neck and they embraced and cried together for White Flower. Over his daughter's head, Badger could see other villagers wailing for their lost loved ones. The village was shattered and many of their horses had been stolen.

As the village leaders assessed the amount of deaths, injuries, and damage, it was recognized that the quick action of their war chief, Badger, had prevented a greater loss to the Atsina. All of the villagers praised him for organizing the rapid defense of the village. For his bravery and sacrifice, Chief Black Elk declared, "I am promoting you from the Dog Society to the Drum Society. I now name you One Ear, so all will recall your brave deeds."

After the burials and four moons of mourning had ended, the village celebrated defeating the Hidatsa. Many enemy scalps hung from poles for all to witness. Though Shining Sun still grieved over the loss of her mother, she assisted her elderly grandmother, who took over the duties of cooking and tending their lodge. The seasons continued to change while Shining Sun grew larger and stronger, becoming ever more helpful to her grandmother. However, old Doe Eyes was frail and sickly and the two had a hard time maintaining their home.

One night while Shining Sun struggled to prepare the evening meal, One Ear realized he needed a strong wife to provide the labor needed for his lodge. He believed Doe Eyes would not live much longer and he felt he needed a mother for his daughter, a younger woman who could teach her in the ways of a proper White Clay maiden. Her clothes and hair were in disarray as she came before him, but she smiled with pride at her womanly accomplishments.

"Come, daughter," spoke One Ear, "let us eat."

Shining Sun observed her father as he sat across the fire eating his buffalo stew. Since her mother's death his eyes seemed dull and distant. Although she was secure and happy in her father's lodge, and he always provided more food, furs, and skins than any hunter in the village did, she still felt unworthy. She had tried hard to please him but he seemed dissatisfied with her efforts. She felt unworthy in other ways, too, believing that the village boys only kick-fought with her because she was the daughter of the famous One Ear. They invited her to participate in all their activities, the only girl allowed to pull their small bows with them, but she longed to be accepted for herself, to *earn* their respect.

After the meal, One Ear lit his pipe and Shining Sun watched the smoke rise through the lodge smoke hole. After awhile One Ear began telling one of his many stories about hunting trips and horse-stealing raids. Shining Sun devoured the details as he relayed them and visualized each event as if she had been with him. She dreamed of being a fine hunter and brave warrior just like her father. Although she tried very hard to stay awake, at last she passed into slumber; One Ear gathered her in his strong arms, placing her into the sleeping robes next to old Doe Eyes, who was already fast asleep.

He looked upon her round, peaceful face and determined he must soon take a woman into his tipi. Somewhat relieved of his melancholy, he bedded down and finally dozed off, pondering which of the village women he should take for his wife.

At daybreak, One Ear woke his daughter saying, "My daughter, I must leave to raid the Crow to the south. We need some of their fine buffalo-chasers. You will remain in the lodge with grandmother until I return."

"Yes, my father," she replied. "I will wait for your gift of success." Then she repeated a previous request. "I wish for a pony of my own to ride. My friends think we must be poor because the daughter of the great One Ear does not have a pony." He smiled with fatherly pride as she helped gather his medicine bag, war paint and armaments. He remembered trying to shame his own father for a pony in much the same manner. However, he did not commit to her request. He reasoned that she was still too young, and besides that, she was only a girl.

One Ear mounted his favorite mare, Nootka, and led Thunder, his war stallion. The big horse had been keenly trained for battle and One Ear had already ridden him on several raids. Shining Sun waved until the armed party rode out of sight as women, children and dogs ran around excitedly. Soon the barking and yelling subsided, and village life returned to normal. Shining Sun spent the morning cleaning the tipi and helping her frail grandmother. She finally laid down for a nap when the sun reached its zenith. Because she had risen early and worked hard, she slept soundly.

In the late afternoon, she arose. Leaving her grandmother asleep, Shining Sun went to the river for her bath. She spent the rest of the afternoon playing in the water with other boys and girls her age. When she returned to her tipi, Snow Woman, her dead mother's sister, greeted her in front of One Ear's lodge. Because her face was swollen and her hair was cut in swatches, Shining Sun knew there had been a death in the family.

"Not father! Not my father!" she shrieked.

Snow Woman wrapped her large, soft arms around Shining Sun to comfort her. "No, Little One, not your father. Our beloved Doe Eyes has passed into the Great Spirit world beyond our Mother Earth. She died softly and peacefully." Shining Sun began to weep. Snow Woman continued, "Do not worry Little One, your father will return soon with many fine ponies, and he will nurture and provide for you. Come now. I have prepared some rabbit stew. You will need your strength." She then hugged Shining Sun as they grieved the loss of their mother and grandmother.

For several days Shining Sun had little appetite, she could only think of her father and longed for his return. At night she bedded down and lulled herself to sleep listening to coyote mating calls and the occasional barking of camp dogs. Her aunt, Snow Woman, was kind to her, but the woman could not fill the emptiness in her niece's small, aching heart.

CHAPTER 2

The early morning uproar jolted Shining Sun out of a deep sleep—noisy barking dogs and excited yelling of women, children and old men alerted her that she had better get up immediately. They may be under attack again. Quickly she dressed and rushed from the lodge.

Their raiding party had returned!

Several of the men had been wounded, some barely clinging to their ponies. These warriors were tended to first by being taken from their mounts by the women and assisted into the medicine lodge of Horned Owl. Some of the younger braves herded a large string of newly captured horses while those children old enough helped hobble the warrior's mounts and lead the others to a corral.

But Shining Sun was only interested in finding her father. Where would she be without him? Her spirits lifted when she saw him, riding straight and dignified atop Thunder, leading his mare. But mounted on Nootka sat a young woman whose feet were bound together under the mare's belly. The young Atsina girl stared in bewilderment at the newcomer.

This was the first enemy woman she had ever seen; surely this stranger was more attractive than any female in the village. Her long, shiny hair had a polished shell affixed to one side; she'd never seen anything like it. Her short nose was turned up slightly, her large eyes adorned by long, thick lashes, were set under high, full eyebrows. Her thin cheeks led to a narrow chin, which had a small dimple at the end, and her round lips seemed the color of a dark plum.

The stranger's frightened, dark eyes swept the village before finally settling on the small girl running toward her and the man who brought her here. She watched as the girl affectionately grasped the warrior's foot, while he in turn placed his large hand gently upon her head. Although only sixteen, Red Plum already knew her destiny—first, the tribe's young warriors would ravage her, and then she would be turned over to the women to work as their slave. She had been told this long before by the older Sparrow Hawk women of her own tribe. Capture by enemy tribes was a fearful thing, especially for a female. For the males the end was usually quick. Though her insides quivered, she determined to show no fear; she knew what she had to do. She would kill herself the first chance she had.

It seemed everyone was speaking at the same time, but the captive didn't understand the Algonquin language of the Atsina. As a Sparrow Hawk, she only spoke the Siouan dialect, but she recognized some of the sign language that all Plains people used for trading and hunting together. She tried to keep her composure and closely observed everything around her, hoping to gain a clearer picture of her predicament.

7

The warrior spoke to the little girl. "My daughter," he said, "I have brought you a mother." Then he dismounted and walked toward the captive woman astride Nootka. He untied her feet and lifted her from the mare. A young boy led the horses to a corral behind the lodges where he would feed them and brush them down. "Come!" One Ear commanded of the captive, then he led her to his lodge. Shining Sun followed, still not understanding why he had brought this intruder into her life.

After entering the lodge, One Ear ordered the captive and Shining Sun to sit on two well-worn buffalo robes. Without a word, One Ear kindled a small fire and took out his favorite pipe. He placed some of his precious tobacco in the pipe and lit it with an ember from the fire. He then closed his eyes and puffed deeply. Shining Sun knew her father was meditating and thanking the Great Spirit for his success and safe return. She looked at the captive woman, who showed fear in her eyes. Shining Sun knew to keep quiet while her father meditated, so she just looked back and forth between One Ear and the stranger, waiting for her father to speak.

Truly, Red Plum *was* confused. She had not been beaten or molested since her capture, and she had not yet been given to the old women as a slave. She knew she needed protection, and if she could impress this warrior, perhaps he would take her for his wife. Then the Great Spirit would smile upon her and some day she could escape to return to her beloved Absaroka . There she could tell everyone about her life as the wife of a great Atsina warrior. Red Plum studied Shining Sun. The warrior's daughter wasn't particularly pretty, but she had good skin on her round face and bright, expressive eyes. Her dull hair was crudely woven into twin braids; her clothing needed repair and certainly didn't reflect the wealth of One Ear's lodge. If Red Plum could show One Ear how much he needed her, surely she could remain in the safety of his lodge.

After he finished his smoke, One Ear cleaned his pipe and began speaking to the maiden in sign language. "You will be my woman," he signed. "You will be mother to my daughter. You will teach her the ways of a woman."

He signed by pointing upward with his index finger and his thumb. He moved his hand from east to west with wrist movement then extended and closed his fingers to indicate rays from the sun. As he did this he pointed to his daughter, saying the words, "Shining Sun. Shining Sun." Next he pointed to himself and his missing ear, saying "One Ear. One Ear." Red Plum looked at his missing ear and understood.

One Ear repeated this procedure several times, hoping she would remember the words he had spoken, then signed to Red Plum. "What are you called?" he asked. Although Red Plum understood the question, she found herself afraid to move or speak.

Suddenly One Ear shouted the question in his Atsina language and raised his arm as if to strike the young woman. "Red Plum!" she answered in her own language. She reasoned she must not offend this warrior if she wanted to survive the day intact. In an effort to help them understand, she signed and motioned, as if to suck and bite at the ends of her fingers, repeating, "Red Plum. Red Plum."

One Ear could not comprehend her meaning, although he figured she must have been referring to berries or fruit of some kind. But it really didn't matter that much to him because he would give her a new name after their marriage. One Ear directed Shining Sun to get him something to eat, after which he laid down on his sleeping robes for a long needed rest. The raid south of the waters of the Elk River had exhausted him, both physically and mentally. His daughter and his new captive would just have to manage with each other.

And manage they did. The captive taught her name to the girl by finding a wild red plum and pointing to it then herself. The next morning One Ear awoke to the aroma of simmering stew. Through the lodge door he observed Red Plum busily preparing the morning meal and realized he had slept longer than he intended. His daughter sat by the fire watching the young woman's every move. The warrior noticed that Shining Sun was as pretty as he had ever seen her. He absorbed the care and grooming she had been given and a lump slowly rose in his throat. He thought to himself, "This is good."

While her father had slept, Shining Sun grew more fascinated with the strange woman. She ceased holding hostility for the newcomer and started to feel a greater need for her attention and companionship. When she finally saw her father come out of the lodge, she exclaimed, "Father, you have been asleep for a moon and a sun. We have been very busy with the lodge and Red Plum has fixed my hair."

Now One Ear understood the maiden's name. Since he found it agreeable, he decided she could keep it. He yawned widely as Red Plum removed the heated stones from the paunch of elk stew. Keeping her head bowed so her eyes would not meet his, she topped the stew with fresh berries and served it to him. Tentatively he dipped in his favorite horn spoon then drew it up to his mouth. It tasted great! Much time had passed since he had eaten such fine cooking and he quickly devoured his meal.

He could now see that Red Plum was no stranger to the work of keeping a lodge. He studied her as he ate, assuring himself that he had made a good choice for a wife.

After finishing, One Ear walked over to the village council fire. Some of the warriors were still recounting their great raid on the Crow for the council members and old men, but now it was time they heard from One Ear. "I counted coup four times," he said. "I took thirty horses and I captured a Crow maiden, who was out gathering plums. I wish to share half of my horses but I wish to take the young woman for my wife, to be a mother to my daughter."

Impressed and pleased with the raid's success, Chief Black Elk told the council, "I know you will agree with me that One Ear has honored the White Clay People. He shows great humility in sharing his captured horses. Therefore, I grant him his request to take the Crow girl as his wife."

The council grunted its approval of the chief's words. When he was finished with the council, One Ear left to examine his newly acquired horse herd. He could tell the good news to his new wife later.

In the meantime, Red Plum cleared away the meal, cleaned the lodge, and shook out the sleeping robes. She then followed Shining Sun down the trail to the river, the same trail where Shining Sun had lost her mother and One Ear had gained his new name. The two veered off to a minor trail that led to a cut in the riverbank.

9

Here, the river's water slowed and eddied. In this place they would find seclusion for their bath.

Red Plum removed her clothes first, then began undressing Shining Sun. She untied the girl's braids and led her into the water. She bathed the small girl and washed her hair thoroughly. She would rather be at home with her own people, but if she could not, being here with the quiet man and pleasant little girl was better than some other alternatives. As Shining Sun wiped the water from her round eyes, she looked up at Red Plum. The newcomer had round, firm breasts, a small waist, and tight hips like a young colt's. Her own chubby, little body seemed egg-shaped and awkward by comparison. Deciding she could never be as beautiful as Red Plum, Shining Sun decided to continue dreaming of the day that she would become a great warrior like her father. "If I became a warrior," she reasoned, "no brave would dare show me disrespect. And they would dare not tease me for being homely."

When they finished bathing, the two of them sat on the grass and let the sun dry their bodies and hair. Red Plum combed Shining Sun's hair, then oiled it with flax so it wouldn't be dull when dry. She also rubbed it with sweet grass to give it a pleasant aroma. Red Plum's own tresses hung all the way down to her curving hips. The Sparrow Hawk people had always been proud of their long black hair and took compulsive care of it.

When they had finished and redressed, Shining Sun led Red Plum to the Peoples Creek delta, an area especially rich in food supplements. This bottomland had become a major source of onions, plums, berries, roots and herbs. Shining Sun ate several dark, red berries and the sweet juice ran down her chin. Red Plum ate a few herself before prodding the girl to get back to work. Soon their basket was full.

Shining Sun carried the basket while Red Plum toted the buffalo paunch of fresh water as they trekked up the trail to their lodge. After their return, Red Plum took a porcupine quill comb from her tunic and began combing Shining Sun's hair. The young girl continued to be impressed with the woman's caring actions. She grew mesmerized by Red Plum's gentle strokes. Faint memories of her mother returned to her as she closed her eyes, enjoying the much-needed attention.

Red Plum braided the small girl's hair, tying pieces of doeskin at the end of each braid. She then hooked her polished seashell into the girl's hair. They smiled at each other warmly. Red Plum then took some sinew and a bird-bone needle and began mending Shining Sun's dress. Because the little girl's moccasins were too badly worn to repair, she softened some new doeskin by chewing it, then stitched the pieces together to make a new pair. The shoes were plain but they fit, and the two could paint them later, or even sew on some beads.

Red Plum groomed herself as best she could, then began preparing the afternoon meal. She cut off a chunk of buffalo hump and placed it into a large hanging paunch, partly filled with water. With two flat sticks she dug several round, hot stones from the fire pit and placed them in the water; she also added roots, herbs and wild onions. As the stones cooled, she replaced them with fresh hot ones.

When One Ear returned to his lodge, he observed the results of Red Plum's activity. It was good to see she was not lazy. He noticed that Shining Sun had been neatly groomed again. This pleased him very much and he decided to reward Red Plum by waiting until she grew accustomed to her new life before consummating their marriage. After the meal, One Ear restocked the fire and lit his pipe. He thanked his secret protector and the six directions of the Great Spirit for his good fortune. Content and secure with his new wife, he undressed and climbed into his sleeping robes.

Red Plum lay apprehensively in her own robes. Eventually she heard his breathing get deeper, then she wondered what could be wrong with her. Was she not attractive or pleasing to One Ear? She believed that if he did not lie with her, he might dismiss her from his lodge. She went to sleep thinking of new ways to make herself more appealing to him.

After several weeks, Red Plum learned the routine of the village, as well as the daily habits of One Ear. Although he still made no attempt to sleep with her, she felt that she did bring him pleasure. She made new clothing from the skins and furs stored in the lodge. She made One Ear new moccasins, decorating them with small beads. She also finally painted a small sun design on each of Shining Sun's new shoes. The girl's eyes lit up with delight as she ran from the lodge to show all her friends.

When One Ear returned for the evening meal his excited daughter greeted him. "Father! Father!" she squealed, "Look at my new shoes!"

The warrior admired the fine Crow beadwork on his new shoes and those of his daughter. He watched Red Plum closely during the evening meal, finding her even more beautiful now than when he had first abducted her from the shores of the Bighorn River. She had adjusted well to her new life, and now he wanted her very much. It was time.

When One Ear finally finished his pipe, Shining Sun had fallen sound asleep and Red Plum lay quietly in her robes. Without a word the strong warrior undressed and climbed into Red Plum's bed. Her naked body felt hot beside his quivering flesh, and he snuggled up to her round buttocks. Red Plum pretended to slowly awaken, then accepted her new husband with all her young energy and instinct.

The night was cool and clear and a full moon lit up the entire countryside. The whole village seemed to be enjoying a peaceful sleep; even coyotes grew unusually quiet as the lodge of One Ear became united again.

CHAPTER 3

Daily Red Plum and Shining Sun traveled to the Milk River to bathe and fill their water paunch. Together they watched the geese, swans, herons and ducks, but watching the large water birds only served to make Red Plum more homesick for the Elk River and the Sparrow Hawk people of Absaroka.

Her homeland lay in the shadow of the Shining Mountains, which the white men called the Rocky Mountains. Due to her melancholy, she began sharing her knowledge of her culture with Shining Sun. While Red Plum learned the Algonquin language of the Atsina—the Gros Ventre of the Prairie—she taught Shining Sun the Siouan language of the Sparrow Hawks. By sharing their knowledge, they grew closer together, emotionally and spiritually.

"I lived among the River Sparrow Hawks in the Elk River Valley" Red Plum said. "The white men call it the Yellowstone. We wintered on the Horses River and roamed the waters of the Bighorn, Tongue, Rosebud, Powder and Musselshell. We hunted elk in the Shining Mountains, sheep in the Big Horn's, and along the valley of the Powder River, grazing buffalo roamed as numerous as the stars in the sky."

Shining Sun was always interested in anything Red Plum had to say and she proved an apt pupil. "Our relatives, the Mountain Sparrow Hawks," continued Red Plum, "live on the Wind River under Chief Long Hair. My chief is named Rotten Belly, and at least once each summer our people gather for a celebration, including a big feast." As it would turn out much later, Red Plum's stories had more of an influence on Shining Sun than either of them could ever have imagined.

When summer finally ended and fall came to a close, thin ice formed on the Milk River; the waterfowl began flying south and Red Plum became more melancholy, longing for her people. Shining Sun did not understand her young stepmother's mood swings but she found herself without Red Plum's company more and more.

When the snow-falling season began, One Ear and his men brought in large amounts of meat, fur and buffalo hides to succor the tribe through to the next green-grass season. Frozen-grass seasons on the Milk River were so harsh that many old and infirm Atsina would die, despite the meat and stacks of firewood harvested to keep their lodge fires burning.

The women, including Red Plum and Shining Sun, did their part by gathering extra roots, seeds and herbs—as many as they could find and store. Red Plum taught her stepdaughter how to prepare jerked meat and pemmican, how to tan hides, and how to use animal brains for making the skins soft and pliable. The youngster showed more interest in tanning hides than gathering roots and cooking.

She did not care much for the frozen-grass season, because it so often forced her indoors.

Shining Sun did not care for lodge duties; she worked quickly but only half-heartedly. She could hardly wait until her chores were completed each day because she would much rather be exploring the Milk River and Peoples Creek, hunting rabbits and playing war games with the village boys. After the snows began, with the accompanying cold north winds, the girl's father spent more of his time in the robes of her new mother, leaving Shining Sun pretty much free to do what she pleased.

Shining Sun spent many of her idle hours daydreaming, where she would lead horse raids and hunt buffalo. When the green-grass season finally began to emerge, she again hunted rabbits with Little Feather, the son of Chief Black Elk.

Little Feather had reached twelve winters of age, and it was he who taught her to hunt and track; he also protected her from the older boys in the village. Near Snake Creek the two found their favorite hunting place, for in this area a unique hole in a big cottonwood tree offered Little Feather a place to keep his bow and arrows. They stashed their secret rocks there also, because *special* rocks could be secret helpers.

One day, after they approached the hollow tree, Little Feather took off his large robe and displayed a new, small bow. Beautifully decorated with ornate carvings, it had hawk feathers tied to each end with a leather thong. A shriek emitted from Shining Sun's throat.

"Oh! Little Feather," she gasped. "Is this bow for me?"

He smiled coyly, "Perhaps, if you will keep all my secrets." He strung the bow and pulled several arrows from a small quiver. He had selected the best bowmaker in the village to prepare this *special* bow for her, because he loved the small girl of seven winters and hoped someday to make her his wife. Little Feather softly told her, "I know you desire to become a hunter, so you must have a bow to learn to shoot. However, to protect us both, you must practice in secret." Quietly he pondered, "After we are married, I will see that you learn your proper role, that of serving as the wife of a great chief as I succeed my father." For now, however, he would teach her how to use the bow.

As Little Feather held the bow out to her, Shining Sun took it from him, then hugged it with all her might. "I owe my soul to you for this wonderful gift, Little Feather. But I must give you something in return. What can I give you?"

When he didn't respond, she gushed, "I know, I will trade you my new seashell ornament for the bow…for your mother's beautiful hair. She will be very pleased."

Proudly he took the seashell from her, then he showed her the more efficient way of placing an arrow on the bowstring and arrowrest. "Pull the notched arrow with these three fingers, not with your thumb and finger like the small boys do," he instructed. "For sighting over the tip of the arrow, I have cut small marks above the arrowrest to help determine the distance to your target. This I have been taught by my father." He also taught her to hold the string with the arrow notch tight against the corner of her mouth, while sighting over the tip of the arrowhead. She practiced shooting the remainder of the day; from time to time, Little Feather gave

13

suggestions to improve her technique, but he was careful not to discourage or anger her.

When they finished shooting at trees, rabbits and rodents, they hid their bows and arrows in the hollow of the large tree. From that moment Shining Sun used every opportunity to return to practice with her new weapon, but they kept their secret from their parents and the other children. Several moons later the two began hunting small animals, such as porcupines, martins, wolverines, beavers, ermine, and even small deer. Little Feather began telling her some society secrets, including those of the Crazy, Fox, Soldier (police) and other societies. He explained that each society held sacred ceremonies in performance lodges.

"The lodge must always face eastward," he explained, "and consists of two tipis placed together to make one large double lodge. Each member of the society secures the aid of an old man, called his grandfather, who is versed in the ritual of the society. Each morning of the ceremony, the 'grandfathers' paint the dancers and the dancers' wives, and each night the 'grandfather' leaves the camp with the wives to teach other rites. By these rites the old men give their medicine to the dancers through the medium of their wives."

Curious about her father's Dog and Drum Societies, she asked about them. Solemnly Little Feather told her, "The dance of the Dog Society consists of two leaders, one with a yellow shirt and the other with a red one. Black feathers from a raven trim each shirt and each leader wears a headdress of owl feathers. All members wear leather sashes, worn over the right shoulders and under their left arms. When the White Clay warriors are in danger of losing a battle, the sash ends are staked to the ground with lances. This ties them down like a dog. Then the sashwearers cannot retreat until their comrades drive the enemy off by yelling at them as if they were dogs."

She urged him on and he continued.

"The members of that society wear eagle bone whistles, hung by thongs around their necks, and for dances, they carry small deer-hoof rattles. The leaders also carry a long rattle made of forked stick with dewclaw rattles, which has feathers at each end. All members are brave veterans of battle and are entitled to wear eagle feather headdresses in combat. The ceremony usually lasts four days."

Her eyes wide with interest, Shining Sun thanked Little Feather. "Can you tell me of the Drum Society she asked. "My father was appointed to the Drums by your father in recognition of his bravery."

He smiled and resumed his all-knowing air of importance.

"The Drums are comprised of the bravest and most powerful warriors in the village," he continued. "They have a special drum in their medicine bundle that they can throw toward the enemy during a battle. The Drum members then run to the drum and stand beside it where they fight until either the enemy backs away or the drum owner is killed. During their ceremony, four leaders carry staffs, hooked at one end, and wrapped with a white buffalo skin. All members paint themselves red from top to toe and cover themselves with white dots, which represent hail, and a white zigzag line, which represents lightning. They wear only breechcloths for clothing and an eagle down-feather is attached to the sides of their heads."

14

The girl committed to memory everything her friend told her. She wanted to become a member of these societies when she grew up. As he spoke, Shining Sun reaffirmed her desire to never become a member of the Buffalo Cow Society like other women. At every opportunity, she practiced her shooting in earnest and even tried her hand at tracking deer. She continued to keep her bow a secret from One Ear and Red Plum.

Even at this early age, Shining Sun knew she wanted to become a great hunter despite her father's desire that she take her place with the tribe as a lodge woman when she grew up.

CHAPTER 4

With the change of season, One Ear and the other village men resumed their hunts; this time they selected Little Feather to accompany them as their horse tender. Though a normal part of his warrior training, he still felt proud to be selected for such an honorable position.

Now that hunting trips kept One Ear and Little Feather away from the village much of the time, Red Plum and Shining Sun rekindled their strong relationship, picking up where they had left off, comparing differences and similarities between the Sparrow Hawks and the White Clay People. One day Shining Sun confided, "Red Plum, I have learned some of the secrets of our warrior societies!"

Communication between the two females took a more secretive turn. Shining Sun told her stepmother and friend what she had learned from Little Feather, while Red Plum shared what she knew about the Hammer Owners society of the Sparrow Hawks, the society to which her brother had belonged. Before her capture she had eavesdropped on him and his friends as they discussed their exciting and mysterious new activities.

"Most Sparrow Hawk boys become Hammer Owners by their sixteenth winter," said Red Plum, as the two slowly gathered berries and roots northeast of the village. "The men and older boys instruct them and make four wands for the leaders. Four willow sticks are laid against the outside of the lodge, then two instructors go outside to discuss potential leaders. When they return with a pipe, they choose two leaders, two rear officers, four staff-bearers and four belt-wearers. The society separates into four companies and sticks are bestowed upon each while everyone feasts and sings, then the celebration culminates in a dance. The staff-bearers are to be brave in battle, while the belt-wearers are to be brave when faced by wolves or counting coup on game animals, including wapiti. Their emblem is a wooden hammer with a hole for the insertion of a tall staff; the staff is over two horses long. The tall hammer is painted with white clay and topped by an eagle feather. Bands are painted on the hammers, either yellow and red or yellow and blue, then they paint the owner's body with the same colors."

While they talked, Red Plum found it necessary to remind the distracted Shining Sun which fruits they needed most. Then she would continue.

"The society's purpose is to train young men to become warriors," Red Plum said. "Occasionally, new initiates are allowed to participate in real battles with their elders, but because they are generally more reckless than the adults, those who do participate are often killed before they reach manhood." When Shining Sun and Red Plum shared this sacred knowledge, they made certain they were alone; they didn't want to be heard discussing matters that pertained to males only.

These revelations from Little Feather and Red Plum fascinated Shining Sun so much that she recited the information over and over in her young, fertile mind, committing the details to memory. She soaked up the hunting and warring information like the dry, hot ground soaked up a summer's rain. She silently vowed to some day use this knowledge to gain entry to one of their training societies.

Too soon the yellow-grass season turned into the leaf-falling season. Once again One Ear led his hunters in obtaining necessary meat and robes to keep them fed and warm through the snow-falling season. This time they left Little Feather behind, which gave Shining Sun new opportunities to hunt with him. By now Red Plum had to keep busy making pemmican, tanning hides, jerking meat, and sewing new clothing for the coming cold months.

Shining Sun often pouted about her horse. "I am nine winters of age," she thought, "and I still have not received the horse my father promised me. All the boys of the village have *their* own horses and I get left behind when they ride off on their outings. Sometimes Little Feather allows me to ride behind him on his horse, but then he can't chase the other boys in their mock wars. At times father allows me to ride Nootka around the pasture, but he forbids me to ride her with my friends."

Shining Sun had much to be grateful for, but she had a tendency for centering on what she did *not* have.

When ice and snow finally closed in the Milk River and the major hunts ceased, Shining Sun approached her father once again about a horse. "Father, I am belittled by all of my friends, because the daughter of the Great One Ear does not have her own pony. They say we must be very poor."

One Ear studied his daughter and smiled. As he studied her intently for the first time in many moons, he realized that she was growing rapidly. He thought, "I have stalled her as long as I can. Nootka is getting too old for long trips and Shining Sun should have the mare as her own. Nootka is still dependable and as experienced as any horse in the village." At last he exhaled a large puff of tobacco and spoke.

"When the green-grass season comes," he said, "you shall have Nootka as your very own."

"Oh! Thank you father! Thank you!" she exclaimed. "I will always take care of her and will never abuse her. Thank you! Thank you!" She hugged her father then raced from the lodge.

All through the winter Shining Sun tended to Nootka, brushing her, watering her, and feeding her grass or cottonwood bark. On the coldest nights, she would tie a buffalo robe on the mare's back for added protection against the freezing chill. When the wind died down and the sun shone for a few hours, she joined the boys in their games. She could run as fast as any of them and she *always* played to win. Sometimes she and the boys would throw spears through a small hoop they rolled upon the frozen Milk River or Snake Creek. They tracked snow rabbits and practiced shooting at them with their small bows and arrows. The girl's love for hunting was no longer a *secret* and all the young boys were impressed indeed.

When Shining Sun killed her first rabbit, she ran to her lodge. "Father! Father!" she exclaimed proudly, "I have killed a beautiful rabbit for your meal."

Although One Ear realized his daughter was not accepting her training as a woman and potential wife, he complimented her efforts. "You have done well, my daughter," he offered. Then he jested, "Someday you will make a fine hunter and provide food for me in my old age." As they laughed at his joke, her father failed to realize the extent to which he had reinforced his daughter's desire to assume traditional male roles.

When the river finally thawed, green grass began growing in the meadows and on the hillsides, and Shining Sun started riding Nootka every day. She rode everywhere with the boys but she had difficulty keeping up. For one thing, she didn't have much experience riding and for another thing, she was protective of Nootka, which slowed her down. The mare always responded, but was older than most of the other horses and grew winded after a chase.

With steady practice Shining Sun learned to shoot while riding horseback, firing her arrows as she raced past a target. She had learned to squeeze her knees together and to lock her left heel on the horse's ribs in order to keep the mare under her. However, she had difficulty keeping her balance while pulling her bow aboard Nootka at full speed.

Little Feather said, "Wrap the mare's mane around your fingers before grasping the bow, like this. It will stabilize your left hand and when you lean forward and to your right, you can sight in on your target. With practice you can ride a galloping horse and shoot while holding onto nothing at all."

Shining Sun was delighted. She affectionately responded, "Thank you, Little Feather. I will never forget your guidance and friendship. We shall hunt together for life so we can forever feed our people." With that declaration, she raced off to practice until dark.

Shining Sun regretted seeing the next snow-falling season arrive in full force, for now she had to hobble Nootka on days too cold to ride.

As the white man's year of 1809 approached, all was not well in One Ear's lodge. He gambled much of the time and every evening drank rum with the older warriors. He grew less interested in sleeping with Red Plum and was no longer providing enough robes and food for his lodge. The more he drank, the more he wanted to drink, and his body weakened from the excessive alcohol and lack of nourishment.

One Ear brooded, "For many moons now my medicine has been bad. My wife is still without child and my manhood will no longer respond. I have failed to make meat on my hunting trips and fewer of the hunters will accompany me. I have to rely more and more on the young, untried boys to follow me. What will become of me? What will I do? I must have goods to trade for more firewater."

During the last leaf-falling season, One Ear had nearly been killed by a Cheyenne war party because he had been careless when charging a small herd of buffalo. The noise of his young hunters attracted the enemy party, which had been tracking the same herd. During the ensuing stampede, he managed to escape, but returned home without meat once again.

Although no longer depressed about being torn from her homeland, Red Plum still felt anxious about her life. Although she had been with One Ear for several years, she still remained without child. "Perhaps I am being punished by the Great Spirit," she thought, "for being happy among my enemies." But her happiness waned as she and Shining Sun carried the full load of work that winter; it was as though One Ear wasn't even there.

During the frozen-grass season, French traders from the Northwest Fur Company, including Jean Baptiste Lepage, Antoine Larocque and Rene' Jussome, visited the village. Shining Sun learned that these bearded white men came to their village to trade guns, pots, knives and trinkets for Atsina furs.

Chief Black Elk cautioned his people. "Be shrewd in your trades," he said, "or you will lose all your wealth. We need their goods but they cannot be trusted." They built a large council fire and the great feasting that followed lasted for four days.

One Ear bartered for a British trade gun then began to brood and drink by trading the few furs he had left. The traders' rum warmed One Ear's belly but his resultant anger and frustration turned toward Red Plum. He came to the conclusion that the Crow woman had brought bad medicine to his lodge. "She is turning my protector against me," he thought. "My medicine was strong until I captured *that* woman."

After consuming nearly two bottles of alcohol, he returned to his lodge and approached Red Plum. Suddenly he ripped off her robes. Startled, she jumped up and stood facing him. With one of his big hands he knocked her to the floor of the tipi while he still held onto a bottle of rum with his other hand. He gulped down the last of the bottle, tossed it aside, and then quickly disrobed. Roughly he grabbed Red Plum and attempted to rape her, but found himself too drunk to perform. In his fury, he beat her, knocking her about until she lay in a ball, covering her head with her arms. At last he grew exhausted and staggered from his lodge into the night.

Hurt emotionally more than physically, Red Plum was in tears as she tried to console her adopted daughter, who sobbed and clung to her stepmother. The Crow woman's heart ached and her bruised body hurt.

"What has happened to father?" Shining Sun cried. "Doesn't he love us anymore?" But there were no easy answers. The youngster had noticed her father's dull, distant eyes for some time. She had thought his demeanor must have been *her* fault. Here she was, busy growing and learning, developing her independence, and suddenly her whole world seemed to be crashing down around her. She thought, "I love my father, he hasn't always been like this. But I also love and need Red Plum."

Although she had been young when she lost her mother, she remembered the loneliness and fear. When Red Plum arrived, the young woman not only reminded her of what her mother had meant to her, but helped fill the void left by her mother's death. Now she feared losing her new mother, she feared being alone again. Despite Red Plum's consolation, Shining Sun cried herself to sleep.

Early the next morning Red Plum slipped from the lodge as Shining Sun slept. Stealthily, she followed the path to the French camp by the frozen river. As she approached, she noticed a few of the strange traders stirring, one already putting a coffeepot on the fire. Lepage noticed her first.

"Sacre bleu!" Lepage said in French. Then in Hidatsa he asked, "What do you wish, lovely one?"

"Please take me with you," she replied. She understood the language of the Sparrow Hawk's relatives, the Hidatsa, and replied in the Siouan dialect of her people. "My husband no longer wants me."

Larocque, the trading party leader, was shocked to hear what sounded like the Hidatsa language, spoken by an Atsina woman. "What are you called?" he asked her.

"My Sparrow Hawk name is Red Plum," she replied eagerly, "and my people are the River Sparrow Hawks. I was captured by the Atsina warrior, One Ear, to become his slave. Now he has beaten me and does not want me anymore."

Larocque looked at the bruises already forming on her face and noticed the dried blood crusting at the corner of her round lips. He spoke to his men in French, "If you try to assist this girl, we will have the entire village upon our heads. They could follow us all the way to Saskatchewan to avenge her loss." Reluctantly he turned to Red Plum and spoke slowly in the Hidatsa dialect. "I am sorry pretty one, but we wish only to trade with the Atsina and return to our homes." Disappointed, Red Plum lowered her head, tears flowing down her discolored cheeks.

Despite Larocque's warning, Lepage came forward. "I will trade some of my traps and one rifle for her," he announced. Though Red Plum did not understand his words, the tone of his voice and the lascivious look in his eyes gave her chills. Slowly she backed away from them, then turned and ran all the way back to her lodge. As she raced into the early morning fog she could hear the frightening trapper laugh aloud. When she reentered the tipi, she found Shining Sun still asleep; as she expected, One Ear had not returned.

Quickly she made a fire, then began preparing the morning meal. Shining Sun awoke to the aroma of elk stew. Sitting by the small fire, she ate quietly, observing her stepmother's bruises and tired eyes. The girl didn't know what to say and Red Plum just stared at the wall of the tipi while clasping her hands over a small bag containing her personal belongings.

When she finished eating, Shining Sun wanted to talk to Little Feather. Grabbing her bow and arrows, she hurried out to seek solace from her friend. She felt more and more helpless now and her childhood friend seemed her only symbol of security in a very confusing world.

CHAPTER 5

Painfully, One Ear rolled over under his robes. His head felt like a battleground for two bull elks and his tongue tasted like water from Stinking Creek. As he raised up on one elbow, he recognized the lodge interior of the wanton Rabbit Woman. Not only was she fat, dirty and homely, but most villagers knew she would sleep with anyone for a fur or for food. Since she could not attract a husband, the village women looked upon her with disdain and because of her impurity, no self-respecting brave would touch her before going on a hunt or raid.

Disgusted with himself, One Ear rose from her robes and staggered out of the smelly lodge. Slowly he headed down the path leading to the river, thinking perhaps a bath would clear his aching head and revive his weary body.

Before he reached the river, he ran into the French camp. Recognizing One Ear as the husband of the Crow maiden, Lepage approached him with a goatskin of red wine.

The Frenchman called, *"Allo! Bon ami,"* then signed to One Ear to drink the hair of the coyote, which was playing tricks in his head. One Ear grunted, then squeezed the red liquid from the bag into his stale mouth. After moistening his dry lips with his swollen tongue, he raised the bag several more times. The liquid seemed to raise his spirits, and he grunted appreciation to his new friend. Meanwhile Larocque and the other traders nervously watched this odd interchange. Most had tried to discourage Lepage from his perfidious course, but their colleague remained persistent in his plans to obtain the attractive Crow girl. Fearing the worst they could only watch as Lepage continued to lay his trap for One Ear.

Feeling much relieved, One Ear no longer had an aching in his head or ringing in his ears. Forgetting about his bath, he and Lepage walked back to the village, sharing the goatskin of wine. When they reached the trading fire, they observed several warriors and old men sitting on their blankets in a circle throwing bones. Hunkering down in their robes to keep out the cold, they showed little enthusiasm for the day's game, but they became interested when Lepage signed to them that he wished to play. Excitement mounted as the wine diminished and Lepage became very lucky indeed. He won several rifles and many of the trade trinkets or foofooraw he had previously exchanged to them for furs and hides. Lepage repeatedly tried to get One Ear to gamble but all the warrior had was his precious rifle; he knew he could not part with his main tool for survival.

This was how the Frenchman wanted it, and he signed to One Ear that he would bet most of his rifles against the Crow maiden. Pondering the wager, One ear took another long drink of wine. Though his mind felt cloudy, he knew that if he won he would have many rifles to trade for rum; if he lost, he would be rid of Red Plum and the whispers from the villagers about his waning manhood. He reasoned that since he could no longer perform his reproductive rites, and Shining Sun was getting older, then he no longer needed a wife. He could trade for a slave to keep his lodge and a slave would not remind him of his sexual inadequacies.

At last One Ear agreed to the wager and picked up the bones. The tribesmen in the circle gasped and grunted. This was an unusual wager and One Ear had the opportunity to become wealthy from it. Closing his blurry eyes, the unhappy man fondled the bones, then tossed them to the center of the circle. Then Lepage tossed the bones and after much shouting and whistling from the group it became clear to the still inebriated One Ear that he had lost Red Plum.

"So be it," he said and struggled to his feet. He staggered over to his lodge and entered. Composing himself as best he could, he lunged at Red Plum, grabbing both her arms and yanking her up. "Go to the evil-eyed Frenchman," One Ear slurred. "He owns you now. You can have his hairy children. I will look upon you no more and you will never enter my lodge again." Red Plum looked up at his glassy eyes, observed his slovenly condition, and knew he spoke the truth. The man named Lepage would have her after all.

Shortly after One Ear sent Red Plum away, Shining Sun ran tearfully into her father's lodge. Shocked at the news that her father had gambled away her stepmother, she yelled at him. "Father, no! What is wrong with you? You cannot give my mother away. I love her. Why have you done this vile thing?"

Angered, One Ear struck her hard with the back of his big hand, knocking her backward through the tent flap. The girl clutched her stinging face while blinking lights danced before her eyes, but another type of pain now raged through her throbbing heart. As soon as she could get up, she fled to find solace and comfort from Little Feather.

Meanwhile Red Plum was choked with fright. In the nineteen winters her life had now taken two traumatic turns. She looked around for help but the villagers knew Lepage and the fat French trader with him had won her fair and square. There was nothing they could do. Many of the drunken gamblers laughed and hooted as Lepage drug her toward his camp. When they approached the French camp, Larocque looked upon Lepage with disgust and anxiety. He surmised what had happened and decided they must pack and leave the area at once. Lepage would surely get them killed if they didn't leave quickly.

But Lepage saw no danger. "I now have me a new wife," he boasted. "She will teach me the ways of the Crow and the Atsina. I will become a great interpreter and guide along the Missouri like my friend Charbonneau."

Larocque and his men ignored Lepage's delusions. Quickly they packed their furs, supplies and traps onto the packhorses and the travois. Hurriedly they mounted and headed east toward the Red River of the North, hoping to reach the safety of their homeland before suffering any repercussions from Lepage's foolish act.

CHAPTER 6

Confused and fearful, Shining Sun finally returned to her lodge. Her life had been turned upside down, once again. Her remorse over losing Red Plum brought back the emptiness she felt when her real mother had been slain. At that time she hated the Hidatsa; now she hated the Frenchmen who took away her second mother. Grateful to be alone, she lay down and prayed to the Great Spirit to deliver her from this horrible pain and sorrow and to give her a vision of the *purpose* of her life. Then she snuggled under her robes and sobbed until she fell asleep.

Emotionally exhausted, Shining Sun slept deeply at first, then fretfully as she dreamed. She saw herself leading a war party across the snow-shrouded plains, riding hard and searching for Red Plum and the Frenchmen. One of her scouts rode up hard, spraying snow on her before his snorting horse could stop. "I have located the French camp," he reported. "Come, follow me." She spurred Thunder with both heels and led her warriors after the scout, screaming for vengeance.

In her dream all the French traders scattered in fear as the maiden warrior and her Atsina braves charged. The white men didn't even have time to unwrap their encased guns before Shining Sun attacked Lepage, felling him with her war club; then she dismounted and scalped him. Proudly she tied his wavy black hair to the end of her war club. After remounting Thunder, she pulled the grateful Red Plum up behind her and her stepmother wrapped her trembling arms around her stepdaughter in tearful gratitude. After killing or scattering the traders, the young war party pillaged the camp before reorganizing for their return. They felt jubilant as they followed their leader back toward the Milk River. However, their joy was cut short as they topped a rise and found themselves surrounded by a Cree hunting party, which was twice their size in number.

Shining Sun turned back to Red Plum. "Hold on tight!" she yelled as she charged Thunder right into the midst of the Cree, scattering the enemy before her. She counted many coup and slew several warriors before the Cree fled, demoralized and humiliated by this crazy girl and her fearsome followers. By now Shining Sun and her party had collected many scalps, along with guns and other plunder she intended to share with her friends and relatives. As she rode into her village, she saw Little Feather and Chief Black Elk waiting to welcome her home. Proudly she rode around the camp while the village crier proclaimed her exploits to all who could hear him. Then Black Elk and the elders applauded Shining Sun for her bravery. The girl filled with pride and her body felt as though it could contain no more joy. In her exuberance she waved two Cree scalps and the hair of the ugly Frenchman.

Suddenly, Shining Sun was torn from her dream—One Ear had returned.

The ailing warrior staggered around the lodge, still reeking of stale wine. "Daughter," he growled, "get me food! I have not eaten in two suns. Now that I have dismissed the Crow woman, you will be the woman of my lodge." He stood over her like a mad man. "It is time you were trained to do the work you were born to," he bellowed. "You must develop skills of womanhood so you can attract a rich husband to take care of me in my old age."

Shining Sun felt heartbroken, but she was powerless in the face of her father's wrath. She pitied her haggard father because he seemed but a shell of the great warrior she had admired and loved. Dutifully, she rose and fixed him a meal, then watched in disgust as he ate like a lobo wolf feeding on carrion left behind by vultures. As time passed, One Ear's depression grew deeper as his mind receded even further into dark recesses created by alcohol. As the days grew warmer, Shining Sun attempted to hunt for food for their lodge. However, it proved difficult for her to obtain enough food for both of them, so Little Feather helped by bringing meat to them when he could. She gathered roots with the village women, and Snow Woman taught her how to locate burrows of peas stored up by field mice and ground squirrels. Everyone showed kindness to her because they sympathized with her situation and because One Ear had once been a respected warrior.

Other than finding food and fixing two meals a day, Shining Sun had no restrictions on her activities; therefore, she rode with Little Feather and his friends as often as she could. Although she still rode Nootka, she often led Thunder while on hunts, so she could use him for the chase. Nootka had grown too old to keep up with the younger ponies, while Thunder was the fastest mount on the Milk River. When she rode Thunder, she rode the stallion fearlessly, with her long, black hair flying out behind her like the tail feathers of the sparrow hawk. Often she rode with the boys when they ran after elk or antelope, but as a female, she was still not allowed to hunt buffalo.

As One Ear's appetite diminished, his body became weak and emaciated. Finally the day came when he traded his last rifle for more rum; after all, he could no longer afford lead or powder for the gun, and without ammunition it was useless to him. As the provider for their lodge, Shining Sun began trading cured skins and furs for arrows. She also traded for a new, stronger bow made from Osage orangewood. As she grew taller, she gradually lost her baby fat; she could run faster than most of the boys her age. She could even compete with some of the boys several years older.

In the spring of Shining Sun's tenth winter, Little Feather approached her lodge and entered to warm himself by her fire. He stared into the flames for several moments without speaking.

"What is it, Little Feather?" she queried. "You look troubled. Is there anything I can do?"

The boy allowed the drama to build as he slowly rose from the fire and somberly faced her. "I have just been told by my father that our people need fresh meat," he said. "I am to organize a hunting party and attempt to find a herd of wapiti. I must kill and pack as much meat as I can without scattering the herd." Little Feather definitely had her attention now. "If I cannot approach them," he continued, "I am to follow their migration, while sending one scout each day to the

24

village to report our location until our adult hunters can come to us. I am allowed to take anyone I choose with me, therefore, I must call upon our friendship and request your assistance."

Shining Sun was shocked. Little Feather had just invited her to accompany him on her very *first* buffalo hunt! "Oh, Little Feather," she shrieked, "I will love you forever! I will always follow your bidding. I will make you proud to be my friend." In her exuberance, she grabbed him around his lean, muscular frame, almost knocking him into the fire.

Although startled by her behavior, he quickly regained his poise and solemnly added, "You will only attend to our extra horses, and you will not be allowed to charge the herd. You will carry my extra gun and ammunition, and if we are successful, you will share in the division of meat and robes." Shining Sun nodded that she understood her role. As soon as Little Feather left her lodge, she began checking her hunting gear. Gathering the last of her furs, she left the lodge to trade for more of the precious cedar shafts that were made by the village arrowmaker. She felt confident that she could perform any task Little Feather asked of her. She would show them *all* that she was dependable—including her father.

CHAPTER 7

As the last spring storm of 1810 slowly subsided, Shining Sun and the young Atsina men set forth from the Milk River on their hunt for fresh meat. They traveled south across the Missouri River hoping to find herds that might be returning to the northern grasslands. Shining Sun rode Thunder because she feared the trip might be too hard for Nootka.

Since One Ear was no longer capable of hunting, he had little fight left in him to deny her access to his buffalo chaser. Thunder pranced nervously in the cool spring air, eager for the opportunity to run on the prairie. Like Shining Sun, Thunder was also ten winters of age, and while that was young for the girl, the age was considered prime for a war-horse or a buffalo chaser. Because of the horse's excitement, it took some time for Shining Sun to bring him under control.

As the only female in the party, she nearly exploded with excitement and anticipation, fantasizing that this hunt would bring her the praise and recognition she craved. She rode point beside Little Feather, thinking of herself as his lieutenant. Whenever Little Feather looked at Shining Sun he smiled; he thought of her as his future wife and was eager to ask his father to contract with One Ear for his marriage to Shining Sun as soon as she reached her fifteenth winter. He felt secure when she accompanied him on his hunts; he even considered her his talisman. As long as she attended him, he believed he would have success; she seemed to have enough confidence for both of them.

The young hunting party rode south for several days, trying to keep clear of any contact with the Assiniboine or Crow. They tried to camp each night in a coulee, not only to escape the frigid winds, but to also hide their campfires from their enemies. When they reached a deep ravine on Box Elder Creek, they unpacked and built a fire. Little Feather sent scouts to look for game, while the rest of the party dug through the snow to uncover firewood for their camp and clump grass for their horses. After Shining Sun fed Thunder, she sat by the fire next to Little Feather, who shared his large robe with her by wrapping it around her shoulders.

"Will we see many wapiti?" she asked.

The young hunter looked to the sky before replying, "We will see as many wapiti as there are stars in the Great Spirit's lodge in the sky. Our people will praise this hunt until the sweet grass gets tall and the fat deer return to Peoples Creek."

Shining Sun smiled, hoping that should would be among those praised. She prayed that her people would come to boast of her deeds as they once had her father's. Finally, she went to her own robes to get some sleep, still scheming of a way she could participate in the hunt itself.

Before dawn Little Feather awakened her with a shake. "It is time," he said. "We must now ride south."

It seemed as if she had just laid down, but she rose with great anticipation. Just in case she should get the opportunity to use them, she checked her bow and arrows.

The party quickly decamped, mounted and rode stealthily over the rolling hills, steam rising from the noses and mouths of the horses and their riders. Thunder nervously pranced around again; he seemed to smell the buffalo herd through the brisk air. Leading his stallions, Black Hand and Spotted Nose, Little Feather guided his party across patches of melting snow and around snowdrifts until they topped another ridge.

Looking down upon the sprawling grassland below, the hunters beheld a valley laden with black and brown buffalo. Steam billowed from the animals' nostrils and hoarfrost clung to their whiskers. They snorted as they pawed at the hard ground, working to loosen the frozen grass. War Horse Lake shimmered like a black glassy stone in the center of the valley. Viewing the idyllic scene, Shining Sun thought, "This must surely be home to the wapiti Gods." Her heart beat so strongly she nearly became light-headed. She could not wait!

Little Feather split his young men into two groups, sending one group to the east and staying with the westbound group. Shining Sun followed him closely as they quietly descended the slope downwind of the unsuspecting herd. When they reached the valley floor, Little Feather stopped, then handed the girl the halter ropes of Black Hand and Spotted Nose.

"Stay at this location," he directed. "If I wave my hand that my horse is tired, bring me Spotted Nose or Black Hand at once. Keep my spare gun in case I need it."

Calmly the leader turned to his men. "Little Elk, you begin firing on the herd from the east, so they will run up the valley to our location. We will turn the lead bulls into the oncoming herd, causing them to stop, circle and mill in confusion until they get exhausted. Then we must shoot accurately and quickly before a lead bull can stampede them again." Little Elk headed out, circling around the herd. Little Feather held his hunters until he heard gunfire from down the valley. He had stationed his young men at twenty horse-length intervals across the edge of the slope.

Shining Sun took a position south of them, near some brush. Here she waited excitedly. Before long she felt the ground vibrate, then the dull vibration gradually rose to a thundering roar like the sound of a great waterfall. Snow and mud sprayed about the herd as their hooves tore into the valley soil. The herd came snorting toward them, as the hunters charged, shouting and shooting at the lead bulls. Then the herd split, with one portion turning north until it ran headlong into other oncoming animals. This group milled about until they finally formed a circle, where the bulls lowered their heads and backed up to the herd to protect the cows and calves.

The other portion of the herd, led by a large black bull, turned south heading straight for Shining Sun and the horses. In panic, she kicked Thunder and dashed up the slope, leading Spotted Nose and Black Hand while riding for safety. She raced up the foothills of Big Snowy Mountains, then fled south across Flat Willow Creek.

She would worry about getting back to the hunters when she was sure she was out of danger. Exhausted, she finally pulled up; she had narrowly escaped. The buffalo and the pursuing hunters raced east of her now, so she could safely return to her assigned post.

As she watched and calmed the three horses, a sea of strange faces stared at her out of the nearby trees. She had escaped the wild buffalo charge only to fall into the hands of an *enemy* hunting party!

SECTION II

1810 - 1820

CHAPTER 8

Two of the enemy quickly rushed up and grabbed the halters of Thunder, Spotted Nose and Black Hand as their comrades raced after the stampeding herd. One brave pulled her from Thunder's back, pinning her arms to his hard body. Her heart seemed to lodge in her throat and she could hardly breathe. She struggled but she was no match for the brave's size and strength.

The girl hoped this was just another of her fanciful dreams and that Little Feather would wake her at any moment to continue the hunt. However, she felt real pain from being squeezed so hard she could scarcely breathe, and she almost gagged from the bad breath of her captor. These conditions assured her that her situation was indeed *real.*

She knew she must regain her composure if she were to survive this ordeal. Although she was still very young, she had seen and felt many events, but nothing had prepared her for her present situation. She listened as the two braves talked; to her joy she discovered they were speaking the language taught her by Red Plum! From their language and dress she determined they must be Crow hunters from the Shining Mountains.

Taking a deep breath, she spoke with more courage than she felt. "Brave Sparrow Hawk hunters, can you share your water with me?"

The startled braves glanced at each other and then stared at her. The man holding her released his grip in order to get a better look. "How do you speak our language?" asked the one holding the horses. Lying was all she could think of doing. Thinking of Red Plum, Shining Sun replied, "I am from the River Sparrow Hawks. The Atsina captured me when I was very small. I am called Shining Sun because I was considered a child of the Shining Mountains."

Certainly she and her friends were outnumbered and outsized. The braves listened to her tale and looked like they just might believe her. While one hunter rode off to locate the rest of their hunting party, Shining Sun sat upon a large rock and continued to develop her story with the ever-cautious brave who remained. The brave said he was called Cracked-Ice.

She knew there was no way Little Feather could find her now, and even if he did, he could not defeat these adult warriors of the Crow Nation. She needed time to plan an escape, and the best way to do so was to convince these braves she was, indeed, a young Crow girl.

Cracked-Ice stayed with Shining Sun until late in the afternoon when the other hunter who had captured her—called Yellow Belly—returned with about twenty hunters. The hunters had many hides, buffalo humps, tongues and hindquarters tied on their packhorses. The leader of the group dismounted and walked up to her. The man was as dark as a moonless night and very muscular; he possessed the darkest eyes she'd ever seen—cold, piercing eyes. The knife scar on his face ran from one nostril all the way to his jaw and made him appear menacing. He had strange curly hair that was shaped like a tumbleweed. He didn't look at all like the other hunters.

After examining her, the dark man spoke in a deep voice with a heavy accent. "I am called Five Scalps. What are you called?"

"I am called Shining Sun," she said, choosing her words carefully. She understood that her life depended on convincing this fearful man of the truth of her story. "I was captured by the Atsina when I was very young," she continued. "My parents and my relatives were killed in the raid."

Shining Sun may not have been so brave had she known this great Crow warrior was a well-traveled and much feared guide, interpreter and Indian fighter. Part Negro and part Cherokee, Five Scalps (whose real name was Edward Rose) had been adopted by the Sparrow Hawks. Not only was he a fierce hunter and fighter, he spoke several Indian languages along with French and Spanish. In 1807, Five Scalps had helped Manuel Lisa establish Fort Raymond at the mouth of the Bighorn River.

Five Scalps observed her more closely by turning her around and feeling her skin. Her sharp features and long frame *could* be Sparrow Hawk, but he wanted to be sure. Continuing to speak in Crow, he asked, "Why was a child like you with that hunting party?"

At this point Shining Sun decided to be even more creative, since it appeared the Crow didn't realize that her hunting party only consisted of only young boys, all untried and on their first buffalo hunt. "I was given a bow, gun and these three fine stallions by Chief Black Elk," she answered, "the leader who adopted me as his daughter. The chief believed that because I was a Sparrow Hawk, I could one day become a great hunter and warrior for the Atsina."

Five Scalps, called *"Chee-ho-carte,"* had defeated the Atsina several times. He had often thought that the Atsina were poor warriors. "Perhaps this gesture on their chief's part is some religious gesture to restore honor to their warriors," he thought, "or perhaps it is the chief's attempt to embarrass his braves by promoting this young Sparrow Hawk maiden to outperform them." He felt satisfied that she might indeed be Crow. Even though her story made little sense, he had to admit that she spoke Crow quite well.

At last he signaled to the other men, who hooted excitedly before starting their return trek to the mouth of the Little Horn River. Shining Sun was mounted behind Cracked-Ice in the custom of a Sparrow Hawk captive. This would insure her safety until she was delivered to their chief. She did her best to act relaxed during the trip. It certainly would not do for her to show fear if she *really* was a Crow girl who was going home to her people.

Along the way she carefully studied the creeks, rivers and the terrain so she would remember the way back home if she found a way to escape. She talked incessantly with Cracked-Ice to learn as much as she could about the Crow village before her arrival. Among other useful items, she learned that her captors were from the *Mine'sepere* village called *Dung-on-the-River-Banks*, and that they belonged to the River Sparrow Hawks.

"When a Sparrow Hawk warrior captures a maiden," Cracked-Ice told her, "he must adopt her as his sister. This means that Yellow Belly and I will become your brothers. We cannot have relations with you or marry you." This news much relieved Shining Sun; she now realized that even if they did not believe she was Crow, she would be safe from physical harm. "According to custom, our leader Five Scalps will become your protector," he added.

The girl pondered this bit of information. Five Scalps seemed both wise and fearless; the other men followed his decisions and directions without question. She already understood that warriors will only willingly follow those leaders who demonstrate courage, strength and wisdom. Shining Sun surmised that this dark man's medicine must be strong *indeed*. She vowed to get to know the man better.

CHAPTER 9

The party rode so long that Shining Sun became sore, but she said nothing. Finally, the party topped a rise and she saw smoke plumes curling lazily into the sky. Under the thin cloud of smoke lay almost three hundred strange-looking lodges. To Shining Sun, these homes seemed oddly made; the lodgepoles extended far above the hides of the lodge. They looked as if an inverted tipi sat atop each lower lodge and that someone had simply forgotten to cover the top with buffalo hides. An excited throng of people met them as they rode into the village, all eager to obtain the fresh meat.

After being told that she had been taken from the Sparrow Hawks as a small child, many of the tribe's women carefully examined Shining Sun. They searched her features for something to identify her as a long-lost relative.

Five Scalps stopped at the lodge of *A-ra-poo-ash* (Chief Rotten Belly), dismounted and entered. "Chief," he said, "we have captured a strange girl from the Atsina. She claims to have been taken captive from us in a raid about five winters ago. She also claims to be a hunter." Rotten Belly stared into his sacred fire, contemplating this news. Five Scalps was indeed intelligent and fearless, he was not easily fooled. He knew many things about the white world beyond the great Muddy River. If he believed this girl to be a daughter of the Sparrow Hawk people, then it must be true.

"Bring this hunter girl to me," directed the chief. Cracked-Ice and Yellow Belly escorted their captive into the chief's lodge, where they found Rotten Belly sitting in his position of honor at the rear of the tipi. Rotten Belly was surprised. He had not expected to see such a young girl claiming to be a hunter of wapiti.

"Where are your people?" he asked.

Struggling to keep her composure she replied, "Oh, great chief, they were slain by the cowardly Atsina when they raided our village five winters ago. My mother hid me in a plum thicket before they killed her, but their famous warrior, One Ear, captured me. He gave me to Chief Black Elk, who adopted me." She paused to catch her breath then continued. "The Atsina stole many Sparrow Hawk horses and drove them to their villages on the Milk River. I do not believe I have any relatives left alive."

Rotten Belly stared into her eyes before finally nodding. He remembered such a raid; at least twenty of his people had been killed and the village had lost over seventy head of horses. "Surely this young maiden is one of our people," he thought, "I must welcome her home."

"As our custom dictates, Five Scalps will become our new daughter's protector," he announced. "This maiden will become the adopted sister of Yellow Belly and Cracked-Ice, due to their rights of capture."

But Yellow Belly did not want to be associated with the captive girl. "I, Yellow Belly, decline this offer," he announced. "I am much too busy leading the Big Dogs to watch over this petulant child. I do not believe she is of our people. I have spoken."

Rotten Belly scowled at his younger brother, then he said, "It is your privilege to decline. So be it. Cracked-Ice shall serve as her brother and tutor. He will be prohibited from having relations with her or taking her as a wife in accordance with Sparrow Hawk law."

Turning to Shining Sun, the chief asked, "Do you wish anything my child?"

"Yes, my father," she replied. "I wish to retain ownership of my three fine horses and my gun. They were given me by Chief Black Elk."

Rotten Belly grunted at her request, but grudgingly nodded his consent. The courageous girl continued, "I was a member of the Hammer Owners society among the Atsina. I would like to join this society among the Sparrow Hawk."

Before the chief could refuse her, Shining Sun quickly recited the rituals taught her by Little Feather and Red Plum. While Rotten Belly marveled at the brashness of the young girl, Yellow Belly stormed from the lodge. He didn't believe a word of her claim. Meanwhile the Chief pondered this ever-widening turn of events. He reasoned, "It is true that the Atsina Hammer Owner rituals sound similar to those of the Sparrow Hawks; however, my people have not allowed females to be trained as hunters or warriors." He knew this was an unusual request.

While Five Scalps and Shining Sun waited, he deliberated further. "On the other hand," he speculated, "if the Atsina chose to accept her as a warrior, perhaps this is a good omen. After all, the Great Spirit now returns her to us and her medicine seems strong."

At the end of his deliberation, Rotten Belly spoke. "My secret-helper tells me our returned daughter will bring good fortune to the River Sparrow Hawks." Having ceded to Shining Sun's request, he appointed Five Scalps and Cracked-Ice as her counselors. He reasoned that if she proved unsuited for war, they could make that determination before any harm had been done to Sparrow Hawk order. Cracked-Ice gladly accepted his new responsibilities; he was proud of the honor the chief bestowed upon him. Besides, he liked the confident, young girl and this situation would place him even closer to Five Scalps, whom he idolized.

Though showing little expression, Five Scalps also felt intrigued by Shining Sun. "This future warrior-woman must have a Sparrow Hawk name," he said. "I propose she be called *Bar-che-ampe*." Cracked-Ice responded, "I agree with Five Scalps."

"Then it is so," said the chief. "From this day forward she shall be known as *Bar-che-ampe,* our beloved Pine Leaf."

Shining Sun, now called Pine Leaf, lived in the buffalo-hide lodge of Cracked-Ice and Five Scalps. Although Five Scalps showed little interest in her, she was drawn to the mysterious black warrior like snow was drawn to the Shining Mountains.

One day Cracked-Ice told her how Five Scalps got his name. "Once some Hidatsa warriors killed a Sparrow Hawk warrior and Five Scalps took fifty Sparrow Hawk warriors with him to avenge the death. The revenge party chased a Hidatsa hunting party into a heavy-timbered, rocky shelf. Our war chiefs surveyed the strong defensive position of the enemy and promptly gave up. But Five Scalps would not quit and he shamed them by attacking the fortress himself, killing and scalping five of the Hidatsa. When the victorious party returned to Absaroka, Rotten Belly honored our dark warrior by proclaiming him *Five Scalps*."

Stories of Five Scalps thrilled the girl but she felt fortunate that her new brother, Cracked-Ice, was warm, sincere and patient in answering her abundant questions. He seemed ready to assimilate her into Sparrow Hawk society. Though Yellow Belly continued to ignore her, Pine Leaf and Cracked-Ice became each other's *'i'rapa'tse,* where loyalty became a bond, an honor usually reserved only among males.

Their lodge consisted of twenty fir lodgepoles, each of them two horse-lengths long. After the poles crossed at the smokehole opening, they reached one horse length into the air. Above the cross, the bare poles extended far beyond the living area of the lodge. She learned that no other tribe used this unique shape. It took sixteen buffalo hides to cover the lower lodgepoles. Many of these hides had been painted with illustrious scenes depicting accomplishments of the inhabitants. Where Pine Leaf dwelt, Five Scalp's deeds dominated the hides although Yellow Belly's were well represented too. Cracked-Ice had only one scene—the capture of thirty Cheyenne ponies in a raid. Now, however, he could add the rescue of Pine Leaf from the Atsina.

Initially, her counselors assigned Pine Leaf to guard their horses; she continually moved the animals to new grazing areas as the snow receded and the green-grass season emerged. Her duties included taking the horses to water and grooming them. In addition, she cared for the three horses she brought with her from the White Clay People. She enjoyed working outside and often shared her dreams with the horses. Only occasionally would one respond with raised ears; then it would snort and turn to search out new sprouts of grass. Sometimes she thought of just mounting up and galloping away from these Crow people but she feared Five Scalps; his men could easily overtake her and then her claims to being one of them would be discredited and she might no longer be safe.

Although she debated whether to stay or to run, day after day she became more settled into Crow life. She decided to wait where she was and see what developed. She missed Little Feather very much, and promised herself that some day she would return to the White Clay people to share with him her experiences of living among the Crow.

Five Scalps was the leader of the Big Dog society and Pine Leaf envied him the rank and prestige accorded him by the *Mine'sepere,* or River Sparrow Hawks. The Big Dogs comprised the most experienced and mature warriors among Sparrow Hawk men. All the men were paired; Yellow Belly had been paired with Five

Scalps and he seemed to be resentful of that. Although he was becoming a fearless leader in his own right, Yellow Belly still rode in Five Scalp's shadow. During the Big Dog ceremony, Five Scalps and Yellow Belly led the procession, followed by two rear men and four sash-owners. Some sash-owners wore a single sash and some wore two sashes crossed over their chests.

Cracked-Ice was paired with Tall Eagle; they wore belts of skin and were called belt-wearers. They daubed their bodies with mud and tied their hair on the sides of their heads to resemble bear's ears. Belt-wearers were required to walk up to an enemy in order to rescue a fellow clansman from enemy attack. Due to their bravery, they were allowed to eat first at the feasts and to dance first at society dances. Cracked-Ice and Tall Eagle were highly regarded by the Big Dogs as future war leaders.

As Five Scalps became more tolerant of Pine Leaf, his manner toward her softened. When he took her shooting, he was amazed at the accuracy she had with her three-fingered pull on the old orangewood bow. He tried it himself and found he could pull a much heavier bow. He restored Little Feather's rifle to her, then taught her to shoot it; though she was natural with a bow, he discovered she knew very little about guns. Pine Leaf found Five Scalps to be bright and moody, but he always took her training seriously. In fact, he seemed serious about almost everything, never joining in the stories and ribald joke telling of the other warriors. The dark, sullen man taught Pine Leaf a few words of the white man's English. He discussed war strategy with her and even spoke of some of the Sparrow Hawk customs with which he disagreed.

"It is not wise to mutilate yourself during mourning," he told her. "One can never become a great warrior if he loses fingers."

The green-grass season passed peacefully enough and as the brown-grass season began, Pine Leaf was finally inducted into the young Hammer Owner society. She outran nearly all of the young boys and shot her arrows as accurately as the best. She outraced her competitors when she rode Thunder and was quickly selected by any team conducting a mock battle or counting coup on small game animals. Because she was not as strong as the older boys, and could not wrestle competitively with them, she relied upon her agile mind. The war club became her favorite weapon and she practiced relentlessly.

CHAPTER 10

Pine Leaf heard a great commotion rising from the river. After running to investigate, she saw a large wooden boat being rowed upstream by three bearded white men. She recognized the leader as Frances Antoine Larocque, accompanied by the fat man who had helped take Red Plum from her. She still hated Lepage and did not trust Larocque. She eased back into the bushes to observe, but curiosity kept her from leaving. As she peered out through the leaves, she saw the boat land, then observed Five Scalps greeting the Frenchmen in their own language.

Five Scalps spoke in French, "Chief Rotten Belly gives you greetings and welcomes you to the River Sparrow Hawks. Do you still labor for the North West Company?"

Larocque took hold of Five Scalp's strong hand as he alighted from his bateau. *"Oui,"* he replied. "I still labor for the North West Company. But *Monsieur*, the Hudson Bay Company tries to put us out of business. I do not know how much longer we can endure their financial injury."

Five Scalps nodded and grunted as the two spoke. Larocque offered, "I have Charles McKenzie, Baptiste Lepage and John Evans with me. We have guns, knives, needles, pots, powder, shot and tradecloth, but not as much as in former years. Our supplies are being cut short from England due to the influence of Hudson Bay Company. They seem to think that HBC means "here before Christ!"

The village set up a trading feast and for two days the Sparrow Hawks bartered skins, hides and furs for traps and other essentials they could not provide for themselves. Pine Leaf observed Lepage from a distance. She would not try approaching him for fear of being recognized and giving away her deep secret. She also feared what she might do if she came too close to the Frenchman.

After the feast, Larocque talked business with Five Scalps. *"Monsieur,"* he said, "your old friend Manuel Lisa is leading a fur brigade up the river this summer. We also hear that the American Fur Company is sending Wilson Price Hunt to set up a trading post at the mouth of the Columbia. Hunt works for *Monsieur* Jacob Astor and wants to establish a fur trading post in Oregon for the American Fur Company. But I believe the Hudson Bay Company will never allow competition on the Pacific. They control the Columbia from its mouth to its sources. Maybe you can make Hunt smart enough to save his life."

This news excited Five Scalps. He felt confident Lisa would hire him again in spite of their past conflicts. "Manuel Lisa and I fought before I left Fort Raymond but he knows I am the best interpreter on the Missouri," he said. "Besides the Crow and Arikara love me. Thank you, my friend, for the information." Silently Five Scalps hoped that if he did not get work with Lisa, perhaps he could guide the greenhorn, Wilson Hunt, to the Pacific. He had heard of this great ocean and wished to see it.

After several days, Larocque and his party left, descending the Yellowstone River toward its confluence with the Missouri. Pine Leaf was once more melancholy, thinking of home and Red Plum. Despite her attempt at eavesdropping on the traders, she had learned nothing of her tribespeople or her stepmother.

After the trading ended, Pine Leaf's training resumed. "All braves must enter the sweatlodge for purification prior to a raid," Cracked-Ice informed her. "They must drink much water to thin their blood and pray to their secret-helpers. Drinking a lot of water also keeps the men getting up during the night, so that they may be more alert and not oversleep. Many braves keep special rocks wrapped in animal skins for power. You must also take a pair of new moccasins to wear on your homeward journey. If possible, you should take along a dog to carry your shoes, water paunch and halter ropes."

Cracked-Ice offered, "Scouts are called *akt'site* and they wear wolf skins when sent to locate enemy camps. They even howl like wolves to deceive the enemy." He continued, "When preparing for the raid, braves must tie sacred objects to their clothing, paint their faces, and sing toward the enemy camp. During a raid the party must fast and make a camp constructed of sticks, bark and foliage. The party sends out the scouts and when they return they kick over piles of wapiti dung before reporting their findings. Finally, a brave is chosen to lead the raiding party to success."

"What do they do after a raid?" asked Pine Leaf. Cracked-Ice smiled at her never-ending curiosity, then took another drink of water from his buffalo hide bag.

He responded, "After a raid, the party rides or runs at full speed to get home. A celebration pudding, called *batsikyaraku,* is prepared for the homecoming feast and a long dance, or *bahatsge,* is held, where young women sit behind the braves, singing songs about his bravery. If you become a warrior, you will also have a young maiden to sing to you, but you cannot lie with her as we do."

Pine Leaf had no desire to lie with a woman. Besides she rarely associated with any of the girls here because they treated her like she had no relatives instead of like a long lost sister. She might as well be a captive as far as her social life was concerned.

Her new brother continued talking. "Scalps are scraped, dried, and blackened with charcoal before being placed on a scalp-stick. When reciting deeds, a brave can never boast of scalps, but he can tell of *dakce,* counting of coup on the enemy, by touching them with his hands or with his coup stick." Pine Leaf proved an apt pupil, taking every opportunity to learn more about the societies and their customs. She would need to know everything the men did if she were to succeed as a warrior.

During the leaf-falling season, Cracked-Ice and Five Scalps allowed Pine Leaf to attend hunts, where she served as a horse tender and rifle bearer, just as she had with Little Feather on that fateful, last trip with him.

Although she was excited to be learning the ways of warriors and hunters, she couldn't help but notice that Five Scalps acted restless and often looked expectantly toward the east. *Something was on his mind.* But Pine Leaf was certainly in no position to ask him about his concerns. She was still a child.

CHAPTER 11

Emanating from the Hidatsa, word rippled across the plains that the Astorian group had reached the mouth of the Nodaway River and would winter there. After hearing the news, Five Scalps announced, "I am going to winter with the Arikara on the Heart River." *And with that, he left.*

Pine Leaf continued to look to Cracked-Ice for guidance, security and companionship. He had always shown a great deal of sensitivity while giving her instruction and she believed he was fond of her.

In the fall of the white man's year of 1811, Chief Rotten Belly gathered an assembly of the River Sparrow Hawk. He announced, "We will move to the Bighorn Basin for the winter and join with our relatives, the Mountain Sparrow Hawks. Chief Long Hair has sent his personal messengers to invite us."

Pine Leaf remembered that Red Plum had told her that the *A'c'araho* and *Erarapi'o* tribes were part of the Mountain Sparrow Hawks. She was told that their chief had hair over a horse's length long but that he usually kept it rolled up and placed in a leather case. She thought, "I can't imagine hair so long; surely my hair will never reach such a magnificent length." She grew anxious to see this Chief Long Hair.

Excitement rose among the villagers as three thousand people dismantled their lodges and packed their belongings in preparation for their journey up the Bighorn. As they readied to leave, Cracked-Ice shyly informed Pine Leaf of his impending plans.

"I am taking Little Blossom as my wife," he said. "You may continue living in my lodge but I ask you to consider Little Blossom as your sister." At first she felt hurt and jealous, for she had been the only woman in Cracked-Ice's lodge since her capture. Her guide and protector had given her plenty of attention, but now he would be spending most of his time with his new wife. However, Pine Leaf's jealousy over Little Blossom proved short-lived.

As she came to know the small, pleasant girl of sixteen summers, she found her to be excellent company whenever Cracked-Ice left to hunt or raid. Little Blossom was not particularly pretty, but she was friendly and comfortable. She treated Pine Leaf as a sister and held her in high esteem. She never discouraged Pine Leaf from pursuing the dream of becoming a warrior, but she did attempt to educate her about the mysteries of womanhood.

Pine Leaf listened to her sister's woman-talk, but at the age of eleven she did not fully understand the menses, childbirth or motherhood. She did envy Little Blossom's open caressing and playful fondling of Cracked-Ice, but she tried to give them as much privacy as she could when they camped each night.

Although their travel proved slow, Rotten Belly's people finally arrived at the home of the Mountain Sparrow Hawks, near the mouth of the Nowood. Cries of "ka'he'! ka'he'!" arose as they were greeted by old friends and relatives. The festivities lasted for four days. *As-as-to* (Chief Long Hair) and *A-ra-poo-ash* (Chief Rotten Belly) smoked the sacred pipe to reunite the two main divisions of the Sparrow Hawk people. Pine Leaf noticed that each chief took his turn pointing the pipe upwards, downwards, then to each of the four directions. She listened as they spoke of their great raids, coups and battles and called each other brother.

While Cracked-Ice and Little Blossom reassembled their lodge, Pine Leaf visited the youth of the village. They rode off to explore the basin and become better acquainted with her new friends. Although curious about her at first, the Mountain Sparrow Hawk boys soon learned they could consider her one of them, and that she could compete with the best of them.

With the early thaws of the green-grass season, Rotten Belly moved his River Sparrow Hawks down to the mouth of the Greybull, while Long Hair moved his Mountain Sparrow Hawks up to the Wind River Valley. From the Greybull, Pine Leaf spent the green-grass and yellow-grass seasons exploring the Bighorn and Shell Creek. One day in late brown-grass season, she and a small party of Hammer Owners were hunting in the upper reaches of Shell Canyon when they noticed a large party of white men coming through Granite Pass.

Their first impulse was to flee down the canyon, but they stopped when they heard an echoing, "Ka'he! Ka'he!" They held their defensive position until they recognized the caller—who was none other than their old war leader, Five Scalps. Pine Leaf rejoiced at the sight of the scarred black man who had been her protector and who now lead four pack mules laden with supplies. He left the others behind and rode up to the young Hammer Owners.

"I am guiding the white men to the great ocean across the Shining Mountains," he said. "We have sixty-five chiefs, led by a greenhorn who doesn't know a bear's behind from wapiti humps. Their headman will not listen to me and he trusts no one. Because he refuses to trade with the Sparrow Hawks, I am taking Rotten Belly as many presents as my mules will carry before the white fools can stop me." Five Scalps, Pine Leaf and the Hammer Owners hurried down to the mouth of the Greybull River and into the village. Here Five Scalps called everyone to assemble by the chief's lodge.

"I have fine gifts for everyone from the white men who follow me," he announced. "Treat them as our brothers and we will earn great favors. Five Scalps has spoken." Five Scalps quickly unpacked the mules, passing out awls, knives, cloth, glass beads, fusil guns and spearpoints. The villagers clamored to obtain as many gifts and trade goods as they could.

When Wilson Price Hunt and his entourage finally reached the excited Crow, he was furious that Five Scalps had given away so many of his goods. Already suspicious and frightened by this savage-looking black man, Hunt now believed him to be a thief as well. He feared he would have nothing left for Astoria unless he got rid of this heathen guide. Turning to his other guide, he said, "Pierre, that fool has given away half of my trade goods. I may not have anything left when we reach

Astoria. I am going to set up camp as far away from these damn thieves as I can. Go see if you can trade with the Crow for more horses. Tell that damn *nigger* I will pay him off but I no longer need his services."

Though Pierre Dorion felt nervous about these directions, he obeyed his unpleasant boss. He hoped that his friend Five Scalps would not blame him for being dismissed by Hunt. Pierre was also concerned because, while he was also an interpreter and guide, Five Scalps knew the passes over the mountains better than he did, and he knew they were headed for rough times, trying to cross those passes during the snow-falling season.

Dutifully, Dorion rode into the village. When he found Five Scalps he said, "Friend, that fool wants me to trade for horses. He is offering you four traps and four rifles if you will stay with the Crow because he feels that you stole his goods."

Dorion's announcement surprised Five Scalps, but he agreed to the deal, and advised the man as best he could. He advised, "Take the fools up to the Mountain Sparrow Hawks on the Wind River. When the snows melt, you can cross over the mountains by ascending the Popo Agie and crossing over a broad pass to the south of the Wind River Mountains at the sources of the Sweetwater River." Five Scalps kept his smoldering anger in check with a deep breath. "Good luck to you," offered Five Scalps, "and if that fancy ass refuses to listen to you, leave him where he stands—save yourself and your family. If he does not do as you tell him, he will never reach the Columbia." Dorion thanked the dark guide, then finished his trading before returning to the new camp of the Astorians.

After Hunt and his party departed, the village moved down river to a point below the mouth of the Shoshone River. Because the tribe was running low on fresh meat, Five Scalps planned a large hunt. Approaching Pine Leaf, he said, "I would like for you to select seven of the Hammer Owners to hunt with me as part of your training. All of you will serve us as our horsetenders."

Thrilled, Pine Leaf ran swiftly to gather the young apprentices, thinking that now they would look up to her for gaining them the honor of participating in a major hunt. She knew that since Little Blossom was expecting her first child, Cracked-Ice would not be going with them.

The hunting party retraced the very steps made after Pine Leaf's capture and she felt despondent again. Although she felt content most of the time, she still longed to see her White Clay people, sometimes more than others, but she always felt a little homesick.

When they neared War Horse Lake her longing deepened. This was where she had last seen Little Feather. She remembered thinking the place was ideal for buffalo and sure enough, as they arrived, they sighted a good-sized herd.

"You and the other Hammer Owners will hold our spare horses but stay away from the surround," Five Scalps told her. Then spreading out his hunters he directed them to proceed slowly toward the herd from three directions. "When the herd shows alarm," he told them, "rush toward the wapiti and drive them into the lake."

Pine Leaf watched with renewed excitement as the lead bulls began snorting and pawing the ground, then a few of the old bulls made their break. She observed, as the hunters followed, firing their guns to stampede the herd toward the water; however, the herd split into three distinct groups. One ran around the northwest shore, one went around the southeast shore, and the third group began milling around, snorting and pressing each other back into the lake, trying to form a circle for defense. Some of the frantic cows even tried to swim away as the hunters fired arrows and guns into their midst. The frightened animals trampled each other in panic as the shoreline turned crimson with blood. Quickly the sand and shallow water became strewn with buffalo carcasses.

As Pine Leaf noticed a small band of leaderless cows and calves headed directly toward her and the Hammer Owners. The boys let loose their extra ponies and hooted loudly as they gave chase. Pine Leaf fired six arrows in rapid succession, just as she did in her dreams, and a fine cow went down. As she stopped Thunder and dismounted, the horse raised his ears and walleyed the fallen cow. As she approached the slain animal, she suddenly became aware for the first time that she had killed her first buffalo. Now she began to tremble from her great excitement. Quickly she cut the animal's throat, drinking some of the warm, sticky blood to enhance her personal medicine. Knowing her arrows would identify her kill, she quickly remounted and gave chase to round up the spare ponies she had released in her excitement. She realized that if she lost any of the hunters' mounts, she would be condemned for not doing her duty; she may even be prevented from accompanying them on future hunts.

Several of the young Hammer Owners had also made kills and they too were quickly trying to regain their lost ponies. As Pine Leaf turned her attention to the lake, she saw several hunters using their horses and hide ropes to drag their kills from the water. Other hunters were already skinning and dressing their retrieved kills.

"I will have to get assistance to prepare my beautiful cow," she thought. "I will ask Five Scalps for help. He will be proud of me."

Camaraderie grew between the seasoned hunters and the young Hammer Owners, as everyone celebrated their success. That night they camped by the lake, building large fires from buffalo dung. They roasted ribs and ate tongues and buffalo humps. Some men even chewed long strands of intestines, with one man at each end. They all sang songs and told of brave deeds well into the night. This night Pine Leaf's melancholy did not visit her as she went to sleep, for now she felt complete. This kind of life was indeed her destiny and she prayed to the Great Spirit that it would be her way of life from now on. She missed the White Clay people less than ever, and even her need to be with Little Feather waned in light of her new experiences among the Crow.

By noon of the next day all meat and hides were packed on their spare horses and the tired but jovial party began their triumphant return to Absaroka. The village welcomed the fresh meat and held four days of feasting, four days of smoking meat, four days of making pemmican, and four additional days to cure the hides.

Finally, the village moved on, traveling upriver to rejoin Long Hair's Mountain Sparrow Hawks. On their third day of travel, Pine Leaf and the others noticed a bright light moving across the sky. Some of the Sparrow Hawk leaders feared this sign may portend the end of the world and refused to move further; but the girl took it as a good omen, declaring success for her new life. For several weeks she watched its glittering illumination. In the evening she would lie on her back, gazing up at the light, daring to dream of greatness.

After the comet traveled to the other side of the sky and disappeared, the village renewed their migration up the Bighorn. They recrossed the Flat Willow, the North Willow, and the Musselshell. After stopping for a rest they crossed the Elk and traveled to the mouth of the Shoshone. Rotten Belly finally located Long Hair at the hot springs below Wind River Canyon.

From this great spring flowed huge volumes of steaming water day and night, and had been doing so even before the Sparrow Hawk people first arrived in the Bighorn Basin. Great stone-like formations had formed from its cooling waters, as they emptied into the Bighorn River. Once settled, Pine Leaf explored the hot springs area, marveling at the steamy water. In the river she could find all temperature ranges, from boiling hot to icy cold. She loved to move about in the water until she found the right temperature for her current mood. Sometimes she stayed in the warm water until her fingers and toes became wrinkled, only moving to cooler waters when she felt faint.

She much preferred this method of bathing to squirting water from her mouth into her hands to wash her body. She also preferred it to sitting in a sweatlodge until her pores were open, and then racing outside and rolling in the snow. Pine Leaf explored the upper Elk, past a large rock formation that had been named Pompey's Pillar by the great redheaded Indian Agent, William Clark.

She thought, "This has truly been my finest season," and her dreams continued to soar.

CHAPTER 12

When the green-grass season began, Rotten Belly moved his people down the Bighorn and the Elk to the mouth of the Powder. Game proved plentiful and Pine Leaf participated in more of the hunts. She was now accepted by most of the hunt leaders and at last began using her gun to kill game, but most of the time she still preferred her orangewood bow.

Cracked-Ice and Little Blossom became proud parents of a baby girl, who they named Doe Eyes. Pine Leaf remembered the name was the same as that of her dearly departed grandmother, but figuring it would not be safe for her to tell anyone here, she kept it to herself.

Shortly thereafter, Five Scalps brought a young wife, Sparrow, to live with them. She was dark, small, pleasant and a hard worker. Sparrow had known Little Blossom all her life and the two were good friends. Due to their closeness and the crowded conditions of the lodge, Pine Leaf again felt she had lost the companionship of a good friend, so she concentrated more and more on her Hammer Owner training.

In late green-grass season, Pine Leaf observed a trapping party making their way up the Elk. Five Scalps informed her that his old employer, Manuel Lisa, led the party. He told her, "Lisa hired George Drouillard, John Coulter, Andrew Henry, Daniel Potts and me to ascend the Yellowstone to the mouth of the Bighorn in the white man's year of 1807. During that winter Lisa sent me to trade merchandise to the Sparrow Hawks for furs. However, Lisa accused me of giving away most of the trade goods without gaining many furs, and although I told him that I awarded the merchandise to build good relations for future trading, he attacked me anyway. I then beat him until Daniel Potts finally pulled me off."

Five Scalps concluded his story by chuckling as he told her, "I then decided to stay among my newfound friends, the Sparrow Hawks, figuring it would be a lot safer for me."

The arriving party was clerked by John C. Luttig, with old Toussaint Charbonneau acting as interpreter. Other members of the party were Alexander Carson, Ben Jones, John Coulter, John Hoback, Jacob Reznor, Ed Robinson and Caleb Greenwood —Five Scalps knew them all.

After landing, Lisa approached and spoke in Spanish, "Señor Five Scalps, I would like you to keep Greenwood with you here on the Bighorn and teach him how to trap and trade among the Crow. I'll place you on the usual retainer and share the profits with you. I know we do not always agree, but I have great respect for your influence among the Crow and I wish you to teach Greenwood their language and customs."

Five Scalps responded sternly. "I also have respect for you as a businessman and a trader. I will assist my old friend Greenwood if you will give me a free hand and accept my judgment in all matters concerning the Crow."

Lisa shook his hand, saying, "You drive a hard bargain, however, I understand and agree. Now, can you get me into the council with Rotten Belly and will you interpret for me?" Five Scalps nodded, then led Lisa and his men to Rotten Belly's large lodge.

After smoking with Rotten Belly, Lisa said, "Chief, I wish to leave Greenwood among you to trade and learn your language. I will pay Five Scalps to be his host and teacher and to provide trade goods for your people." Chief Rotten Belly grunted his acceptance of Lisa's proposal. To seal the relationship, Lisa gave the Crow numerous needles, awls, knives, shot and powder. After Lisa left, Greenwood settled in to begin learning the ways of the Crow. Five Scalps took Pine Leaf and some of the Hammer Owners on a hunting expedition up the Tongue River then up the Powder. After several days they reached its headwaters, where they established a temporary camp.

Before long a band of Hidatsa appeared at their camp begging for food. Their leader, Chief Two Wolves, spoke to Five Scalps. "We have been chasing a raiding party of Blackfeet but we ran out of food. When we have regained our strength, we will camp upstream so that your horses will not tempt my braves."

Five Scalps examined them coolly; they did not appear to be suffering from hunger. Fearing a ruse, he responded, "We will supply you with meat but I must insist that you move your men upstream immediately. I don't wish to make my young braves feel nervous because of the presence of your warriors."

Two Wolves smiled. "I understand, my friend," he said. "I don't wish to upset your fine young men and I don't want to tempt any of my men." Five Scalps and the Hammer Owners gave the Hidatsa some food, but as the visitors rode out of sight Five Scalps quickly turned to his charges.

"Pen up all of the horses and take turns guarding them through the night," he ordered. "They will return before dawn to steal them." Although the sentinels tried to stay alert, the night grew so dark that they could see very little and they heard nothing. Near dawn, Pine Leaf was awakened with a sound of alarm.

"The Hidatsa have stolen seven of our horses!" said one of the young hunters. Pine Leaf immediately grabbed her weapons and began saddling Thunder. Along with the hunters who still had mounts, she rode out in pursuit of the horse thieves. As Five Scalps followed the thieves' tracks beyond the Powder, he spotted a straggler and gave chase.

The frightened Hidatsa abandoned his horse and began climbing a high bank, trying to reach the plains above. Five Scalps stopped his horse and loaded a double ball shot into his Hawken rifle. Taking careful aim he shot and killed the thief, however, the man's body lodged against a rock. Pine Leaf had to climb the bluff to dislodge it so it could fall. By the time she climbed back down, the young Hammer Owners had already scalped the dead Hidatsa. Then everyone remounted, resuming pursuit of the fleeing horse thieves.

As they raced across the prairie they soon caught up with a man and a boy. When they surrounded the two, the boy gave up his weapons, but the man refused.

Five Scalps turned to his young warriors. "I'll take care of the old fool," he announced.

As he leapt from his horse onto the defiant man, the two began a fight to the death, rolling and clawing each other in mortal combat. Both were strong and tenacious, and the fight seemed even at first. Suddenly, a nervous young Hammer Owner shot the captive boy, which made the older man go berserk. Apparently, the boy was the Hidatsa warrior's son, and the father began growling like an angry bear. With a great burst of energy, he broke away from Five Scalps and raced across the prairie. Almost every gun in the Crow party blasted the warrior's large body until he fell writhing on the grass, finally dying.

From a distance, the Hidatsa chieftain watched as two of his men and the boy met with their violent deaths. He did not fear the young Crow braves, but in order to stop their crazy black leader from following him, he turned the stolen horses loose and fled back toward his earthen lodges at the mouth of the Heart River.

Five Scalps sent Pine Leaf and the Hammer Owners back to the Bighorn so he could be alone with his thoughts. "I have to get away from the Crow demands for war and revenge," he decided. "I am getting too old to continue living this way. If I go to wait on the Missouri, perhaps I can get a job with Lisa or some new trapping party entering the fur trade from St. Louis."

When he finally caught up with his protégés, he told them about his decision. "I have to go and live for a while with the Arikara. I will return during the next green-grass season. Pine Leaf, you must lead them home. Farewell!" She hated to see her mentor leave again but she was more secure with herself now. She felt the young men would follow her, as Five Scalps had requested. Soberly, she led the Hammer Owners safely back to the Bighorn.

CHAPTER 13

While the War of 1812 between Britain and the United States raged on, tension among the Indians along the Missouri River continued to swell. Many tribes became hesitant to move too far out on the plains due to continual fighting instigated by British trade representatives. With Five Scalps gone, Yellow Belly was the only Sparrow Hawk leader strong enough to attract hunters to follow the buffalo migrations; horse raids were almost forgotten during this time.

Yellow Belly led his hunters to the Tongue River where they were ambushed by a large Cheyenne band. The enemy was in superior force and charged the Sparrow Hawks from every direction. Pine Leaf tried to follow the retreating Big Dogs, but the Cheyenne got in front of her and cut off her flank. She feigned a run for the water, then raced along the riverbank, forcing her horse to jump driftwood and logs along the way.

It seemed as if her pursuers were gaining on her when suddenly Yellow Belly raced in and shot two of the lead warriors. Not stopping to scalp them, he immediately led Pine Leaf up the bank toward the Sparrow Hawk Big Dogs, who set up a firing line along the high ground. As the Sparrow Hawk battle line laid down its deadly fire, the charging Cheyenne quickly abandoned their attack and disappeared back up the river. Yellow Belly regrouped his warriors and headed back toward the Bighorn.

Pine Leaf admonished herself. "Even in retreat Yellow Belly is a hero. I have proven that I am not yet ready to become a warrior." The narrow escape had left her trembling. She vowed, "I will resume my training more seriously and I will get to know every inch of our tribal lands. I also vow to fast and meditate with my secret-helpers so the Great Spirit can make me stronger."

She located a rock pillar, about two horses high, on the prairie near the upper reaches of the Tongue River. Whenever she became melancholy, she would ride to this sacred place to meditate, fast and pray, sometimes for days. Nevertheless, she couldn't completely relax as she had to remain continually vigilant for the approach of the Teton Sioux or the Cheyenne, who traveled through this area on their raids and buffalo hunts.

On the Missouri, cold weather persisted throughout the summer. From June to July, frost occurred every night and snow fell off and on through July. The game herds turned back due to unusually frigid weather and did not migrate to the upper Missouri until August. The only meat obtained was from mountain sheep and elk forced out of the mountains by the freakish weather. The Sparrow Hawks had to travel to the Platte River grasslands in order to obtain enough buffalo to sustain them. Many of the children and old people suffered from hunger until the weather finally broke.

In late summer of the white man's year of 1816, Pine Leaf finally attended Yellow Belly on a horse raid against the Blackfeet, also known as Pecuni. He led sixty-five Big Dogs on foot across the shallow Elk River. They carried their war weapons, rawhide and horsehair ropes, jerked meat, pemmican, and fire steels. He led them northwest until they struck the Musselshell, then ascended that river westerly until they reached the mineral springs of the upper Smith. After resting, they descended the Smith to the Missouri and crossed to the mouth of the Sun. They then traveled westerly up the Sun for one long day before turning north, where they crossed the Deep and Teton, then rested again while they replenished their food supply.

Now that the party had entered enemy territory, they knew they needed to be more cautious than ever. They had not seen any hunting or raiding parties and felt that their presence was still unknown to the Blackfeet. Pine Leaf prayed to her secret helpers and attached her medicine bundle to her body before following Yellow Belly to the Dupuyer, where they ascended to the mouth of the Medicine River. They secreted themselves while Yellow Belly went to reconnoiter the Blackfeet. As the quarter moon set, Yellow Belly returned to his Big Dogs. He had located twenty lodges and hundreds of horses at the big bend of the Medicine. He gave directions to the warriors.

"Grizzly Bear, take twenty braves and charge the Pecuni from above the river. Bear's Head, you take twenty braves and attack from below the river. I will lead our main party to capture the horses and provide mounts for each of you as you enter the village."

Pine Leaf stayed with Yellow Belly as he moved his command upriver, where they maneuvered close to the Pecuni horse herd. At this time of the morning, the herds were unattended. The Sparrow Hawks moved quietly among the nervous animals, taking off their hobbles and selecting the finest for their personal mounts. Pine Leaf selected a tall, white stallion with black spots covering his hindquarters. She mounted the stallion and led four other horses toward the place where she expected to rendezvous with her men.

The bend of the Medicine River became bedlam as the Sparrow Hawk braves charged the enemy village yelling and firing. Blackfeet poured out of their lodges, as women and children ran screaming across the stream. Yellow Belly and his mounted Big Dogs joined into the fray just as some of the Blackfeet warriors attempted to develop a counterattack. Pine Leaf raced up to offer mounts to four of her friends when, suddenly, she saw a Blackfoot brave riding toward her with his lance held high above his head. She raised her war club and kicked her mount to meet the challenge. As the enemy brave reached for the halter of her horse, he saw she was a girl and hesitated. Instinctively, she seized the moment to jerk her horse's head sharply to the left, while striking the brave viciously across the head with her war club, dropping him to the ground. Without hesitation, she dismounted and cut off his coiffured topknot. Then she quickly remounted and charged again with a high-pitched war-scream. The Blackfeet broke into disorder and retreated across the Medicine to defend their families.

Yellow Belly gave the sparrow hawk call to reassemble. He directed his braves to round up the hundreds of panicked ponies. The Big Dogs then drove the horses due south as fast as they could to the headwaters of the Dupuyer. They continued along the east base of the mountains, crossed the Deep and finally reached the headwater of the Sun. Yellow Belly estimated they had captured approximately six hundred horses and had not lost one warrior. He decided to place herders out and to rotate them periodically while his tired braves feasted and slept. At noon the next day they resumed their journey at a more leisurely pace. They painted their faces black to show their success before they drove the herd across the Elk and up the Bighorn.

The Sparrow Hawk village had already heard of the success of their raiding party and had prepared a feast for their returning warriors. Yellow Belly's party arrived with over five hundred fine mounts, having lost some in their struggle to cross streams and traverse thick woods. Pine Leaf received five fine ponies, but her spotted stallion became the fleetest one in the herd. She named him *Spotted Rump*.

During the homecoming feast, Yellow Belly recounted the raid to the village. He announced, "Our woman warrior, Pine Leaf, charged and slew a charging Blackfoot brave. She stopped the Pecuni's counterattack."

The more experienced warriors were skeptical of Yellow Belly's pronouncement and questioned how this maiden of sixteen winters could accomplish such a feat. Pine Leaf then stood up and displayed the enemy topknot she had taken. Grunts of approval and acceptance of her bravery rose from the crowd. Even the stoic Yellow Belly was pleased that this woman-warrior had taken the time to obtain this trophy in the midst of battle. The camp sang praises to Pine Leaf while she blushed with pride at her initiation as a Sparrow Hawk warrior.

During the brown-grass season, known as July to the white man, the River Sparrow Hawks moved easterly across the Rosebud to the Tongue. Here they found good grass and hunted as far as the Powder River. The Blackfeet had not retaliated for Yellow Belly's raid and the Sparrow Hawks were at peace with *their* small world.

CHAPTER 14

Chief Rotten Belly learned that Joseph La Framboise had built Fort Teton near the mouth of the Bad River. The chief wondered if this development would keep the Teton Sioux from traveling into Absaroka. While he thought that might be a good thing, he also knew more and more forts would be built in this country and he prayed that his people would survive the coming of the white man. The chief voiced his concern to the elders and the Council, but unlike Rotten Belly, the members were not able to envision what could *really* happen to the world of Absaroka.

Manuel Lisa became Indian sub-agent for the Missouri tribes. He knew Indian culture well and took several tribal chiefs to St. Louis to sign treaties with William Clark. Lisa ran several trading posts along the Missouri and headed the Missouri Fur Company. Clark was also a partner in the successful enterprise and jointly they continued to push their financial interests and influence farther and farther up the Missouri river.

When the leaves began to fall, the Sparrow Hawks journeyed up the Tongue to the Bighorn Mountains and crossed Granite Pass to Shell Canyon. From there, they ascended the Bighorn and the Wind River to the mouth of the Beaver, where they wintered with the Mountain Sparrow Hawks and the Mountain Shoshone. After the spring thaws, the River Sparrow Hawks decamped and traveled east to the headwater of the south fork of the Powder. Here they ranged until the brown-grass season, then descended the river to the mouth of the Mizpah.

Pine Leaf grew increasingly restless; she was definitely ready for the challenge of another raid. She had already traded Little Feather's old Northwest Company gun for a Model 1803, which had been first manufactured for the Lewis and Clark Expedition. Though she found this gun to be much more accurate and reliable than her old one, she still used her Osage orangewood bow for hunting buffalo.

At last she was invited to attend Yellow Belly and twenty-five Hammer Owners on a horse raid against the Teton Sioux. During the white man's year of 1818, their old enemies had been ranging in the prairie between the Tongue and the Rosebud, and the Sparrow Hawk Nation had long defended these lands as their own. Yellow Belly led his young followers across the Little Bighorn, the Rosebud Mountains and down Rosebud Creek; where the Rosebud met Deer Creek they discovered signs left by Sioux horses. Excitement grew within members of the party as Yellow Belly led them up the Deer until they located the enemy camp near a large bend of the creek. After spotting the camp, they retreated downstream to set up their own cold camp, without fires. The scouting wolves located a large horse herd further out on the prairie, above the creek and opposite the village. Ignoring the Sioux village, they concentrated on the horseherds.

"Take your ropes and quietly enter the herds on foot," directed Yellow Belly. "Take only two of the best ponies you can find. Ride one and lead the other back to our camp. When you return, give two calls of the sparrow hawk to let us know who you are. Remember, take only two horses; if you get greedy, you will frighten the herd and betray us to the enemy. I will punish anyone who disobeys or fails in this trial. I will guard your retreat and fire two rifle shots if we are discovered. Little Fox and Antelope will guard your horses while you are gone."

Yellow Belly then scattered sacred tobacco to the four winds as the young men and Pine Leaf disappeared over the bluff and into the dark night.

Pine Leaf climbed the bluff to find the ground covered with a few inches of snow. The reflection off of it offered her some slight illumination, which she much appreciated, because the night only granted a sliver of moon.

After traveling parallel with the creek for a while, she then moved out onto the prairie, where she believed she could actually smell the milling horses. She located a snowdrift, under which she dug to retrieve clumps of grass to attract the hungry horses. She held grass in both hands and stuffed some under her belt. Pine Leaf crept nearer until she could actually see the horses and feel their body heat, then she moved slowly and cautiously into the herd. As she walked among them she tried to soothe and calm the animals with soft sounds and words. She spotted a large, shimmering black gelding, which had excellent shoulders and long legs. Extending her bunched grass toward his mouth, she called softly. The horse had an irregular white spot between his alert, protruding eyes. The spot reminded her of the northern star, surrounded as it was with midnight blackness.

"Come to me, Black Star, and become my brother," she cooed. "I will care for you and protect you from the wolf packs. I will keep you safe from old man winter. Come, beautiful one." The cautious gelding slowly inched toward her, taking a few gingerly steps while stretching out his strong neck as far as he could towards the offered grass. As if drawn magnetically, he measured each step as he reached to nibble at the newfound food. As his lips and teeth took the first handful of grass, Pine Leaf took a cautious step forward and softly stroked his quivering muzzle. He flinched slightly but didn't pull away. After giving him some more grass, she deftly circled his neck with her horsehair rope. She then eased a halter over his muzzle and erect ears, all the while stroking his neck and singing softly to keep him calm.

Suddenly a large, muscular sorrel approached; with his ears laid back, he shouldered Black Star, almost shoving him on top of Pine Leaf. Evidently the sorrel wanted a handout too. Aggressively the new horse chewed the bunch grass she gave him, showing total disregard for the young girl holding it. With smooth regular movements Pine Leaf slipped her other rope around his stout neck, then gave each horse another mouthful of grass from the stash she'd tucked under her belt.

"What great fortune," she thought. "Another gelding and a magnificent one, too." The red horse had long white stockings on his forelegs and short white socks on his hind legs. "I will call you Red Devil," she whispered. Due to his aggressive nature she decided to ride Red Devil and lead Black Star.

Swiftly and quietly Pine Leaf swung atop the red horse, then stealthily moved out of the herd, back toward Deer Creek. When she reached the bluff above the camp, she gave two calls of the sparrow hawk. Both she and her horses jerked back as Yellow Belly startled them by stepping out of the dark night. Holding Black Star's halter he examined Pine Leaf's catch.

"You are the first to return," he said finally, "and you have two excellent ponies, sister. I think you have counted three fine coups on your brothers." His grin revealed his large white teeth, which contrasted against his dark skin and the dark night. Since he rarely smiled, Pine Leaf couldn't have felt more complimented. Beaming with pride, Pine Leaf rode down to the creek side camp. She confidently greeted Little Fox and Antelope, who excitedly examined her fine new horses. Slowly the other Hammer Owners straggled into camp with their horses. Lone Wolf arrived last, and although he came in behind the others, he too had a couple of fine geldings in tow.

"Hammer Owners," Yellow Belly said, "you have all passed your trial. Each of you has caught fine Sioux horses. However, Pine Leaf excelled for not only catching two of the best, but also for arriving first. Thus, she will have the honor of leading our return to our village. You have all done well and some of you will be pledged soon to become Big Dog warriors, learning to lead our people against our enemies. Now let us get our horses out of here and leave our enemy to his shame."

Eagerly they rode back toward Bighorn Canyon to share their triumph with their elders and families.

Unfortunately, their joy was short-lived as they found the entire village in mourning. Pine Leaf led the Hammer Owners to the chief's lodge, where with tears in his eyes, Rotten Belly solemnly greeted her.

"My child," he began, "Tall Eagle and your brother, Cracked-Ice, have been slain by the Blackfeet." Pine Leaf froze where she sat, not believing what she had just heard. "They were leading a Big Dog raid," he continued, "when they were surprised and overwhelmed. They fought bravely as the rearguard so that their comrades could escape. The Big Dogs regrouped and mounted a counterattack, but it was too late. Our warriors were able to retrieve their bodies and we have held up their burial until your return."

Pine Leaf felt faint. Without a word, she leapt from her horse and raced to find Little Blossom. As she entered Cracked-Ice's lodge, she saw dried blood clinging to the bloody stubs of two of Little Blossom's fingers. The girl was wailing and Pine Leaf could see where she'd been pulling out her hair. Her emotions were already strained to the breaking point, but became heightened by the sight of Little Blossom's grief; without thinking of the warning Five Scalps had given her, Pine Leaf drew her knife and cut off the first joint of the little finger on her left hand. But the pain that followed did not relieve the grief she felt at the loss of her brother.

Due to the absence of Five Scalps, Sparrow continued to live in their lodge. Though she certainly mourned her friends' loss, she didn't mutilate herself. However, until their mourning period was over, it would fall upon Pine Leaf to keep up the lodge. After four additional days of mourning, a council was held to honor the achievements of the young Hammer Owners, pledging some of them to various adult societies. Yellow Belly related the achievements of each young man, praising each in turn, but he saved his greatest praise for Pine Leaf. When she rose to speak, she was still in grief for Cracked-Ice.

"I will wed no warrior until I have killed one hundred of the enemy with my own hands," she declared. "Let no man underestimate my resolve. I will also adopt Little Blossom and Doe Eyes as my own family. I will become their protector and provider." She then raised her long arms to the Sun God and said, *"Bac' dak' k' o' mbawiky,"* which meant "While I live, I will carry on." To the Sparrow Hawks such declarations showed great commitment. Admiration for Pine Leaf grew among the villagers and even among the old experienced warriors, who had not yet taken her seriously.

Chief Rotten Belly rose and spoke, "Big Dogs, I ask that you apprentice Pine Leaf as a replacement for her brave, deceased brother Cracked-Ice." He continued, "From this day forward respect her as a young warrior, allowing her every opportunity to become an equal among you. I wish it to be so."

The Big Dogs obeyed their beloved chief, accepting the young woman as one of their own. Little Blossom was pleased to have Pine Leaf as her provider and pledged herself to become her *i'rapa' tse,* or loyal sister. The girl did not wish to ever remarry, and she believed Pine Leaf would make an excellent provider and substitute for her husband.

After the council meeting, Pine Leaf left the village to travel up the Bighorn to her favorite rock pillar. Here, she meditated and fasted, then dug a hole under the large rock at the base of the pillar, where she deposited some of the remains and belongings of Cracked-Ice. Here is where she could commune with him. Here is where she could be alone with him. Whenever her sadness became too great to bear, whenever her loneliness became too deep to share, she could come here and feel comforted.

She wept and prayed for one more day. While she was there, she found an additional pebble for her medicine bag, a rugged quartz stone with a shiny jagged line through the middle. At last Pine Leaf started home. After all, she had people depending on her as *never* before.

In time the Big Dogs attempted several raids against the Blackfeet confederacy of Bloods and Piegans, but they proved unsuccessful. However, Pine Leaf felt exhilarated and gained confidence with each new raid, or *sortie.* Her adept hunting skills provided plenty of meat, hides and furs for Little Blossom, who in turn kept up Pine Leaf's wardrobe. During quiet times Pine Leaf played with little Doe Eyes, who now began taking her first steps.

Though some of the Sparrow Hawks trapped beaver for the white men, Pine Leaf considered it beneath her dignity to do so. After all, she was a warrior. When she wasn't hunting, she practiced her war skills, greatly improving her accuracy with the rifle. Periodically, she traded hides and buffalo robes for shot, flints and powder.

Yellow Belly watched his protégé bloom, knowing she could become a fierce warrior someday. Certainly she had more dedication and desire than he had observed in most of the tribe's young men, and though she may never equal Rotten Belly or Grizzly Bear, she should make a fine war leader. She had grown tall and wiry and was becoming a fairly attractive young woman. Among the Sparrow Hawks, he considered her very comely, and she was also unique because she was still a virgin.

The war chief knew that though Pine Leaf seemed reserved most of the time, she had a boiling cauldron roiling inside, a mixture of anger and sadness. She reminded him of the geysers he had seen at the headwaters of the Elk, and he feared for the enemy warrior who would ever corner her or cause her to release those pent-up emotions.

CHAPTER 15

Pine Leaf finally became a journeyman Big Dog, but she still had not been given permission to participate in the Sun Dance Ceremony, as all the other members had. At twenty-one winters of age she felt persecuted, knowing her exclusion was because she was a woman. She constantly badgered Yellow Belly and the other Big Dogs for her right to this high honor, but they evaded the issue. One day she spoke up during a feast, confronting her leaders in public.

"I have been fearless in battle and no one can surpass me in running or in raiding for horses," she argued. "I now lay my claim before the Big Dog members." The surprised group stopped eating, looking to Yellow Belly and Grizzly Bear for a response.

"I do not like this woman," thought Yellow Belly. "She pretends to be a man. However, she is one of our best warriors and she is fearless. If we allow her to challenge the Sun Dance, she will either be disgraced or she will shame those who are too cautious to become true Big Dogs." The group waited for his response but he deliberated more, wondering how they would suspend her. Most young men were hung from slits in the flesh of their chests. He knew they could not hang her from her milk pouches. However, sometimes braves were suspended from the flesh of their backs; perhaps that would work for this female.

Finally, Yellow Belly faced her and made his reply for everyone to hear. "Pine Leaf is correct. She has proven true to all Big Dog ideals ever since she replaced her brother, Cracked-Ice. Although she is a woman, she is fearless, skilled at riding, an excellent hunter, and a fine warrior. She should not be denied the rites of the Sun Dance. However, because she is a woman, she should be tethered to the Sun Dance lodgepole by her back. Do all agree?"

Both grunts and cheers arose from the group as the Big Dog membership agreed with Yellow Belly's decision. Although she had dreamed of this very answer, Pine Leaf felt stunned at his response. She wanted to thank and even hug the stoic Yellow Belly, but she controlled herself. Instead, she slapped the backs of those around her and grinned her appreciation for their support. Now she had to prepare for the grueling ordeal and take her challenge seriously.

When Pine Leaf returned to her lodge, she excitedly told Little Blossom and Sparrow of the impending ceremony. Immediately Little Blossom began to cry.

"Oh! No, Pine Leaf," she begged, "You will surely die. No woman has ever attempted the Sun Dance. Even some of the young men have died in this ceremony. I cried for a week for the recovery of my sweetheart, Cracked-Ice, after his initiation. Now he is dead because of his brave training. I pray to you, do not do this thing. Little Doe Eyes and I need you and we love you."

After her initial shock, Sparrow calmly stated, "Little Blossom, our sister, Pine Leaf, needs our support and assistance more than we need her right now. Come, let us help her prepare for this challenge. She can show up those pompous warriors who have denied her this right for so long. In order to reach full warrior status, she *must* complete the Sun Dance. You know that."

Little Blossom slowed her crying to a sob as she realized that Sparrow was correct. Although she wished it could be untrue, she too began thinking of ways she could help and said, "I still have Cracked-Ice's Sun Dance doll and ceremonial instruments. He would have been proud to pass them on to you, Pine Leaf." Thrilled by this new revelation Pine Leaf's excitement grew as they unwrapped the bundle holding the precious personal effects of Cracked-Ice. Little Blossom had kept a few articles as remembrances, although most of his belongings had been buried with him.

But before much preparation could be accomplished, it was again time to move. Chief Rotten Belly led the River Sparrow Hawks to the greasy grass area of the Little Bighorn. Here the Big Dogs began construction of a large tipi lodge for the Sun Dance ceremony, built under the supervision of Yellow Belly.

Pine Leaf rode alone up the east fork of the river to her sacred rock pillar. Here she fasted for two days, praying to her secret-helper and calling out for guidance from Cracked-Ice, waiting for a vision of her future. As her body weakened, her mind and spirit gained strength. She returned to the Sparrow Hawk village full of confidence, ready to concentrate on the awesome task before her.

Pine Leaf saw the tall Sun Dance lodge as she neared the camp. In the forks of the extended lodgepoles rested a pile of ceremonial effigies, offerings and ornaments; they looked like an eagle's nest up there. Inside the lodge a large pole crossed the center pole. This log would be used to suspend the young warriors attempting the dance. From the pole already hung small bags of ceremonial tobacco, buffalo effigies and other secret pouches. This year Pine Leaf and three young men would be allowed to participate in the Sun Dance and, although she was the oldest, she was the only woman so honored.

When Pine Leaf entered her own lodge, Sparrow and Little Blossom began preparing her for the coming ceremony. The doll of Cracked-Ice had been made of ermine, stuffed with sweet grass, sacred tobacco and a buffalo hairball. The face and breastplate had been fashioned from white doeskin. The face bore a red smile and Little Blossom had painted fifty-four red marks on the breastplate to indicate a long life and many deeds. She had attached feathers of the sparrow hawk to the head to indicate long hair and a tiny skirt made of baby rabbit skin had been sewn around the waist to show that the doll represented a female.

Pine Leaf placed her favorite eagle-bone whistle around her neck and wore her finest white buckskin skirt, adorned by fifty-four elk's teeth, considered the richest skirt in the village. She wore beautiful, knee-high white buckskin moccasins, highly decorated with dyed porcupine quills. Since her back had to remain exposed, she could not wear a dress or tunic, so Little Blossom fashioned a beautiful apron to go around Pine Leaf's neck. The apron served to cover her breasts and was composed of otter skin, with tassels of mink attached on the sides and bottom. The women parted her hair with vermilion, tying the two long strands in front of the apron so it would not become tangled with the hanging ropes.

By the time they were prepared, it was almost sundown; this was to be a rare nighttime Sun Dance. Pine Leaf hurried to the ceremonial lodge. Since women spectators were forbidden, Little Blossom and Sparrow had to remain in their lodge where they could only wait and pray. If she survived, they would be ready to treat her wounds.

When Pine Leaf entered the lodge, she faced Chief Rotten Belly, Yellow Belly, Grizzly Bear, the elders of the council, and her Big Dog peers. All of them sat in a semicircle around a large fire at the rear of the lodge. Though weak from fasting she felt wild with anticipation. At Chief Rotten Belly's command, the chanting and drum beating began. As the sun reached the western horizon, Pine Leaf turned to face the chanters. She did not want to watch as the three young braves were skewered in the chest and drawn into the air to be suspended by their own flesh.

But her time was coming.

Suddenly, she felt the skin behind her left shoulder being pinched hard and then felt the cut of a sharp knife. Just as she was recovering from this shock, she felt the insertion of a wooden peg and could tell they were tying buffalo sinew to each end of the peg. She sighed to relieve the pain, and just as she regained her composure, they began the same procedure on her right shoulder.

To overcome the pain, the female warrior began to meditate, sending her mind on a vision quest to her sacred rock pillar. She felt no additional pain as the rope tied to the sinew lifted her into the air, leaving her dangling by the skin of her back from the Sun Dance pole. Pine Leaf sank deeper into her trance, but she endeavored to keep her head high. She maintained a soft smile on her lips while keeping her eyes softly closed. It was as if she were asleep in a peaceful meadow, near a river. She could see the grave of Cracked-Ice and saw hundreds of beautiful ponies grazing upon the prairie. For her, time was suspended, and she felt little pain.

She didn't know how long she hung there, but shock and pain returned to her as her soft flesh tore away from the wooden skewers, plunging her to the earthen floor of the lodge. It took several moments for her to realize that she had successfully completed the ceremony and now lay safely on the ground. As her vision cleared, she could see the faint light of the sunrise creeping through the smoke hole of the lodge.

She attempted to stand, but her numb legs would not obey her. Like a newborn colt, she tried again and again, wobbling and falling over until at last she stood. She heard a cheer rise from the Big Dogs and with blurry eyes saw the three brave young men still suspended by their own bloody flesh. However, all of them appeared to be unconscious. As Pine Leaf felt herself falling again, Grizzly Bear quickly rushed up to catch her and carry her to her lodge for medical attention.

Little Blossom and Sparrow had not slept much that night and immediately began ministering to their sister. Before Grizzly Bear left, he told them of her bravery during the ordeal. Quickly they undressed her and began applying herbal salves to her bloody back; they cleansed her wounds and cleaned the dried blood from the rest of her body. Though, she remained unconscious all day, they continued to attend to her wounds by placing moist, pulverized sinew into her mouth to relieve her swollen tongue and cracked lips.

On the second day, Pine Leaf was coherent, able to take both water and buffalo broth. Her wounds were fastened with a poultice and her nursemaids kept watch to see that she did not get an infection. But she would have to continue lying on her stomach until her torn flesh mended. She learned later that two of her companions had to be cut down, and one almost died from the ordeal.

Her back would forever bear the scars of her ordeal, but they would be scars of honor and pride. The white man's year of 1821 had been good for Pine Leaf.

Jerry A. Matney with D. A. Gordon

SECTION III

1821 - 1827

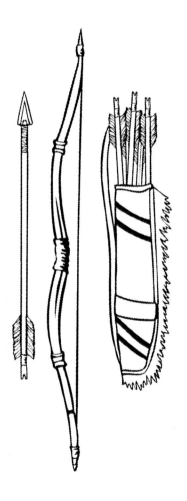

CHAPTER 16

Although they moved around a lot, the Plains people still received news. Word reached the tribe that Manuel Lisa, who'd had both an Indian wife and a white wife, had succumbed to an illness and died in St. Louis.

Fort Raymond, which had been built by Manuel Lisa, had not been in service for years. The Sparrow Hawk people learned that Joshua Pilcher, new head of the Missouri Fur Company, would build a trading post for them near the old site of Fort Raymond. The people grew excited about the prospect of having a trading post in Absaroka again.

The entire village moved to the mouth of the Bighorn on the Elk to see the white men work. Chief Rotten Belly encouraged his younger men to trap for beaver so that they would have a commodity for trade when the post was completed. However, most of these youths much preferred going on hunts and raids. The young maidens wore their finest garments, beads and necklaces around the fort, seeking sexual alliances with the strange, bearded foreigners. In this way they hoped to gain many trade credits for future trade.

Pine Leaf had never learned to trap and she had no desire to learn now. She told Yellow Belly and Grizzly Bear of her feelings.

"I will get my robes and furs by hunting," she said. "I do not wish to kill the beaver unless I can find nothing else for the sustenance of my family." They could only grunt in agreement, for neither of them wished to trap either.

Yellow Belly led the Big Dog Society on a large hunt to obtain meat for the village and robes for trade. Many of the hunters took their wives and packhorses so they could more quickly butcher and transport their kills. Pine Leaf took Little Blossom and Sparrow.

They located a large buffalo herd north of the Elk River, near Big Lake. With only her bow, Pine Leaf charged into the herd, carefully selecting the animals with the best hides rather than just killing the fattest cows. Five Scalps had taught her that the white men favored light brown or yellow robes and would pay dearly for a rare white buffalo robe. Leaning off the left side of Black Star, she shot her first animal right through the heart. As soon as she saw the beast fall, she selected another target. When she at last retired from the field, she had seven browns and five yellows on the ground.

Pine Leaf then rode over to help Little Blossom and Sparrow butcher the kills. Little Blossom approached her as she dismounted and hobbled her lathered-up horse.

"Sister," Little Blossom said, "these are beautiful robes and should bring many riches to our lodge."

Then Sparrow added, "However, you will have to help us locate some of your kills, because it seems some of your arrow feathers have disappeared inside the animals. We can only guess they are yours by the color of the hides."

Pine Leaf laughed. "I was so excited that I practically pushed the arrows into my kills instead of shooting from farther away. And Black Star! He almost rode on top of several of the buffalo to get me closer to them. He is a great buffalo-chaser and fears nothing." Surveying the work that lay before them, Pine Leaf said, "Hand me some knives and I will assist you."

Together they butchered the carcasses, placing the meat securely inside the hides. These they tied to the packhorses and travois to transport their precious cargo to their temporary camp at Big Lake.

After everyone had come in, they roasted humps and tongues, sang songs of praise and gave thanks to the Great Spirit for a good hunt. Later they began singing dirty songs and telling ribald jokes on each other.

Yellow Belly began to tease Pine Leaf. "Oh, great hunter," he said, "is your little wife with child yet?" The Big Dogs laughed while Pine Leaf and Little Blossom blushed. Then Yellow Belly continued his harangue. "I hear you *squat* when you relieve yourself, because your enemies cut off your *manhood*." The laughter and snickers continued, making Yellow Belly more confident in his humor.

"Dear Little Blossom," he said, "if your great warrior cannot give you another child or comfort your womanly desires, come to Yellow Belly's lodge. I always have an extra robe and my women smile with satisfaction."

This time there was less laughter; many felt that Yellow Belly had finally gone too far. Pine Leaf tried to compose herself but Little Blossom hid her face and began to cry from the sting of the crude joke. As Pine Leaf rose to face Yellow Belly across the fire, a hush fell over the camp.

"Thank you great warrior and fellow Big Dog," she said softly. "I am truly honored to have such a *faithful* and *loyal* comrade. I know you brag much about and think highly of your *manhood*, Yellow Belly. But when we were hunting together last spring, I was with you when we had to bathe in the icy Greybull." Now the assemblage held their collective breaths. *This* they wanted to hear.

"I decided to take a peek and see what you were so proud of," she continued, "and I was shocked to see what looked like a plum worm hiding in a sparrow's nest. Brother Yellow Belly, I am afraid *you* do not have much more to offer poor Little Blossom than I do."

As the entire camp rolled and howled in laughter at her response to Yellow Belly, Pine Leaf sat down. In uncharacteristic style, even Yellow Belly laughed until he had tears in his eyes. Everyone shared the good mood but no one else tried to make Pine Leaf the butt of their jokes. She had proven herself to be too quick-witted to mock or verbally challenge.

By afternoon, the Big Dogs and others proceeded south to the Elk, continued down river past the mouth of the Bighorn, and proceeded to the new trading post named Fort Benton. They received a grand welcome and held another feast to celebrate the hunt.

Pine Leaf, Sparrow and Little Blossom worked for days slicing and drying meat. They scraped the inside of the hides and tanned the robes by using buffalo brains and tallow. The work proved arduous but their efforts provided an abundance of food for themselves and their friends. They had the finest trade robes in the group. When Joshua Pilcher finally opened Fort Benton for trade, the Sparrow Hawks took in thirty packs of beaver, seven hundred buffalo and elk robes and two hundred fine deerskins.

Pilcher spoke to two of his men. "Boys, we've made a fine start. Now Bob, see what you and Mike can obtain this winter. Try to teach these Crow how to trap their streams, encourage them to help you locate some new trapping areas." But Jones had his doubts about Pilcher's orders.

"Hell, Josh," Jones argued, "we can't get them Crow warriors to work, like we did them Assiniboines and Atsina. All's the Crow wants to do is hunt, steal horses, and fight with the other tribes."

"I know Bob," Pilcher answered, "but tell them I will bring up some rich goods in the spring and they are going to wish they had plenty of furs to offer for my treasures." To both of them he warned, "Be alert and be careful of the Blackfeet. They still don't like Americans and I think those damned British keep them agitated against us with their lies."

Pilcher and his other men loaded their flatboats and headed downstream with the furs, while Robert Jones and Michael Immel prepared to winter with the Crow.

"I'll see you boys in the spring," Pilcher said as he left.

While the villagers camped near the fort, Pine Leaf stayed away from the white men as much as she could, only dealing with them to trade a precious skin for ammunition and necessities for her lodge.

As the white men received her periodic trade robes, Jones remarked, "Mike, why does a good-lookin' gal like thet want to be a man? She could have any rich buck in this country if she'd just be a woman."

"Yeah," Immel replied, "I'd like to winter with her myself. If'n I had her down in St. Louie, I could make my fortune by just rentin 'er out fer the night."

They both chucked heartily, looking forward to the rare occasions when they would see her, because she was truly unique. She appeared almost queenly with her body posture, poise and charismatic beauty. Though she kept her distance, she was always pleasant and quiet in her trading.

Jones and Immel became restless and they tired of their squaws. Not only were the women homely, they seemed to be getting fatter as the winter grew colder. Finally Immel could take it no longer. "Bob," he said, "I got to git out of here for awhile. Why don't we go up to the Three Forks and check it out?"

Jones too felt lodge fever closing in on him. "Yeah, let's go," he agreed. "We can check out the Gallatin, Madison and Jefferson. I hear tell it's great beaver country." They packed their food, supplies and traps on two packhorses and covered their feet with the furry hide of a bull buffalo. This would keep their animals' feet warm and give them added traction as they traveled up the frozen river. They ascended the Elk until they reached Pompey's Pillar that evening and camped for the night. The next night they camped at Indian Caves. When they reached the mouth of the Shields, they took the buffalo shoes off the hooves of their horses and cut out overland, due west across the snow. They crossed through a pass into the valley of the Gallatin River. Here they located a hot spring near the river and set up camp.

Jones scouted around and then yelled to Immel, "Hot damn! Look at the beaver sign! As soon as we build a shelter, let's start settin' them traps."

"You build the lean-to and I'll set the traps," Immel replied. "You don't like the way I build a lodge anyhow." Jones began chopping small trees as Immel unpacked their traps. After Immel had headed toward the river, Jones began to notch and lay the logs for their lean-to.

Before long he heard a rifle shot. Grabbing his own weapon, he raced toward Immel. As Jones approached, he saw Immel standing near a cow elk and said, "You scairt the hell out of me, Mike. I thought you'd done been kilt." Immel just stood by the elk, staring across the frozen river. Jones looked at him in confusion and asked, "Now what's wrong?"

Immel pointed to the far bank and whispered, "Blackfeet." Jones froze and tightened his grip on his rifle. Then he spied about a dozen braves on horseback, slowly descending the opposite bank of the river. He didn't breathe or blink until they went out of sight around the bend of the stream.

"Damn," Jones exhaled. "I thought we was gonners for sure."

The perspiring Immel replied, "They ignored us this time, but they know we're here and we got to be cautious. Now help me butcher this here camp meat." They worked quickly on the cooling carcass and carried the meat inside the elk's hide to their new camp.

They slowly trapped where they could find ice holes made by the beavers. When they reached the three forks of the Missouri, they started to trap up the Madison. One evening Jones looked up and froze.

Hoarsely he called to Immel, "Blackfeet!" But again the savages completely ignored them. However, the two took turns guarding their camp for several nights before their nerves calmed. Within three weeks they had accumulated a large number of pelts, but they detected a large storm brewing over the mountains. Retreating to their log shelter on the Gallatin, they built a hot fire and soon fell fast asleep, safe from the oncoming storm.

Jones awoke early and crawled out of the lean-to to relieve his full bladder. After looking around he yelled, "Mike! Mike! Them damn Injuns has stole our horses. *Now* we're in fer it!"

Immel stumbled toward the door and tried to focus on where the horses had been tethered. Not only were all the horses gone, but the Indians had carefully brushed away all their tracks.

"Let's cache them furs and get the hell out of here," Immel gushed. They wasted no time in digging a pit near a knoll to bury the furs and traps. Immel swept the area clean then packed all the supplies and food they could carry on their backs. Jones made some crude snowshoes out of willow branches and rawhide, then together they trudged off, heading back to the safety of the Crow.

Pine Leaf saw two lone figures slowly making their way down the frozen Elk. She primed her gun and checked her arrows before riding steadily toward them. As she approached, she recognized them to be the white, bearded fur traders from the Missouri Fur Company.

Since she could only speak a few words of the white man's language and knew one of the trappers spoke Atsina, she hailed them in the language of her former people, "Where are your horses?" Jones spoke the language of the Atsina fairly well and replied, "The Blackfeet attacked us and robbed us of all of our animals and furs. They were many, but we drove them off, leaving their dead for the great white bear."

As Jones attempted to impress the female warrior with tales of his heroics, Immel almost choked, but he said nothing. Pine Leaf had been taught to believe white men, so she proudly escorted the tired travelers back to the Sparrow Hawk village in Bighorn Canyon.

Jones and Immel were well received by the village and they were happy to again be in their warm lodges with their fat squaws.

Heavy storms came once again over the Rockies and everyone battened down their lodge flaps to avoid the icy winds and blowing snow. For two months, one storm after another rolled in until at last the sky cleared and the healing warmth of the sun once again came to Bighorn Valley.

Jones turned to Immel. "I think we better try diggin' up them furs before Pilcher comes back with them trade goods," Jones said. Immel agreed and was able to trade for four fairly good horses and although the animals were thin from lack of forage, the two loaded them with their necessary supplies and headed back to their cache on the Gallatin.

While they prepared to depart, Pine Leaf gave them a warning. "There will be large parties of Blackfeet out looking for fresh meat. I think you should wait for your white brothers before returning to avenge your losses."

However, they ignored her warning because they had to retrieve their furs for Pilcher. Pine Leaf watched as they rode out of sight. "Why do white men always seem so foolish," she wondered. "They take great chances for wealth, but do not even seek honor," she thought. She knew that she would not die for wealth, but that she would die for honor.

She could not understand these strange *foreigners* and their strange customs.

CHAPTER 17

Missouri became a State in 1821. During this time, the state representative, Senator Benton, began clamoring for the United States to open up the fur trade to compete with the British. Since the Northwest Company and the Hudson Bay Company of England had merged, the new company had become a formidable challenger to the St. Louis firms. General William Henry Ashley (Lt. Governor of Missouri), Major Andrew Henry and Senator Benton made alliances with the prairie Indians and entered the fur trade in earnest. Their Rocky Mountain Fur Company would change the west forever. A new era was dawning as the American trappers began a new assault on the upper Missouri. However, few prairie dwellers could read the warning signs.

That winter proved particularly harsh. Snow had piled deep in the Shining Mountains, causing food and forage to become scarce. Pine Leaf and other Sparrow Hawk hunters had to range to the lowlands and secluded canyons to secure game. In Bighorn Canyon and the foothills they obtained big horn sheep and some scattered elk, but they needed to find buffalo.

Traveling beyond the Bighorn Mountains, Pine Leaf and her hunters finally located a herd of buffalo near the Tongue River. As they approached the herd, she noticed the bulls were already forming into a solid ring to protect the cows and calves. The bulls stood horn to horn without budging, and she figured they must have been recently attacked by a wolf pack. Even though the hunters successfully shot several of the bulls, the remainder of the bulls held their positions and even filled in the gaps left by the dead bulls.

She knew from experience that the buffalo could hold this position for days or as long as they felt threatened. She had seen many large fertile grass circles on the prairie caused by the deep dung of circled buffalo. She decided to withdraw her hunters, allowing the herd to calm down, break up and move on so her hunters could retrieve their kills. On this expedition, they would be denied the tender meat of the calves and the fat meat of the cows, but at least they would still have fresh meat and warm robes.

They set up camp behind a nearby hill and after several hours of absence, she and the young braves returned to find the herd had moved on across the Tongue River. They butchered and packed the old bulls, heading for home with their meager results.

When the green-grass season came, the Sparrow Hawks left the hot springs and crossed the Bighorn Mountains through Ten Sleep Canyon and Powder River Pass to the North Fork of Crazy Woman Creek. They followed the ancient trails along the Crazy Woman until they met the upper reaches of the Powder River.

They avoided the Bighorn Canyon, where they knew the heavy snow pack would create torrents of floodwaters when it melted. As spring continued, the rivers rose over their banks, flooding the valleys and lowlands. For the mountain men, trapping became very difficult in the swollen streams. Indians and white men alike moved to high ground to wait out the danger of the raging waters.

After Rotten Belly's River Sparrow Hawks reached the Elk, they camped near the mouth of the Powder on its west bank. They had several days of activity, such as hunting, building new lodges and tanning new robes. Just when everything seemed to be settling down, a young brave raced into camp.

"Blackfeet! Blackfeet!" the brave yelled. Rotten Belly mounted, and with his best warriors, he rode to the riverbank. Peering across the water he saw many smokes indicating a large village of Blackfeet was staying across the swollen river.

Although it caused him some concern, Rotten Belly reassured his people. "Do not worry, the Blackfeet cannot cross the swollen waters of the river. I will post wolf scouts at this point to follow their movements and to monitor the river level."

Armed with the knowledge that the river was too high and swift for anyone to cross, the young warriors and women began mocking and taunting their enemy. On opposite banks, people from both tribes rode their horses back and forth, often feinting as if to dash across the river. Some of the Sparrow Hawks made lewd gestures, such as dropping their breechcloths and showing their bare buttocks to their old enemy.

Though the rushing water created a great deal of noise, some of the Sparrow Hawks could be heard to shout, "You are without relatives!" This meant the Blackfeet were of no account or were of no importance. This declaration was a great insult to any Indian.

Prominent leaders of the Blackfeet were White Buffalo, Buffalo's Back Fat, Eagle Ribs, Iron Horn, Bear's Child and Buffalo's Child. After several days of feasting and taunting, Chief Buffalo's Back Fat moved his village farther up the Elk. The Sparrow Hawks returned to their normal routines, including mending their badly worn personal effects, which had barely made it through a harsh winter.

It wasn't long before Pine Leaf spotted a large party on the east bank of the Powder River. Quickly she rode into camp giving the call, "To arms! To arms! The enemy approaches." Rotten Belly again scrutinized the situation and assured the villagers, "We are in no danger. Place scouts along the river to keep a watch on the flood level."

The large party became a five-hundred-lodge village of Sioux. It was true that the Sioux were their enemy, but the Sparrow Hawks did not consider them a threat at this time because the group was on the opposite side of the flooded Powder and because the Sioux were not well mounted. The Sioux proved formidable as foot soldiers, but since they were new to the plains, they were not as expert in horse warfare as the older plains tribes.

At times, the Sparrow Hawk leaders of Two Crows, Four Wolves, Red Bear and Yellow Belly would ride back and forth along the river, demonstrating their superior horsemanship to their rivals on the opposite bank. The Sioux were being led by Black Rock, Tobacco, Stone Horns, Torn Belly, Corn, No Heart, Little Bear, Grizzly Bear, Dog, Elk's Head, Shell and the famous warrior, One Horn.

As each side tried to impress the other, the Sioux chief challenged the Crow to a foot race along the banks of the Powder. The chief knew that One Horn could outrun anyone in the Shining Mountains and had been noted for running down buffalo on the open prairie.

The Sparrow Hawks enthusiastically accepted the challenge and in addition to entering his leading young male warriors, Chief Rotten Belly entered Pine Leaf. He had been watching her race since she was a girl and knew she had an excellent chance of winning. If she could beat One Horn, the Sioux would be humiliated because a woman, particularly a Sparrow Hawk woman, could beat their greatest brave. People of both villages grew excited as the distance for the race was agreed upon. The race would begin upriver at the horseshoe bend of the Powder and end at the two opposite villages. The judges would be Chief Black Rock and Chief Rotten Belly.

As Pine Leaf and her companions rode upstream to begin the race, she observed her challengers across the Powder. "I have heard of the great running ability of One Horn," she thought, "but I think I have more speed than he does. If I can stay close to him until we near our village, I think I can out-sprint him to the finish."

The distance agreed upon by the two chiefs was equivalent to ten consecutive rifle shots. As the opposing warriors reached the horseshoe bend, they dismounted and began to strip their clothing down to their breechcloths and moccasins.

Pine Leaf tied on a loincloth and removed her doeskin dress. Her firm, small breasts quickly caused a stir of attraction among the Sioux. While they stared at her across the river, the guns went off and the Sparrow Hawk runners broke into a sprint. The Sioux sprinted to catch up and were soon passing their challengers. Pine Leaf allowed the excited young men about her to race on while she tried to develop a pace she could handle well. She had never raced this distance before and feared she might tire too quickly if she started out too fast.

The spring sun felt hot on her bare skin, but her legs and arms felt strong and relaxed. She was aware of the bouncing of her breasts, but as she developed her stride, her entire body seemed to coordinate into a fluid motion, like that of an antelope. She pictured in her mind the antelope's beautiful strides as they fled across the plains and willed her body to emulate that movement; meanwhile she planned when and how she would begin her challenge. As her mind rehearsed her strategy, she began to pass her fellow warriors and the Sioux runners across the river.

At the halfway point, she was greeted by a large number of her friends on horseback. They told her she was gaining on her colleague, Yellow Belly. She felt strong and confident when she finally passed Yellow Belly and began to gain ground on her friend, Four Wolves.

She admired Four Wolves, who stood over six feet tall and had beautiful hair that reached clear down his back. He was a good runner but he had gone out too quickly and was beginning to weaken. His tied-up hair was soaked with perspiration and beginning to come untied from the top and sides of his head. As she passed him, she noticed his pained face and heard his harsh breathing.

Pine Leaf only had one Sparrow Hawk runner ahead of her as she drew within sight of the villages near the mouth of the Powder. She pumped her arms even more and lengthened her stride, she caught up with Red Bear, then began her sprint to the village. Across the river she could see the powerful Sioux warrior, One Horn, running smoothly, but his speed wasn't as great as hers. She left him behind as she raced into the village and then collapsed from exhaustion.

When the sound of her own heart finally quieted, she began to interpret the shouts of praise from the village crier, Good Herald. Rotten Belly picked her up in his strong arms and embraced her nearly nude body. Across the river the humiliated Sioux withdrew to their village while the Sparrow Hawks partied and danced.

Pine Leaf, having lived twenty-six winters, was in her prime in both health and acclaim. However, she was still not allowed to attend council meetings or to listen to the warpath secrets of the other warriors; she thought about this slight often. She wanted the honor of participating, even if she had no secrets to divulge.

Meanwhile, in the valley of the Green River, a black trapper named Jim Beckwith felt he was getting nowhere.

He had as much experience as any of his comrades but they owned the best damned trapping firm in the mountains, the Rocky Mountain Fur Company. Jed Smith did not want Jim to go with him to California so Jim decided to accompany Smith's partners David Jackson and William Sublette up into the Yellowstone country. Although he hunted as a free trapper, he was still having financial difficulties.

Much of Beckwith's income went to his many and varied female alliances and the cost of necessities was rising. Even though he received three dollars a pound for his beaver skins, his expenses were high. He had to pay a dollar for lead, a dollar and fifty cents for gunpowder, a dollar and twenty-five cents for shot, nine dollars for blankets, nine dollars for traps, a dollar a pound for sugar, a dollar and twenty-five cents a pound for coffee, and a dollar and fifty cents a pound for flour.

"At these prices," he thought, "I cain't get ahead a'tall. Howsomever, I'm better off than them company trappers and I can damn well go anywheres I want to, but still, I want more than this."

Jim decided that he would jump at his next opportunity, even if it was just to do something different. Unknown to him, his opportunity would come soon enough.

CHAPTER 18

With Five Scalps still away from Absaroka, Pine Leaf took on more of a leader role within the Big Dog Society. She stood third in ranking behind Yellow Belly and Grizzly Bear. She still could not develop a brotherly relationship with Yellow Belly, but she had to admire him as a warrior and leader. Chief Rotten Belly appointed his brother Yellow Belly as the primary war chief of the River Sparrow Hawks. Yellow Belly took his new role with great pride, but he also showed a great deal of arrogance.

Members of the Big Dogs were always paired. Pine Leaf was now paired with Grizzly Bear. He felt she was beneath him, but he admired her grit and determination and treated her with dignity. Her new role allowed her to become more of a leader, but wisely she never tried to upstage Yellow Belly or Grizzly Bear. She expressed her open confidence only when they were in battle with the enemy or during a raid or a buffalo surround. It was in that atmosphere that she knew she could hold her own, with only her weapons and her skills to depend upon.

When she was alone, she prayed to her secret-helper and the Great Spirit for guidance, confidence and strength. Though her achievements were applauded, she only received limited personal reward from them, becoming sullen and melancholy when she did not have outstanding achievements in battle. Whenever this sadness overtook her, and if the tribe were anywhere near the Tongue River, she tried to return to her sacred rock to be with the spirit of Cracked-Ice. Sparrow Hawks did not fear death, believing that their ghost spirit would rise to the happy hunting ground in the sky.

"Then why do I mourn so for Cracked-Ice?" she asked herself. "I fear no warrior and yet I fear for my death spirit." She did not know that she had inherited a common belief of her former Atsina people through her own father.

More of the white men's pack trains passed through the Absaroka buffalo grounds as they headed into the Shining Mountains. Pine Leaf and others noticed these travelers killed their game and altered the migration patterns of the buffalo and elk. Because of this, it was getting harder to predict when these much-needed animals would return. She could remember when the council and the elders could predict within a few days when and where buffalo could be found. Each spring they even burned large pastures of dead grass, so that new green shoots would attract the returning herds. Now it seemed useless to try to guess the location and time of their next arrival.

Word reached the Sparrow Hawks that Immel and Jones had been killed. After retrieving their furs, they had been attacked by Blackfeet and had fled to Henry's Fort. Andrew Henry survived the subsequent attack of the fort and he fled to St.

Louis, where he reported the disaster to Joshua Pilcher. Not only were their men gone, but also were their furs and trapping equipment.

Pine Leaf could tell when the belligerent Pecunis were on the warpath, because the Shoshone and the white trappers would flee across the mountains to the Wind River or to the Bighorn, seeking Sparrow Hawk protection.

The changing patterns of the buffalo also caused more contact and conflict between the Sparrow Hawks, Cheyenne, Piegans, Blackfeet, Teton Sioux, Plains Cree, Atsina, Mandan, Arikara and the Assiniboine tribes. At times there was even conflict between the Sparrow Hawks and their relatives, the Hidatsa.

In the white man's year of 1825, the persistent warring and raiding prompted Pine Leaf to seek out assistance in making replacements for her war weapons, so she employed old Lodge Skin to help her make a new war shield. She obtained the thick hide off the neck and hump of an old bull and had Little Blossom scrape it clean of flesh and hair. Lodge Skin then dug a circular hole in the ground.

But Pine Leaf quickly told him, "No, Lodge Skin. I want a shield shaped like this," and she drew the shape of a wild pear in the dirt with her knife.

Lodge Skin shaped the hole as she wanted, then heated large rocks in the pit. After the fire went out, he staked the hide over the hot stones, explaining, "The heat will shrink the hide and make it tougher." He then dampened it, turned it over and placed several medium sized stones in the center, which caused it to droop toward the heat. Lodge Skin nodded to her as he said, "This will give the shield a hollow shape to protect your body."

After being shrunken and shaped, the hide was removed by Lodge Skin to cool before cutting. He trimmed the hide, then made a frame of green willow branches to stabilize it. After he cut the hide to her satisfaction, he punched holes in it and tied it to the frame with rawhide and sinew. Pine Leaf watched him closely. He knew his work, but she alone knew just how she wanted it.

Lodge Skin made a long strap to attach to the upper portion of the shield so Pine Leaf could carry it over her shoulder or attach it to her saddle horn. In the rear of the shield's upper middle, he attached a handhold, made of a piece of bone wrapped and glued with rawhide.

When the shield was completed, Pine Leaf held it up to her—it covered her entire torso—when she set its end on the ground, it reached to her waist. It was perfect. Little Blossom painted the front of the shield with the sun, to represent the Sun Dance ceremony; four horses, to represent her skill at raiding; and a rock pillar in the lower center to represent her sacred rock. On the fringe, Little Blossom attached scalps of their enemies, to show Pine Leaf's prowess in battle.

Lodge Skin then hung the shield from the lodge smoke hole for two full moons, for curing and waterproofing. When he finally took it down, Pine Leaf could hardly wait to test it. She bade young Hammer Owner's to shoot arrows at her as she warded them off with her beautiful shield. She foolishly believed it would even deflect the white man's rifle balls.

As she displayed the shield around the village, old Lodge Skin proudly received many new requests for war shields.

CHAPTER 19

After the summer hunt and meat drying activities were completed, Chief Rotten Belly moved the River Sparrow Hawks high up the Elk to escape the debilitating heat. They camped around a large lake and began repairing their war and hunting weapons; most of the women continued to cure the animal hides for making clothing and moccasins.

Pine Leaf started to grow bored again, so she decided to go on a hunt for mountain sheep. She needed some large horns for a new bow anyway. She hired Arrowmaker to go with her and advise her. He was reputed to be the best arrow and bowmaker in Absaroka. "I will pay you with the very finest sheepskins you have ever received," she promised.

They ascended the rugged Elk to a large hot spring, setting up camp with a lean-to and a fire pit. They erected several pole tripods to keep their goods and food out of the reach of pesky animals. Nothing would be safe, however, if they were visited by a silver-tipped grizzly. Often called a white bear, they had no defenses against a grizzly bear on the prowl.

While Pine Leaf ascended the rugged Elk in her quest, Arrowmaker remained in camp preparing his tools and straightening his bundle of cedar arrow shafts.

After some hours, she climbed the rocks near a spring and noticed a small flock of the elusive white sheep. The breeze was with her, they had not scented her presence yet. Slowly she placed three arrows in her mouth and nocked one on her old *bois d' arc* bow. As the animals grazed she selected several large rams as her primary targets. Holding her breath, she began firing the arrows. In less than a minute she shot three rams and a ewe. The rest of the flock ran from the spring and climbed the walls of the canyon.

Pine Leaf carefully skinned her kills, saving the horns, tendons, sinew, brains, hooves and hides. She hated to waste most of the precious meat, but she could not pack it all down to the hot springs. She packed only that meat which she could easily carry, along with her trophies, and started back across the stream.

In a small eddy she spied a black, glassy object about the length of her hand. It was shaped rather like a large spear point. Laying down her pack, she bent down to examine it and cut her thumb on its sharp edges. The rock fascinated her, so she decided to see if Arrowmaker could put it to good use. If not, she would make it one of her sacred rocks. Carefully she wrapped it in a piece of leather and stuffed it in her pack.

It was after dark by the time Pine Leaf returned to the hot springs; she found Arrowmaker asleep. Early the next morning she woke him to show off her heavy load of treasures. He expressed pleasure at her success and immediately began preparing the hides by scraping the flesh from them. He then staked them on the ground and began tanning them with the animal's brains. While he worked, Pine Leaf remembered the black stone and dug it out of her parfleche. Arrowmaker became excited over her find.

"This black glass is created in the bowels of mother earth," he said. "When her stomach is full of glass, she regurgitates it as some of the buffalo regurgitate hair balls. Our ancient ones used this rock for arrowpoints and spearpoints, because it does not have to be sharpened. Also, it will not rust like the white man's iron does." Examining the stone closer, he said, "I can make a new point for your lance with this piece and if you will get me more, I can also make points for your new arrows. They would be the finest weapons in the Shining Mountains." They didn't know it at the time, but white men called this black stone *obsidian*.

While Arrowmaker worked, Pine Leaf retraced her steps up the river, back to the source of the wonderful black rock. When she came to the spring where she had killed the sheep, she continued climbing higher and higher until she reached a large black cliff. Here she found several large black stones, but they were too heavy to carry. Then she noticed that much of the face of the cliff consisted of columns of the black glass. At the base of the cliff she found shattered pieces of the rock in every size and shape imaginable. She began to fill her two parfleches with stones she felt would be appropriate for Arrowmaker's use, but this time she was careful not to cut herself.

When she had all she could carry, she proceeded to drag her cargo back to the spring; this was not an easy task, trudging such a load down the steep incline. At the base of the cliff she spent the night, arising early to make her way back to the hot springs and Arrowmaker.

By afternoon she dragged her load into camp and lay down, exhausted.

As she rested, Arrowmaker examined the black stones; they were magnificent and he could hardly wait to begin work on several points. From his tool bag he picked out the prong of a deer antler and a piece of buffalo hide, then he placed a piece of the black rock into the hide with his left hand, and began pressing against its edges with the antler prong held in his right hand. As he pressed, little pieces of the glass would flake off, and gradually he shaped the rock into a point. He then repeated the process to form two small notches at the other end so it could be attached to an arrow shaft.

Pine Leaf awoke from the nap to find Arrowmaker busy with her newfound raw materials. He sat in a cross-legged position with small black flakes covering his bare legs. She observed him a moment, then picked up a finished point.

"Oh, Arrowmaker! It is beautiful!" she exclaimed. "And so very sharp too." The man smiled as he continued working on his next point.

"I have only made a few to show you how they are superior to iron," he explained. "Tomorrow I must get to work on your bow. It will take much time to prepare." After dinner they told stories and went to bed. The artisan had already suspended some of the horns in the hot springs to soften them.

Early the next day he retrieved one and held it with a piece of buckskin while he delicately sliced off the two sides with a knife. He slightly curved the ends and tied them together while directing Pine Leaf to pour cold spring water on them until they stiffened and held their shape.

As he prepared more horns, he had Pine Leaf get a gourd of hot water and place fire pit stones into it to make the water even hotter. He then had her scrape shavings off the hooves into the water until she had a gooey consistency. Here he took over and stirred the glue until he was satisfied it was ready. He then separated one of the horn slices, wiped glue all over the inside of it and placed shredded sinew on top of the glue before giving it another coat. About two hands from the tip he glued another two strips of horn. He filed the end of the top piece after it set and again applied glue and sinew. He then attached the top outside mate to the bow's wing and glued it. When he had both front and back matched, he wrapped the entire piece tightly with rawhide until it could cure. With this procedure he created only half of the bow.

In preparing the second half, he retied another horn and repeated the process of slicing the horn, curving it to match the already partially completed bow and then cooling the tied bundle with spring water.

When he was satisfied, he glued one outside piece to the main bow as if it were part of a jigsaw puzzle. He filed the bow with sandstone and glued on the final outer half of the lower wing. He then glued slices of bone in the middle on each side of the overlapping joint to serve as bowgrips and to strengthen the joint. Finally he tied the bow in his new furs and placed them on a tripod of poles above the campfire. From time to time he would place punk wood, moss or wet grass in the fire pit to make more of the curing smoke.

Arrowmaker spent two more days making arrow points, then he directed Pine Leaf to stick out her left arm so he could measure it. Unrolling his bundle of cedar shafts, he held one up to her, then measured the shaft from the tip of her left fingers to her right shoulder and marked it.

"This shall be the length of all of these arrows," he explained, "so they will all fly straight and true each time you shoot. If they are not all the same length, then you cannot be consistent in your accuracy. Remember, do not use these arrows for hunting, but only use them as sacred arrows against our enemies."

After he cut all the shafts the same length, he carefully split the ends and attached the completed glass points. He bound the ends of the shafts with sinew fibers and lightly coated them with glue, then he glued three matched feathers near the end of each shaft.

As a final step, he cut horseshoe-shaped notches at the end of each shaft, again binding the area between the notch and the feather fletchings with sinew and a light coating of glue to keep them from splitting.

Pine Leaf could hardly wait to use a completed arrow; she could already feel their excellent balance. Arrowmaker sensed her excitement. "Take only two," he said, "and practice shooting them with your old bow." For a target he wrapped his old buffalo robe around a bundle of moss and grass then placed it next to a soft grassy knoll. "If she hits the robe," he reasoned, "she can recover the arrows, and if she hits the hill, maybe I can repair the damage."

He continued working as he watched her shoot both arrows into the center of the robe bundle. He smiled to himself, "If she thinks she can shoot now, just wait until I complete her new bow."

The two had been gone almost three weeks when Pine Leaf and Arrowmaker returned to the Sparrow Hawk village. Chief Rotten Belly had grown eager to prepare for the fall hunt and promptly directed everyone to decamp. Pine Leaf did not show anyone her new sacred weapons. She gave her old lance to Arrowmaker and as he found time on the trail, he applied her new black point to it; he also continued to file and shape her new bow.

The long Sparrow Hawk train stretched out for half a day as they descended the Elk to the mouth of the Stillwater River. Here, Rotten Belly directed them north until they came to another large lake. Scouts had reported herds of buffalo northwest of there and the Big Dog police had great difficulty keeping the excited young men in camp until a hunting party could be organized by the council.

On the second day, Rotten Belly directed Yellow Belly to lead the surround. Their women would follow with their knives and packhorses to butcher the carcasses. He assigned Pine Leaf to prepare a defense of the village in case the Pecunis should learn that most of their warriors were off hunting. Her scouts and defenders consisted mainly of older men and young Hammer Owners. She sent them in the four sacred directions, rotating them often to gather reports and to keep them from becoming bored. She also needed to make sure none of them ran off to join the hunt.

As it turned out they only had to keep up this vigil for three days before the main hunting party returned, laden with meat and robes. For four days the villagers celebrated and feasted on roasted tongues and humps. For several more days, the women stripped and dried the meat, cured robes and hides with buffalo brains, then smoked them slowly to waterproof them and make them pliable.

Now it was time to move on. They dismantled their lodges and attached the lodgepoles and skins to their many horses. By tying two poles together to form a travois they could haul all of their robes, lodge hides and personal effects. Some of them even hauled old people and young children, but most of the able-bodied either walked or rode on their horses. They traveled due east until reaching the Elk River, near Indian caves, then they stopped.

It would take them two days to pack all of their belongings across the river.

To tote their stacks of robes, lodge skins and large packs across the stream, they tied poles together to make rafts. The regular-sized rafts were usually four-sided, while the larger ones were only three-sided. Between the poles they tied waterproof hides, placing a stone in the center for ballast, then they tied their goods on the rafts. On some of the rafts they constructed pole tripods to suspend precious items high above the splash of the water.

Swimming men or gentle older horses towed the rafts across the river, using hide or horsehair ropes. Most of the goods crossed without mishap, and once the caravan reached the other side, everything had to be reloaded as it was before. Then the group headed southeast toward Bighorn Canyon.

Once settled, the villagers often kept to their lodges as the snow began falling and piled up against their lodges. As usual, Pine Leaf grew melancholy as the storms passed, but her spirits were lifted when Arrowmaker approached.

"I have a gift for the finest hunter in Absaroka," he said, handing her a fur bundle. After opening the hide she hesitated, almost fearful of handling something this precious.

"It's beautiful, Arrowmaker!" she exclaimed after uncovering the bow. "I have never seen such a marvelous bow!"

He had strung it with strong sinew fibers taken from young buffalo bulls, hand rolling the fibers to the thickness his experience dictated would withstand her strongest pull. He had shaped a roughened handgrip that would not slip from a wet grasp and on the left side, above the grip, he had glued a short feather to serve as an arrowrest.

The bow had a beautiful double curve, which bent backward when it was strung; this would give the bow more thrust. Pulling the cord to the corner of her mouth Pine Leaf felt its strength and power. Arrowmaker had also lightly carved geometric designs on both sides of the bow's wings. Because of its tremendous power, Arrowmaker demonstrated how she would have to string and unstring this bow.

The movements were much the same as she'd used before, but the technique and especially the muscles involved were different due to the bow's size and strength. She would place the bow in front of her with the bottom, recurve tip against her right instep. She would then take the top recurve in her right hand and pull and bend the bow over her right hip until it curved downward. Slowly she would then move up the sinew string loop until it fitted into the holding grove at the top of the recurve. With practice this could be done safely and quickly.

"Go practice your new bow," Arrowmaker advised. "It will not break. As you consistently hit targets at a given distance, sight along the bow and file a mark to indicate that distance; eventually you will know which mark to use for the distance of your desired target. This will increase your accuracy immensely. You should always carry the bow with you, or secure it in your lodge, for it will make a tempting trophy for your enemies."

Pine Leaf hugged Arrowmaker, an odd gesture indeed, especially for her, then raced off to the hills to practice with her new treasure.

Eventually, she shared the beauty of her new bow and arrows with her fellow Big Dogs and other villagers. Everyone marveled as they examined each item, and after she demonstrated her accuracy with them, Arrowmaker received more orders for new weapons than he would ever be able to complete.

Pine Leaf also revealed the source of the magical black stone used to make her arrowheads, but she would not trade any of her precious supply. She continued to use her old *bois d' arc* bow and iron-tipped arrows for hunting, but anytime she felt she might come in contact with the enemy, she took her new weapons.

Pine Leaf gave Arrowmaker another trade robe and in turn he made her a new leather arm shield for her left arm, so the heavy bow would not cut or bruise her forearm. He also cut a four-sided piece of elk skin and cut two finger holes at one end. This would strengthen her fingers and protect them from the friction of the bowstring as it was released when she shot the bow. He then made a new quiver for her sacred arrows and attached it to the bow's case. By tying them together with thongs, they could always be stored or carried as one unit.

Now that she had new weapons, Pine Leaf felt she would surely be a successful warrior. *She could hardly wait to see what this new season would bring.*

CHAPTER 20

When the early shoots of grass began cropping up from the prairie floor, Chief Rotten Belly moved his village eastward across the north front of the Bighorn Mountains. For several months their only fresh meat had been elk and mountain sheep. They had again grown hungry for buffalo and he wanted to attempt to locate them in their northern migration.

After the Sparrow Hawks crossed branches of the Little Bighorn they moved southeast toward the Tongue. Here Pine Leaf took a side trip to her sacred rock pillar to tell the spirit of Cracked-Ice about her new war weapons.

"Now, my brother," she said, "I will be more capable of my promise to slay one hundred of our enemies to avenge your death. I have remained a virgin in your honor and I do not intend to ever marry. I will carry your spirit with me as I continue to live the life of a Sparrow Hawk brave. It is my desire to become the greatest warrior our people have ever seen."

After several hours of prayer and conversation with the spirit of Cracked-Ice, Pine Leaf rode hard to catch up with her moving people.

The Sparrow Hawks headed east to the Powder then ascended Spotted Horse Creek to the head of Horse Creek; after descending the Little Powder they established a base camp.

Scouts soon returned to the newly established village to report that they had seen buffalo on the grasslands to the east. Camp police held the excited people in check as the chief and council designed a plan for the hunt. They also developed a defense plan for the village, since they were outside their home grounds of Absaroka.

"We are now close to the sacred hills of the Teton Sioux and their allies, the Cheyenne," said Rotten Belly, "so our hunters must remain vigilant." The hunters were excited to get going, but they also understood the gravity of the situation.

"Pine Leaf," he said, "you will take fifty Big Dogs to act as scouts and defenders of the buffalo surround. Yellow Belly, you will lead the actual surround. Grizzly Bear, you will be in charge of defending our camp. Good hunting!"

When dawn broke over Thunder Basin, Pine Leaf led her warriors south, downwind from the herd of buffalo. She figured that if danger came, it would come from the Brulé or the Teton Dakota.

She and her warriors had ridden across the Little Muddy headwaters and between the prairie buttes, when Pine Leaf suddenly stopped. She thought, "I must be seeing a ghost spirit." Before them was a larger-than-life replica of her sacred rock pillar. She had to ride closer to investigate. It was much taller and wider than her rock column and it rose up majestically, high above the valley of the white man's Bell Fourche River. Though edged by bushes and even trees at its base, the large rock column was slick and mostly bare.

Although the other Big Dogs were impressed with the huge rock formation, they feared it might be a sacred place for the Cheyenne or the Sioux and wanted to leave right away. At last Pine Leaf gave in, and they continued their trek to the buffalo hunting grounds.

They neared Prairie Creek in the afternoon, where the point rider returned to tell them he had located an enemy camp. Quickly they dismounted and Pine Leaf sent two scouts to investigate.

Pine Leaf wondered, "Who could be this close to our hunting party without being detected?" She would soon have her answer.

When the scouts returned, they reported, "Cheyenne war dogs are hidden in the coulees by the creek. They are only waiting until it is dark before they attack our hunters."

Leaping upon her war-horse, Red Devil, Pine Leaf shouted, "Big Dogs, prepare for battle!" Loosening the case from her horn bow, she stuck two of her new arrows between her teeth. She then placed one on her bowstring and held one in her left bowhand with the point facing down; this would make it easier to reach the nock for shooting.

"I want you to spread out by four horse's lengths each," she said, "and then charge as if we are the entire Sparrow Hawk Nation."

The Big Dogs charged over the ridge and down the hill toward the hiding Cheyenne. The would-be raiders were visibly startled by the surprise attack. They couldn't believe the stupid Crow had successfully surrounded them. Quickly they fled down the creek toward the Little Missouri; some were on foot and some were on horseback, but all proved equally swift in their departure.

As Red Devil concentrated on his footing, Pine Leaf took her time, aiming from the marks on the upper wing of her bow.

She fired one arrow, then reached for the arrow in her bowhand. In a smooth motion, she placed it on the bowstring, drew it to the point of her chin and let the second arrow fly. She then fired the two arrows that had been held in her mouth, before she realized the fleeing Cheyenne had scattered and were pulling out of range.

She stopped and recalled her warriors with her loud eagle-bone whistle. She then rode back to retrieve her arrows and scalps.

When she dismounted by the last warrior she had shot, she found the arrow had passed completely through his body, landing several feet beyond on a slope. The tough arrow did not even seem to be damaged. She found that two more of her arrows had passed through the enemy warriors she hit and neither of them had been broken. Only two of her four arrows had even lost a fletch feather.

Arrowmaker had designed them well.

When she regrouped her warriors, Pine Leaf learned that most of them had counted coup and many had killed more than one of the enemy. They rode toward the Sparrow Hawk camp, arriving just after dark. Yellow Belly was shocked when he learned that the enemy had been so close to his camp.

Though relieved that Pine Leaf and the Big Dogs had been so successful, the chief thought, "Perhaps I have not taken this woman seriously enough. One day she *will* surely become a war chief and I shall have to place her on my council of advisors. I will have to observe her more closely in the future."

The hunt had been very successful as well as their swift victory over the Cheyenne hunting party, so the entire camp celebrated by roasting tongues and buffalo humps.

After the celebration, Pine Leaf approached the old master craftsman of their tribe. "Arrowmaker," she teased, "I have damaged two of my fine arrows and I need them repaired. They didn't seem to hold up very well in combat."

The irritated, older man looked painfully at her and curtly asked, "What did you shoot, buffalo skulls?" Pine Leaf smiled as she showed him the arrows; none were broken and only two were missing feathers. She answered, "No, just four lowly Cheyenne."

She then presented the four scalplocks to the beaming but surprised Arrowmaker, saying, "These are for you, my friend."

He took her to his fire, lit his pipe and made her tell him every detail of the battle. As she proudly recited her deeds, he marveled at her prowess as a woman warrior. He had seen a few female hunters in his time, but he had never known of a female warrior.

SECTION IV

1828 - 1832

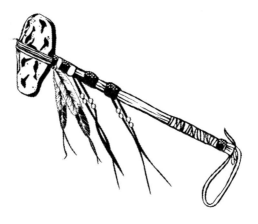

Jerry A. Matney with D. A. Gordon

CHAPTER 21

At the 1828 rendezvous, old Caleb Greenwood told a group of Crow Indian traders a big story about trapper Jim Beckwith. Greenwood was great at telling tall tales, so he told them of how the black man, Beckwith, was really a Crow Indian, who had been captured as a child by the Cheyenne. He told them he was raised as a young Cheyenne warrior, but was later sold to the white people, who trained him to become a mountain man and fur trapper.

The Sparrow Hawk braves present grew fascinated by the story and some examined Jim at length. They had heard of his bravery and had witnessed his fine rifle marksmanship, so they felt proud that this man had actually come from their tribe.

Even though his skin was quite dark, so some of the Sparrow Hawks were nearly as dark themselves. However, they were curious about his curly hair; it seemed almost as curly as that of Five Scalps, and yet Sparrow Hawk people had straight hair. After the Indians left, all of the mountain men had a great laugh at the joke Caleb had pulled on the Crow.

Jim also laughed at the good joke, but he was impressed with the obvious pride the Crow braves seemed to take in his being one of them. "Thank you Caleb," he thought. "I may be able to use this story myself someday. I still ain't gettin nowhere and I got as much experience as any man in these here mountains. Smith don't want me to go with him to Californi and Jackson and Sublette act like I got the pox." *He would show them all yet, by God.*

In 1829, Beckwith signed a promissory note with the firm of Smith, Jackson and Sublette for two hundred seventy-five dollars. He agreed to repay the note with beaver pelts at the rate of three dollars per pound. He seemed to forever remain in debt to the company even though he was considered a *free trapper*.

One night Beckwith began telling some of his tall tales.

"I war down on the Laramie trappin a couple years ago when I found my best trap missin. Now, I knowed no beaver war gonna steal that thar trap, cause it weighed nigh onto twenty pounds. I looked up an' down that consarned river until it emptied into the Platte and still found no hide nor hair of that damn trap. After I broke camp and was a ridin over to the Sweetwater, I seen this small herd of buffler an' decided to get me some fresh campmeat. I downed this big bull, and would you believe, I found my missin trap tangled up in his neck hair. Har! Har! He were a wearin it like a damn cow bell!"

Everyone roared at Jim's tale except La Bonde. The Frenchman stood up, saying, "Monsieur, I am an rester baba at your mensonge. I believe you are a coquin and a menteur." Jim didn't understand all that the man said, but he did realize La Bonde was calling him a scoundrel and a liar.

That was all the insult he needed; Jim attacked the big French-Canadian with a vengeance. Once he had fought and killed a grizzly in a dark cave, so he sure as hell was not going to be put down by a mere Frenchie.

The black man's first punch downed La Bonde, then he leapt upon the prone figure and began hammering his body. Just as he reached for his Green River knife, Bridger and Greenwood pulled Jim off.

The big Frenchman lay prone on the ground, unconscious.

Bridger grabbed Jim saying, "Come here Beckwith, let's you and me go on a hunt until you cool down. Come on now." Jim knew he had lost control, so he followed Bridger without resistance.

After they set up camp on a stream, Jim rode off to think. "I gotta get out a here or I'm gonna kill somebody," he thought. "I'm not treated with the respect I deserve and I'm tired of them damn Frenchies, Creoles and Brits—they're tryin to take over these mountains."

As he staked his traps out on a stream, Jim came upon a herd of horses in a small grove of trees; curious, he rode closer. He thought, "They could belong to Blackfeet, Shoshone, Bannock or Crow, I cain't tell." As he moved closer he murmured, "They are mighty fine horses." Jim always had a hankering for good horseflesh.

Suddenly two braves jumped up from each side of him, grabbed his horse and led him to their hunting camp. They talked rapidly, then began touching his skin and hair. Finally Jim recognized one of them as a Crow brave who had attended the rendezvous with him, Greenwood and the other trappers.

"I'm a friend," he exclaimed! "This here brave should remember me." He augmented his mountain English with sign language and when the braves finished eating, they packed up their gear and escorted Jim to their village in Absaroka.

Meanwhile Bridger returned to the Rocky Mountain Fur Company camp to report that Indians had captured Beckwith.

Jim felt confident as they rode into the village. His experienced and watchful eyes took in everything around him. He knew the tall hourglass shaped lodges were distinctive of the Crow. When they rode into camp, dogs, squaws and children were running around in an excited frenzy trying to get a better view their dark visitor.

Jim calculated that there were at least two thousand tribal members present. As more men and women gathered around, he waited for the right moment to play out his drama. Although he did not understand much of their discussion, he could tell they were curious about his physical appearance.

They could tell he was not a white man, Jim gathered that much. He could tell they had seen dark people like himself before. Jim tried to follow the proceedings via words he had learned and from signings that he recognized as common on the plains. One of them told the story related to him by Greenwood.

Jim definitely wanted to stay. Not only would this be a change of pace, but he would be treated with the respect he deserved. He spotted the civil chief of the clan and signed to him that he wanted to parlay.

In sign language Jim said, "I am the famous mountain man, Beckwith, who was born a Sparrow Hawk but was captured by the Cheyenne as a child." He signed to Chief Bowl, that he had been sold to the white-eyes who trained him to be a mountain man and fur trapper.

When Jim finished, Chief Bowl directed the village crier to make an announcement to all women who had lost children in past raids. He wanted them to come to the council fire to inspect the strange captive.

As the crier rode through the village calling out the news, Pine Leaf stood a short distance away examining this strange black man. Even though she had heard tales of his bravery and his daring deeds, she did not believe his story of being a Sparrow Hawk. Nevertheless she was curious about his skills of war and knowledge of the white man's ways.

Jim stood half naked as the Sparrow Hawk women examined him from head to foot. Suddenly, a woman began crying and wailing for her lost son. She identified Jim as being her long lost son, by a mole she had located on his right eyelid. Jim was amazed when he learned that his new mother was none other than the head wife of Chief Bowl. He also learned that he now had several brothers and four attractive sisters. *This pleased him greatly.*

Immediately they took him to Chief Bowl's lodge, where his new sisters lavished him with affection and started to dress him in the finest skins and robes. They also prepared his bed, a soft bed built up high in the air; such a bed was considered a great honor. Jim was then paraded around the village, where he was hugged and kissed by all who claimed to be a long lost relative.

His new mother named her long lost son, "Medicine Calf."

Pine Leaf went about her business but she kept an eye on Jim, who remained the center of attention and gossip around the village for some time. He reminded her of her old friend and former Sparrow Hawk war chief, Five Scalps, who also had coarse, black, curly hair and dark skin. Seeing this newcomer renewed her longing to see Five Scalps again.

Jim's new brothers gave him twenty trained war-horses and a full compliment of hunting and war weapons to go along with his fifty caliber Hawken rifle, his pistol, and his Green River knife. The warrior Black Lodge offered one of his daughters to Jim, who chose the quiet and docile maiden named Still-water. Jim had his own lodge built then spent a long time out of sight of the rest of the village.

Though Still-water proved an obedient wife to Jim, he nevertheless grew bored with just one mate and eventually took additional wives. Providing for his ever-expanding family required Jim to spend more time hunting and trapping. But when he was with the tribe, Jim still flirted with other village wives and maidens. This caused a great deal of tension and jealousy among the village's males and many refused to invite him on their raids and hunts.

Being left out frustrated Jim, so he approached Pine Leaf. He knew she was preparing to lead a raid against the Blackfeet. Jim examined the comely woman who appeared to be around twenty-five years of age. He looked over her tall, sinewy body and took in her piercing, dark eyes. She seemed alert, intelligent, well coordinated and quick. He also noticed that half of the little finger on her left hand had been cut off and he understood that she had previously been in mourning. This so-called *female warrior* fascinated him; he had already heard tales of her bravery. Because he did not feel a similar sexual attraction for her that he felt for most women, he figured that perhaps they could raid together after all.

Pine Leaf signed to Jim saying, "Oh! Brave Medicine Calf, will you follow me on this raid? I have forty braves who have agreed to support me. Are you brave enough to join us?"

"I will follow your lead and match your every deed," he signed. "I am the greatest warrior in the Shining Mountains." Pine Leaf knew that Jim had a powerful body but she scoffed at his air of self-importance. It was obvious he considered her inferior to him and that he intended to best her on the raid.

"We shall see, Medicine Calf," she responded. "We shall see."

She led her party northwesterly for three suns. As they rose from their third sleep, she heard her scout yell, "Pecuni! Pecuni!" She mounted quickly, then she spied the approaching enemy. Approximately fifty Blackfeet rode toward her camp.

"Charge, brave warriors!" she yelled. "Charge!"

She rode hard because she wanted to stay in front of her braves, but in her peripheral vision she saw Medicine Calf strike down an enemy before she had made contact herself. Medicine Calf then flew into hand-to-hand combat while she directed her warriors to launch a counterattack to extricate him from the crazed Blackfeet. Some of the Blackfeet had already begun singing their death songs, but they still fought, intending to take as many Crow with them as they could.

The Sparrow Hawks dispatched the enemy quickly; Pine Leaf herself had lanced one Blackfoot and shot another. "I have never seen a brave fight in Medicine Calf's style," she thought. "He fights with more ferociousness and daring than our famous war chief, Five Scalps, or even Chief Rotten Belly." She decided that she would definitely have to watch this black warrior more closely. After the dust settled, the warriors broke camp and prepared to leave.

Pine Leaf instructed her followers to paint their faces black. This would announce to everyone that they had been victorious.

The entire village turned out to celebrate their return.

"Medicine Calf was the first to count coup and to strike the enemy," Pine Leaf announced. "He is truly one of us and a great warrior. I will follow his war trail anytime he calls out. I will even sponsor him for initiation into the Big Dog Society. He is one of us now. I have spoken."

Because of Jim's success at drawing first blood, Chief Bowl had to give away his property, which was a Sparrow Hawk custom. Jim celebrated and basked in his newfound glory, vowing to restore his new father's lost riches.

From that day on Jim was allowed to follow any raiding party and when he led, he had many followers, especially the admiring Pine Leaf. He had seen her in combat and had witnessed her skill, quickness, courage, and fine horsemanship. In the weeks and months that followed, Jim observed she was also deadly accurate with a rifle and bow.

Jim started teaching Pine Leaf the battle tactics he had learned from the military and from listening to General Ashley. The General would often tell tales of battle when seating with others around a campfire. Jim also used some of the ideas learned from his fellow trappers.

Jim struck up a friendship with Black Panther, a fellow warrior who had no family. Through Black Panther, Jim began learning their language. The two trapped together and confided in each other, but since they had become each other's protectors, they could not attend raids together. This custom had been designed to allow the survivor to mourn the other and exact revenge upon the other's killer.

Jim Beckwith fit in well with the Crow; he had found a home at last.

CHAPTER 22

As Pine Leaf had requested, Yellow Belly initiated Jim Beckwith into the Big Dog Society. After the initiation, Yellow Belly, the brother of Chief Rotten Belly, led the Big Dogs on a raid against the Atsina on the Milk River. For this trip, he teamed Jim with Pine Leaf. This suited Jim just fine, for he had become more interested in this strange woman.

As they rode side by side, Jim said, "Pine Leaf, we are both the bravest of the brave. We are both very comely, tall and strong. Together we could produce generations of great Sparrow Hawk warriors. Why don't you move to my lodge and become my head wife?"

The offer from the loud-mouthed but brave warrior only amused Pine Leaf. He stood over eighteen hands tall, had a muscular build, was fleet of foot, and proved to be an excellent marksman. Though he wasn't much darker than some members of her tribe, his black hair was very curly instead of straight, so he didn't really look like a Sparrow Hawk to her. While the other warriors shrunk from courting her, this braggart seemed to believe that she would simply leap into his robes at his request.

But Pine Leaf wouldn't dream of it.

"Oh, Brave Medicine Calf!" she replied. "I will marry you as soon as the pine leaves turn yellow." Then she left him as she rode ahead, chuckling.

Even though Jim's Big Dog friends poked fun at him because of Pine Leaf's rejection, he just smiled and became more open in his calls for her attention and affection.

When Yellow Belly's Big Dogs arrived at Citadel Rock on the Missouri, the warriors placed their powder, flint, primers, and guns into hide tubs. Some of the braves would swim across the river with these bags in tow. The remaining men and Pine Leaf crossed the river on the backs of their horses while leading the remaining mounts through the slow-moving current. Upon reaching the opposite shore, they regrouped and rode north to Big Sandy Creek, where their scouts reported they had located an Atsina.

Jim, Pine Leaf and some thirty warriors rode together to circle and attack the north side of the village. Yellow Belly and the main force planned to steal the Atsina horse herd, leaving their enemies on foot. While Pine Leaf followed Medicine Calf and their small party north to encircle the camp, Pine Leaf worried about attacking her old tribe.

"The White Clay people are my relatives," she thought. "Perhaps Little Feather has become a warrior, he may even be the chief of this village by now. What would I do if I recognized Little Feather or any of my other childhood friends or relatives?" She felt reluctant about participating in the raid, but of course she could not voice her concerns to anyone. After all, they believed her to be Sparrow Hawk. What would it do to her reputation and her future if they believed her to be soft on the big-bellied Atsina?

She felt depressed as her group rode up the Milk River.

After lining up his warriors and directing them to leave their horses with the tenders, Jim led them across the Milk River, shouting a murderous, "Aihee!" Jim's warriors formed a skirmish line; while one group fired, one stood ready and one reloaded. His heavy firepower prevented the Atsina from mounting a counterattack. As Jim's warriors fired, Atsina warriors, women and children scattered in panic.

Caught up in the quick action, Pine Leaf stopped thinking of the White Clay people as her relatives and joined in the raid. She realized that before her stood enemies of the Sparrow Hawk people. Therefore, she must attack. While Jim's forces pinned down the enemy troops, Yellow Belly's men stole twelve hundred ponies, which they drove back to the Big Sandy and across the Big Muddy.

By the time they reached the village, they still retained over a thousand fine horses. Though the raid was considered a big success and dealt a crushing blow to the Atsina, Pine Leaf knew for certain that after this attack, she could never again return to her people.

The River Sparrow Hawks moved their encampment toward the mouth of the Little Bighorn. Jim rode off to scout the area ahead of the caravan. When he saw smoke he immediately rode into a copse of cottonwoods and dismounted. Slowly he crept forward to investigate. Before him lay a temporary village of a Cheyenne hunting party. Watching the lodge smoke rise lazily into the clear skies, he assumed the Cheyenne were not expecting visitors. After creeping back into the wooded grove, he quietly mounted then rode back to the Crow caravan.

As he rode up, Jim hailed Chief Rotten Belly.

"Chief, I have located a village of Cheyenne on the Sparrow Hawk hunting grounds. They do not seem to be aware of our approach. I believe we can surround them."

The news excited the chief. "Take the Big Dogs," Rotten Belly directed, "and engage them until I can organize my main force for the attack." Then he yelled, "Warriors, gather around me! Warriors, hear me!"

"Big Dogs, follow me," yelled Jim. "We will teach the Cheyenne to stay out of Absaroka. Who will be the first to count coup?" The excited warriors raced to make contact with their age-old enemy. For the time being, Pine Leaf remained with Rotten Belly; they needed to locate a suitable site near wood and water for establishing a defensive position. Rotten Belly was a great warrior, but as the chief and army general, he needed to remain in the rear to direct the main battle.

Leaving the camp police to guard his village, the chief led five hundred mounted cavalry toward the fortifications of the Cheyenne. Near the battle site he set up a temporary camp to wait for daylight; he also needed intelligence reports from the Big Dogs.

That evening Jim Beckwith rode into the camp exhausted. "We have killed about fifty Cheyenne," he reported, "and have lost twenty Sparrow Hawks. Because they received reinforcements in the late afternoon, they were able to keep us at bay. I have sent out some of my wolves to locate the origin of their recruits. We must send a relief patrol so my men can get some sleep and renew their armaments." After delivering the bad news, Jim left to locate a lodge for his much needed rest.

"Pine Leaf," Yellow Belly directed, "take out a command to relieve the Big Dogs. Do not attack tonight—wait for our main forces to arrive at sunrise. Only engage the Cheyenne if they try to leave their fortifications."

Obediently the woman warrior organized fifty of her best men, then proceeded to lead them up the Elk until they located the Big Dogs near the mouth of the Bighorn. She found that the tired warriors were losing their enthusiasm for the battle with the reinforced Cheyenne. Pine Leaf sent those Big Dogs back to the bivouac area, then sent some of her scouts to keep an eye on the Cheyenne until Rotten Belly and Yellow Belly could arrive at dawn.

But things didn't turn out as she had planned.

Sporadic gunfire broke the silence of early morning and a wounded scout raced up to her. "The Cheyenne have broken out of their fort!" he exclaimed. "They are mounted well and are trying to reach their main village near the Tongue. We must head them off quickly before they escape our main forces."

Pine Leaf mounted. "Go to Rotten Belly with your news," she directed. "Tell him we are headed for the Tongue in an attempt to turn the Cheyenne. We will fight them until you arrive with our army. Now, warriors, follow me!" Pine Leaf rode in a southeasterly direction, toward the enemy. As daylight broke over the prairie, her outriders waved, gesturing that they had detected the fleeing Cheyenne.

Pine Leaf gathered her forces and engaged the Cheyenne, trying to force them to fort up until the Sparrow Hawk reinforcements could arrive. She sent sortie after sortie into the enemy's flank until they were forced into a coulee, then she quickly placed her troops along the southern perimeter to prevent escape. She knew better than trying to enter the deep wash with her limited forces. She directed some of her men to start cooking the morning meal so the aroma would further demoralize the hungry Cheyenne.

By mid-morning Pine Leaf's scouts detected a large force of Sparrow Hawk warriors approaching from across the prairie. Pine Leaf sent a rider to lead them in. When Rotten Belly arrived, Pine Leaf recounted the events.

"Chief, I would like to return to the Bighorn with my braves," she said. "We have fought hard and have ridden all night in order to cut off the Cheyenne. We need a rest and we will need fresh horses. Each of us has counted coup, and many of us have enemy scalps. Although I have not lost any braves, I do have ten wounded who need attention. Caution your men to be on the lookout for more Cheyenne reinforcements. We could not stop all of the enemy from escaping, and some of them may have taken word to one of their main villages."

Although Pine Leaf had already tired of this war with her old enemy, little did she know that the running battle would last for a full moon, with both sides suffering numerous losses.

Near the end of the conflict, Medicine Calf approached Pine Leaf with great sadness in his eyes. "I have lost the only male friend I've ever had," Jim confessed.

"The Cheyenne have killed Black Panther and for that I will never forgive them. I will name my first son in his honor. Will you follow me to avenge my friend?"

For the first time, Pine Leaf felt sympathy and compassion for Medicine Calf. She too still longed for her dead friend, Cracked-Ice. "I will follow you anytime, my friend," she responded.

Angry and vengeful, Jim led one hundred thirty warriors against the remaining Cheyenne village. His party took sixteen scalps before they scattered the enemy. Pine Leaf, who attended him, counted three coup—killing three warriors with her long lance.

Although the Sparrow Hawks did not defeat them, the Cheyenne had been forced from the Absaroka hunting grounds in disgrace.

CHAPTER 23

Peace in Absaroka allowed Jim to do some trapping in the rich beaver streams of the River Crow. He laid his traps along the bend of the Rosebud before starting to build a lean-to. One day, as he gathered firewood, he detected men and animals descending along the edge of the creek. After checking his rifle and pistol, he secreted himself in a plum thicket. The small party rode right into his camp, stopping to study the fresh campfire. The leader looked around the nearby trees and underbrush.

"Halloo, the camp!" he yelled. "We are friends. We bring trade goods and gifts." The man called out in English, Sioux, Cheyenne and Crow, while looking around expectantly. Jim understood the party leader's words in all the languages he spoke; he also recognized that the high voice belonged to his old trapping partner, James Kipp.

"Halloo, James," Jim hollered from the thicket. "It's me, Jim Beckwith." When the black man stepped out of the plum thicket, Kipp stared in amazement.

"Well, I'll be damned," he exclaimed. "I thought yee were dead fur shur. What air ya doin in Crow country?"

Jim laughed. "I've been seekin some squaw pleasure fer muh youth and beaver wampum fer muh old age. So far I cain't complain about either one." They both laughed. "Tell me," asked Jim, "what the hell air ya doin in these parts? I could'a had ya from that thicket."

Kipp grinned. "I smelled yee from over thar and muh men was at the ready all the time. I knowed you was an American cause of yore camp. Indians is smarter than to camp out in the open alone. Besides, yee smell like sour mash and most Redskins bathe ever day or so. Hey, since I found me such a good man, how would you like to represent me in tradin among the Crow?"

Jim grinned broadly, showing all of his large, white teeth. "Done, James. Done," he replied. "Now I'll have foofooraw fer muh women and money fer muh old age too. I've found Crow squaws to be very expensive indeed."

After the men settled into the small camp, Jim traded thirty prime pelts for ammunition, tobacco and small supplies. Then the men spent the next two days checking traps and making detailed arrangements for future trade.

Kipp and his trappers rode off to locate new trapping territories, while Jim rode toward Pryor Creek to locate the River Crow village. The Sparrow Hawks called the creek Horses River, considering it the center of Absaroka. As Jim entered the large village he saw signs that there had been a great battle; he noticed women in mourning and a great deal of agitation among the young men.

Pine Leaf rode up to meet him. "We were attacked by over two thousand Sioux warriors," she reported. "We have lost thirty-one of our finest braves, but the Sioux lost fifty-three of theirs. We finally drove them off when they couldn't dislodge us from our barricades."

As Jim looked around him, he growled in disgust and anger. In his best Crow language he said, "I will seek revenge for our dead." *Pine Leaf knew he would.*

After the camp recovered and held services for their dead, Chief Rotten Belly directed his village to ascend the Elk to the Stillwater. It would be some time before Jim would get the chance to make good on his promise to avenge his dead comrades.

After the move, the villagers began gathering much-needed berries, roots and fruits. Dried chokeberries were pulverized with crushed buffalo meat to make pemmican. Gumbo lily roots were used for food, but also boiled in water to treat coughs and respiratory infections. The small nutlets of the rose tree were pounded into a meal and baked into cakes. While wild onions were eaten raw, they were also dried for food flavoring or cooked in water to treat sore throats.

Strawberries were eaten ripe, while their leaves were boiled to make tea. Sego lily bulbs, a real delicacy, were boiled or baked; they tasted like potatoes. Sumac fruit was used as tea, while the seeds were pounded into a flour for gruel.

Pinecone and sunflower seeds were roasted and eaten, while pinecone flowers made a fine tea when boiled. Prairie dog weed leaves were pulverized and snuffed into the nostrils to cure headaches. The yellow gumweed flower was smoked for asthma, while blazing star sap produced a juice used to treat fevers.

Food supplements found here included Pomme Blanche (called prairie turnips) along with wild plums and artichokes. This area provided gooseberries, currants, buffalo-berries and many other edible plants to augment the heavy meat diet of the Crow. They called the bearberry leaves *kinnikinnick* and the dried leaves were mixed with tobacco or the leaves of the big bluebell plant before smoking.

During this time, Jim and Pine Leaf often hunted together. Jim continued to make light sexual overtures toward the female warrior, even renewing his request for her to marry him. She continued to reply in riddles, such as, "Yes Medicine Calf, I will marry you when you can find me a red-headed Indian."

Riding toward the Musselshell Pine Leaf topped a rise and then stopped suddenly. She leapt from her horse and grabbed its muzzle to keep the animal quiet. Jim quickly followed suit as he looked to Pine Leaf for the cause of her alarm. She pointed down river to a thin column of smoke rising high into the sky. Slowly they led their horses along a coulee until they could get close enough to make out the size of the camp.

Jim counted one hundred thirty-five lodges. Figuring five warriors to a lodge, he calculated the village contained over six hundred fighting men. A large horseherd grazed beyond the village. To Pine Leaf, the villagers looked like Blackfeet.

"Pecuni" she whispered. Jim agreed and after quietly leading their horses back down the hill, they raced all the way back to the mouth of the Stillwater.

"Pecunis! Pecunis!" they yelled as they galloped into the village.

Rotten Belly quickly organized his warriors and issued provisions, then he led his small army toward the Musselshell. Jim and Pine Leaf guided them northeasterly until they came to Big Lake, where they watered their animals and Rotten Belly split his troops. He sent Yellow Belly and four hundred warriors due north, while he led the main force, including Jim and Pine Leaf, northwest.

At dusk the latter group crossed the Musselshell and prepared a cold camp. Since the night air was still very cool, the warriors bedded down in pairs or in small groups for warmth. Since Pine Leaf was not particularly close to any of the Sparrow Hawk warriors, she bedded next to her new friend, Jim. Although she allowed his body against hers for warmth, she continually rejected his aggressive, sexual advances. She smiled as she thought of his torment, being so close to her yet unable to have his way.

As it turned out, she not only enjoyed the comfort of Medicine Calf's warm body, but she even felt a tingling sensation from being so close to him. She could feel his strong muscles twitch and his lungs expand and contract. She could also feel his strong heart beat as she snuggled against his broad back, but she would never let him know how much she enjoyed the contact. Contentedly, she finally slipped into deep slumber.

Early in the morning the camped warriors rose, keeping their noise level as low as possible. They spread out in various directions to make their toilet calls, then they painted themselves for battle and prepared their weapons.

Above the river Rotten Belly held his troops until he heard the charge of Yellow Belly. After the first group stormed the village, Blackfeet women and children began scurrying across the Musselshell, running from Yellow Belly's forces, but running right into Rotten Belly's warriors. As Blackfeet warriors tried to organize a defense against Yellow Belly's men, Rotten Belly yelled at his warriors to charge. Pine Leaf had fired off a few volleys when she saw Medicine Calf surrounded by some of the desperate Blackfoot defenders. She charged the mass of their bodies and drove her lance through the heart of a war chief.

Her momentum scattered the astonished enemy warriors allowing her to extricate Medicine Calf from certain death by pulling him up onto her horse. His mount had been mortally wounded, and Jim himself had a bullet crease on the side of his head.

Despite his injury, Jim would not stay out of the foray. He quickly took advantage of his newfound freedom to resume his attack on the remaining Blackfeet. The fleeing foe left over one hundred seventy dead on the battlefield, and the Sparrow Hawks captured one hundred fifty women and children. The defeated enemy abandoned weapons, food, equipage and horses, which were readily confiscated by the victors.

Losses to the Sparrow Hawks consisted of twenty-nine wounded men and some of their mounts. Pine Leaf counted six coups and killed four Pecunis. Jim killed ten of the Blackfeet and wounded many more, but he had lost his favorite horse. He also suffered a severe headache from his scalp wound.

The defeat of the Blackfeet had proven decisive, and the remaining Pecuni warriors fled back to the Sun River in disgrace.

CHAPTER 24

In the fall of 1830, Jim received a letter from Kenneth McKenzie requesting his presence at Fort Union. Jim had already learned that McKenzie recently built Fort Union on the Missouri above the mouth of the Elk.

In 1828 McKenzie built a post at the mouth of the Milk River, but the post had failed. Jim knew his influence with the Crow was needed to control their trade for the American Fur Company, so he traveled over six hundred miles to the mouth of the Elk.

Whenever Jim traveled among the white men he learned how his friends and acquaintances were doing in the fur trading business. The French Fur Company had built a post on the Teton River but it too had failed. The Columbia Fur Company had been absorbed by the American Fur Company and the Rocky Mountain Fur Company had changed hands. This last company was now run by Jim's old associates: Jim Bridger, Milton Sublette, Tom Fitzpatrick and Henry Fraeb. Jim felt depressed that he had not prospered along with his old trapping companions.

"I used to trap with all those men," he thought, "Now they're all big booshways and I'm just a Crow warrior and occasional trader. I wonder if I'll ever make anything of this business or just die *forgotten?*"

As Jim suspected, he and S. P. Winter were being hired by McKenzie to develop the Crow trade. The two received ten packhorses loaded down with trade goods, then Jim guided Winter back to the Mountain Crow to introduce him to Chief Long Hair. Since the two divisions of the Crow only occasionally camped together, Jim decided it would work to their advantage for Winter to be situated with Long Hair and the Mountain Crow while he himself would remain with Rotten Belly and his River Crow.

Each went about the business of living with the Crow and trading their goods for furs, as per their agreement with McKenzie.

In the spring, Chief Rotten Belly moved his river tribe to the mouth of Rosebud Creek. One morning they were rousted from slumber by an attack from a large party of Blackfeet. Since most of the Sparrow Hawk warriors kept their war ponies tied to their lodgepoles, they quickly mounted and initiated a counterattack. The Blackfeet were driven back to the prairie, where each tribe charged and countercharged for the rest of the day. The Sparrow Hawks slowly but surely gained an advantage. Pine Leaf repeatedly wielded her battle-ax against the heads of the stubborn Blackfeet warriors.

Jim signaled Pine Leaf and her nearest braves to follow his lead back through the village to attack a large party of Blackfeet trying to enter from the rear. The defenders charged down the hill, directly into the Blackfeet, scattering horses and bodies everywhere. The force of their charge split the enemy forces.

As Jim passed through them, a Blackfoot lance grazed his leg, hitting Jim's horse and killing it. Jim was pinned under the fallen animal until Pine Leaf tied a leather thong around the horse's front leg and with the aid of her own pony, rolled the dead animal off of Jim. He quickly retrieved a riderless horse and rejoined the fray. Pine Leaf felt relieved when she saw that Medicine Calf was basically uninjured. She followed him to reengage the enemy but soon her own mount, Red Devil, received an arrow in its side, sending Pine Leaf crashing to the ground. She leapt free with her lance and battle-ax in hand.

Several Blackfeet had her in retreat when suddenly Jim drove his horse into them, bowling them over. She drove her lance through one of them and on foot pursued the rest behind Jim's charge. She too located another horse and followed the retreating Blackfeet across the plain. The Sparrow Hawks captured twelve hundred horses. Ninety-one Blackfeet were killed while the Sparrow Hawks lost thirty-one braves. When they arrived back home they did not celebrate because they had lost many warriors. However, it would be some time before the Blackfeet attacked the people of Absaroka again.

Pine Leaf was not jealous of her friend and fellow warrior, but she seethed with anger because she had not been heralded and publicly honored by the council or the chief for her war efforts as he had been. This snub added one more wound to her fragile psyche. She was still not allowed to sit in council and she was never allowed to share in the warpath secret ceremony while on a raid.

Being excluded from the warpath ceremony galled her more than anything else. In this ritual, each brave could recount his sexual alliances with any woman or maiden in the village without fear of retaliation by the boyfriend, husband or father. By thus cleansing his soul and conscience, a warrior believed he would be entering battle with a pure heart, which would gain him a better chance of success. The Great Spirit would offer him protection after forgiving him of his transgressions. Sarcastically Pine Leaf thought that some warriors probably used this occasion to brag about their conquests or to psychologically torture someone whom they did not like.

She did notice however that most of the braves took the warpath secret seriously, believing that to repeat any of the secrets so divulged would surely result in death. Her exclusion from such an honor bothered her greatly, so one day she complained to Jim about it.

"I have killed many men," she said, "counted many coups and have led where no other dared to lead, yet I am still denied the right to the warpath secret ceremony. Why am I sent off by myself while warriors inferior to me are allowed to participate?"

Jim hopelessly tried to explain the situation to her. "You are a woman and can never be trusted with a man's secrets because you don't have anything to protect. If you ever broke the secret trust, you would be killed by your own warriors."

Pine Leaf glared at Jim with fire in her eyes. "Let their secrets protect them the next time they are surrounded by the Pecuni or Cheyenne," she replied, then she dug her heels into her poor pony's sides and galloped out of sight. Jim had to laugh at her spunk and her anger; he chuckled, but he was sure glad her ire was not directed at him.

Not long afterwards Jim was riding with a small hunting party when Big Robber rode out to find him.

"Aieeee!" he called. "Our beloved Pine Leaf led a raid against the Pecuni and she was severely wounded. She counted two coups and secured eight scalps before they stopped her; we were able to defeat them but we lost two braves."

Jim quickly turned his party around and headed back to the village. After several days Pine Leaf was able to talk again and she asked for Medicine Calf. As Jim entered her lodge, she begged, "You must avenge our losses to the Pecunis. I cannot wash my face until we have killed our enemies."

Although she was doing better, Jim could see she needed much more time to heal. "I must go to Fort Cass on business and I cannot avenge your losses until I return. Recover from your wounds and I will assist you." Pine Leaf endured her blackened face until she healed, but she was disappointed with Medicine Calf. If he had needed avenging, she would not have left him in humiliation.

After one moon, Medicine Calf had still not returned and Pine Leaf began to worry about him. Even though she had not fully recovered, she rode to Fort Cass. When she arrived she learned that a white hunter had been killed near the post. But she was more interested in finding Medicine Calf and when she did, she angrily pulled him aside. "I'm tired of waiting for you," she railed. "Will you go to war with me so I can wash my face?"

Jim smiled. "Yes, I will go with you and the white men will even pay me to avenge *their* dead hunter. I now have two reasons to find the Pecuni."

Together they led fifty warriors north to the Musselshell, then descended the river northward. As they neared the forks they detected a small Blackfoot camp. Thinking it only fair, Jim opted for Pine Leaf to count the first coup.

"You will have the honor of leading the charge and we will follow you." Although still recovering from her wounds, she felt a surge of renewed energy from Medicine Calf's words. Raising her lance she called to her followers, "Charge, brave warriors. Avenge our loved ones! Follow me!" Pine Leaf lowered her body over Black Star and broke into a full gallop. The Sparrow Hawks caught the Pecuni unaware and quickly killed two braves before the Blackfeet could mount any opposition. After she and her warriors killed several more of the Pecunis, they scattered the rest, then began to drive as many horses as they could round up. They finally controlled seventy horses in their flight away from their old enemy.

When they reached Dead Man's Basin they stopped to rest. Pine Leaf counted the men but she could not find Medicine Calf. Nervously she rode back up the river until she spied two lone riders coming slowly toward her. One of them was an injured Medicine Calf.

"What happened?" she asked.

Big Robber held onto Jim's reins as he spoke. "My brother has killed two of the enemy, but he caught an arrow in his head. If his head were not so hard, he would surely be dead now." Jim slowly raised his bandaged and bloody head. "Don't ever count me out my friend. As soon as I rest I will tell everyone how I avenged my beloved Pine Leaf so she would marry me. Now that she can wash her face again, we can be wedded and settle down." At first his words infuriated Pine Leaf, but then it dawned on her that this was his way of telling her he was not mortally wounded. Realizing that he would be all right, she laughed aloud.

They had lost no warriors this time and Pine Leaf was finally allowed to wash her dirty face.

As a war chief, Jim rose in rank until he became the third-ranking counselor in the Sparrow Hawk Nation. Pine Leaf was proud of him, but she quietly seethed because she was the second-greatest Sparrow Hawk warrior, yet she was not a counselor or even a war chief. She deplored the double standard under which she lived and vowed to someday earn her rightful place on the council.

Even though Jim had taken seven wives, he still became bored and wanted new sexual adventures. When a new young maiden began pursuing him, he approached Pine Leaf to explain the situation. "Pine Leaf," he said, "since you will not marry me, I want to marry Little Doe. However, she is young and inexperienced. Will you take her into your lodge and have your squaws teach her in the ways of a warrior's wife until I come for her?" Pine Leaf admired Medicine Calf and would do most anything for him, but this situation annoyed her. She knew Little Doe and liked her, so it would be difficult for her to turn this child over to her womanizing friend.

Reluctantly she agreed to the proposal, but with a provision.

"If you promise to cherish her, provide for her, and not abandon her," she said, "I will do as you ask. Because we are Big Dog warriors, we must honor each other's requests; therefore, I will take care of Little Doe until she is ready and willing to move into your lodge." Jim agreed. He thought he detected a note of jealousy on Pine Leaf's part, but then again, perhaps not. He disregarded this suspicion as concern for Little Doe's future.

For several months Pine Leaf boarded Little Doe in her lodge, teaching her and protecting the girl's virginity. She became very fond of the youngster's wonderful disposition, her keen intellect, and her prompt absorption of everything she was taught.

"Little Doe," she advised, "Medicine Calf may not always show his affection for you, but he is a great warrior. He has a large sexual appetite and roaming eyes so you will have to share him with many other women. Can you live with this?"

Little Doe looked up at Pine Leaf with large black eyes, which brimmed with innocence and devotion. "My Sister, I love Medicine Calf dearly and will always be devoted to him. I know he has weaknesses but I will make him love me above all others. I will be patient until I can give him a son and that will convert him."

Jim readied for his wedding hunt and approached the lodge of his bride confidently. At last Jim called upon Little Doe and took her to the Bighorn Mountains. While camped in a high valley, she confessed her innermost desires to him.

"I love you, Medicine Calf, and I want to bear your children. I will always remain faithful to you."

Jim felt the pull of her softness and vulnerability. "Although I love you very much," he said, "I do have other wives and I must provide for them and make them happy. However, I will consider you my number one wife and will provide you with your own lodge."

Little Doe seemed overjoyed by this statement and gave herself fully to Jim while they camped with only the Great Spirit as their witness. Because she was a virgin, she was not prepared for his aggressive love making. On the other hand, Jim couldn't have been more pleased. He had Little Doe as his eighth wife and for the first time in ages, his sexual appetite had been satisfied. While the new bride was still trying to share more of her devotion with him, Jim slipped into a deep slumber, with her delicate body entwined around his muscular but tired frame.

After they arose the next morning, Jim killed several sheep with his bow. When he brought them to camp, Little Doe displayed her further talents by helping him skin and butcher their carcasses. Jim loaded the meat and hides onto the pack animals and they began their trip back to the village.

Upon their arrival, Jim announced to the village that he and Little Doe were indeed married and that he had changed her name to *Nom-ne-dit-chee,* meaning Little Wife. He stayed in the village for a week, then joined Pine Leaf and a large hunting party assembled to locate the migrating buffalo.

On the second day, the party located a large herd and Rotten Belly directed his soldiers to cut out several hundred for the surround. To their great surprise they found they had also trapped seven Blackfeet, who had been hunting the same buffalo. Though the enemy hastily erected a sand fort for defense, Jim rode forward and struck one warrior with his coup stick then quickly retreated.

As he turned to accept the honor of the first coup, a Blackfoot bullet struck him where he wore his Green River knife, knocking him to the ground. He hit his face as he fell and began bleeding from the mouth. He realized he was not seriously injured and encouraged Pine Leaf and the others to proceed with the attack. This bravery spurred the Big Dogs into a frenzy and in a few moments they annihilated all seven of the enemy. Not only was the hunt a complete success, but they had taken seven scalps and they suffered no casualties except for Jim's near disaster.

When they returned to Absaroka, Jim received great honor for counting first coup and the warriors and villagers alike praised his remarkable medicine for not being seriously injured by the Pecuni bullet. While the village held a great feast and dance in his honor, Pine Leaf again stood in his shadow. She suffered from mixed emotions about her friend. She felt proud of him but jealousy over his accomplishments had crept into her heart.

Pine Leaf rode off to the foothills alone to pray to her spirits.

CHAPTER 25

During the falling-leaf season of 1830, Jim and a party of Sparrow Hawks journeyed to Fort Clark, below the mouth of the Knife River on the Missouri. He had several thousand dollars worth of beaver pelts and wanted to make sure he received top dollar in trade for his hard work. His party paralleled the Elk until they reached the old earthlodge ruins. He then led his men east to Beaver Creek, which they followed until it emptied into the Little Missouri; they then crossed overland until they found the headwaters of the Knife. By following the south side of the Knife, they reached Fort Clark.

Jim now had the appearance of a Crow warrior and he could speak Crow quite well. The fort clerk could not understand his request for a new knife, so he called the chief factor, James Kipp, to interpret. When Kipp arrived, Jim spoke in English. "I want me a damned Green River knife so's I can scalp thet dumb bastard!"

It shocked Kipp and the clerk to hear a Crow speak understandable mountain man English. "Where did you learn English?" asked Kipp.

Jim smiled. "Mr. Kipp," he said, "you hired me to trade among the Crow for you. Don't you remember Jim Beckwith?" Jim's presence indeed surprised Kipp because traders and travelers continually told yarns about each new death Jim had allegedly suffered at the hands of one Indian tribe or another. They spent several hours swapping lies and stories along with news from St. Louis. Finally Kipp saw to it that Jim received a favorable exchange for all of his pelts and they bid each other farewell.

After leaving Fort Clark, Jim and his party of two hundred men and women ran into two hundred fifty Cheyenne braves. Since the Sparrow Hawks could not leave their women, they had to do battle rather than try to outrun them. Each warrior mounted his best war pony and met the Cheyenne charge head on, driving them back onto the plain. They killed about fifty Cheyenne before the enemy regrouped. Then once again the Cheyenne charged and the Sparrow Hawks chased them into the thick timber of the Knife River bottom. This time the Sparrow Hawks retreated because they had lost nine warriors and a number of them had been wounded. Jim received another arrow wound, but he knew he would heal in time.

The Sparrow Hawks gathered their women and trade goods, then headed off for the Bighorn Basin. Absaroka remained quiet until the spring of 1831.

After Jim's wounds healed, he decided to take a small party up the Bighorn and Wind Rivers to trade with the Shoshone. After they arrived at the Shoshone village, near Ocean Lake, Jim discovered a large party of Utes riding under Chief Walkara. Jim's familiarity with the Ute tribe had taught him that these people could be treacherous, so he limited his trading and kept a constant vigil. His men traded some of their guns and ammunition to the Shoshone for some spotted horses.

"Come Medicine Calf," they coaxed, "you too must trade for some of these fine ponies." Jim stared at them angrily, as if they were ignorant children.

"You fools!" he yelled. "We are among wolves and you have given your weapons away to the cunning coyotes. Mount your worthless ponies and let us leave this place. Now!" As they rode down the Wind River, Jim kept an eye on their rear.

They rounded the great bend and moved on toward Wind River Canyon, but before they could reach the narrow security of the canyon, the Utes attacked, killing the rear guard and scalping him immediately. Jim took over the lead and raced for the entrance to the canyon. When he entered its high walled security, he pulled up behind a large boulder and quickly climbed to the top with his rifle and pistol.

He watched as his braves tried to outrun the Utes on their poor, jaded, Shoshone horses. He began to fire and reload his Hawken as fast as he could but he watched in disgust and anguish as five more of his men were overtaken by the Utes. He killed three of the attackers before he was able to turn them back, but they had already scalped his men and recovered their own fallen comrades.

He was angry with his old enemies, the Utes, but he blamed his old friends, the Snakes, for allowing his men to be set up and for selling his men the useless ponies. He vowed to reap harsh revenge on Chief Mowoomhah of the Shoshone as he moved on down the canyon with his survivors.

CHAPTER 26

Jim rested as the Sparrow Hawks painted their faces and mourned for four days over the loss of their braves. He then enlisted five hundred warriors to exact punishment upon the Shoshone. Pine Leaf volunteered to lead one hundred braves while Grizzly Bear would lead another hundred.

They retraced the Bighorn and the Wind rivers to the big bend of the Wind at the mouth of the Beaver River. They then ascended the Beaver to its source. They crossed southerly over the mountains to the Sweetwater River and followed it to its source near South Pass. From there they rode over the Shining Mountains to the headwaters of the Big Sandy River.

Sparrow Hawk scouts reported two upper encampments of the Shoshone on the Prairie Hen River, called the Green River by the mountain men. The encampments lay near the mouth of Big Sandy. They also located the main village about five miles below the lower camp. Jim took three hundred warriors and made a circle to the south in order to approach the main village from the east. Pine Leaf split her forces and charged her assigned encampment from both the north and the south. Her party killed or wounded thirty Snakes before the unprepared tribe could escape across the Green River. She and her braves rounded up many Shoshone horses before they proceeded down the Green. When Pine Leaf caught up with Grizzly Bear she learned that he too had achieved great success, and together they approached the smoky battle scene downstream.

By the time Pine Leaf and Grizzly Bear arrived, the battle had ended and the Shoshone chief was suing for peace. Medicine Calf sat before Chief Mowoomhah, calmly smoking a large calumet pipe and dictating the terms of peace.

The Shoshone surrendered five hundred good horses, chosen by Yellow Belly, as a sign of their renewed brotherhood. Jim accepted their offer and the proud Sparrow Hawks rode toward the Bighorn, moving slowly in order to nurse their forty wounded soldiers. Since the Sparrow Hawks lost no warriors in the battle, they were entitled to wash their faces.

After settling back down to village life, Jim again became restless. This time he began lusting for the shapely wife of Chief Big Rain, the civil chief of the Mountain Sparrow Hawks and leader of the tribal police.

Jim located Chief Big Rain's encampment near the great hot springs on the Bighorn, below Wind River Canyon. Jim's village was located on Shell Creek, where it emptied into the Bighorn. One day he complained to Little Wife and his other wives about his rheumatism, which had been caused by trapping too many years in the cold streams of the Shining Mountains. He then excused himself to go the hot springs for treatments.

While he was soaking in the steamy water of the Bighorn, below the great mineral floes, he plied Yellow Belly to take a large amount of tobacco into the village and offer a big smoke in honor of Chief Big Rain. While the camp warriors smoked, Big Rain proudly recounted his many deeds and battles as a young warrior.

Jim took the opportunity to slip into Big Rain's darkened lodge. He found Red Cherry asleep on a high bed laden with soft robes. Gently he began stroking her long, shapely body.

Half awake, she asked, "Who is there?"

"It is I, Medicine Calf, your idol," Jim replied softly. I have seen you look upon me and I can no longer resist your love. I have come to receive your nurture in order to restore my warrior powers. You kindle my dying spirit and I need you to inspire me to greater deeds. Let our hearts merge into one."

Though Red Cherry was flattered and aroused, she worried over the consequences of being caught. "I am the wife of Chief Big Rain and he will beat me and banish you from Absaroka," she warned.

Caressing her further, he replied, "I will bring you fine horses, make passionate love to you, and paint your face after counting coup. Big Rain is only a civil chief and he can never paint your beautiful face."

Red Cherry again tried to dissuade Jim. "Big Rain will kill you and your father will lose all of his horses and property."

"Then every brave will know I died for a beautiful woman," argued Jim, "and it will make you the most popular woman in our nation. If my father loses his horses, I will simply steal more from our enemies. If I am dead, my Big Dogs will steal them in my honor. I will not leave until you vow to join me on the war trail."

Red Cherry trembled at Jim's touch; her feelings were intensified by her fear. Nevertheless, in the darkness she took one of the rings off a slender finger and placed it into Jim's hand in the darkness. He took her pledge and slipped from Big Rain's lodge to return to his lean-to next to the source of the hot spring.

Jim gloated over his near conquest when Yellow Belly returned to their small camp. Jim showed him the ring he had received from Red Cherry, and although Yellow Belly had little sense of humor over such things, he smiled at the trick that had been played on Big Rain. He thought it served the pompous old goat right that he should be cuckolded under his very nose. Yellow Belly and Jim talked into the night of their plans to get Red Cherry out of Big Rain's village. The next day Jim sent a message to Red Cherry to meet him below the falls at full moon. He was leading thirty warriors on a raid against the Blackfeet and asked her to lead his war pony and carry his war shield—which was considered a great honor.

About midnight, Jim heard the soft call of an owl and he answered with two ghostly moans. Through the willows emerged Red Cherry, riding a small gray mare. She leapt from the mare into Jim's waiting arms. He could feel her heart fluttering through her large breasts. Her soft, round lips kissed every inch of his rough face until his loins ached. Finally the two fell to the ground and began making love. After almost uprooting the surrounding willows with their active lovemaking, they weakly mounted their horses and rode down the Bighorn to rendezvous with Yellow Belly and the Big Dogs.

Jim and Red Cherry found Yellow Belly and his men at the mouth of the Nowood and proceeded down the Big Horn to the Shoshone River. Here they cut overland across Clark's Fork of the Elk, or Yellowstone River, to the Musselshell. While the group rested, Jim and Red Cherry went off to be by themselves. The party resumed their travels by crossing Judith Gap to the Judith River, where they finally located a Blackfoot village.

After two days of reconnoitering, the Big Dogs found an unguarded horseherd. They stole one hundred seventeen fine ponies and hastily retreated into the stillness of the night.

When the valiant party returned to the Mountain Sparrow Hawks, the camp police promptly arrested Jim. Red Cherry was not harmed, but the police tied Jim to a tethering pole. Big Rain and his sisters proceeded to whip and lash Jim for his transgressions. In addition, Chief Bowl had to forfeit five hundred horses to the angered chief and Jim lost all of his stable. Although sore and bruised from the beating, Jim danced the Horse Dance, even though he did not have any horses left.

Undaunted, Jim danced up beside Red Cherry and whispered to her. "Meet me at the same place and time as before," he said. "We shall again set the wild prairies afire." Red Cherry blushed nervously, but nodded in agreement.

Pine Leaf felt sad when she learned of Medicine Calf's elopement with Red Cherry. The escapades of her warrior friend disappointed her greatly.

However, Big Dog and Sparrow Hawk codes did not allow her to side with her friend, Little Wife. The codes forbid a warrior from betraying a comrade-in-arms, but she certainly wanted to. It galled her that even though she was not permitted to attend the warpath secret ceremony, she was still bound by its codes. Once more she rode up into the Bighorn Mountains in disgust.

The next day Little Wife arrived at Jim's lean-to, surprising him with her outburst. "You have dishonored me and your parents by losing all of your horses and your father's horses. You were only spared your hunting and war weapons. Now only your mother and your wives have property. If you do not cease this display, you will have no relatives and no one will associate with you or call you their brother." With her tirade concluded, a pregnant Little Wife remounted and rode back to Shell Creek.

His wife's diatribe meant little to Jim. That night he met Red Cherry and they left with seventeen followers. They made love for four days before they luckily happened upon a Blackfoot war party of nine warriors. Jim and his men were able to kill three of the enemy before they escaped. With scalps from their enemies and seventy-five captured horses, they finally returned to the Mountain Sparrow Hawk village. Once again Jim was arrested and whipped by Big Rain. To make matters even worse, Big Rain confiscated all his newly captured horses. As Jim lay in his lean-to, trying to recuperate from his latest beating, he was awakened by a kick in the back.

As he rolled over, Little Wife started screaming at him. "Here is something you cannot find in Big Rain's bed. I have given you a war chief and I have named him 'Black Panther' in honor of your deceased friend."

Jim slowly raised up his pained body and through his bleary eyes observed the small, black baby boy held in Little Wife's delicate arms. He packed what little gear he had left and followed her back to Shell Creek. Although Jim was truly proud of his new son, holding him and checking out every inch of the baby, his wandering mind soon returned to thoughts of Red Cherry.

When Jim finally headed out on another raid, he once again took Red Cherry with him. This time Big Rain gave up his ownership of her. He let her go because of the pressure he had been receiving from Yellow Belly and the Big Dogs. "If you beat Medicine Calf again," Yellow Belly had warned, "the Big Dogs will cut off your manhood."

Jim paid Big Rain one horse, one bolt of scarlet cloth, ten guns, ten chief's coats, ten pairs of leggings, and ten pairs of moccasins. *Now he could keep Red Cherry legally.*

He took his newest wife to Shell Creek and set up a new lodge. He had to divide his wives into three lodges, making certain Little Wife was separated from Red Cherry. Although unhappy over her situation, Little Wife rationalized that she was still the head wife. "I am the only one to give him a son and heir," she thought. "He will return to me after he has tired of their flesh."

CHAPTER 27

During the brown-grass season, the River Sparrow Hawks moved to the upper valley of the Bighorn. They had adequate meat supplies and the river bottom was ripe with berries, plums, roots and herbs. But shortly after they arrived, they lost several young men in a surprise raid by the Cheyenne.

Jim raised two hundred men to head south in search of the ever-mobile Cheyenne enemy. They traveled around the northern foothills of the Bighorn Mountains and then headed south until they reached the North Platte. A trail led them down the Platte to the mouth of the Laramie River, where they located a Cheyenne village. As the warriors reconnoitered the enemy, some of them located eleven Cheyenne hunters, encamped and dressing out a fresh kill. Jim immediately secreted his men and waited until dark. He then charged through the small camp, quickly killing and scalping the entire party. They loaded the Cheyenne meat, guns, ammunition and horses before dashing north toward the Bighorn.

In Jim's absence, Pine Leaf organized a horse raid against the Shoshone. She attracted about ninety followers who followed her along the Bighorn to the Wind, then following that river in search of the enemy. They crossed the Shining Mountains at Union Pass. It grew colder and even snowed before they descended again to the Green River.

While Pine Leaf sought out a favorable campsite, her scouts spotted smoke and the signs of a large encampment below the Green River Lakes which they called *Seeds-ka-dee* or "Prairie Hen River." She felt certain these were Shoshone, but as they cautiously approached the camp, she discovered about seventy white trappers. Grizzly Bear hailed the camp to inform them they were the friendly Sparrow Hawks and wished to approach; after some hesitation, the trappers allowed the party to enter.

Captains Jefferson Blackwell and John Gantt, along with a clerk named Zenas Leonard, led the free trappers. The Sparrow Hawks smoked and signed their purpose for being in Shoshone country. While they parleyed, Pine Leaf examined the trappers' fine horses. She stayed in the background during the talks because she knew white men did not involve women in business or war. She believed these men considered women only good for tending to their sexual needs and taking care of domestic chores. But even in the distance, Pine Leaf could make out much of their conversation.

Grizzly Bear told the white men, "We are making war against the Snake. We followed them through the Shining Mountains but now we have lost them to the snow and wind."

Captain Gantt did not understand Crow, but one of his men had been their captive some years ago and claimed to know their language. He called on John Saunders who explained to Grizzly Bear that the white men were on a trapping expedition and had just left the Great Salt Lake. After the two groups smoked their allotment of tobacco, the Sparrow Hawks moved on down the Green River to set up their own camp.

After everyone was asleep, Pine Leaf slipped out of her own camp, returning on foot to the white camp. She noticed only two posted guards. The men were bundled up, obviously tired and cold. She watched until they nodded off to sleep. Slowly she entered the horseherd, gently rubbing the horses' noses to keep them from alarming the guards. The horses were hunkered backwards, braced against the cold wind; they did not seem frightened by her presence. Stealthily Pine Leaf picked out five of the best horses she could find then led them out of the rope corral and back to her own camp.

At daybreak, she awakened her followers. "Great warriors," she said, "I have found five beautiful war ponies, but I fear the white-eyes will try to claim them. Let us return to our villages and forget the Shoshone." Her frightened men mounted and rode south to the Big Sandy where they crossed the mountains at South Pass without difficulty. They descended the Sweetwater until they could cross over the foothills and gain the headwaters of the Beaver, which they followed to the Wind River.

After Captain Gantt and his men arose, they soon learned they had lost five of their best hunting horses. His guides reported that Union Pass and Togwotee Pass were surely closed by the storm, so Gantt decided to follow the Crow trail in order to locate a pass over the Rockies. He desperately wanted to regain their valuable horses.

Because they had such a big head start, the Sparrow Hawks had not attempted to cover their tracks. Pine Leaf led her party down the Bighorn, then found the River Sparrow Hawks camped at the mouth of the Stinking Water River. She was so proud of her acquisitions that she immediately showed her new horses to Jim.

"Medicine Calf," she announced proudly, "I have taken five fine horses from the white-eyes we found in Shoshone country." Jim was impressed at her deed but he became alarmed when he discovered the quality of the thoroughbreds. Even in the dark he saw that the trappers could easily identify these animals; they did not look like other Indian horses. Jim scolded his protégé.

"I have told the Sparrow Hawks to never steal from or attack the white men! These people are as numerous as the buffalo and they have many soldiers and guns. They have guns so big they can blow up any of our fortifications. They could even blow up the Shining Mountains themselves." By now he was yelling. "We need the white men for our guns, ammunition, knives and supplies. How can we defeat our enemies if we do not have these weapons?"

Like a chastised child, Pine Leaf dropped her head. She handed him the halter ropes. "Here, Medicine Calf," she replied meekly. "Take my new horses. You fix it so the white-eyes will not attack and kill our people. I will never steal their horses again." Afterwards she rode into the Bighorn Mountains in shame.

Exasperated, Jim led the thoroughbreds away and hobbled them near his own horses to keep them from being taken by anyone else. As he tried to think of a way out of his latest predicament, he received the message that a large party of white men were traveling down the valley towards the village. He cursed, because he knew they would locate their horses and he would have some tall explaining to do. Perhaps he could make up another good story.

As Gantt's party rode up, Saunders asked the Crow about their missing animals. Jim stepped forward. In his best English he said, "I am York, the black slave who accompanied Captain Clark and the Corps of Discovery to the Pacific. When we returned in 1806, Captain Clark gave me my freedom and I have returned to these beloved mountains to live with my friends, the Crow."

Gantt recovered from his surprise and stared at this strange black man. He knew William Clark, now an Indian Agent for the Missouri Territory, and he knew that Clark at one time owned a slave named York. He also knew that York had disappeared after he was freed and Clark never heard from him again. It made sense that the old rascal had returned to the land where he had become so famous and popular when he was with the Lewis and Clark Expedition.

Gantt approached Jim. "We believe your people have stolen five of our fine horses and we have tracked them to this village," he said. "We will hold no ill will if our animals are returned."

Jim smiled. "Yes, some of our warriors did bring in some purebreds and I took the horses from them, as I figured they must belong to some wealthy white men. No Indian nor even any mountain man owns such animals as these." Jim continued explaining as best he could. "The Crow thought you were in Shoshone country to trade them guns and ammunition, therefore, they considered you their enemy. I have already admonished them for their actions and their leader has been banished into the hills."

Jim quickly returned the stolen horses to Gantt's party then invited them to spend the winter with the tribe as they waited for spring on the Bighorn.

After much trepidation and with all precaution, the white men settled down among the Crow to wait for the thaw.

Because Jim was a field agent for the American Fur Company, he had to make periodic trips to Fort Union or Fort Clark to sell furs and trade for supplies. He often bought cloth, beads and trinkets for his many wives. However, McKenzie was displeased with the small amount of furs Jim and S. P. Winter were able to bring in from the Crow country, and he wrote scathing memorandums about the two to his St. Louis associates.

Jim and Winter were well aware of the problems encountered in trying to teach young warriors how to trap beaver in cold streams. They knew the Crow would rather be astride their horses on an exciting raid. Besides, the braves could get more in trade from a live stolen horse than they could from a dead beaver skin.

In exasperation, McKenzie sent a thirty-year-old Scot named Robert Meldrum to the Crow country to work with Jim and Winter. McKenzie knew Meldrum could never supervise Jim, but at least he could observe him and develop trade contacts with the Crow.

Jim did not like being spied upon, but he helped Meldrum get accepted by the River Crow and Winter introduced him among the Mountain Crow. Jim and Winter both needed their pay from the American Fur Company, so they were willing to play McKenzie's game, up to a point that is. Jim taught Meldrum the rudiments of the Crow language and some of the Crow codes and taboos. He found Meldrum to be intelligent enough but the man seemed to have no sense of humor. Meldrum soon became fast friends with the angry young warrior, Big Robber. As time went on, Meldrum continued to draw about him the more militant and undesirable Crow elements. Although Jim felt uneasy about the man, he maintained a civil relationship with his colleague for the sake of his job.

Meldrum's ambition was to become fully established into Crow leadership so he could ultimately strip Winter and Jim of their influence. Then he would be the sole fur agent among the Crow. Meldrum assimilated into the Indian way of life so well that he soon purchased two wives to provide him comfort and to care for his new lodge.

CHAPTER 28

In the early spring of 1832, McKenzie summoned Jim to Fort Union. The American Fur Company decided to build a new fort in the Crow country to make trade goods more accessible to them. They hoped to make the Crow dependent on trade articles and further encourage them to trap their streams.

The arrogant McKenzie had new plans for Jim. "I want you to select the best site for a fort in Crow country and supervise its construction. Later I will send Sam Tulloch up the Yellowstone to assist you."

The news elated Jim; it appeared at last that he would become a head trader or a *booshway*. He would be as important as his old friends, Fitzpatrick and Bridger.

Jim selected the old site of Fort Raymond at the mouth of the Bighorn River. Fifty men from Fort Union arrived by boat and the erection of the post began. The walls were built of hewn logs erected in the ground in a perpendicular position. They were about eighteen feet in height after they had been anchored into the ground. For defense, a wooden parapet was erected along the entire length of each wall, about one hundred twenty yards. Wooden steps led to the parapet every thirty yards. Two blockhouses were constructed at opposite corners and small cabins and shops were built between the blockhouses.

Six weeks after the fort's completion, Chief Rotten Belly directed four hundred of the River Sparrow Hawks to move next to the newly constructed Fort Cass. Jim loaded five Mackinaw boats with pelts and sent them down river to Fort Union. He needed more trade goods and Johnson Gardner had not yet arrived from Fort Union with new supplies. Everyone wondered about Gardner's whereabouts and from Fort Union, Sam Tulloch sent Hugh Glass, Five Scalps and Louis Menard to locate Gardner.

Bad news greeted Jim the next morning. Arikara marauders had killed Five Scalps, Glass and Menard. Jim raced from his lodge to find Glass butchered and scalped near the fort. He then rode down the river and found two more bodies on the frozen edges of the Yellowstone. As he approached, he recognized his old black friend, Five Scalps. The other body belonged to the French trapper, Louis Menard.

Pine Leaf raced up behind Jim and knelt beside the remains of her old protector and friend, Five Scalps. Even though he had been a part of the war party that had captured her from the Atsina, she had learned a great deal from him and he had been her mentor.

She gazed at the dried blood on what was left of his graying, curly hair. His face appeared tired and old. This was not a proper death for the fiercest warrior she had ever known. She remembered his piercing eyes and his deadly, serious demeanor. Although Five Scalps could be ferocious, he had always been reliable and his tongue did not lie. He had been as dependable as the flow of water down the Bighorn. How ironic that he had been killed by the same tribe that had adopted him after he left the Sparrow Hawks. He had become the first counselor of the Arikara and was highly admired and respected by most of the young braves for his famous war escapades. Five Scalps' heroics and fearless deeds among the Sparrow Hawks had exceeded even those of Medicine Calf—but now Five Scalps was dead.

Jim and Pine Leaf gathered a large posse to travel down river in pursuit of the Arikara. After they journeyed about eighteen miles, they found Gardner's camp and Jim hailed him. After some assurances, Gardner allowed them to enter and Jim queried him about the fleeing renegades.

"Gardner," Jim said, "they have killed old Glass, Five Scalps and Menard—three of the best damn mountain men who ever came up the Missouri. Who in the hell is leading those savages?"

"That old scoundrel, Antoine Garreau," Garner replied. "He distracted me while his red devils stole every damned horse I had. We couldn't pursue them, but we caught us three of the heathens. We turned one loose to tell Garreau that if he don't return the horses, we'll kill the two we have left. We ain't heard another word."

Jim followed Gardner to a large bonfire where Gardner's men had the two braves bound in trapper chains. Just as Jim and Pine Leaf approached, the trappers threw the two braves into the bonfire. At first there was screaming and writhing but it quickly subsided, as a high blue flame emitted from the fuel of human body fluids. Slowly the flames returned to an orange glow and everyone who could borrow one of Jim's horses mounted and gave chase down river.

By morning the large posse reached a point where they could hear gunfire, a great deal of it. They paused to rest their horses when a large explosion rocked the countryside. Jim led the mixed party of Crow warriors and mountain men over the hill and attacked the still shocked Arikara. Pine Leaf fought with a vengeance to atone for the death of Five Scalps. Her arrows and battle-ax hit their targets repeatedly, and she lanced two of the enemy as they tried to drag her from her horse.

Jim observed the ground that had been blackened for many feet in all directions. Apparently, when the fleeing Arikara attacked the white traders, the traders feared they would be scalped and tortured, so they set off their kegs of gunpowder. Charred bodies of white men and Indians were everywhere. When the Arikara survivors broke off the fight and fled the avenging posse, they left seventy-two dead warriors. They had paid dearly and had also lost most of their stolen horses and ill-gotten plunder.

Pine Leaf rode to the top of a knoll in further pursuit of the fleeing Arikara. As she paused to observe their retreat, one of the tribe's rear guardsmen shot her in her upper left arm. Even as she felt the impact of hot lead, she dashed toward them in retaliation. She overtook and lanced three stragglers before fainting from loss of blood; she fell off her horse into a bank of snow. As Pine Leaf lay there, her blood turned the surrounding snow crimson.

As soon as Jim arrived, he placed a tourniquet on her wounded arm. He lifted her limp body onto his horse and rode back to Gardner's camp.

Luck was with Pine Leaf, because Dr. John Walton had accompanied Gardner's party on his trip to the mountains. Dr. Walton cleaned Pine Leaf's wound and set the bone so that her arm would heal properly. When she awoke, she met the doctor.

For giving her medical attention she gave him one of her secret helpers, a large gold nugget she had found in the mysterious Black Hills during a raid against the Sioux. Dr. Walton was very pleased with the gift, but the nugget caused him to wonder about the riches those hills must conceal. However, every white man knew it would be certain death to enter those hallowed, Sioux mountains. Even so, the good doctor not only had a great souvenir, but he had a story he could share over a thousand future campfires, dinners and bar rails.

The large party finally moved on to Fort Cass, where the Sparrow Hawk Nation arrived to mourn Five Scalps, Glass and Menard. They held these famous men in high esteem and in their honor, there was much chopping of fingers, cutting of hair and gouging of flesh. Since Jim had taught Pine Leaf not to mutilate herself any further, she meekly cut off long lengths of her beautiful hair. Chiefs Long Hair and Rotten Belly held a great council and elected Jim First Counselor of the Sparrow Hawks for defeating the Arikara and avenging Five Scalps, Glass and Menard.

Because Chief Bowl was getting old, he decided to retire from the six-man council. This left a vacancy on the council. Pine Leaf wanted to believe that now, at last, she would be appointed as Chief Bowl's replacement. She had avenged her friend, Five Scalps, and had ridden right alongside Medicine Calf; no one had achieved more coups and honors than she. But she would be passed over again.

When Chief Long Hair raised his resonant voice and passed the calumet, he announced, "The council has selected the great warrior, Grizzly Bear, to be our new counselor. May he always give us sage advice and provide leadership for the Sparrow Hawk Nation."

Pine Leaf felt faint and nauseous. She had fought with Grizzly Bear many times but she thought him too conservative and methodical in his actions; he was not as aggressive, creative or spontaneous as she. She liked him well enough, but believed she was more intelligent and a better leader than he. "If only I weren't a woman," she thought. "Why was I not born a man?"

At the first signs of thaw, Jim loaded his Mackinaws with seven hundred packs of buffalo robes and forty-five packs of beaver pelts. In places, he had to break the ice to travel down river, but he had run out of patience waiting for nature to prepare the river for him. He would gouge his way to Fort Union.

Pine Leaf's recovery took several weeks. During this time, she stayed at Fort Cass, while most of the River Sparrow Hawks moved to the Little Bighorn Valley. At Fort Cass, Pine Leaf's only friends consisted of old Chief Red Bird and his small band of followers. When the grass grew higher, Pine Leaf emerged from her self-imposed exile and began the task of strengthening and rebuilding her left arm. The sun warmed her and as she exercised with her bow, she could feel her muscle tone begin to return. Soon she was wielding her battle-ax and practicing with her rifle.

She learned that Red Bird's band was headed for Fort Union to trade. They had learned that the great fire-eating raft of the white men had brought many beautiful goods to the fort for barter. Even though Pine Leaf had not fully recovered, she decided to travel with Red Bird; there would be no Sparrow Hawks left at Fort Cass.

When they arrived at Fort Union, Pine Leaf saw Blackfoot, Assiniboine and other tribes with which the Sparrow Hawks were usually at war. Because the fort was neutral ground, they were forced to remain at peace with each other while they were there. She was disappointed to learn that Medicine Calf had decided to take his furs to St. Louis to get a better price. He had told McKenzie he would return to the Crow by crossing overland from St. Louis.

While at the fort, Pine Leaf heard the strange tale of a white man who could paint pictures onto cloth. He could paint a picture of anything he saw. She became curious about what a white man's painting would look like, wondering how they would compare to the rock paintings of the ancient ones.

After wedging herself through the crowd to get a better view, she saw a thin, pale man in strange clothing. He wore a cloth robe that reached from his neck to his knees. His cloth leggings stretched from his waist to his feet, which were covered with decorative moccasins. The most unique thing about him was his hat, which stuck out in front to shade him from the sun. It had two strange ears on each side, with their ends pulled up and tied together at the top of the hat.

Pine Leaf noticed that his painting contained beautiful shades of red and vermilion—then she was aghast! He was painting the likeness of the head Pecuni chief, Buffalo's Back Fat. As she leaned forward for a better look, she discovered that the grand chief himself was there, standing just beyond the red picture. Quickly, she withdrew from the crowd, easing away from her mortal enemy.

Twice in the past year the Sparrow Hawks had stolen Chief Back Fat's grandson and twice the Blackfeet had recaptured the boy. In the last battle, Back Fat's son, Medicine Shield, had been killed while trying to protect his son. Now Back Fat's grandson was the sole heir to replace the great chief when he retired or died. Pine Leaf had heard that the young prince was under the protection of the American Fur Company, but her skin crawled from her encounter with the old Pecuni chief. She quickly left Fort Union to rejoin Red Bird's Greasy Mouth clan.

Red Bird led his people back up the Elk. Since they could not trade at Fort Union, they would set up camp and wait for Tulloch's replacement supplies to arrive at Fort Cass.

As the yellow-grass season approached, Pine Leaf grew restless; she wanted to go hunting, so she rode into the fort to trade for shot and powder. She was still debating the price with Tulloch when she heard shots and screams from Red Bird's camp. Climbing the nearest steps to the fort parapet, she peered over the stockade. She yelled out when she saw a large party of Pecuni attacking Red Bird's camp.

Men, women and children ran for the gates of the fort, dodging the bullets and arrows of their age-old enemies. Pine Leaf and the fort engagees began firing frantic volleys of bullets and arrows at the Pecuni so that Red Bird's people could enter the fort. But before they could get inside the gate, a dozen men, women and children were slain, then their bodies were scalped and mutilated. Pine Leaf cried out as she watched the bodies of her friends being defiled by the Pecuni.

The entire throng looked on as the Blackfeet withdrew out of fusil range and laid siege to the fort. They taunted the fort dwellers by exposing their genitals and bare buttocks. After awhile the Blackfeet sent five men forward to counsel for peace, but no one at the fort would leave their temporary haven of safety to talk with them.

Pine Leaf was the only person present who could understand the language of the Blackfeet. She was furious at them for their utter disdain for the Sparrow Hawks and for their disrespect for the white men and the fort. When she could no longer control her anger and shame, she jumped to the ground and began arming herself. She loaded her fusil, tied her battle-ax to her saddle, checked her bow and arrows, picked up her lance, and mounted her horse.

"You are not warriors," she yelled at the people in the fort. "You have opossum guts. Who will ride with me to uphold Sparrow Hawk honor and teach these crazy dogs how to fight? Is there a grizzly among you?" Although no one responded to her challenge, they nevertheless tried to keep her from leaving the fort. Ignoring them, she raised her lance.

"Open the gate or I will carry you to the enemy on my own spear," she yelled. Reluctantly they opened the gate and she galloped out to meet the Blackfeet, her long hair and beautiful skirt flying behind her. The Blackfeet watched in amusement as this foolish woman rode out to meet certain death. They admired any brave person, but these cowards had sent a woman to plead for their lives. The Blackfeet laughed and yelled epithets at both her and the fort, but they were surprised when Pine Leaf began to yell epithets back at them in their own language.

"You are the children of the same clan members," she yelled insultingly. "You have no relatives. You have intercourse with your mothers-in-law."

Her insults angered the young men and some of them made a blind charge at her. She shot the lead war chief with her fusil, then cast it aside. Taking up her bow she began firing arrows as rapidly as she could pull and reload. Two more Blackfeet went down and they halted their charge. She used the lull in the battle to turn her horse around and race back to the fort. Suddenly, a young warrior bore down on her from the side, trying to cut off her escape. Rising high in her saddle, she cast her spear into his erect body. As he fell, she leaned over the side of her horse and raced into the fort just as the protective gates opened.

Even before she could dismount, Pine Leaf heard white men and Sparrow Hawks alike shouting, "Woman Chief! Woman Chief!"

She rushed to join them on the parapet as they poured volley after volley of shot at the Pecuni. The engagees even fired the small cannon filled with scrap metal at the Blackfeet. In frustration and humiliation, the enemy finally retreated with their dead.

Pine Leaf swelled with pride at her new name, but she was saddened to learn that old Red Bird had been one of the people killed in the Pecuni attack. As soon as she felt it was safe, she took over the small band and led them back to Bighorn Valley.

Upon their arrival, Pine Leaf was surprised to learn that there would be great feasting and dancing in honor of her heroics at Fort Cass. Tales of her battle with the Blackfeet were repeated over and over around the campfires, and after four days of festivities, Rotten Belly finally held council.

"From this day forward," he said, "our beloved Pine Leaf will be known as 'Woman Chief'. The Sparrow Hawk chiefs have appointed her to the Nation's Council." He then sent the herald to tell everyone in the village of her new name and her new station.

Woman Chief was ecstatic!

She had now attained most of her childhood dreams. She could not wait until Medicine Calf returned from the white man's town, so she could share her good fortune with him.

After the announcement and congratulations, she left the village to ride to her sacred rock pillar, where she could meditate and pray to her secret helpers. She would share her success with the spirit of Cracked-Ice. She could hardly believe that she was the first woman to become a member of the Sparrow Hawk council. After this, she would be an advisor in all matters concerning Absaroka.

As the night closed in around her, tears of joy streamed down her face.

SECTION V

1833 - 1839

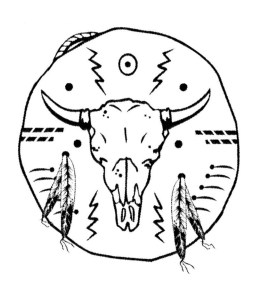

CHAPTER 29

When Jim Beckwith returned to the Bighorn from Fort Union, he could not believe that his friend Pine Leaf had finally become a war chief *and* a counselor. This was totally unheard of among any Indian tribe he had ever known. He became even more enamored with her, but he controlled his advances for fear of more of her embarrassing rejections. But Jim continued to tease her with innuendoes.

"I told you we could breed fine Crow warriors," he reminded her. "Our children would have a mother chief and a father chief, and no son could shirk that heritage!"

Woman Chief always had a quick reply. "What about our daughters?" she responded. "Could they also not be chiefs like their mother?" They both laughed at their jokes as they prepared for the summer hunts.

Long Hair and Rotten Belly moved the entire Sparrow Hawk Nation north to the Musselshell, then followed the groups westward to the Castle Mountains. They descended the Smith River to the Missouri and moved downstream to the mouth of the Sun River. They stopped above the Great Falls of the Missouri River, which the Crow called the Big Muddy. Once the Crow people had encamped and everyone was settled, Rotten Belly began to brood. He spoke of bad medicine.

"Medicine Calf, I will soon die," he confided to Jim. "But I want to die like a warrior. I am tired of no one listening to my counsel, and I grow weary listening to all the bickering among my relatives. I wish to ride on a raid and never come back. I want you to come with me to rescue my bones and return them to Horses River in Absaroka."

Jim could tell that Rotten Belly was distraught; he also knew that the chief meant what he had said. Jim tried to humor Rotten Belly by reassuring him that he had much for which to be grateful, telling him that the Sparrow Hawks respected and needed him. But it was no use; Rotten Belly's mind was set.

That evening the chief placed his war shield on edge in a pile of buffalo dung. "Warriors," he announced to those who stood nearby, "if my shield rises, I will die before I return to Absaroka—if not, I will return from this raid alive." After praying to the sun, Rotten Belly began swinging his lance around his head. After a few minutes, the shield rose slowly into the air, rising as high as a horse's back, then it quickly fell to the ground. Although Jim did not believe in such tricks and sorcery, nevertheless he could not explain what had just happened right before his eyes.

Everyone was talking about the extraordinary event, when some of their scouts entered the village. The scouts reported a raiding party of fourteen Pecuni approaching on foot. To the Sparrow Hawks, this meant the enemy raiders were after their horses.

Rotten Belly mounted and led the charge against the Pecuni. He rode through the enemy party wielding his war-ax and killed two before being pierced by an arrow in his chest. Jim led an aggressive counterattack, quickly disposing of the remaining Blackfeet. Then Jim gathered his men around the dying Rotten Belly.

"I came here to die as a warrior," the fallen chief whispered. "My final wish is for Grizzly Bear and Medicine Calf to replace me as head chiefs of the River Sparrow Hawks. Bury me here," he groaned, "and in one year return to my grave and rescue my bones for burial near our beloved Horses River." Rotten Belly sighed as his eyes half closed.

"Hear me my braves," he gasped. Then he gave his final order. "Listen to the counsel of Grizzly Bear and Medicine Calf. Follow their leadership. I have spoken."

Rotten Belly's eyes became glazed, and his mouth fell open. Jim checked the chief's pulse, then nodded. "Our chief's spirit has left his body," he said. "Come; let us bury him where he has fallen. We will mark his grave with four large stones and then drag brush over the grave so the Pecuni cannot find it."

When Grizzly Bear, Jim and the defense party returned to the village, the screaming and crying of villagers greeted them. Jim observed several mutilations, and general chaos prevailed in every lodge. Even the great Long Hair cut off a strand of his proud hair; the strand was the length of a horse. On the second day of mourning, Long hair moved the entire Nation back to Little Horn Valley. He feared that a larger party of Pecuni might be near and, if so, they may retaliate for the attack.

In honor of Rotten Belly's dying wish, Grizzly Bear was proclaimed chief of the Upper River Sparrow Hawks and Jim was named the leader of the Lower River Sparrow Hawks. Both chiefs still recognized Long Hair as the chief of the Sparrow Hawk Nation.

After things returned to normal, Jim pleaded with his men to stay in the rich beaver country and put more time into trapping for wealth instead of raiding for horses and warrior status. He had seen enough fighting and raiding for a lifetime. He would offer speeches in an effort to sway the men to his way of thinking. "We have lost Chief Rotten Belly along with many of our best young braves. Let us hunt and trap for a richer life and only go to war in defense of our families and our hunting grounds."

Although Woman Chief respected Medicine Calf, she still did not want to trap beaver. Instead, she used her beautiful buffalo robes for trade. She reasoned that she could also steal horses to trade for her necessities and weapons. She made up her mind to continue raiding. She knew sooner or later that she would be able to goad Medicine Calf into joining her in battle for one cause or another.

Jim slipped off on a buffalo-scouting trip without telling the brooding Woman Chief. He led his small party into the Assiniboine hunting territory. After he left, Woman Chief took a war party in search of Cheyenne horses. On the fourth sun, her party found a large number of Cheyenne and charged into them. During the battle, Woman Chief felt the familiar hot impact of a rifle ball as it hit her chest. The impact knocked her from her charging pony. Immediately her men rallied around her, driving the Cheyenne from the field.

Woman Chief lay unconscious in a pool of her own dark red, coagulating blood. Her braves observed that the ball had entered her left breast, barely missing her heart and then it had passed out of her left shoulder blade, taking part of the bone with it. They thought for sure she would die, but they wrapped her wound with sweetgrass covered with doeskin, then carried her back to their Rosebud camp.

When Jim returned from his buffalo-scouting trip, he learned of Woman Chief's debacle. Although he feared that this time her wound might prove fatal, he angrily chastised her for going on a raid against his wishes. "Because you disobeyed me," he rankled, "you are now dying."

Smiling weakly, Woman Chief responded, "I am sorry I disobeyed my great chief but I counted *two coups*." After her declaration, she promptly passed out. Despite his worry, Jim had to smile at her. This tough little warrior was not done for yet. Her will to survive was too strong to be stopped by one rifle ball.

Jim then led a war party to avenge the attack on Woman Chief and the death of four of her warriors. He and his followers drove the Cheyenne to the south side of the North Platte before returning to the Little Bighorn. When he returned to Absaroka, Jim displayed a Cheyenne scalp for every downed Sparrow Hawk warrior. Although he felt better, he could no longer be called Good War Road. Once again be would be expected to lead revenge raids against all Crow enemies.

Woman Chief slowly recovered, much to the astonishment of her followers, but not to Jim.

In the late summer, Grizzly Bear and Jim led his River Crow up the Musselshell, down the Smith, and on to the Sun River once again. Here they intended to recover Rotten Belly's bones for burial; but when they reached the burial site, they detected a band of Blackfeet had crossed over their former chief's grave, *vilifying* it. This made the Sparrow Hawk warriors furious and they made a vicious attack on the transgressors, killing most of the warriors and even some of the women and children before Jim could bring them under control.

He was only able to rescue about one hundred fifty women and children while his men plundered an abundance of horses, weapons, ammunition, cloth, beads and trade trinkets. Apparently, the Blackfeet were returning from Fort Union laden with goods. Grizzly Bear had Rotten Belly's bones disinterred, then reburied near the Horses River, as he and Jim had previously promised.

The entire party then returned to the Bighorn, where Jim was honored for his success against the Blackfeet.

During the falling-leaf season, a white trapping party, led by Joseph Walker, arrived on the Bighorn. With them was a young clerk named, Zenas Leonard.

Walker and Jim had a good laugh about the time Jim told Leonard, Gantt and Blackwell that his name was York, and that he had accompanied Lewis and Clark on their expedition to the Pacific. Leonard took the ribbing in good spirit and Jim invited him to go on a big buffalo surround. The Crow needed to put up their winter supply of meat and pemmican. Leonard, two others from Walker's party, and Robert Meldrum followed the River Crow as they crossed over the Big Snowy Mountains.

The party numbered several thousand and it took them three days to wade through the huge snowdrifts. They lost several hundred horses to the elements before they wearily preceded around the Judith Mountains to Box Elder Creek. Here they found a good area to set up the main camp. Jim then took three of his wives and three packhorses to search for a buffalo herd.

After a half-day's ride, he observed fifty Sparrow Hawk hunters engaged with a Blackfoot hunting party of about one hundred sixty braves. The enemy had secured themselves in a natural rock fortress, holding the excited Sparrow Hawks at bay. The fort was made of granite and its walls formed a shape like a large horseshoe. The perpendicular walls varied in height from four feet to ten feet with the open part of the horseshoe facing up the steep hill.

While Jim studied the situation, he sent a runner back to the hunting camp to bring reinforcements. When the hunters arrived, Jim noticed that Robert Meldrum, Zenas Leonard, and two other white men had come with them to observe the battle.

The Sparrow Hawks made numerous charges against the fort but they met with little success. They soon had three dead braves and fifteen more wounded from their futile attempts to charge the fort.

At last Chief Grizzly Bear rose to speak. "Warriors, we are paying too dearly. The enemy has too strong a position and we will make too many widows and orphans by continuing. Let us move on and prepare for our winter hunt. Retreat!"

Jim turned to Meldrum. "Will ya jine me in battle," he asked, "er do ya tend to stay in yer hidey-hole?"

Meldrum did not want to be disgraced in front of the Crow. "I want my share of the adventure Beckwith, and I want to keep my reputation among the Crow," he answered. "But be you brave enough to lead me?"

Jim smiled slyly. "I'll get er done, Mr. Meldrum; I'll damn sure get er done!"

With that, he jumped upon a rock and yelled, "Hold on warriors! If these old men cannot fight, let them retire with the women and children. You and I can defeat these Pecuni cowards and save Sparrow Hawk face."

Excitedly he tried to reason with his followers. "If we run, they will always brag of how they beat the mighty Sparrow Hawks at the Battle of Pecuni Fort. If we are killed in battle, we will be praised for bravery and mourned by our loved ones. The Great Spirit gave us this opportunity for a mighty victory that will long live in Sparrow Hawk history. Come and follow Meldrum, Woman Chief and me. Let us show these white-eyed observers how we Sparrow Hawks can fight!"

Woman Chief dropped slightly over one side of her pony and, holding on to its mane, raced for the fortress with a wild screech. Jim, Meldrum and the Big Dogs followed as fast as they could run on foot.

Since Woman Chief had momentarily distracted the enemy, Jim and his party were able to get to the walls without being detected. When her horse was shot from under her, Woman Chief rolled to the safety of the granite wall. Other Sparrow Hawk warriors began attacking on foot as Jim, Woman Chief, Meldrum and the Big Dogs helped each other over the walls.

When Jim yelled "Hoo-ki-hi!" they leaped upon the unsuspecting Blackfeet below. They hacked with battle-axes, knives and lances until the rocks ran red with blood and the ground became too slick to stand on. The Blackfeet fought valiantly

124

and desperately until they were completely overwhelmed by the Sparrow Hawks. The sounds of gunfire, thuds of weapons, smell of gunpowder, and the screams of combat permeated the entire valley.

As the horrified white trappers looked on, the Sparrow Hawk women who had been left behind began to wail and mutilate themselves. One returning warrior even told Little Wife that her husband, Medicine Calf, had been killed. She too began to wail loudly; she cut off one knuckle from her left hand and gashed her forehead with her knife.

After a short but violent period, all became quiet at the battle site. Jim surveyed the carnage, the blood, brains and human viscera, strewn all over the rocks. Over a hundred Blackfeet scalps had been taken, along with many guns, bows, arrows, ammunition, knives, lances and some freshly butchered meat. The Sparrow Hawks had lost forty warriors and another fifty had been wounded, including Meldrum.

As Little Wife stood bleeding and contemplating suicide, she saw the ghost of her late husband arise from the smoldering battle scene. Loaded down with plunder, Jim didn't notice his wife's condition until he drew near and spied her bloody face.

"Who the hell are you mourning for?" he demanded.

Little Wife yelled with joy. "I heard you were dead and I was only going to go on living until I could rescue your precious body from the Pecuni."

Jim laughed, wiped the blood from her face, bound her mutilated finger, and carried their trophies back to his warm lodge. Woman Chief loved Little Wife but she was jealous of her time with Medicine Calf. She longed to sit with him and recount their every movement in the battle. They had fought side-by-side, each counting eleven coups and each killing twelve of the enemy. As they fought, their very lives depended upon each other, and she wanted to share this excitement and camaraderie with him. But all she could do was go home to her working squaws who did not understand the skill and excitement of battle.

They could not even be honored by her success because she was herself only a woman. She could not paint their faces and they could not dance with her in the victory dance. But even in her loneliness, she was still living out her dreams. At thirty-three winters, she was now the sixth-ranked counselor and the second greatest warrior in Absaroka.

Zenas Leonard and the white trappers went up the Bighorn to Walker's camp to report their experience. The bloody battle soon became famous and for years would be told and retold across the plains by both Indians and mountain men alike.

Due to his leadership and tenacity, Chief Long Hair named Jim *Bloody Arm*. Jim had to reconsider his future as a trapper. "Perhaps leading warriors is what I do best," he thought.

CHAPTER 30

After the battle of Blackfoot Fort, Long Hair and Grizzly Bear moved the Sparrow Hawk encampment to a new location closer to the mouth of Box Elder Creek, near the Musselshell.

Jim placed his lodge on the outer edge of the camp so he could have more privacy. He always felt sexually aroused after battle, and he went to bed with the sensual Red Cherry while Little Wife recuperated from her wounds. Around midnight, the uncanny stillness awakened Jim; it was too quiet. As the hairs on the back of his neck strained to unravel their tight curls, he grew increasingly uneasy. Jim slowly moved from under the long arms of Red Cherry and slipped to the lodge floor. Silently he slithered to the tent flap and peered into the night. His lodge fire had long since burned out and he lay swathed in darkness. Although the sky was clear, only a quarter moon illuminated the night darkness. However, his practiced eyes and sensitive ears picked out a foreign movement.

Someone was slowly advancing toward his hobbled ponies, which were tied to his lodgepole. The stranger held a pointed stick and softly moved twigs and leaves from his path as he inched himself toward Jim's horses. Whenever the nervous horses moved or snorted, the intruder would stop, and then when all was still again, he would continue to advance. Just as he reached out to cut the tethers of the horses, Jim rushed. He leaped upon the intruder's back, wrapped his arms around him and pinned the man's arms to his sides. The would-be horse thief couldn't even go for his knife.

Jim yelled, "Hoo-ki-hi!" and armed braves emerged from all of the nearby lodges. When he saw he had reinforcements, he released the Blackfoot brave and leapt backwards. The foreign intruder was immediately spiked with Sparrow Hawk arrows until his fallen body resembled an aroused porcupine.

The rest of the Nation awoke, joined in the excitement, and then washed their faces. They feasted and danced through the remainder of the night. After the revelry waned, Jim retired, exhausted. He slept for two days, not even capable of responding to the ever-stimulating Red Cherry.

Walker's party left the area just as a new party arrived. Jim's old booshway, Tom Fitzpatrick, rode in with thirty-five men and over two hundred horses. Fitzpatrick hailed, "Halloo, Beckwith. How air the Crow squaws treatin yee?" Jim waved. Fitzpatrick bellowed, "I hear they done made you some high muck-ee-dee-muck of a war chief."

Jim roared, "Since y'all white men don't 'preciate my talents, I figured ta give the Crow the benefit of muh thinkin and experience. They've treated me mighty fine and the squaws fight to bed me, just like you heerd."

Fitzpatrick chuckled. "These two duded up fellers with me is Sir William Drummond Stewart and Dr. Benjamin Harrison. Then Fitzpatrick whispered, Sir William is a pompous Scottish nobleman and Dr. Harrison is the alcoholic son of ole William Henry Harrison, who is a politician and a lawyer."

After the party made camp, Fitzpatrick left Sir William in charge of the camp while he went with Jim to set up a trade feast with the Crow. After Jim left, Meldrum incited some of his Crazy Dog followers to invade Fitzpatrick's camp. Led by Big Robber, they bullied Sir William then stole his watch and his fine gray thoroughbred. They then pilfered the remainder of Fitzpatrick's guns, goods, pelts and horses. When Fitzpatrick returned to his camp, Sir William was furious.

"I say," he threatened, "why don't we annihilate the entire Crow Nation. They are nothing but a bunch of damnable thieves and scoundrels."

Fitzpatrick calmed Sir William, then returned to the Crow village to confront Jim. He yelled, "Goddam! Beckwith, I never took yee for a horse thief and a yellow dog. Yore Crow has wiped me out."

Jim responded, "Tom, I swear my followers didn't do this. Wait here so's I can get this mess unkinked."

Since Winter was in camp, Jim ran to his lodge, only to find him captive of the Crazy Dog friends of Meldrum. He coldly yelled, "Get out of this camp. If I get any of you in my sights again, I will kill you, Crow law or not."

Winter sputtered, "I found out about their plans, but the damn heathens wouldn't let me leave my lodge. Besides, our own American Fur Company has put Meldrum up to them dirty tricks so as ta bankrupt ole Fitz and Bridger."

Jim knew he could not prove his claims against Meldrum and even if he could, the American Fur Company would just fire him and Winter. All he could do was to try and restore the stolen goods and horses to Fitzpatrick and Sir William.

Jim took his Big Dogs and rode to the Wind River Canyon to rescue Fitzpatrick's men. He then returned to the Crow village which he and his men surrounded and searched every lodge. He located all of the stolen goods except some scarlet and blue cloth, five horses, and Sir William's prize gray gelding.

Fitzpatrick was satisfied with Jim's effort but Sir William was not, and he still blamed Jim for the thievery. It became obvious to Jim that Sir William did not trust him because he was black and because he lived with the Crow.

Finally at the urging of Fitzpatrick, Sir William showed some humility and approached Jim. He said, "Mr. Beckwith, my good man, can you regain my valuable horse for me?"

"Cap'n Stewart," Jim replied, "I'm a poor man. High Bull has yore horse and he's one of my company's best customers. He also has many friends and relatives that'll no longer trade with me if I accuse 'im. If'n I lose my customers, Mr. McKenzie and the American Fur Company'll terminate me. I'll lose my livelihood fer shore."

Sir William decided to show up Jim. "If your company discharges you for returning my horse," he said, "I will give you six thousand dollars a year for ten years."

This put Jim on the spot in front of Fitzpatrick and his men. "I'll see what I kin do," he replied.

127

After negotiating with High Bull all night, Jim rode the gray horse into camp and turned him over to Sir William. Then he and the Big Dogs escorted Fitzpatrick's party through the Wind River Canyon and instructed them, "Keep a close watch fer them horse thieves, Fitz."

However, the very next day, Jim saw several of Fitzpatrick's horses around the village. He knew that the Crow had once again robbed the white hunting party. He was just sorry he did not see Sir William's gray horse among the stolen animals. It would have served the pompous ass right to have it taken again.

On November 12 and 13, 1833, shortly after Fitzpatrick left, meteor showers assaulted the skies. Although many of the superstitious Indians became frightened, Jim used this occasion to admonish them.

"The Great Spirit is angry because you robbed the white men," he warned. "The great white father has requested that the Great Spirit punish you. If we are not faithful, we will lose our gun and ammunition trade and we will lose the migration of the buffalo and we will surely starve." Jim had their utmost attention. "Be loyal to the whites and they will protect you from our enemies," he concluded. In spite of Meldrum's agitation, the Crow did not molest any more of the white visitors to Absaroka.

In the spring of 1834, Sam Tulloch summoned Jim to Fort Cass. "Beckwith, them Blackfeet air a constantly harassin' my woodcutters and haycutters," he complained. "Now my traders 'n trappers air too damned scairt to leave the post. I need some help gettin these worthless bastards to get off'n they asses and git to work."

Jim looked about the stockade. It appeared that Sam really did have a sorry bunch of recruits to work with. "I'll stick round fer a few days," he told Sam, "and observe they's behavior. Mebbey I kin git them to show ya more respect."

The next morning Tulloch sent seven men to cut logs. Just before noon they were attacked. Before they could defend themselves, one man was killed and scalped right within sight of the fort. Jim quickly mounted his war-horse and prepared to rescue the remaining woodcutters. "Men," he yelled, "grab your guns and foller me."

Thirty of the workers mounted but they followed slowly and at a safe distance behind him. Jim observed about forty Blackfeet surrounding the six remaining woodcutters, so he quickly picked out a war chief and dropped him with his Hawken rifle.

This panicked some of the Blackfeet, which gave the woodcutters an opportunity to break out of hiding and flee toward the fort. When the enemy charged Jim on foot, he turned to see not only the six woodcutters running, but his own rescue party fleeing toward Fort Cass. This sure wasn't like fighting with his own Big Dog followers. Quickly he reloaded, fired his rifle, then his pistol, and finally turned and raced for his life.

Gunfire from the fort forced the Blackfeet to retreat while he safely entered and dismounted. Angrily he looked around the post at the sorry men he found himself with. "You are nothing but a bunch of wet-nursed cowards," he exclaimed. "How the hell have you survived this long? My female friend, Woman Chief, and her squaws could whip this whole damn fort."

No one challenged his fiery assertion; the French-Canadian engages retreated in disgrace while the previously surrounded woodcutters expressed their adulation and indebtedness to him for saving their lives.

Jim gave strict instructions to Tulloch. "Sam, you need to send out a guard detail every time your men go for wood or hay. If they are guarded, they can work faster and harder and the Blackfeet will hesitate to attack them." He stayed on for several days until the Blackfeet quit the area and the operation of the post returned to normal. Finally, even the French trappers were brave enough to head back to the beaver streams.

Jim returned to the Bighorn and again tried to get the Crow interested in trapping but without much success. He tried to seduce Woman Chief again, but she continued to put him off.

Woman Chief knew Jim was attracted to her, but she reasoned that if she ever gave in to him, he would soon tire of her, as he did with most of his female conquests.

Another reason Woman Chief disregarded his advances was because she did not know how to submit to a man. It seemed to her that she would be giving up her identity in some way. It also seemed like a surrender of sorts and such a surrender would be contrary to everything for which she had been trained. As a Sparrow Hawk woman she may have submitted, but now, as a counselor and a war chief, she certainly did not intend to give that up, not for anyone, no matter how compelling.

To some extent, Woman Chief also feared she may not measure up as a woman. By being fearless, she did not have to face emotional rejection. The tougher she appeared, the more her peers admired her, which then reinforced her bravery. She often wondered at the relationship between a man and a woman, but she had war to keep her mind busy. Someday, perhaps, she would take a mate, but for now she only looked up to one man, and he was an arrogant ass indeed. She repeatedly assured herself, "I would never marry Medicine Calf."

Woman Chief continued to be close to Little Wife and Medicine Calf's son, Black Panther. He was a strong little boy, ever curious about everything with which he came in contact. In the ways of the Sparrow Hawks, Little Wife did not discipline or punish him. She explained the value or the danger of the elements and nature's animals then allowed Black Panther to judge or experiment for himself.

Black Panther's favorite dog, Sniffing One, became his constant companion and protector. Once, when the lad approached a black and white furry animal, Sniffing One interceded and was sprayed by a foul odor that lasted for a week. Black Panther learned to avoid that animal from then on.

As Woman Chief watched the little boy mature, she struggled over the issue of ever bearing children. She desired the life of a warrior, but at times her hormones and female urges confused her. The only man for whom she held secret desires was Medicine Calf, but she continued to fight these feelings so she could remain his equal and never become subservient to him. She saw how Medicine Calf had abandoned his son to his old father, Big Bowl, while he came and went freely with Red Cherry or any other girl who would join his group of wives.

He had not proven to be a reliable or responsible father or husband, but he was nevertheless a great warrior. She still respected him for his fighting prowess.

During the falling-leaf season, Medicine Calf and Woman Chief led three hundred warriors and their families to Fort Cass. While camped at Fallen Creek, the Cheyenne crept into the horseherd and stole fifty horses. Woman Chief immediately mounted her war pony and followed Medicine Calf and about two hundred fifty Sparrow Hawk warriors who rode off in hopes of retrieving their stock.

After a short run, they came in sight of the Cheyenne. Before they could attack, Medicine Calf's horse was shot through the head, which threw the rider against a large rock, knocking him unconscious. Woman Chief led members of the war party to surround his fallen figure. She had to leave him to engage in hand-to-hand combat, but she noticed that Medicine Calf was bleeding from his mouth, nose and ears. She fought furiously with her war club in her left hand and her lance in her right.

Jim awoke to find his Sparrow Hawk warriors battling the Cheyenne all around him. The Sparrow Hawks had gained a slight advantage, when suddenly the Cheyenne fled as another fifty Sparrow Hawk warriors with all of their women and children approached. The Cheyenne apparently thought they were all warrior reinforcements.

Although they had only taken three scalps, the victorious party and the bruised Medicine Calf sang the rest of the way to Fort Cass. Sam Tulloch was much surprised to find that Jim was still alive, for the prairie telegraph had reported him as being dead for months.

After everyone finished their greetings and feasting, Jim and Woman Chief led one hundred warriors on a Blackfoot raid. They found a camp where most of the warriors were out hunting buffalo and attacked. They captured eighteen women and a like number of children, along with over two hundred horses.

While they calmed those in the captured camp, Woman Chief spotted a young teenage Pecuni running down a coulee. She immediately gave chase, still carrying her lance above her head. He tried every maneuver to outdistance her or to throw her off his trail, but she dogged his every move. In exhaustion he finally stopped, tossed away his war weapons, and stood ready to die. Woman Chief drew back her lance, but something about the boy touched her and she could not murder someone who stood so brave, yet defenseless.

He was moderately tall and very handsome, with long black hair that reached almost to his waist. She motioned to him then solemnly marched him back to the camp. Since a captive becomes the captor's responsibility, Woman Chief declared the young Pecuni to be her adopted brother. She named him Little Feather, in honor of her childhood friend among the White Clay people.

When Jim learned what she had done, he began heartily teasing her. "I see," he stated loudly. "You have refused to marry a Sparrow Hawk warrior but you are willing to capture an enemy boy for a husband. You must be afraid of a man you cannot control." To the others nearby he announced: "Woman Chief desires to rob the cradleboard."

The other warriors roared with glee at the fine joke Medicine Calf had played on Woman Chief. Woman Chief felt her face grow red as she flushed. In order to control her anger, she quickly mounted her captive on an extra pony and rode back to the fort.

But after the raiding party reached Fort Cass, Jim continued his game. "Your captive told me he only surrendered because you promised to marry him."

Woman Chief sputtered, "He lies! You all lie!" Then she bravely announced, "The only man I would have ever married was you, but now I will not even marry you." After she stormed away, Jim wondered if he had gone too far this time.

There was great merriment at the fort for four days as the Sparrow Hawks celebrated the Blackfoot raid. Jim allowed his young son, Black Panther, to give a fine horse to Sam Tulloch. His son could now speak and curse in both French and English.

CHAPTER 31

The Sparrow Hawks left Fort Cass to return to the Bighorn Basin. They arrived at the main village to learn that some three thousand Cheyenne had attacked the village. They lost hundreds of prime horses and several warriors before the enemy fled across the Tongue River. Chief Grizzly Bear ordered the Big Dogs to not pursue the attackers. He feared that his men would be ambushed.

Jim and Woman Chief joined the council meeting to discuss the attack. Woman Chief spoke, "Let us chase the lowly Cheyenne dogs before they can leave Absaroka. We know our territory and they do not."

"I agree with Chief Grizzly Bear," said Jim. "We still have plenty of horses and the Cheyenne will be waiting in ambush for us. Wait until we can pick our time to avenge our losses." Woman Chief stormed out of the council meeting in disgust.

Jim encouraged the young men to trap for a few weeks after the attack to allow a cooling off period. In this way he could gather furs for the American Fur Company and develop a plan for attacking the Cheyenne. He would much rather plan than charge straight into a trap.

By October the Sparrow Hawks had obtained numerous packs of furs and all the hot bloods had cooled down. Jim called a council. "Who will follow me against our old enemy, the Cheyenne?" he asked. Four hundred warriors joined him in search of the Cheyenne, but because Woman Chief was still angry, she would not join in the raid. She rode into the hills to sulk and meditate.

After ten suns, Jim's scouts—called wolves—located a large village with a great number of horses. He and three of his men descended the hill to the edge of the encampment. The Cheyenne had just concluded a successful buffalo hunt, so there was great merriment and eating in the camp; tonight they would sleep well.

About midnight Jim led his troops into the horseherd to cut out around eight hundred head. They drove them hard all night, then camped the next day in a small canyon to rest the horses and avoid pursuers. As they rested, they detected over two hundred Cheyenne approaching. Jim's men made several charges before routing the smaller enemy force; his group took numerous scalps before the enemy fled, while Jim had not lost any men.

They rode home to great jubilation and celebration. After four days of celebration, the Sparrow Hawks moved the entire Nation to Fort Cass for their winter trading. They bartered forty packs of beaver and over two thousand elk and buffalo robes. They reveled and traded for seven days before splitting their forces and heading for winter quarters.

After settling in camp, Jim called out, "Who will follow me to obtain some fine Comanche ponies?" He had many volunteers and although he led over two hundred fifty of his followers into Comanche country, he still could not get Woman Chief to raid with him.

Jim's party traveled on foot at a leisurely pace in search of horses, and it took days for them to reach the headwaters of the south fork of the Powder. From here they crossed over to the big bend of the North Platte and descended it to the mouth of the Chugwater. They turned up this stream to its headwaters and crossed over Lodgepole Creek to Crow Creek. As they descended the Crow, they kept their eyes out for Pawnee, but spotted none.

Where Crow Creek empties into the South Platte, Jim turned westerly, traveling upstream until he came to Cherry Creek, where he turned south to its source. He then led his men over to the Black Squirrel Creek and descended it to the Arkansas River. Here he turned east until he found Timpas Creek then headed south into the heart of the Comanche Nation.

They found a large enemy camp hunting buffalo in the great Comanche grasslands. The enemy had a large number of horses enclosed in a wide canyon; these were evidently being held for use as fresh mounts to chase the migrating buffalo. Although there were thousands of horses scattered on the prairie, Jim decided to attempt taking those already rounded up in the canyon.

At about midnight he and his men gathered as many horses as they could into a herd and then they drove them all night. Retracing their route as closely as they could, they changed mounts frequently so they would always have fresh horses under them in case they had to make a run for it. As Jim and his large party topped a hill on the Arkansas River, they spied a large Cheyenne village directly in their path. Jim led his group to the left of the village through a hollow in the hills. Although the Cheyenne were alarmed, they did not pursue the Sparrow Hawks. But when the fast-charging Comanches came up the hill, they charged right into the waiting Cheyenne.

The Comanches assumed the Cheyenne were the perpetrators of the horse raid and a fierce battle ensued. Meanwhile, Jim and his men drove the stolen Comanche horses swiftly toward Absaroka.

They had not lost a single warrior and yet had captured over two thousand horses. When they reached the North Platte, they traveled upstream past the Laramie, to the Sweetwater. After crossing over to the Beaver, they located Long Hair's Mountain Sparrow Hawks on the Wind River.

Jim greeted Long Hair, "Chief, we have just concluded a raid on the Comanche, and we need food and rest."

Long Hair responded, "Medicine Calf and our cousins are always welcome among the Mountain Sparrow Hawks. Join our lodges and rest your fine ponies."

Leaving Long Hair about five hundred ponies, they descended the Bighorn northward to Fort Cass, where they learned that the River Sparrow Hawks were encamped on the Rosebud. When Jim arrived, his group still had nearly fifteen hundred head. He gave horses to all his friends and gave a beautiful red and white speckled roan to Woman Chief. The entire village celebrated while they listened for hours as Jim and his men recounted tales of their hair-raising trip and told how they had tricked the Comanche braves into attacking the Cheyenne.

This episode remained a favorite story among the Sparrow Hawks for many winters.

Two weeks later, Jim led about a thousand of the Sparrow Hawks to a camp in the cottonwood bottoms near Fort Cass. On their third day, fifteen hundred Blackfeet attacked them. To assist them, the fort sent out two Frenchmen dragging a cannon, but the Blackfeet attacked and soon captured the weapon. This infuriated the Sparrow Hawks and they vigorously counterattacked until they retook it. In anger they loaded the cannon with musketballs and fired into the band of Blackfeet, but their efforts caused little damage. They abandoned the cannon as worthless and fought as they always had. The Blackfeet finally fled, taking over one thousand horses with them.

Jim used cottonwood timbers to make a fort for his women and children, and then he raised a posse of five hundred men to pursue the Blackfeet. Even the pouting Woman Chief said, "I will join Medicine Calf against the Pecuni. I have two hundred followers who will join your forces."

They rode for seven days before locating an enemy village of Blackfeet on the headwaters of the Milk River. Before attacking, Jim said, "Let us rest our bodies and our horses. At sunrise, we will punish the Pecuni."

Early the next morning Woman Chief led fifty warriors against the village; her group was to act as a diversion. The Blackfeet immediately attacked like a swarm of angry bees. Her warriors slowly retreated, drawing the enemy ever farther from their village. The enemy was so close she had to lance three charging warriors to keep the rest away from her.

At last Jim led the main Sparrow Hawk force against the village from the rear. In total chaos, the startled Blackfeet fled in every direction. As Woman Chief charged back into battle, she saw two little boys hiding behind a sweatlodge. Speaking in Blackfoot she ordered, "Quickly, Pecunis, climb up here behind me and I will protect you." The frightened boys responded swiftly and climbed up behind Woman Chief. Because she was a female, they were less fearful than if she had been a male enemy warrior.

When the smoke cleared, the Sparrow Hawks had accounted for over sixty scalps and had taken many children and women as prisoners. They also drove home approximately two thousand horses, many of which had just been taken from them in the raid at Fort Cass.

It took five suns before they arrived safely back in Absaroka. Although several men were wounded, Jim had not lost any warriors, so they rejoiced and feasted for four days to celebrate their revenge against the Blackfeet.

Woman Chief adopted her two little boys as her newest brothers and added them to her already crowded lodge. She still had Cracked-Ice's wife, Little Blossom, her daughter, Doe Eyes, Sparrow, Little Feather and three squaws to take care of the lodge. She decided she would train the two Pecuni boys to take care of her horseherd; Little Feather would help train them and they could relate to him, since he too was a Pecuni.

Due to the high level of activity and noise in her lodge, Woman Chief did not spend much time in it. She used every excuse she could find to either go on a raid or go hunting. Often she simply went into the hills to meditate or to pray to her secret helper. Although she still suffered from periodic bouts of melancholy and depression, meditation seemed to improve her spirits and lessen the load of life's burdens.

In spite of his gift of the beautiful pony, Woman Chief was still unable to restore her former close relationship with Jim. She thought highly of herself and was hurt when others did not respect her as she felt she should be respected. She sensed prejudice against her because she chose to become a warrior instead of taking her place as a lodge woman.

Since Jim was the one man who had totally accepted her for her fighting talents and horsemanship, it hurt her even more that he would belittle her and make her the butt of his jokes in front of her fellow warriors. Not one of the others would dare treat her as he did. She could not understand how he could admire her as a warrior, and yet lust after her as if she were just another woman.

What she didn't know was that because he could not conquer her, Jim retaliated by putting her down at every opportunity. His actions confused Woman Chief, but they helped elevate his ego.

During the winter, Long Hair's band made several successful raids against the Blackfeet and took over one hundred scalps. The year of 1834 had been an outstanding one for the Sparrow Hawk Nation, and for Jim Beckwith in particular. He stood at the zenith of his leadership among the Sparrow Hawks, and he also had a good year in the fur trade.

The Crow had grown in number, partly due to the many women and children they had captured; also they had suffered fewer deaths in battle.

The captives adjusted well to their new environment and to the freedom allowed in Crow culture. The Crow treated their women with greater respect than many other tribes, because their society was matrilineal. The women owned all property except their husband's war weapons. When a man married, he had to join his wife's clan and become a part of her family's unit.

With the Crow adopted captive children and women instead of raping them or turning them into slaves; the women were taught domestic chores and could marry anyone in the Sparrow Hawk Nation except their captor. Young boys were taught to ride, shoot both bow and gun, and were trained to become warriors. Many of them became greater warriors than their captors, as Woman Chief had done.

Woman Chief allowed Little Feather to lead her spare horses on her raids and hunts to give him the experience of observing her techniques and skills. The experiences also taught him how to think and react under fire. He displayed a great deal of confidence, but was very impatient to participate in battle, even if it meant fighting his former tribe, the Blackfeet.

She encouraged his patience and complimented his every accomplishment with the bow, rifle, battle-ax or lance. Little Feather in turn continued to tutor Woman Chief in speaking the Blackfeet dialect.

Jim was finally able to persuade his lower river clan to trap more beaver and collect elk and deer robes for the spring trade. He came across some trappers from the Delaware tribe, who informed him, "The raids on the Crow that have been blamed on the Blackfoot Confederacy have actually been committed by the Assiniboine. We have observed their raids."

In anger Jim returned to his followers, saying, "Hear me Big Dogs. Our enemy is the sneaky Assiniboine. Who will follow me?"

Chief Yellow Belly organized over eight hundred warriors and followed Jim across the Missouri to attack their old enemy. After following Big Sandy Creek to its mouth on the Milk River, they found an Assiniboine trading party on their way to Fort Union. Jim called out, "Attack, brave Sparrow Hawks! Attack!"

The Sparrow Hawks slaughtered over twenty-five of the enemy, with the survivors suing for peace. At the council fire, Yellow Belly roared, "You cowards have continuously been treacherous toward our Sparrow Hawk people. We will not forgive you. I, Yellow Belly, have spoken." His voice seemed to speak for the entire Sparrow Hawk Council and the Assiniboine were chased back up the Milk River without their furs and hides.

Upon their return to Absaroka, Jim led a trading party to Fort Cass. When he arrived, he found a letter waiting for him from Jacob Halsey of Fort Union. Halsey chastised him for allowing the Crow to attack all the other northern tribes, who just happened to trade with Halsey.

The year of 1834 had been a trading disaster for Fort Union, even though Fort Cass had done quite well by the Crow. Halsey accused the Crow of placing so much fear into the Blackfeet, Piegan, Blood, Atsina and Assiniboine that these people had become reluctant to leave the safety of their villages in order to trap.

In closing, Halsey wrote, "For God's sake, do keep your damned Indians at home, so that the other tribes may have a chance to work a little and the Company may drive a more profitable business."

J. Archdale Hamilton of the Company even threatened Sam Tulloch that he might close Fort Cass to the Crow if the raiding did not stop. Jim believed that if he could make the surrounding tribes fear the Sparrow Hawks, then his people would be left alone to hunt and trap without fear of being attacked. Now he was frustrated as to which approach would benefit his objectives more.

Jim knew that he must remain vigilant because Robert Meldrum was now in control of the trade with Long Hair's Mountain Crow. Jim knew that Meldrum continually undermined him. It seemed as though 1835 would have to be a feeling-out year for Jim if he planned to remain employed by the American Fur Company.

CHAPTER 32

In late summer, the entire Sparrow Hawk Nation moved up the Elk to the hot springs. While they rested at the hot springs, the Blackfeet raided their camp and the Sparrow Hawks lost almost three thousand horses. They moved farther up near the headwaters of the Yellowstone, while scouting parties attempted to locate the marauding Blackfeet.

Meanwhile, Jim tried to keep the young warriors in camp in an attempt to obey Halsey's edict.

"Stay in camp and the Pecuni will not dare attack us," Jim directed. "If we scatter or divide our forces, they will kill a few of us at a time until we are defeated. I will punish those who go on raiding parties." But even the old warriors became angry with Jim because they could not seek their revenge against their enemies. He finally gave into the pressure and took one hundred fifty of his best men into Blackfoot country.

As Jim and his followers headed for the upper reaches of the Sun River, once again Woman Chief refused to accompany him. The group crossed a low pass to the Gallatin, descended to Three Forks, then traveled down the Missouri to the mouth of the Sun, all the time in search of the Blackfeet. When they finally located a Blood village, they raided the horseherd at night, netting over six hundred ponies and taking one scalp. Quickly they regrouped then headed back for the Yellowstone.

While Jim was gone, Woman Chief led a raid against the Arapaho. She gathered over one hundred young warriors who didn't have much experience. Her party crossed the Shoshone and the Greybull, traveling until they came to the Bighorn. They ascended the Nowood and crossed the Bighorn Mountains, to the south fork of the Powder, where they located an Arapaho village on the Thunder Basin grasslands.

She waited patiently until the middle of the night, then made off with over a thousand horses. Excitedly, she drove her young party hard until daybreak. Desiring to rest her warriors and the horses, she threw caution to the wind and rested in a coulee without placing outriders or scouts.

While they rested, a strong party of Arapahos located them and attacked; due to her precarious position, she and her warriors had to abandon all the horses and flee for their lives. Three of her men were overtaken and scalped. When Woman Chief returned to her people, her face was black with mourning.

When she learned that Jim had been highly successful against the Blackfeet, her depression grew deeper. She seemed to only have success when she was with him;

she seemed to fail when she led her own raids. Because this made her feel like a second-rate warrior, in despair she rode alone into the hills.

During the falling-leaf season, the Sparrow Hawks descended the Yellowstone to Fort Cass to spend the winter and to trade. Jim had experienced another good year, while Woman Chief had enjoyed very little success in her last few years. Now in her thirty-sixth year, and still only the sixth-ranked counselor among the Sparrow Hawks, she was no longer a leading warrior. She prayed to her secret helper for a vision, asking her secret helper to place her on the good-war road.

In the green-grass season, the River Sparrow Hawks moved to Shell Creek Valley to plant their tobacco. After the planting, Woman Chief followed Jim and over one hundred fifty warriors up Shell Canyon and over Granite Pass to the Tongue River. Here they descended to the Little Powder, where they located a Cheyenne camp moving to the buffalo hunting grounds.

Jim gathered his warriors into a wedge and charged the surprised Cheyenne. They took nine scalps before the Cheyenne fled, leaving much of their goods and supplies. Again Woman Chief could not count one coup and in her frustration she blamed Jim for calling off the charge too soon. Jim knew she was angry but he was anxious to leave the area without losing any of his men. Even Woman Chief's adopted son, Little Feather, counted coup and took one scalp. Because the boy worshipped Woman Chief, he did not understand her unhappiness. Jim worried about her also and began to feel uneasy about her mood swings.

In addition, Jim had begun seriously considering his life in the mountains among the Crow. He thought, "What do I have to show for my many years of fighting, hunting and trapping? At age forty, I have very little in the way of material wealth and I no longer enjoy the simple life of the Crow. I'm getting too old for this constant raiding and killing, and I am weary of trying to keep these damn Crow under control. On top of it all, the American Fur Company keeps pressure on me to produce more furs and to keep the peace, which I just can't do."

In the brown-grass season, Jim took more pelts and robes to Fort Cass. After several days of trading, his braves left the fort area to hunt buffalo, but the Blackfeet ambushed them. The Sparrow Hawks counter-attacked and chased eleven of the enemy into the old Sparrow Hawk fortress that Jim had built the previous year. When he learned of the battle, Jim went to the aid of his men.

After surveying the situation, he yelled for his Big Dogs to follow him and kill the Pecuni warriors, but no sooner had he engaged in battle than he was down, bleeding from his mouth. Jim did not know what had hit him, but he felt a terrible impact before he lost consciousness. His men thought he was dying and hurriedly carried him back to Fort Cass.

Most of the trade boats had already left for Fort Union but Sam Tulloch was still around. When Sam looked at Jim, he believed the dark man's wound would probably prove fatal. Since there was nothing he could do, he left and boated down river, reporting to everyone he saw that the Blackfeet had killed Jim Beckwith.

After Sam left, Jim's men revived him, discovering that his Green River hunting knife had blunted the bullet, saving his life once again. Although he recovered soon enough, Jim remained sore for a long time due to the severity of the bruise.

Three weeks later the River Sparrow Hawks traveled up the Bighorn River to Fort Cass in order to see their war leader. But scarcely had they arrived when the Blackfeet stole eight hundred of their horses.

Woman Chief wanted action and vengeance. She cried out, "Who will follow me?" This time two hundred warriors followed her up the Elk River in pursuit of the enemy.

Jim had partially recovered and knew the Blackfeet would have to cross the river and turn east to the Musselshell crossing in order to return to their country. He called out, "Follow me! We will cut the Pecunis off at the Musselshell." Over one hundred of his best men mounted and rode with Jim directly over the hills to the Musselshell where they set up an ambush. After several hours the celebrating Blackfeet leisurely drew near, leading the Sparrow Hawk horses.

Jim's braves charged, chopping the Blackfeet to pieces. They took twenty scalps before the enemy could flee, abandoning all of their stolen horses. By the time Woman Chief's party arrived, the battle was already over. She was shocked to see Jim, since he was supposed to be seriously injured. She inwardly groaned because even when wounded, Jim was a better warrior than she was. She grew furious with him for showing her up in front of their warriors. She knew in her heart that he was actually smarter than her and she blamed herself for being too hasty and impulsive.

Instead of riding back with the others, she rode off alone, disgusted.

When Jim returned to Fort Cass, he met the five trappers whose lives he had saved in the spring. They were again penniless and the American Fur Company would not allow them any credit for traps or supplies. Because they were ready to quit the mountains and return to St. Louis, they tried to talk Jim into going with them. Instead, he talked them into staying, outfitting them as his partners. He then gave some new directions to the Sparrow Hawks.

"Take the white men to the best beaver streams in Absaroka, and protect them from the Pecuni until I return." All five of the visitors agreed to stay for one more season to see if they could make their fortunes. Jim called a council. "My friends," he announced, "I desire to visit my old white friends and relatives in St. Louis. I will return to you when the next green-grass season comes."

News of his leaving saddened the Sparrow Hawks because only under his leadership had they been consistently successful, like they had been in the old days under their other black war chief, Five Scalps.

CHAPTER 33

On July 15, 1836, Jim arrived at Fort Union; once again he surprised everyone by still being alive. After a short respite, he was placed in charge of two horse thieves and sent on to St. Louis.

As the falling-leaf season approached, Robert Meldrum tried to take over the trading and counseling of the River Crow, but due to their loyalty to the absent Medicine Calf, they rejected his intrusion. Meldrum believed Jim did not want to return to the mountains; he also knew the Company did not want to retain him any longer, so he pressed further for what he wanted.

"My friends," Meldrum said to the Crow, "Medicine Calf has been killed in St. Louis by his white enemies. His dying wish was that I become your counselor and trade agent for the American Fur Company." Though his bid for becoming their counselor failed, he had succeeded in convincing them that Medicine Calf had died.

The entire village went into mourning for the death of their beloved war leader. Woman Chief would not cut off any more joints of her fingers, but she did cut off lengths of her long hair.

After four days of wailing and gashing themselves, the River Sparrow Hawks moved up the Wind River to join the Mountain Sparrow Hawks and the Shoshone in their winter quarters. They continued to brood over the loss of their war chief. Woman Chief called out for vengeance against the white-eyes for Jim's death. She then rode into the Owl Mountains to pray to her secret helpers.

In February 1837, the angry Sparrow Hawk Nation laid siege to Fort Cass in retaliation for the death of Medicine Calf. Led by Woman Chief, they blamed all whites, including Meldrum, for Jim's loss. Alarmed, Sam Tulloch boarded up the fort with Meldrum inside. He would have enjoyed throwing him to the Crow wolves, but he knew Meldrum had great influence with the Company. Though he was their fair-haired boy, Sam did not like the man's ambitious conniving. Tulloch knew he could not hole up indefinitely because he needed new supplies.

One night Sam slipped a French Canadian voyageur over the wall, sending the man down the Yellowstone to Fort Union. His message requested Beckwith's return to Fort Cass, with great speed and at all costs. While he waited for word from Beckwith, he tried to convince Grizzly Bear, Woman Chief and Yellow Belly that Jim Beckwith was still alive and was on his way back to Absaroka. But the Sparrow Hawks did not believe him and continued the siege.

Meanwhile in St. Louis, Joseph Pappen located Jim, telling him of the Crow blockade on Fort Cass. Jim laughed heartily. "I've always tole the Company that I'm the onliest one what ken control them Crow. They love me, they would die for me 'cause I'm their spiritual leader."

"I'm authorized to pay you the sum of five thousand dollars to return to Fort Cass as quickly as possible," said Pappen.

Jim's eyes lit up for the first time in months. "I'll return if'n you'll accompany me fer one third of th' payment."

"Done," Pappen replied, "but let's hurry, please." After purchasing good horses and hiring an additional man to assist them, they rode up the Missouri to Fort Clark and ascended the Knife River to Golden Valley. They crossed the Little Missouri, the Beaver, the O'Fallon, the Powder, the Tongue, the Rosebud and at last reached Fort Cass in late April, after fifty-three days of arduous travel.

Jim stopped on a knoll and observed the entire Crow Nation still surrounding the little fort. He angrily rode in among the Crow, chastising them for threatening the white men. When Tulloch saw Beckwith, he opened the gates, welcoming everyone in to celebrate and to trade. Then he sent hunters out to get fresh game for food.

After a joyous reunion and celebration, Woman Chief addressed the fort. "When my brother Cracked-Ice was killed, I swore to never marry until I had killed one hundred of the enemy. I have kept my word and henceforth, I will remain a warrior no more. I have fought my last battle among you. Today, Medicine Calf has returned to us. The Big Dogs believe that he loves me and if I marry him, he will stay among us forever." Though this speech proved difficult for Woman Chief, she continued. "Therefore, today I will become his woman and I will always remain faithful to him and to honor him. I only ask that you continue to follow and obey him, as I shall."

Woman Chief's words both surprised and excited Jim. He immediately renamed her Pine Leaf and accepted her as his wife. In turn she agreed to put away her weapons of war and take on the domestic duties of a Sparrow Hawk wife.

That evening they visited the nuptial lodge for a short wedding ceremony. Pine Leaf looked like a queen in her white fawn skin dress, brilliantly decorated with beads, elk's teeth and porcupine quills. Her hair was braided and adorned with seashells; at thirty-seven, she was still attractive and slim. After the ceremony, Jim and Pine Leaf went on a hunting expedition to consummate their marriage. Pine Leaf felt confused about giving up her life as a warrior, but she did not want her feelings to interfere with her marriage. She also feared giving herself to Medicine Calf, but she wanted to keep him in Absaroka at any cost, even one this dear to her.

First they set up camp and built a fire, then they lay down under the stars upon the white robes of the mountain goat. Pine Leaf had no training as a sexual partner and was very tense when Medicine Calf mounted her. As Jim had not been with a woman for several months, his desire for Pine Leaf overcame his common sense. Besides being a virgin, Pine Leaf remained quite rigid and was certainly not ready for his large member. She felt as if she had been shot by a rifle ball when he forced his way into her body. She bled profusely from the tearing of her hymen and from the dryness of her female organs. Jim did not seem to notice and rode her several times that night; by morning she could barely walk to the nearby cold stream. She felt extreme pain and sat in the cold water to stem the flow of blood and to help numb the pain.

Pine Leaf felt shocked from the bloody ordeal. She thought, "If this is what women have to go through, I would rather be a warrior and die on the battlefield." Painfully, she sighed, "Medicine Calf should be renamed *Bloody Arm* after all."

Jim was dumbfounded at Pine Leaf's lack of skill and response to his lovemaking. He thought, "She shows no affection and even seems to be repulsed by my advances." In disappointment, he went off to kill a deer for dinner and to ponder his new dilemma. He could not reject Pine Leaf as he had others of whom he had tired. His own Big Dog Society would kill him for abandoning their great warrior woman who had sacrificed herself in order to marry him.

In the end Jim reaffirmed his decision to leave the Crow. "Everything in St. Louie has changed," he thought, "and the life of an Indian is no longer satisfyin' to me. I'll try a little longer to make a go with Pine Leaf, but if it don't work out, I'm headin back to St. Louie to look for a new life. I ain't gettin any younger."

After three days, Jim and Pine Leaf returned to Fort Cass where they learned more of the smallpox epidemic along the upper Missouri River. It had spread from Fort Union all the way to the Blackfeet and was killing thousands of natives. Jim called an emergency Sparrow Hawk Council.

"My beloved people," he began, "the white men have brought a dangerous disease to our mountains and streams. It infects everyone and either kills them or scars them for life. It is called smallpox. I advise the chiefs to take their people up to the Wind River Valley until this threat is over. Meanwhile, I will go to the white men and see how bad the outbreak is. I may not return for a while, because I too could become infected with the dreaded disease."

The Sparrow Hawks were terribly frightened; they quickly struck their lodges and began their retreat up the Bighorn while Jim left for Fort Union to survey the effects of the disease.

After arriving at the fort, he learned that not only had the Company canceled his contract, but Robert Meldrum had been accusing him of purposely planting smallpox among the Blackfeet. Jim was not only furious but also hurt; he knew he was innocent of the crime. He had not come to the mountains via Fort Union, but had traveled overland to Fort Cass from Fort Clark, and he had not even contacted any Blackfeet since the previous year, during his last battle with them.

If he had known Meldrum was spreading the rumors about him, Jim would have killed the man. While at Fort Union, Jim contracted the disease himself, but he was strong. With treatment, he recovered. When he was well enough, he proceeded upriver in search of the Crow.

When Jim returned to the Bighorn, he called in his white trapping partners and collected most of their furs. "Boys," he said, "the smallpox epidemic is gettin' pretty bad. I caught it myself and it damned near kilt me. The Indians are gonna blame all white men for bringin this bad medicine. I advise you all to take your pelts and leave these mountains while you still got hair."

After the trappers left, Jim had more time to ponder his situation. He could not survive under the present conditions, and he felt as though he was finished in the mountains. He finally decided to go along with his fellow trappers and headed downstream to catch up with them. At least he had some furs to take with him so he would not return to St. Louis a total failure.

Although he would often think of Woman Chief, Red Cherry, Little Wife and his son, Black Panther, it would be twenty years before Jim would return to the Crow.

CHAPTER 34

Pine Leaf and the Sparrow Hawk people obeyed Jim's advice and traveled to the Wind River Valley to wait out the smallpox epidemic. In late summer she learned that Jim had quit the mountains once more in favor of St. Louis. She also heard that he had left for some foreign place called Florida to fight the Seminoles.

Now convinced that Jim would never again return to her or to the Sparrow Hawks, Pine Leaf dressed as a warrior and once again took up her battle arms. She changed her name back to Woman Chief. To renew her faith in her war powers, she led a raid against the Pawnee.

She took Little Feather and over one hundred warriors up the Beaver to the Sweetwater. They descended the Sweetwater to the North Platte and turned upriver to its headwaters in North Park. Here they came close to battling a pugnacious Ute hunting party, but since neither of the parties had anything to gain, they both withdrew.

In North Park they killed several fine elk and enjoyed the beautiful mountain streams and lush valleys. They continued their journey until they located a Pawnee village at the big bend of Crow Creek. Thousands of horses grazed on the Pawnee grasslands but over five hundred Pawnee lodges camped nearby at the bend of the river. While Woman Chief studied the situation, she secreted her men in a coulee to rest.

She placed her hand on Little Feather, saying, "I have decided to allow you and twenty-five of your Hammer owners to act as a diversion. You and your followers are the youngest and fastest of our raiding party." She equipped them with the best weapons and the fastest horses, then directed them to fake an attack on the Pawnee from across Crow Creek opposite the bend. "After making contact," she directed, "flee east through the grasslands and then north across the Lodgepole to Horse Creek. There you can follow Horse Creek to the North Platte and ascend it to our rendezvous point at the huge rock pillar on the Sweetwater." She wished him good luck and safe hunting.

Woman Chief and the remainder of her warriors scouted the horseherd to determine how many they could round up under a full moon. She noted that only a few young men served as herders and they did not appear very experienced or attentive. Although each of them had a half-shelter lodge located in the various grazing areas, they had congregated at one large lodge for companionship, to alleviate fear and boredom. Because of their large fire, they were visible for a great distance. Woman Chief advised her men to hold the nostrils of their horses until they heard noises from Little Feather's ruse.

As the large, round moon further illuminated the dark sky, the warriors heard gunfire and shouts echo from the bend of the creek. Suddenly many campfires darkened as the Pawnee doused them. After several minutes a roar rose from the village as its defenders organized a counterattack. But Woman Chief and her braves waited patiently. The young horse herders scattered along the valley, panicked, mounted their ponies, and raced each other to aid their besieged village.

Now Woman Chief made her move. "Braves," she directed, "fan out and ride abreast about three horse-lengths apart. Together we can sweep the prairie grasslands of all their ponies." Working through her plan, they gathered over two thousand horses that day, moving them swiftly away from the Pawnee camp. She sent five of her fleetest horsemen to serve as point leaders to guide the large herd northwest along the foothills of the Shining Mountains.

By daybreak, the horses had settled down to a routine and were traveling well, as they had been trained to do by the Pawnee. The group moved on steadily for two days until they found Medicine Bow Creek, which they followed north until they reached the North Platte. She led her caravan across the Platte and followed it to the Sweetwater, stopping in a canyon near the large rock pillar. Here they camped and waited for Little Feather and his young braves.

They waited a full day and night before Woman Chief spied a party coming up river. From her high perch on the rock she counted the faint figures as they slowly came into focus. Though she counted the right number of riders, now she had to wait to see if it was indeed Little Feather's group. Since her eyes were not as sharp as they had once been, she called down for a young warrior named Gray Eagle who had sharp eyes.

By the time he reached her lofty position, Gray Eagle had no trouble identifying the party as Little Feather and his young warriors.

Woman Chief alerted the entire camp, "Our young braves come! They are safe!" In her excitement and relief, she almost fell as she hurried down the rocks, but the young Gray Eagle quickly grabbed her by the arm and she regained her handhold.

Upon reaching the ground, she exclaimed, "We must welcome our young raiders as heroes. Prepare a feast." Then she mounted and rode out to greet Little Feather and his young warriors. Though Little Feather was much fatigued from his ordeal, he beamed with pride as he hugged Woman Chief, almost dragging her off her horse. They rode into camp shouting and yelling, then the party stayed up all night exchanging stories about the raid and the young men's diversionary flight to freedom from the angry Pawnee.

After sleeping most of the morning, the group decamped and drove the large herd over the hills to the Beaver and down Wind River Canyon to the hot springs, where they met with the Mountain Sparrow Hawks. Here they received a grand celebration to reward their first successful raid of the year (in 1837).

This achievement of the River Sparrow Hawk warrior-woman pleased Chief Long Hair very much, so he made an announcement. "From this day forward, Woman Chief shall become the fourth-ranked counselor of Absaroka."

Woman Chief felt like a warrior once more; she had regained her former self-confidence and vowed, "I will never again marry, nor will I try to become a lodge woman." Now she was truly a warrior of the highest rank. She missed the companionship of Medicine Calf, but once again she had her own identity, and this helped her feel more at peace.

The smallpox epidemic continued to spread along the Missouri River. The Blackfeet, Bloods and Piegans suffered greatly. Woman Chief and her Sparrow Hawks stayed in the Bighorn Basin and the Wind River Valley until the green-grass season, but they finally had to leave to hunt for fresh meat. Woman Chief followed Chief Long Hair as he led two hundred lodges and two hundred good hunters in search of buffalo. Though he was getting old, his mind was still clear and he was greatly loved by his people.

At Rock Creek, they met Blanket Chief Bridger and his large band of trappers, who were trapping every creek in the Bighorn and Yellowstone valleys. Bridger stopped to talk to Long Hair. "At the beginning of the brown-grass season, the white men are going to hold a large trade fair on the Seedskadee at Horse Creek. We will welcome your Crows at the fair," added Bridger, "but you must keep a sharp eye out for them Blackfeet, for they have killed four of my Delaware Indian trappers."

Long Hair thought upon these words. "Kash-sha-peece, my friend, we too are constantly harassed by the Pecuni," he replied. "As long as we are in Absaroka, we have the advantage. If we went to the white man's fair, they would have the advantage. My people will stay in Absaroka, but I will send some of my strongest warriors to trade with the white men."

The Sparrow Hawks chased buffalo all over the coulees, valleys and hills. They were making meat and collecting trade robes as fast as the women could butcher. When they could pack no more, they returned to the Bighorn Hot Springs to dry meat, make pemmican and brain tan their many robes. Woman Chief greatly enjoyed the hunt after being cooped up for so long. She was only sorry they had not found any Pecunis to fight.

As the brown-grass season approached, Long Hair sent Chief Yellow Belly, Woman Chief and the Big Dogs as a trading party to the white man's fair on Horse Creek. Woman Chief followed her senior counselor, even though she was now the fourth ranked war chief. Chief Yellow Belly led them up the Wind River to Union Pass and descended the headwaters of the Seedskadee Agie to Horse Creek. Some Flatheads and Pierced Noses had already arrived, but the trade caravan had not yet come in. Also in camp were Bill Williams, Joe Meek, Joseph Walker, Moses Harris, Robert Newell, Reverend William Gray, Osborne Russell and Andrew Drips. Woman Chief and Yellow Belly had traded with Drips many times and they knew several of the other veteran mountain men. Since the Sparrow Hawk representatives made such a small group, they were invited to set up camp with the white men.

The next day twenty-five Delaware trappers arrived and held a wild scalp dance. Woman Chief had never seen such vigorous hopping from one foot to the other; their dance involved more jumping, stomping, firing of guns and yelling than she had ever seen. She watched them for half a sun before they terminated their ceremony and established a camp upstream.

Early the next morning Woman Chief heard yelling. "They come! They come!" The announcement echoed across the valley as word spread from camp to camp; many different languages declared the arrival of the impressive group. Two thousand Snake and Bannock warriors led the trade caravan up Horse Creek, by racing their richly clad horses back and forth, firing their guns, and issuing savage war cries that would have frightened the wits out of less experienced or more civilized people. Chief Mowoomhah of the Shoshone led the warriors, appearing in his finest dress and weaponry.

Broken Hand Fitzpatrick, Lucien Fontenelle, Sir William Drummond Stewart and Alfred Miller led the pack train of trade goods behind the wild-eyed Snakes and Bannocks.

All who attended the trade fair tingled with anticipation.

CHAPTER 35

As Fitzpatrick began unpacking his goods, the Indians and mountain men alike began drinking heavily, increasingly becoming noisy and quarrelsome; some were running amok, bashing each other with anything they held in their hands. Even old Mowoomhah had his snout full and lost control of his braves.

The Sparrow Hawks were the only natives in attendance who did not drink the white man's crazy water. They had been taught by Five Scalps and Medicine Calf both to abstain from this drink, so that they could maintain their senses in battle and trading. Woman Chief watched critically as she saw otherwise brave men making fools of themselves.

When morning came, in spite of many hangovers, the men initiated horse races, gambling, wrestling and many other forms of mountain entertainment. Woman Chief stayed away from these activities, as she had not brought her fastest horse and she did not like the games of bones and hands.

About noon Yellow Belly called the Sparrow Hawks together. "We have been challenged to a foot race by the Snakes, Bannocks and Pierced Noses," he informed them. "We will accept their challenge by spreading the rumor that Little Feather is our swiftest warrior. He will be the rabbit and drain their strength by racing as fast as he can until he drops out. Then Woman Chief will take over and catch them as the mother and father coyote catch the hare."

"Why will they not expect me to be a challenge to them? You know I am the fastest runner in Absaroka," Woman Chief asked.

Yellow Belly smiled. "These tribes don't know that," he said smugly. "I will tell them that we are so sure of Little Feather, that we will even enter a woman, to make the race more sporting. I will tell them that I will bet all I have on Little Feather, and I will even wager my poor old horse on our female runner, to further shame them. Secretly, I want all of you to bet every thing you own on Woman Chief."

In unison the braves agreed. "It is a good plan," they said, and then they gathered many of their belongings in anticipation of placing large bets. Though Woman Chief did not always agree with Yellow Belly, she liked his plan; it took a great deal of the pressure off of her. After all, she was now thirty-seven winters of age. This tactic would allow her to pace herself for a maximum effort. As word of the challenge race spread, trappers and Indians alike gathered to wager on their favorites.

The Nez Perce' entered Spotted Eagle and Looking Glass; the bellicose Bannocks entered Pashego; the Shoshone entered Horned Owl and Washakie.

Because Washakie was a great warrior and about the same age as Woman Chief, he was the favorite. He also had the greatest number of tribesmen present.

Woman Chief entered her lodge to bind her breasts with flannel cloth, then she pulled a short, sleeveless tunic that only reached her waist. Instead of her doeskin skirt, she decided to wear a breechcloth like the men. She pulled her long hair into a ponytail and tied it with a rawhide whang. She wore her low-top moccasins made of buffalo calf with the fur turned inside. This would serve as padding and help protect her from cactus and sharp stones.

Excitement grew high as Andrew Drips started lining up the runners and explaining the racecourse. They were to run from the base camp, down Horse Creek to the Green River, then they would return to the base camp. Spectators began to line the course, so they could have a good vantage point to observe and cheer their favorites.

Drips wagered ten packs of beaver with Sir William Stewart against his beautiful rifle and thoroughbred stallion. He had seen Woman Chief run several times and knew how competitive she was. No one other than the Crow seemed to pay her much heed, and he chuckled to himself as he raised his Hawken pistol into the air, firing a salvo of smoke and fire, to start the race.

Since Little Feather ran very fast for a short distance, he quickly took the lead, setting a furious pace down the banks of Horse Creek. Washakie was mature, experienced and intelligent. He followed closely behind the Crow runner to bide his time. However, he had to keep a sharp eye out for Looking Glass and his old friend, Pashego. He knew they were both fierce warriors, as had fought alongside of them against the Blackfeet. He also knew them to be competitive runners.

Washakie wanted to look good to Chief Mowoomhah and the Shoshone. Though he was only a subchief, he harbored the desire to become the leader of the entire Nation, and this race would add to his war honors. A victory could bring him powerful medicine, indeed.

About two thirds of the way to the Seedskadee, Horned Owl and Spotted Eagle began fading because of Little Feather's fierce pace. As they struggled against each other, they watched with amazement as Woman Chief caught up to them with her smooth stride. She breathed smoothly and maintained her composure, though she still trailed other runners by many paces. But instead of feeling anxious, she concentrated on relaxing, as her mind drifted from her body to follow her secret helper.

When Little Feather saw the Seedskadee Agie ahead of him, he put forth his final burst of speed. The Sparrow Hawk lad surprised Washakie, but he knew he must not take any chances; this unknown runner might embarrass him. The other runners followed Washakie's move and fought harder to catch the fleet Sparrow Hawk. As Little Feather reached the mouth of Horse Creek and made his turn, his lungs burned and his thigh muscles swelled from lack of oxygen. He slowed as he started to bind up, and other runners began passing him. He gasped to Woman Chief, as she ran next to him, "Take them, my sister." Then he collapsed on the trail.

Washakie now knew that Little Feather had fooled him, but he could not determine the lad's objective. He looked at Pashego and Looking Glass, who struggled as much as he did. Though he had no fear of the other runners, his mind grew weary, so he concentrated on glory as he struggled to complete the race. Woman Chief rounded the turn and began picking up her own pace. She kept her arms and legs as loose as possible as she started to gain on the lead runners. When she ran back past the sprawled Little Feather, she could see he would be all right. He had done his part, now it was up to her to bring honor to Absaroka. When she saw the rendezvous lodges in the distance, she began her final challenge. She was gaining with each stride until she found herself even with the gasping Looking Glass.

At first, the runner from the Nez Perce' tried to hold her off, but his body would not respond. The pace had drained him of his strength and his legs felt as wobbly as those of a newborn colt. When he faded behind the older Sparrow Hawk woman, his mind screamed, "How could this be? Who is this woman?"

Washakie was determined to defeat the challenge of Pashego, even though he had been fooled into expending too much of his energy chasing the crazy young Crow. He wondered, "Could it be that my Bannock friend has entered into a plot with our enemy?" Again his tired mind tried to analyze what was happening. Then he realized that all of his tribesmen were yelling something to him. His foggy mind asked, "Why are they so excited? I am in the lead, and even now I can still defeat Pashego. What are they saying?" His mind was just too tired to be rational.

Woman Chief concentrated on keeping her patience and keeping her muscles from tying up as she gained on the struggling Washakie and Pashego. Finally the three ran neck to neck as they neared the finish line.

With one hundred paces to go, Woman Chief pulled on her reserve energy; slowly but surely she eased past the two tired runners. The shock of the Crow woman passing them further constricted their overtaxed muscles; they could only watch helplessly as she ran away from them.

Washakie only beat his old friend Pashego by half a stride, before they both collapsed to the ground.

The crowd roared from the excitement of a great race and from the pain of losing such valuable wagers. The Shoshone were proud of Washakie, so how could a Crow woman have beaten him? Many bystanders fired their guns and most everyone yelled in excitement and bewilderment. The Sparrow Hawks collected their winnings and informed the losers that their old woman was a Sparrow Hawk war chief, who for years had been the fleetest runner east of the Shining Mountains. Many people then admitted to having heard the name of Woman Chief.

Drips smiled as he approached Sir William. "Well, I told ye I had a hunch about the little lady. I seen her defeat the Cheyenne, the Sioux, the Assiniboine, the Hidatsa and the Mandan; if you think she can run now, you should of seen her when she was younger."

Sir William shook his head at Drips. "I say, I think you're a blackguard and a pirate, but I'll pay me debts. It was a bloody good show. Here, take your spoils." When Drips took hold of the beautiful English rifle, he handled it as if it were glass. He had admired this weapon from the first day Sir William brought it to the mountains. He decided he would give the tall, gray thoroughbred to Woman Chief for running her greatest race ever.

In order to approach Woman Chief, Drips had to move through her new admirers. He spoke to her in Crow. "Woman Chief, I wish to present you with this fine stallion, which I won from that rich white man over there."

Woman Chief was shocked. "Captain Drips, I cannot take your winnings," she responded. "You don't understand. We used Little Feather as a rabbit to run down the other runners, so I could save my strength for the finish. Yellow Belly planned it so."

Drips laughed as hard as he could and gasped, "That makes it even better. The Crow have outsmarted the entire nations of the Nez Perce', the Bannock and the Shoshone, and I outsmarted that rich Scotsman, because I bet on you. I will hear no more. You take the stallion, or I will never trade with you again."

Woman Chief smiled, as she affectionately grasped Drips' hand. She then led her newly acquired horse, with its beautiful saddle and bridle, back to the Sparrow Hawk camp. She became the envy of the rendezvous, as she showed her award to all her friends. Woman Chief tied the grand horse inside her lodge—she was taking no chances with her new prize.

All of the Sparrow Hawks won so many goods through the race that they could hardly pack it all. They traded some of them for necessities, but kept the bulk of their winnings to take back home with them.

After they had fully recovered from their ordeal, Washakie and Pashego approached Woman Chief. Though Washakie was almost as old as she, he was an imposing man. He stood about eighteen hands tall and had a very muscular build; he was also handsome, despite a deep scar along his left cheek. The scar made his character more serious.

"You ran an excellent race," he told Woman Chief, "but I was fooled by your rabbit, and I did not know you were the great Woman Chief. If I had known these things, I do not think I would have lost so easily. I would have run a much smarter race."

Washakie continued. "Even though the Crow and Shoshone do not always get along, I pledge you my friendship from this day, forever."

Woman Chief felt flushed as she accepted his greeting and complement. "Thank you, Scar Face," she replied. "I too pledge my friendship as long as the buffalo roams our prairies."

Pashego grunted. "Come, Washakie, do not grovel with this Crow cheat. She is more man than woman and is not fit for our company." In anger, he turned and walked away, while the embarrassed Washakie could only sputter his apologies. Then he too quickly turned and followed the bellicose Pashego. Woman Chief had been insulted before, so Pashego's words did not hurt her. If he only knew, she did not like him very much either; she could never be his friend.

The next day, Blanket Chief Bridger and his men arrived with a roar. Not only did Bridger act like a wild man, but he wore a full suit of metal armor. Woman Chief could not believe her eyes as she watched tossed arrows and war clubs bounce off of Bridger, so she edged over next to Drips. "Where did Blanket Chief get his magical clothes?" she asked.

Drips smiled. "He received the outfit as a gift from that rich Scotsman over there; the one who lost his horse and gun to me on your race. His name is Sir

William Stewart, and he is the son of a long line of chiefs from across the big waters to the east. He fought in many of the great white man's wars; he is chief of a great stone fort, in a land called Scotland. He gave old Gabe that suit as a reward for guiding him through the Rockies for the last several hunting seasons. Gabe just loves to show it off."

Woman Chief looked over at Sir William, then she remembered his accusations against Medicine Calf several seasons ago, down on the Bighorn River. He had accused Medicine Calf of sending the Sparrow Hawks to rob him and his party of their furs, guns and horses. She remembered too that Broken Hand Fitzpatrick went to Medicine Calf and was able to restore the guns and horses, but he never found the furs. She has also heard that Sir William never forgave Medicine Calf, and even spread forked-tongue tales about him among the whites, in the village called St. Louis. She did not want to meet this man, and she now possessed his fine horse. She chuckled as she realized that, in a way, she was getting even with Sir William for his viciousness against her old friend and husband, Medicine Calf.

Woman Chief then turned her attention to a handsome trapper who came in with Bridger. "Who is the trapper with the Blanket Chief?" she asked Drips.

Drips looked where she pointed and laughed, "That is Jean Baptiste Charbonneau. His mother was the Snake woman, Sacagawea, who helped guide our red-haired chief, Clark, across the Shining Mountains to the great salt waters in the west. His brother is the half-breed, Basil, sitting over there. Captain Clark educated him in the white man's schools in St. Louis. Then some foreign chief, called Prince Paul, took him across the great salt waters to the east for several years. He speaks many languages, plays music, and is a very smart fellow."

Woman Chief eyed him as she walked around the camp. He was friendly to everyone but seemed shy and very modest. She preferred people like that as opposed to loud braggarts like Medicine Calf and most of the mountain men.

Walking around some more, Woman Chief observed a young man painting and drawing Indians and mountain men while they posed. She moved closer and learned from Bill Williams that the artist's name was Alfred Miller, another man who had come to the mountains with Sir William. She watched as he painted Blanket Chief Bridger and Joe Walker. She was fascinated by the art of this white man, but in her judgment Miller was not as good as Catlin. the painter she met several seasons ago at Fort Union. Catlin's drawings were more easily recognizable.

Despite everyone's fascination with these artists, she had always resisted being painted for fear of losing her spiritual powers in the process. Many of her friends feared they would lose their shadows if they were painted. When the Indians and trappers began consuming crazy water, she moved back toward her own camp. She watched the white Reverend Gray retreat to his lodge and saw him crouched in prayer to his great spirits. Maybe this was a good time to return to Absaroka.

As the Sparrow Hawks readied to leave, Fontenelle approached them. "Yellow Belly," he said, "I want to send Doc Newell and a couple of his men back with you to trap and trade among your people this season. If you will assist and protect them, I will give you credit for trade goods at Fort William."

Though Yellow Belly knew Fontenelle would keep his word, he did not like the man and did not care for the rotten odor of his breath. Fontenelle always smelled like crazy water. He also did not like the idea of being burdened with the responsibility of more white trappers. Nevertheless, he wanted to stay on good terms with the white men, and he liked the idea of getting free trade goods. At last he nodded and grunted his consent.

After the small party packed their newly acquired horses and all their other winnings and trade goods, Yellow Belly led them up the Seedskadee Agie toward Union Pass. Although it had been entertaining and rewarding to be at the trade fair, it would be even better to get back home.

CHAPTER 36

For the Sparrow Hawks, encounters with the white men became more and more frequent. During the snow-falling season, Grizzly Bear and Woman Chief led a trading party down the Bighorn toward Fort Union. Near the mouth of the Shoshone, they encountered a group of white trappers, which upset Grizzly Bear, because they had not sought permission to enter Absaroka.

"We will take your tobacco and ammunition as payment for taking our beaver," he demanded.

"Chief," answered Osborne Russell, "we will divide what we have, but no more. If we are molested, Bridger will bring all of the white men in the mountains down on your people." Russell hoped his bluff would work. Though this counter threat hurt Grizzly Bear's pride, he did not want to anger Blanket Chief Bridger, so he reluctantly agreed to half of the tobacco, balls and powder, but he followed the white men for two suns. His braves sang vulgar war songs in an attempt to frighten the white men into relinquishing more of their goods.

Woman Chief did not want to be a party to this foolish game so she rode on ahead of the party. One night Grizzly Bear's warriors stole the white men's horses, and then sped down the Bighorn to catch up with Woman Chief. Their actions disgusted Woman Chief, and she felt Grizzly Bear was no longer worthy of his high rank; she did not want to follow him any more. In fact, she thought, this incident could cause problems for the entire Nation.

Unknown to Grizzly Bear's party, Little Soldier and twenty of his braves happened upon Russell's horseless trappers. Little Soldier offered to take the white men to the Sparrow Hawk village for succor, but by this time Russell did not trust the Crow. He refused to go for fear of being further endangered. He and his men cached their furs, buried the bridles, saddles and ropes, then they plodded up the Nowood River toward Fort William. To complicate matters further, it began to snow.

Meanwhile, Grizzly Bear changed his plans. "Woman Chief," he said, "you take the trading party to Fort Union. I will take Big Robber and Two Face back with me to return the white men's horses." This seeming change of heart encouraged Woman Chief, so she consented to proceed on to Fort Union.

The next day Grizzly Bear met Little Soldier's hunting party on the Shoshone River. Little Soldier said, "I see you have met the white trappers; I believe those are the white men's horses you are riding. They were so distrustful of me that they would not even allow me to take them to our village for assistance. I saw them bury their furs and supplies across from the mouth of the Shoshone before they headed up the river."

"We have been trying to catch up with them so we could return their horses," offered Grizzly Bear. "Some of our young braves became too excited about the white men's trespass, but now I am on my way to return the plunder to them. May your hunt be fruitful, Little Soldier."

Opposite the mouth of the Shoshone, Grizzly Bear directed Big Robber and Two Face to look for signs of fresh digging in order to locate the white men's cache. It was a slow process, but finally they located the goods near a ridge and proceeded to dig them up. The warriors loaded the stolen furs and ammunition onto their stolen horses and headed up Shell Canyon; Grizzly Bear knew he could trade the furs and goods at the Portuguese House. Antonio Montero would not make them answer any questions about the ownership of the goods.

Woman Chief reached Fort Union in a light snow and quickly her group set up their lodges. She then went in search of Alexander Culbertson, the chief trader. She learned that he had gone down river to Fort Pierre and had left a new clerk, Edwin Denig, in charge. In Denig she found a confident man who was small and thin, but who had piercing eyes. His beard grew around his face and across his chin, but did not cover his mouth. His fresh facial scars indicated he had recently contracted the white man's pox.

"I am Woman Chief of the Sparrow Hawk people," she said softly.

Denig responded in a language she understood. "I do not speak Crow;" he said, "do you speak Assiniboine?" His response startled Woman Chief. She spoke this language but she wondered how this greenhorn learned it.

"I am Woman Chief, fourth-ranked counselor of Absaroka," she said in the language of the Assiniboine. "I am sent by Chief Long Hair and Chief Grizzly Bear to obtain much needed supplies for our Nation. How do you speak the language of the Assiniboine so well?"

Denig was taken aback by the woman's quiet confidence. He had traded with members of the Missouri tribe since 1833, but he had never seen a female warrior or chief. "I traded at Fort Pierre for the past four winters, and I am the new chief clerk here at Fort Union. I intend to remain here for a long time, and I would like to get to know you and your Crow people. Come with me!" When he led her into his living quarters, she marveled at the chairs, glassware, rugs and other riches adorning his lodge. As she touched and inspected everything within reach, a small, attractive, native woman entered the room.

"This is my wife, Deer Little Woman," said Denig. "She is the sister of Chief First-to-Fly, of the Assiniboine." Woman Chief now understood how he knew the language of the Assiniboine. She also knew of First-to-Fly, for she had fought his warriors many times, and had always been victorious. She respected First-to-Fly, but she considered his braves inferior to her Sparrow Hawk warriors.

Deer Little Woman smiled pleasantly and grasped Woman Chief's arm in an affectionate manner. Deer Little Woman wore a lacy cloth dress and hightop leather shoes, tied with strings through small round metal holes. Woman Chief had never seen such clothing before; she assumed they must be the clothes of a white man's woman, but she felt they did not suit an Assiniboine princess.

Denig left the women to become acquainted while he checked on his traders. While pricing goods, he queried several older Crow warriors about their woman war chief. He learned she was much feared but highly respected among the tribes of the Rocky Mountains. He thought this could be his opportunity to gain the Crow trade, through friendship with this strange woman warrior. "I sure aint gettin' much help from that damned agent Meldrum," he fumed.

Woman Chief liked Deer Little Woman and felt very much at home, even in her strange lodge. Deer Little Woman said, "Welcome to my lodge. My man, Denig, has another wife, who is older than me and very sickly. I take care of her, as well as serve as hostess for Fort Union. We have many important white visitors, who come up the Big Muddy River to us, on great smoking canoes. Come, I want you to try something with me."

Deer Little Woman gave Woman Chief her first cup of coffee, lacing it with sugar and cow's cream. Woman Chief loved this strange dark drink and vowed to use every excuse to return for more of it. "This white man's drink is wonderful," she exclaimed. "When visitors have such a fine brew, why do they drink the crazy firewater?" Deer Little Woman laughed heartily, but she also felt a sadness in her heart. As much as she loved Denig, she knew he had a serious craving for the white man's alcohol.

When Woman Chief returned to her camp she directed her people to gather all their trade goods. "Trade only for shot, powder, balls, salt, knives, needles and other essentials," she admonished. "Our Nation needs these supplies until the green-grass season, so do not trade for gewgaws and foofooraw. I have set up our trades with the head chief."

Denig took charge of the Crow trade. Because of the smallpox epidemic, he had not received as many furs as was normal. The disease had devastated the Missouri tribes, and those tribe members still living were reluctant to visit the forts for fear of catching the disease. As a result, Denig was generous in his trading with those who did come to the fort. Their trading success pleased the Sparrow Hawks and they gave full credit to Woman Chief.

When her turn came, she said, "Chief Denig, I wish to trade for a cap and ball rifle. My old weapon is worn out and has been mended many times. Have you such a weapon as Blanket Chief Bridger carries?" Denig smiled and entered a small storeroom behind him. He returned with a beautiful Hawken fifty-caliber cap and ball rifle. Its stock had been created from walnut and was well oiled. The gun was also trimmed with bright brass accessories.

Woman Chief examined the rifle intently. "How many robes for this fine weapon?" she asked.

Denig played his hold card. "This is my gift to you, for a long and lasting friendship."

His reply surprised Woman Chief while her people grunted their approval and admiration at such a fine gift. She thought, "I want this rifle very much, but I just met this man. Even Medicine Calf has never given me anything but stolen horses. Only Captain Drips ever gave me a real gift, and he had won it at the white man's trade fair because of my success in the foot race."

Receiving such a fine gift worried Woman Chief, so she turned and left the fort to return to her camp. There, she unsaddled her beautiful gray horse and led him back into the fort.

"I will accept your beautiful gift, if you will accept mine as a bond of our friendship," she told him.

Put on the spot, Denig was stunned, but he could not refuse her gift, that would be very bad form. A quick examination of the horse proved to Denig that the animal was a fine thoroughbred stallion. It occurred to him that the horse actually belonged to Sir William Stewart and that it had probably been stolen. "I could get him into serious trouble for accepting this gift," he thought, "but I could also make an enemy of Woman Chief."

Cautiously Denig asked her, "Where did you get such a fine animal? I have never seen such a marvelous horse."

Suspecting his nervousness, Woman Chief endeavored to place his fears at rest. "I won this horse from Sir William Stewart at the last white man's rendezvous. I outraced the Snake, Bannock and Pierced Nose runners to win this fine prize. You can ask any of the mountain men who attended. It is so."

Denig had no reason to doubt her claims and proudly received the grand gift. He did not receive very many gifts; instead he was expected to treat every chief or warlord who entered his fort. Everyone was pleased with their good fortune and the area was peaceful for the next few weeks. As the fort began celebrating the white man's new year, Woman Chief led her band up the frozen Elk toward the Bighorn.

Woman Chief located the Sparrow Hawk village at the Bighorn Hot Springs. Excitement and revelry broke out at their arrival and she led her loaded pack horses to Chief Long Hair's lodge, where the trading party unloaded to expose the goods to eager men and women.

The feeble Long Hair rose and announced, "We again thank our beloved woman warrior for her unselfish gifts to our people. All praise and revere her. Today I announce that she is now the third-ranked counselor of the Sparrow Hawk Nation."

When the large crowd started chanting, "Woman Chief! Woman Chief!" she withdrew in embarrassment. Later she rode into the Owl Creek Mountains to pray to her secret helpers.

The green-grass season of the white man's year of 1838 brought new reports of many deaths among the Blackfoot Confederacy and the Missouri tribes, from smallpox. Even though the damage happened to their old enemies, the Sparrow Hawks feared that they too might suffer from the white man's disease.

In need of fresh meat, Woman Chief led Little Feather, Two Face, Big Robber, Rottentail and Bear's Head up Ten Sleep Canyon to the headwaters of the North Fork of the Powder River. They ran into Doc Newell and a large group of trappers, who informed them of the fall trade fair and rendezvous to be held at the Popo Agie. As Woman Chief led her party on toward the mouth of Crazy Woman Creek, she wondered why Big Robber and Two Face seemed so nervous. She did not know until much later that they were fearful that she would discover that they had robbed the white trappers during the snow-falling season.

The party found many buffalo on the Crazy Woman and soon had all the meat and robes they could pack. But when they returned to Bighorn Basin, she found the entire village in mourning. "What has happened," she asked. "Is it Yellow Belly?

157

Why are we in mourning?" For the first time since her capture by the irascible Yellow Belly, she saw him in tears. He choked as he spoke to her.

"Our father, Long Hair, has passed into the spirit world. We have been in mourning for a moon. We have deposited his remains in the caves above the hot springs. I am now the head chief of Absaroka." Woman Chief screamed in her anguish at the loss of her leader and father figure. She had not grieved this hard since the loss of Chief Rotten Belly many seasons ago. She cut off large strands of her long hair and covered her face, arms and legs with charcoal, then she went to Long Hair's tomb to pray and fast for four days. Afterwards she sat on the bank of the hot springs for a long time in order to recover from her mourning.

When she finally pulled herself together, she returned to camp and started making provisions for taking her warriors to the rendezvous on the Popo Agie. Since the Sparrow Hawks had some pelts, many robes, clothing ornaments, jewelry, moccasins and parfleches for trade, they sent a large trading party to the fair. To Woman Chief's surprise, Chief Grizzly Bear had been banned from the fair for robbing Blanket Chief's men during the snow-falling season. She learned Grizzly Bear had not returned the men's horses as he had promised, and instead had even stolen their furs, trading them to the Portuguese House.

Though he would not disclose who assisted him in the thefts, Woman Chief felt strongly that Big Robber was involved, and possibly Two Face also, but she kept her own counsel with her suspicions.

The Sparrow Hawks enjoyed themselves at the white man's 1838 rendezvous. They received five dollars per pound for beaver pelts and four dollars per robe. These were good prices, but blankets sold for fifteen dollars, tobacco was five dollars a pound, and sugar and coffee were each two dollars a pound.

Woman Chief purchased her first sugar and coffee. She craved the strange drink ever since Deer Little Woman made it for her at Fort Union. She cooked a brew of her new luxury to share with her braves, but when she tasted it she realized hers was not as good as Deer Little Woman's because she did not have any cream. But her friends did not seem to mind and kept coming back for more. She sat in her camp, drank her coffee, and watched the debauchery of the mountain men, particularly those who consumed too much crazy water.

Blanket Chief Bridger finally arrived with one hundred sixty trappers, squaws and children. His arrival always created a stir because of his booming laugh and tall tales. The handsome breed, Charbonneau, came with him and though Woman Chief was pleased with her feelings towards him, she was too shy to approach the man.

Nervously she left her camp and wandered around. Upstream she saw a small camp of white missionaries with their wives. Drips had brought them here. Woman Chief noticed the women dressed much like Deer Little Woman. Lace and fine sewing adorned their cloth dresses. She observed that though Sparrow Hawk women were creative with porcupine quills, beads, tanning and painting on animal skins, they still could not do fine sewing like the white women.

The next day Joe Walker and his men drove in over three hundred well-built horses from a place called California. Woman Chief thought she would like to see such a place if it had so many fine ponies. Walker stayed a few suns to sell some of his animals, then he left for Fort Bent.

Woman Chief enjoyed attending these get-togethers for she saw many of these people once a year. This time she saw Doc Newell, Joe Meek, Bill Williams, Moses Harris, Francis Ermatinger and Osborne Russell. She visited with them to apologize for the actions of Grizzly Bear. She found that they were fully satisfied by the sacking of Portuguese House and the banning of Grizzly Bear by the Sparrow Hawks.

To change the subject, she asked, "Have you heard from Medicine Calf Beckwith?"

"I saw him in St. Louis last winter," said Harris. Williams offered, "Well I saw him at Fort Vasquez this spring. He was trading with your old enemies, the Cheyenne. They will end up poor people, for sure. Har! Har!"

Woman Chief laughed with them, to cover her emotions. She candidly interjected, "The Cheyenne must have buffalo dung for brains if they trust Medicine Calf. He will give them blind ponies and sell them loco weed for tobacco."

They were all laughing as Woman Chief left and walked back toward her Sparrow Hawk camp. She packed her goods and rode down the Bighorn to the Medicine Wheel to cry and pray. She still missed Medicine Calf, her husband, fellow warrior and friend.

CHAPTER 37

As the early winter storms rolled in, the Sparrow Hawks moved up to the Wind River Valley. Everything seemed peaceful as Woman Chief and a small hunting party stalked mountain sheep near the headwaters of the Wind River. Unfortunately that peace was soon broken.

Woman Chief suddenly barked, "Seek cover! A large party is approaching from Togwotee Pass!" As everyone scrambled she added, "Little Feather, you have strong eyes. Move forward and see if they are friend or enemy."

Little Feather left his horse with Two Face and headed up the trail, bracing against a light snowfall. Woman Chief directed her party to hobble their horses in the trees and then gather logs and brush for fortifications. All work feverishly, breaking only when Little Feather returned from the thin clouds of snow. He had been running and was out of breath. When he regained his composure, he delivered his report.

"There are over one hundred white trappers and a few women and children in the party. They are led by Blanket Chief Bridger and Captain Drips." With that welcome news, everyone relaxed. When at last the traveling party drew near the hunting party, Woman Chief hailed them.

"Aiee, Drips! Aiee, Blanket Chief!" she yelled, "Your clever passage caught us by surprise. We are fortunate that you are not the Pecuni warriors—we would have been at a severe disadvantage."

Bridger roared in English. "Yeah, we seen yore fort back thar. With that meat y'all are packin, you could hole up 'til the spring thaw."

Drips laughed at the repartee between them and chimed in with his broken Crow speech, "It looks like you knew we were coming. Can we feast with you?"

Woman Chief gave them both a shy smile and answered in Sparrow Hawk, "The white men are always welcome in Absaroka. While you are here your rifles will discourage our enemies from acts of treachery." Together they all rode to the Sparrow Hawk winter camp at Sage Creek, where there were many greetings among old friends before the white men set up their lodges and settled into village life.

During the subsequent days of catching up on mountain gossip, Woman Chief learned that the redheaded chief named Clark had died in St. Louis. The new Indian superintendent was an old trapper named David Mitchell. She did not know Mitchell, but Drips spoke well of him. She had not met the red-haired chief either but everyone, including Five Scalps and Medicine Calf, spoke highly of him. She remembered Chief Long Hair and Chief Rotten Belly telling of the time they met him.

Clark and the Snake woman were returning down the Elk River from the great salt water west of the Shining Mountains. When he died, Chief Rotten Belly still had the medal of friendship he had received from Clark.

It saddened Woman Chief that now Clark, Five Scalps, Long Hair and Rotten Belly had all gone to the spirit world and she began chewing pieces of tobacco root for solace.

The next evening Woman Chief perked up when Drips told her that the Comanches and Kiowas had fought a big battle with the Cheyenne and the Arapaho down on Wolf Creek. "They damned nigh killed each other off," Drips said, "and now they are tryin to get ole Bent to negotiate a peace." She did not like the Cheyenne or Arapaho and she wished that the Kiowas had wiped them out. The Sparrow Hawks were friendly with the Kiowa, although they no longer had frequent contact.

Woman Chief took Little Wife and her son, Black Panther, into her lodge. It was Sparrow Hawk custom that the nearest relative take in the dependents when the head of a lodge died, and although Medicine Calf may not be dead, he had been absent a long time with no communication. He might just as well be deceased, since she had heard no word from him. Woman Chief added them to her already large family, consisting of Little Blossom, Doe Eyes, Sparrow, Little Feather, Coyote, Badger and the three women she had married to perform the arduous work of keeping up the lodge.

She was very pleased to again be close to Little Wife and Black Panther because they had belonged to Medicine Calf. She could not be a husband to Little Wife but she could act like a father toward Black Panther.

Soon afterwards Chief Bowl and his wife Fawnskin died; pneumonia had overtaken both of them. Chief Bowl had been the civil chief of the Greasy Mouth Clan and Chief Yellow Belly nominated Woman Chief to replace him. Though she was flattered by the honor, she felt apprehensive regarding the additional responsibility. Woman Chief pondered the nomination.

"I have led hundreds of horse raids and dozens of war parties," she thought, "but when they were concluded, I could always go back to my hunting or exploring in the mountains." Being a civil chief for the tribe was a full-time job and she loved her freedom too much to be tied down.

After several days of meditation and praying to her gods, she came to a conclusion. "At this time, there is no one else qualified to take the job," she rationalized. "Besides, I am almost thirty-nine winters of age and perhaps I should take on more responsibility for the people who had given me so much."

After her return she gathered the band to make her announcement. "I will accept the honor of becoming your chief," she said. "I expect everyone to follow my directives without question. If you should ever fail me, I will immediately resign. If I should fail you, I ask that you leave me and select a new leader."

Flattered that the feasting and jubilation lasted for four days, she felt most satisfaction when Chief Yellow Belly personally congratulated and encouraged her. He pledged his undying loyalty to her and to her Greasy Mouth Clan.

At the lodge, Black Panther was delighted to have Coyote and Badger to play with, and the boys were forever getting into mischief. All three were now eight winters of age and Woman Chief and Little Feather began teaching them to care for the horseherd. When no adult was around, the boys wrestled, chased each other, and rode all of the older horses. With their bows, they shot at rabbits, ground squirrels, skunks or any other small game they could find. They did their jobs to please Woman Chief and Little Feather, but they played at every opportunity.

While Badger was aggressive, Coyote was shrewd; however, Black Panther proved both strong and smart. He could outdo either of them; he was taller and quicker than they were and when wrestling, he often fought both of them at the same time.

During the leaf-falling season of the white man's year of 1839, Woman Chief learned that McKenzie and the American Fur Company were building a trading post opposite the mouth of the Rosebud on the Elk River. She took her Greasy Mouth Clan down to watch the white men work. The man in charge was named Charles Larpenter, who had been in the mountains for several years. He was a sour man and Woman Chief did not like him much; besides, the man had difficulties with Medicine Calf when her husband was still among the Sparrow Hawks.

The post was to be called Fort Alexander, in honor of both McKenzie and Culbertson. McKenzie was retiring as the head trader of Fort Union, and Culbertson was taking over for him. The Greasy Mouths were very excited about getting a trading post in Absaroka again, but Woman Chief vowed to shun the post. She would continue to go to Fort William or to Fort Union, preferring to trade with Denig and drink coffee with Deer Little Woman. They always treated her with respect and sincere warmth.

Woman Chief became so busy with civil duties and obtaining more food and skins that she hardly had time to replenish her supplies. She needed powder, shot, a new knife, more brass cooking pots, blankets and other necessities the white man had taught her to depend upon. She learned that another rendezvous would be held on the Seedskadee that year; however, beaver was becoming scarce and when they trapped a few, the pelts could no longer bring in all the trade goods her people needed. She noted that her own lazy Sparrow Hawks had almost depleted their streams of beaver by over trapping.

What concerned her even more was that the white men and tribesmen had almost eliminated the buffalo from the valleys of the Seedskadee and the Snake. They were killing too many animals just for their hides, tongues and humps. As buffalo carcasses began to pile up on the trails and mountain meadows, she continued to counsel the Greasy Mouths, "Only kill the food you need. Do not destroy the very staff of life."

During the snow-falling season, Woman Chief led her Big Dog apprentices up Rock Creek on an elk hunt. After a day's ride, she set up a base camp in a large cave she knew to be hidden behind a rock formation near the stream. Then she sent Little Beaver, Bear's Head and Rottentail to locate some elk. She was hauling in a butchered mountain sheep on her back when Little Feather raced into the camp, breathless.

"Mother," he gasped, "I have detected a large hunting party coming over Beartooth Pass."

Woman Chief alerted her braves. "Retreat with your horses and supplies into the cave. These hunters may be Pecunis." She warned, "Be calm, but alert. If we have to fight, this cave will defend us until Rottentail and Bear's Head can bring us assistance. I will go to greet this party and see who they are." She waited on the trail by the stream, pretending to be drying strips of mutton. She tried to appear as nonchalant as possible, while the approaching party drew nearer. The group stretched out for a long way as they slowly descended Rock Creek. She could tell that they were not painted for war; there had to be nearly two hundred hunters and each of them led pack animals.

At last her aging eyes recognized Washakie. "Aiee, Scar Face!" she yelled. "It is I, Woman Chief of Absaroka." Washakie prodded his horse into a gallop and raced up to her. He was still fascinated by this woman warrior who had outrun him at the rendezvous three seasons ago.

Warmly he said, "Hello, my sister. I did not see you at the last trade fair. Are we no longer a challenge for the great Sparrow Hawk runner?" In spite of herself, this pleased Woman Chief, and her nervousness caused her to giggle. In turn, her reaction pleased Washakie very much. When she regained her composure, she responded.

"No, my friend, I was only afraid to run against you again because you learned my tricks. I could never beat the great Snake chief twice. What brings you to Absaroka?"

Washakie turned in his saddle to point to the hunter just now arriving and answered, "Pashego and his Bannocks have joined my Seedskadee clan on a buffalo hunt. We have none left, west of the Shining Mountains. Our people need meat, skins and robes. We are hungry and our clothes are rotting off. Some of my people do not even have skin lodges and must sleep in brush lodges or caves. I also have with me the black-robed chief, Father de Smet, who is returning to the white world to gain support for a new spirit lodge for the Flatheads."

Woman Chief stared at the large white man in black robes who rode astride a black mule, but as he passed her he acted as if she were of no importance to him. She renewed her decision to stay in her own spirit world, because she did not trust the white man's representatives or his gods.

Washakie spoke up again. "Here comes Pashego now. I wish you two could get along. You are both my friends." He called to Pashego. "Brother, over here. I have found Woman Chief of the Crow. She can direct us to the best hunting grounds."

Pashego gave Woman Chief a cold stare. "I am a Bannock chief, I do not need a Crow woman to help me find game." With that he wheeled away and rode downstream.

Washakie turned a flushed face to Woman Chief. "I apologize for his behavior. He is a vain and proud warrior and he still has not recovered from your outrunning us at the rendezvous. His temper and his arrogance will someday be his downfall, but he is still an excellent fighter and war leader. I want you to know that I will remain your friend for life, just as I declared. We will meet again, under better conditions."

She searched his dark shining eyes before responding, "Thank you, my brother. If you ever do need my assistance, please ask. Keep your scouts alert because there are Pecunis sneaking along the Musselshell and the Elk."

With that they parted and Washakie joined the long line of hunters still moving down Rock Creek. Woman Chief returned to the cave to inform her braves that everything was fine. She then sent them out to continue their hunt for elk.

She sat in the cave by a campfire, roasting mutton and pondering. If the Bannocks and Snakes no longer had any buffalo, then they would continue to put more pressure on the hunting grounds of Absaroka. "Our Sparrow Hawk warriors already fight the Pecunis, Assiniboine, Atsina, Cheyenne and the powerful Sioux for game," she thought.

She did not know what the outcome would be, but it made her stomach churn whenever she dwelled upon it.

The Sparrow Hawks comprised a small nation. Their land and their resources were being squeezed by enemies as well as friends. The Sparrow Hawks were also being exploited by the powerful white men. "Why do things have to change so much?" she thought. "Why must the Sparrow Hawks lose their beautiful lands and animals?" In solitude she sat and chewed her tobacco root. Futile tears streamed down her weathered, aging cheeks as she realized there were no easy answers to her questions.

S E C T I O N VI

1840 - 1854

Jerry A. Matney with D. A. Gordon

CHAPTER 38

As the snow and ice closed in the rivers and streams of Absaroka, the Sparrow Hawks huddled in their lodges near the hot springs in Bighorn Basin. Most game was still plentiful and smallpox had kept the Pecunis away from Crow horseherds.

Woman Chief and the other women had their hands full with Black Panther, Badger and Coyote. The boys had turned nine and seemed to become more rowdy by the season. They would charge each other on bareback ponies and push, kick, grab and try every way possible to dislodge each other from their mounts. The last person left astride was considered the winner, and as usual, most of the time the winner was Black Panther. He had his father's courage, for sure.

When the green-grass season finally arrived in the white man's year of 1840, Woman Chief decided to adopt Black Panther as her protégé. This would mean she had officially become his tutor. He showed great promise, like his father, and she wanted to teach him to think, read sign, stalk game and enemies, and to move without leaving tracks or creating sounds. She wanted to teach him the bow and spear and later how to shoot the white man's rifle. She hoped some day he would be a great warrior and a chief among the Sparrow Hawks; he would be her legacy.

When Little Feather and Woman Chief had time, they taught all of the boys as much as the lads could absorb. Then she would take Black Panther into the mountains or the foothills for days at a time. Together they would explore nature, learn the trails, and read the weather. She knew that in order to be a Sparrow Hawk warrior, he would have to know the area of Absaroka thoroughly. She also taught him about the area's plants and animals along with their uses. He already knew about plums, buffalo berries, strawberries and such, but she took the time to search out plants and herbs he did not know.

"See the native turnip," she would say. "They grow all over the prairies and will supply you with nourishment when you cannot find game. They are good in stew or even eaten raw. Over there is the bitterroot. Only gather it during the green-grass season when the bitter coating can be peeled off. Dig up the squaw root only at the end of the acorn season. See the stunted bushes? They make a good tea, which is not only good to drink, but works for relieving the pain of sexual diseases. Of course, you will learn about that much later." She smiled at the boy's eagerness to learn. She told him of the beneficial uses of stinging nettle tea, sunflower seeds, broomrape and the sego lily.

As they rode up into the Wind River Mountains, often she would dismount and pull up some of the plants so he could taste them. She pointed out the uses of the bear medicine plant and where to pick it; she also had him dig up camas bulbs and rice roots from the ground of a moist meadow.

"There is food and medicine all around you," she explained, "and if you know Absaroka, you shall never go hungry or remain ill." Because of these trips, Black Panther started seeing Woman Chief in a new light. She was no longer his big sister or aunt, she was a wise hunter and warrior. He knew of the stories of her bravery and how she had fought alongside his father. Now he understood that he was learning from the best.

On their third outing he asked, "Woman Chief, was my father brave?" Before replying she stopped her horse and turned in her saddle to face him. "He was the bravest warrior I have ever known. I learned much of my skill and knowledge from Medicine Calf, who saved my life more than once."

His solemn black eyes searched hers as he asked, "Then why did he leave us? Did he not love us?" She quickly turned away in order to hide her pain. She gazed across the valley to Crow Heart Buttes, then to Knife Point Peak, beyond which she knew lay Indian Pass. "This is Absaroka, home of the Sparrow Hawks," she thought. "Why would Medicine Calf leave such a beautiful place? Did I fail him as a wife or as a woman?" Those unanswered questions often drove her to tears, but not today.

At last she turned back to her young, apt pupil and said, "Your father was stolen from us as a child and raised by the powerful white men. Their magic has always held influence over him. They have drawn him back to their lands, across the prairies to the east, but some day he will return to us. Please forgive him, because I know he loves you and Little Wife very much."

Black Panther seemed satisfied with her answer, and they rode on for a great distance in silence, Black Panther wondering about his father and Woman Chief once again analyzing her feelings about Medicine Calf.

The seasons of the next year passed quickly as Woman Chief hunted, provided for her big lodge, and trained her three boys. In addition, she had to provide leadership and counseling services for the Greasy Mouth Clan members. Little Feather now led raids of other young Big Dogs. His own horseherd had grown, and he would soon be seeking a wife and wanting to establish his own lodge. She envied his youth and his freedom to raid and hunt as she had once done. But duty called, and at the moment she needed to decide on the next move for her Greasy Mouths. They must constantly keep on the move to leave their middens and excrements so they would not contract disease. Even though they had hundreds of dogs to eat offal, debris continually built up around their villages.

As the new snow-falling season began, Woman Chief moved the Greasy Mouth band back to the main village under Chief Yellow Belly. They wintered in the valley of Beaver Creek, south of the Wind River. She felt she could finally relax and let Yellow Belly assume the overall responsibility of the community. She knew she could never become a head chief, but her station was fine with her. Being a minor chief was all the responsibility she ever wanted. The prestige was a good feeling, but at the same time, her life was not her own. At times her stomach knotted from the decisions she had to make and the problems she had to solve. No wonder Medicine Calf left Absaroka, he probably could not deal with this much responsibility any longer.

After the storms of the white man's year of 1841 eased, Woman Chief led the Greasy Mouths over Beaver Ridge to the Sweetwater River. Again, she decided to trade at Fort William, instead of traveling to Fort Union or Fort Alexander. The group camped at Split Rock for several days to hunt for fresh meat, but they were careful to avoid contact with the Pawnee, Cheyenne or Sioux. Their old enemies had taken over the buffalo range along the Platte and the Sweetwater. She again noticed that buffalo were becoming more and more scarce. Nevertheless, her hunters secured twelve fat cows.

After drying their meat, they moved south of Devil's Gate, and then back north, past the big rock where the white men were already making many strange markings. They bypassed the narrows and rode past Red Buttes to the mouth of Poison Spider Creek, where they again camped and hunted. Two suns later they reached the mouth of the Elkhorn, where they washed and cleaned up at the Warm Springs. Woman Chief wanted her Greasy Mouth band to look their best when they reached Fort William.

As they rode down the Platte, Woman Chief noticed a large new building near the river. It was made of earth, but she had never seen anything like it. She wondered how the white men could get the earth to go straight up into the air like a stone wall. She had seen the oval earthen lodges of the Hidatsa and the Mandan, but this building greatly differed from those dwellings.

She set up camp and explored the new post. The walls measured twelve hands thick and two horse-lengths tall. She stepped off eighty-five paces for the length, and sixty-five paces for the width. Towers stood at the northwest and southwest corners. Inside the post lay twelve smaller buildings that served as stores and dwellings. The central corral contained over two hundred fine horses of white man's stock, which meant they were taller and a little heavier than Indian ponies. After examining the goods, she found that they only had skins, gunpowder, trinkets, lead and crazy water.

Through an interpreter she learned that the chief of the post was named Lancaster Lupton, and the strange building was called Fort Platte. Woman Chief went back to her camp and approached Little Feather.

"Come with me," she stated. "We are going to Fort William and see what trade goods they have." Little Feather mounted his horse and followed her down river. When they reached the mouth of the Laramie, they crossed the Platte and ascended the Laramie until she saw another large earthen post being built. This one would be located just south of Fort William, and she learned that the trader, John Sarpy, had named this new post Fort John.

When they finally arrived at their destination, they checked the goods and prices at Fort William; the prices were similar to those of Fort Platte, but Fort William had blankets, pots, knives, arrow points, spear points, and other necessities. Here, too, the men tried to sell them crazy water, which the Sparrow Hawks refused to buy. They mounted and began their return to Fort Platte to inform the Greasy Mouths that Fort William would prove more to their liking.

As the Greasy Mouth Clan reached the mouth of the Laramie, the group met a large party with pack mules coming up the river. Little Feather's sharp eyes picked out a familiar face and announced, "It is Broken Hand Fitzpatrick."

Woman Chief plunged across the stream, yelling, "Aiee! Aiee! Broken Hand. It is I, Woman Chief of Absaroka." She galloped forward to meet the surprised Fitzpatrick. As she pulled up she said, "Does Broken Hand bring new supplies for another trade fair?"

"No," he replied. "I'm guiding these pilgrims across South Pass to the western territories. I got me three padres under a priest named Father de Smet, a fire and brimstone preacher named Joe Williams, and sixty-five greenhorns that don't know buffalo's backfat from elk dung. John Bartleson is chief of this group, and the brains behind the outfit belong to young John Bidwell. Bidwell wants to break off at Fort Boise and go across the desert to Californi'. I aim to take the rest to Oregon."

He then changed the subject by asking, "What is being built up there at Fort William?"

She turned in her saddle and looked at the blur up the Laramie as she responded. "Sarpy is building a new earth post called Fort John, and upstream, a man called Lupton has already built an earthen lodge called Fort Platte. I don't think I like either one and they both tried to bribe us with crazy water."

Fitzpatrick laughed. "You best keep your Crow braves away from that firewater, cause there's a heap of Cheyenne and Sioux along the trail. I've already had to rescue one lad who got too damn careless. I advise you to return to Absaroka by going over the Black Hills from the headwaters of the Laramie."

She looked up toward Fort Platte, then said, "I only brought my Greasy Mouth band, and I only have twenty-five good warriors. They can only be used to defend our families if we are attacked. I wish I had a hundred of my Big Dogs, then I would seek out the Cheyenne."

He looked at her soberly, then he gave her a warning. "You must change your old ways of warring against all the other tribes, Woman Chief. The white men will bring peace to the plains, and they want the Indian wars to stop. This party is the first of many white men to come. There are thousands of white people forming trains back on the Missouri, and as these large caravans come up the Platte and the Sweetwater, they will destroy the game and anger the Cheyenne and Sioux. In turn, those tribes will have to hunt the Powder River country, which will bring them in contact with the Crow. If you want to survive, you had best make peace with your enemies, soon."

Woman Chief thanked him and turned to lead Little Feather upstream to Fort Platte. Fitzpatrick led the black-robed padres and the white emigrants across the Platte and up toward Fort William and Fort John. The Greasy Mouths only traded for necessities, then they headed up the Black Hills to the headwaters of the Laramie. Woman Chief decided to avoid the white men and get her people safely back to Absaroka as soon as possible.

At the source of the North Laramie Woman Chief led her party over the Black Hills to Bear Mountain. They descended it to the mouth of the Sweetwater on the North Platte. As they turned back toward Devil's Gate and Split Rock, she considered what Broken Hand had said. When he told of the many white men coming to the west, it reminded her of Medicine Calf's words, that the white men were as plentiful as the buffalo. "They must be running out of room in the east if they are so eager to conquer the land west of the Seedskadee," she thought. She mused over Broken Hand's warning. "The white men will destroy the game and your enemies will try to take over the buffalo grounds. You must do all you can to save Absaroka for Black Panther, Coyote and Badger."

Things were changing rapidly, and life was becoming more complicated. She longed for the days when it was Indian against Indian, living and fighting in concert with nature. The white man had upset nature's balance, and she felt helpless to deal with the consequences.

CHAPTER 39

As the snow-falling season arrived, Woman Chief moved her Greasy Mouth clan up the Wind River to the mouth of Crow Creek. She set up camp and took Black Panther up Horse Creek to hunt sheep. Out of a light snow flurry rode her old friend, Bill Williams, the tall, gaunt man who had become a legend in the Rocky Mountains and who had also become a friend of the Sparrow Hawks.

"Aiee! Crooked Arm," she called. "What brings you to Absaroka?"

Bill recognized Woman Chief and replied in his high-pitched voice, "This child is now a free trapper and a part-time horse thief. I'm a stayin with muh wife among the Snakes this season. Times is a little rough right now, and the Blackfeet are after me for cheatin 'em last year. I took their robes to Fort Hall and drunk up most of their credit. I figure they won't fight the Snakes and the Crow just to get even with me."

Then he looked at Black Panther and asked, "Is this here yore boy?"

Flushed, she responded quickly, "Oh, no. This is the son of Medicine Calf Beckwith, his mother is Little Wife. His name is Black Panther." Black Panther raised his open palm into the air to acknowledge the old man.

"Well, I'll be damned," swore Bill. "He shore resembles ole Jim, all right. He has that curly hair and darky skin like Beckwith, now don't he?"

Black Panther studied the strange man. "Have you seen my father?" he asked.

Williams looked amusedly at the young boy. "Well," he answered, "I whupped him down on the Arkansas last summer. He and some other niggers built a post up thar, called Pueblo Post, and they was a givin alcohol to the Cheyenne an cheatin 'em out of their robes and hides. We ain't spoke since."

To Woman Chief and Black Panther this did not seem like a serious offense. In fact, they felt down right proud that Medicine Calf was cheating their old enemies. As the group talked, Little Feather ran up to them with several excited young men. "Mother!" he shouted. "We have detected a large party coming down the river. Come quickly!"

As Williams, Black Panther and Woman Chief followed Little Feather, she saw the dust of many horses. As they cautiously crept forward and quietly watched, a large party of Seedskadee Shoshone rode in out of the snow. Leading them was a stout warrior on a spotted horse.

"Aiee!" called Woman Chief. "It is Scar Face. I see you cannot live without me; you have again come to Absaroka for succor. Welcome to our valley."

Nervously, Washakie laughed at her brashness. To him, her words always seemed sharp and double-edged, and he never knew quite how to take her. She was the only person he had ever met that made him feel unsure of himself. Ever since she defeated him in that footrace he had felt slightly intimidated by her. If she were simply a woman, he could ravish her and if she were a man, he could fight her in combat, but she was a unique person, and he did not know how to deal with her. He only knew he wanted to keep her as a friend and an ally, so he covered his mixed feelings by joking with her.

He retorted, "I came to protect the Sparrow Hawks. I hear their chiefs have turned the task of fighting over to their women. I started worrying about my old friend and decided to spend the cold nights of winter before her lodge fire, to protect and comfort her. Are your robes warm?"

Williams laughed. "Chief, even you cain't put her fires out. I'm hungry as a she-bear with sucklins; let's go to camp and eat some hump." As Woman Chief blushed, she turned downstream and led them to her Crow Creek camp.

Slowly the harshness of snow-falling season subsided and hunters ventured further into the mountains in search of elk and sheep. One morning, as the villagers began to stir, a Snake hunting party rode in at a rapid gallop yelling, "Blackfeet! Blackfeet!"

Quickly Washakie sent all of the women and children of the village up Crow Creek to hide; then began organizing his warriors. He placed fifty riflemen under the leadership of Williams and directed them to dig rifle pits as a last line of defense. He then took one hundred warriors and ascended the south bank of the Wind River to meet the enemy. Woman Chief took her twenty-five mounted braves up the north bank.

At Bear Creek the combined forces collided head on with the Blackfeet and drove them back up the river. As more of the Blackfeet caught up, they forced an overwhelming counterattack, driving the Sparrow Hawks and the Shoshone downstream. Finally, Washakie and Woman Chief turned and led their forces away, as if in full retreat, and the fooled Blackfeet blindly pursued them. But when the Shoshone and Sparrow Hawks cleared Crow Creek, William's Shoshone riflemen opened fire on the startled Blackfeet, cutting them to pieces. They were routed into a full retreat, leaving dead and wounded on both sides of the river.

Washakie and Woman Chief then hounded, harassed and bit at the heels of the fleeing Blackfeet until they retreated all the way over Union Pass. As the victors returned down the trail, they killed the remaining wounded Blackfeet and scalped every fallen body they could find. After they regrouped to count their own wounded and killed, Washakie said, "I knew you could run, now I know you can fight too. I have never fought along side of a more cable war chief. I will follow you into battle any time you ask."

Woman Chief flushed again. She had only done what she had been doing all her life. Finally she retorted, "It was not I, Scar Face. It was the combination of our medicine that defeated the Pecunis. We have powerful secret helpers, you and I, but thank you anyway, my friend."

Quietly they rode back to the Sparrow Hawk village, where the celebration had already begun with drum beating, dancing and feasting. Apparently word of the victory preceded the party. This battle would long be remembered in Shoshone and Sparrow Hawk history.

Little did Woman Chief know, but by befriending Washakie she had opened the door for the Snake to lay claim to the Wind River Valley. The Snakes now had their blood in the valley, and a great victory to remember it by.

Washakie finally led his Shoshone out of Wind River Valley, and life among the Sparrow Hawks returned to normal. On foot, Bill Williams and Woman Chief ascended Bull Lake Creek to hunt sheep. She turned to Williams and asked, "Broken Arm, now that the beaver are gone and the Pecunis seek your scalp, what will you do? Can you not join your old friend Walkara and his Utes?"

Bill thought for a moment before responding "No. A couple of seasons ago I took a load of Ute furs into Taos fer Walkara. Now, I was in them mountains fer a long time, and I had me a longin fer some of thet Taos lightnin. I traded them furs and drank until I was told that there warn't nothin left in my credit account. I must'a been thar fer a week, cause my head hurt somethin fierce, but I was sober enough to know thet Walkara would skin me alive whilst he had me staked to an ant hill, if'n I returned without his goods."

Williams had his audience's apt attention. "Now I ain't a real smart feller, but I ain't a goin back to Walkara and try to explain what happened to his furs. He's a mean sonofabitch. I just may head back to Californi with old Joe Walker and get me some Meskin horses; I always liked midnight ranchin. I cain't go with old Peg Leg Smith cause he's too tight with Walkara. And me and ole Jim Beckwith ain't got along since we had that big fight down on the Arkansas."

He thought about it for a while, then added, "I been down in Arizoni a few times and I like that country. Howsomever, I shore don't like the Mojaves, Apaches or Yaquis down there. They hates us white folks to a fare-the-well."

After awhile Woman Chief stopped climbing, signaling to Williams to halt. She pointed up the mountain. Bill strained his tired old eyes, but he couldn't see anything except a snow-capped peak. As he strained to see, it dawned on him that he was beginning to get too damn old to be living like this. He needed a more secure livelihood, with a little protection from his growing army of enemies. She signed him to climb higher to determine who these intruders were. He quickly checked his rifle and began to climb the trail on all fours. As they cleared the brush and reached the short grass, they could see that the intruders were white men.

Bill rose from his knees and yelled in his squeaky voice. "Halloo the camp! Halloo up thar!"

Woman Chief too jumped up and screamed, "Aiee, Carson! Broken Arm, it is small chief, Kit Carson."

Williams tried to keep up with her, but she climbed the slope like a mountain goat as Carson came down to meet them. Kit exclaimed, "Well I'll be damned, if'n it ain't old Bill Williams and Woman Chief."

The soldiers behind Carson watched cautiously as the three people hugged and hooted at each other like people who had escaped from old Bedlam itself.

Woman Chief finally said in Shoshone, "What are you doing with these strange white men on top of our mountain?"

Kit laughed at her question, "I'm a guide for that fancy officer over thar. His name is Lieutenant John Charles Fremont, and he's a surveyin a wagon road fer the emigrants goin to Oregon and to Californi. He wanted to climb this peak, to declare it in his name as the highest peak in the Rockies."

Woman Chief looked at Fremont as though he were crazy in the skull. She had hunted over every peak in the Wind River, Tetons, Bighorns and Shining Mountains, and yet she had never named a peak after herself. Not only that, though she was not as smart as the white men, she still did not think this peak was as high as some of the others she had ascended. White men had some funny ideas.

When she returned her attention to Small Chief and Broken Arm, they were talking about getting a job for Broken Arm as a guide for Fremont.

She heard Broken Arm say, "Yep, that's what I been a lookin fer. The Army pays reglar, and I'd be protected from them damn Utes and Blackfeet. I know those mountains across South Park and on into Utah better'n anybody. So you put in a good word fer me with thet young lieutenant. I'd be much obliged to ye fer it."

Kit answered, "Well come on and I will introduce ya, but you got to promise me you won't drink no more of thet lightnin whisky. You get plumb crazy when you do, and you ain't no good to anyone when yore dog drunk."

"I promise Kit, I promise," Bill answered eagerly. "All's I needs is one more good chance and I'll do ya proud."

Woman Chief eyed the young white man as he listened to Little Chief and Broken Arm. The lieutenant seemed pompous, in his dark blue clothing trimmed with brass buttons and gold thread. She decided that she did not like him and did not want to meet him. Self-important people like that bothered her. Besides, she considered such people dangerous. It seemed to her that Little Chief had changed because he was trying too hard to please the cocky, white leader. Finally the parley broke up, and she and Broken Arm waved good-bye and continued their hunt for sheep. They both made several nice shots and went together to retrieve and butcher their kills.

Bill finally spoke, "I learned that old Gabe Bridger is a buildin him a fine tradin post over on Black's Fork of the Seedskadee. He's aim'n to trade with the white wagon train folks thet are goin to Californi and Oregon. I think I might just go and visit old Gabe for a while until I hear from Carson and that mighty fine young lieutenant. Do you want to jine up with me?" Woman Chief felt only sorrow for the desperate attitude of Broken Arm. He had been one of the toughest, brightest and bravest warriors she had ever fought beside. Now he was acting like a broken down old man, begging for buffalo offal.

She answered, "No, I have to lead and take care of the Greasy Mouths. I am no longer free to roam as I did when I was younger; I now have many responsibilities. I need to take my people down to Pryor's River to visit our relatives. But please tell Blanket Chief that someday I will visit his new fort."

Silently the group packed the butchered meat inside of the sheepskins and tied the bundles on their shoulders for transport back to camp. Woman Chief could regularly carry her own weight in meat. By dusk they were back in camp and eating roasted sheep ribs.

After several suns of moping around, Williams directed his Shoshone wife to pack up and they headed up the Popo Agie toward South Pass.

Woman Chief led the Greasy Mouth band down Wind River Canyon to the Bighorn. She left the river at the mouth of the Shoshone and struck out overland for the Pryor Mountains. In Pryor River Valley she found Yellow Belly's group, camped in the grass meadows. They all danced and feasted for four days before settling down to camp life.

Chief Yellow Belly told Woman Chief, "I will winter my people here in the Pryor Mountains. Washakie's Snakes have taken over the Wind River Valley and we have much bad blood between us. You know he is married to a Sparrow Hawk captive who is a relative of mine. I am not even allowed to speak her name."

Woman Chief understood his feelings, but she had learned to like Washakie. Besides, they had defeated the Pecunis together. She had met Washakie's wife, Strawberry, and she seemed very happy with the Shoshone. Yellow Belly and Doe Eyes now had two sons and a daughter, which made Woman Chief a grandmother under Sparrow Hawk law. When Cracked-Ice died, she became the mother of Doe Eyes. She thought, "Since I am in my forty-third winter, I guess I am old enough to be a grandmother."

As the white man's spring of 1843 broke, the River Sparrow Hawks moved to the mouth of Mizpah Creek on the Powder. They found plenty of Buffalo and antelope, once again life was happy and pleasurable. Woman Chief and Little Feather continued training her adopted boys.

When the brown-grass season arrived and the black cherries were all gone, she decided to visit Denig and Deer Little Woman at Fort Union. She called to Black Panther, "Pack your hunting weapons, dried meat and a change of clothing, Brave One. I will teach you how to trade with the white men on the Big Muddy at the mouth of the Elk."

Black Panther ran to get his belongings. He saddled his black pony and tied his personals and weapons on his mother's high horned saddle. As Woman Chief watched him, she decided she would get him a man's saddle. He could not take such a long trip with just his riding pad, and she did not want to embarrass him by having him use a woman's saddle. As they traveled leisurely down the Elk, Woman Chief led two pack animals loaded with elk, sheep, goat and buffalo robes. She still would not trap for beaver, but her robes brought good money, and she was usually able to purchase all the supplies she needed. She even had credit with Denig, just in case she should ever become injured or fall on hard times.

When they finally arrived at the fort, Woman Chief set up a half-shelter camp for herself and Black Panther. She unloaded the horses and hobbled them by the camp. When she entered the post with Black Panther, Denig was talking to a strange white man, so she waited until he addressed her.

"Woman Chief," he called, "I want you to meet John Audubon. He is an artist and a scientist. He wants to study the birds and animals up here on the Missouri River." Then he turned to his guest and said, "Mr. Audubon, this is Woman Chief, who is a chieftain among the Crow Indians. She has been all over this country and can probably find anything you want."

Audubon addressed Woman Chief. "I am pleased to make your acquaintance, my dear lady. I would very much appreciate your assistance in acquiring the skulls

of the bison, elk, prairie wolf, puma, mule deer, and a good Indian specimen."
Denig interpreted Audubon's words for her; after listening intently, she smiled.

"I remember two old caves, near the mouth of Pryor River, where I can find
some ancient ones," she said. "There are also many large animal bones in and about
the cave. It appears the old ones lived in the caves, many winters ago, before they
learned to build skin lodges. There are paintings on the walls, where they show
how they killed the buffalo and elk before they had horses."

"Splendid!" Denig replied. "My men will locate anything you cannot find for
Mr. Audubon." Woman Chief finished her trading, then Denig began talking to the
white man at length. Black Panther and Woman Chief packed and left. The two
rode slowly for several days until they struck the mouth of Pryor's River. Here they
ascended to a trail that led to the caves, just as Woman Chief had remembered.

Black Panther was wary as he entered the darkened cave, whose walls were
carved with ancient paintings and markings. Woman Chief reassured him. "Do not
worry my son, the old ones were not Sparrow Hawk people. We do not seek the
bones of our mothers and fathers. These dwellers were most probably the ancient
ones, whom we defeated to conquer Absaroka."

Slowly they explored the cave, then Black Panther called out, "Mother, I have
found the skull of a huge gray-backed bear. Come quickly."

She looked at the grizzly skull; indeed, it was one of the largest she had ever
seen. "It is good," she said. "Denig will like this head very much."

After searching and scraping around with sticks, they found skulls and bones of
buffalo, elk, panthers, wolves, mule deer and black tail deer. Woman Chief only
selected one of each to take back to Fort Union. It appeared that the inhabitants of
the caves had used the area inside and around the caves for a midden area, where
the ancient ones left their offal and broken weapons. Since they could not move on,
as the Sparrow Hawks did now, wild animals and nature had not carried off the
garbage, nor had the garbage been exposed to wind, rain or snow because it was in a
cave.

She remembered where she had once uncovered some human bones and went
to the back of the cave. After a few minutes of digging in the soft earth, she
uncovered some bones and decayed animal skins. One hardened skin had been
wrapped around its owner, with the fur turned inside, so the skull and several of the
large bones were well preserved. She noticed that it had a flattened forehead with
large ridges above the eyes. She carefully wrapped it and placed it into a parfleche
to tie to the packsaddle. Since Black Panther still felt spooked, they rode on down
to Pompey's Pillar to camp.

As they sat looking into their campfire, Woman Chief told him, "This was an
ancient lookout for our people, to keep a lookout for the Pecunis. Many seasons
ago a great, redheaded white chief came to this place and named it after the son of a
Snake woman. She had guided his party across the Shining Mountains. That young
man is the trapper Jean Baptiste Charbonneau, who is a good friend of your father's.
Baptiste is the one who came to visit us with Blanket Chief Bridger."

Black Panther was all eyes and ears when he heard anything about his father.
He tried to remember the trapper Charbonneau, but could not. All the white men
looked alike to him. At last he said to her, "You are very wise, mother. You know

so many things and have met so many people. Do you think I will ever be wise like you, and meet great people?"

She placed a few more sticks on the fire, as she smiled with pride. "Some day you will be a warrior and a chief like your father was, but you must never abandon your people. You will be a great leader, and will be able to bring permanent peace for our people. Only use war for defense or revenge. It is all right to raid for horses now and then, but try to never kill anyone while raiding, because that only brings about retaliation and revenge." With their thoughts toward a brighter future, they both slipped off to sleep. However, even in this state, their senses were acutely alert to possible danger.

The next morning they rode back to the fort, where they rode right up to the warehouse and began unpacking their treasures. Denig and Audubon examined the specimens excitedly. Denig especially liked an old bison skull, while Audubon almost hyperventilated when he examined the skull.

"By Jove," he said, "I believe this is hundreds of years old. I can't wait to have my scientific friends and colleagues examine it. When the new Smithsonian Museum opens, I shall donate this specimen to their anthropological room."

"My men have all the skins you asked for," Denig added, "and I have personally prepared many birds and small animals. If you need further assistance, please let me know. Woman Chief, I want to thank you and the boy for your great contribution. I would like for you to stay with me and Deer Little Woman for a few days, so we can show our appreciation."

Denig then addressed Black Panther. "So you are the son of ole Jim Beckwith. Well, I'll be damned. I only met him a few times down at Fort Pierre, before I came here, but he had a wild reputation and was a real hellbender. Since I arrived at Fort Union, I have heard many stories about his fighting skills, which rival those of Woman Chief, herself. I hear Beckwith is in Santa Fe or Taos, I forget which."

"I heard last season that he helped build a trading post on the Arkansas, to trade with the Cheyenne," added Woman Chief. "I guess poor Medicine Calf just cannot settle down. I have now adopted Black Panther and his mother, Little Wife. I will raise him as if he were my own son, in the custom of our people." Denig nodded, while Black Panther grinned.

Though Black Panther had only reached twelve winters of age, he wanted to be independent, and he wanted to become a famous warrior, like Woman Chief. It caused him confusion, because sometimes she was like a mother and grandmother, while at other times she was a wizened chief and war leader.

Woman Chief visited with Deer Little Woman and drank her favorite drink, coffee, while Denig showed Black Panther around the post, talking to him about the fur trade. The next day she became restless and started worrying about her Greasy Mouth clan.

Although her band was with Chief Yellow Belly, Woman Chief still felt responsible for their welfare and safety. She also knew that Little Wife would worry about Black Panther until he was safely home again. She packed and bid Denig and Deer Little Woman good-bye.

Woman Chief led the loaded pack animals back across the Big Muddy, then up the Elk towards Absaroka. Black Panther watched the passing terrain wide-eyed, his head still reeling from all the things he had seen and heard during the trip. Woman Chief knew the boy could hardly wait to get home to tell other boys of his amazing travels and the many people he had met.

CHAPTER 40

The Sparrow Hawks elected to spend the winter (1843-1844) on the Elk River, above the mouth of the Shields. However, before they could settle in, heavy snows started to fall. Woman Chief had never seen such harsh weather begin so soon; the trees were frozen before their leaves turned brown. Smoke from the intense lodgefires of the village hung low over the entire valley.

During the occasional breaks in the weather, Woman Chief would travel to the Elk Hot Springs to sweat and cleanse herself. She had to travel by foot up the frozen river and had to wear thick buffalo moccasins, with the fur turned inside, to protect her feet against frostbite.

Chief Big Robber's band stayed on the Rosebud; runners brought word that the people were suffering terribly. The trader, Meldrum, continued to hold too much influence over Big Robber, often talking him into actions that only benefited the American Fur Company. Meldrum tried to keep the band as close to Fort Alexander as possible.

Two other chiefs of the Mountain Sparrow Hawks, Two Face and Rottentail, blindly followed Big Robber, but Yellow Belly's River Sparrow Hawks consisted of the bands of Bear's Head and Woman Chief. More stable and experienced, these bands did not listen to Meldrum.

As the ice and snow continued to pile up, the Sparrow Hawks ran out of fresh meat. The freezing temperatures had driven the game from the mountains. Even the firewood became scarce, so they began chopping down saplings and burning green wood. The group began living on pemmican, dried meat, dried fruits and edible roots.

During the slightest breaks in the weather, Yellow Belly would send out hunters on snowshoes to try to locate goat or sheep. When they finally located a few sheep, they also ran into some hungry silver-backed bears. The bears mauled two of the hunters who had grievous wounds but who lived to tell their stories. After months of winter, the days finally began to lengthen, but by the time the trees should have been budding, ice still remained.

After another month, warm rain fell, causing the ground to thaw. After several days of rain, the sky cleared and father sun began to warm the bones of the grateful Sparrow Hawks. As their icy world became warmer, Yellow Belly decided it was time to move his people to the Powder River Valley, in the hopes of finding buffalo. His hungry people packed their belongings on their horses, along with their lodgeskins and lodgepoles, and then they began traveling in a line along the south side of the icy river. Because of the warm rain, they dared not venture out on the ice.

As they quietly rode along next to the river, a loud roar up river broke their reverie. The rains had created premature melting in the higher elevations. The water easily flowed over the top of the frozen stream, rushing straight toward them.

Immediately Yellow Belly, Bear's Head and Woman Chief urged their people to head for higher ground in order to escape the rushing wall of water. Most of them succeeded in getting out of the water's way, but one group, near the mouth of the Shields, caught the greatest volume of the onslaught.

Caught unprepared, their lodgeskins, lodgepoles, baggage, horses, and even some of their children were swept downstream. Several of the smaller children had been tied to the horse saddles and could not escape. Three mothers and a father also drowned while trying to rescue their children. Yellow Belly regrouped his people and waited for the flood to subside. Many relatives mourned for the loved ones they lost to nature's violence. Eventually the river ice began giving way under the weight and friction of the rushing water. As soon as it was safe, Yellow Belly moved the people toward the Rosebud to see how the other clans had fared.

Travel was slow and laborious, and fords that would allow safe passage over the swollen streams were difficult to find. They crossed the Boulder, Stillwater, Rock Creek, Clark's Fork, and the Horses River before they came to the Bighorn. After two sleeps the river had fallen low enough to ford and they passed on down to the Rosebud.

Although the Mountain tribe had not experienced the severe flooding the River tribe had, the Mountain tribe had suffered severely from the long harsh winter. After their arrival, Yellow Belly, considered head chief, called a council of all the clans. While Yellow Belly represented the Kicked-in-Their-Bellies band, Rottentail was chief of the Thick Lodges, Woman Chief was head of the Greasy Mouths, Bear's Head had the Without-Shooting-They-Bring-Game band, Two Face led the Piegans, and Big Robber was chief of the Whistling Water clan. The smelly, dirty, unkempt Meldrum sat in as Big Robber's advisor. After each councilor passed the pipe to his left four times, Yellow Belly took charge of the conference.

"Chiefs," he began, "we have suffered greatly this winter from freezing weather, and we have lost several of our relatives due to floods on the Elk. I have never seen the snow so deep in the mountains, and I fear more heavy flooding in our valleys as the thaws begin in earnest. What must we do?"

Big Robber rose to speak. "My people have not been effected by the flood, because my friend, Meldrum, chose the valley of the Rosebud for our winter quarters. He now proposes we go to the valley of the Musselshell to await the return of the elk and buffalo. We need to replenish our larders and fill our empty bellies." Two Face grunted in agreement with Big Robber.

Then Woman Chief spoke. "Chief Yellow Belly's concern for the heavy flooding that will come is correct. The Musselshell, Elk and Big Muddy will surely flood entire valleys and remain flooded for many suns. I, myself, have seen it happen before. Because the flooding will restrict the migration of the elk, antelope and buffalo, the Pecunis will be marauding the countryside in search of game. They too have suffered a harsh winter."

After taking notice of the nodding heads around her, she continued. "I say we should go up to the big fork of the Powder to avoid the floods and the Pecunis. There we can meet the early return of the buffalo and rebuild our strength."

All in attendance supported Woman Chief except Big Robber and Two Face. Because of their commitment to Meldrum, these two wanted to stay near the American Fur Company trading posts. Rottentail's Thick Lodge band joined the River tribe under Yellow Belly. After a rest, all of the parties departed.

While Big Robber searched for a safe ford for his mountain tribe to cross the Elk, Yellow Belly moved the River clans easterly across the Tongue and Pumpkin to the Powder. After ascending the Powder to the mouth of the Little Powder, they established a permanent village .

By late green-grass season, the River Sparrow Hawks still had not seen many buffalo. Woman Chief volunteered to take out a scouting party to search for the bison herds. "Little Feather," she called, "bring me your young Big Dogs and we will obtain meat for our people. Black Panther, bring me my best buffalo ponies, and if you are quick, I will take you with me as my horse tender." Little Feather ran to gather his young braves, while Black Panther excitedly raced out into the pastures to gather Woman Chief's horses. As he ran, his playful wolf dogs knocked him down several times, but he kicked at the animals to let them know he couldn't play today. This time, he had important duties to fulfill.

By the time Black Panther brought in the horses, Little Feather was tying weapons and possibles onto his saddle. Woman Chief saddled Dancer while Little Wife, Sparrow and Little Blossom brought her weapons and accouterments. There was much hugging and kissing before the party of twenty finally got underway.

In addition to their mounts, each of them had two extra buffalo ponies. They would alternate their horses and in case of danger, they would ride one mount to exhaustion before abandoning the worn-out pony and quickly sliding over to the next one. In this manner, they could usually escape enemy forces.

Woman Chief led her party east; they made camps on the Box Elder and Little Muddy before turning southeast to the hills at the headwaters of the Moreau River. They established a camp on Sand Creek and hobbled their horses; they still had not seen any buffalo herds, and they found that the further east they traveled, the drier the grass and bushes. At sunrise, Woman Chief and Little Feather climbed the buttes to survey the horizon before them. Further to the east, they spotted a heavy haze over the valley of the Moreau.

"Little Feather," she said, "what can you make of the smoke out there?" Little Feather focused his sharp eyes upon the scene below, then became agitated.

"The prairie is on fire as far as I can see!" he yelled "The buffalo are sweeping before it as ants out of a broken anthill. I can see them near Castle Rock on the Owl. We must warn our camp or they will be trampled."

She said, "You must quickly take your horses and return to our village so you can warn our people; for safety, take them up to Otter Creek. I will follow the herd to determine its destination."

After quickly descending the rock formation, they raced back to camp. Little Feather grabbed his horses and departed in a cloud of dust, while Woman Chief spoke to her gathered party. "Hunters," she gasped, "mount your ponies and ride as high up the hill as you can. We are in the path of a buffalo stampede, and we will be crushed unless we can get to high ground."

Woman Chief grabbed Black Panther and her horses, then fled up a ridge. The ground began to shake and the smoky air became even thicker, with the dust created by a million thundering hooves. When they topped the ridge, they turned to watch leaping antelope and deer, then herds of racing elk, mingled with a sea of large black and brown buffalo. It appeared to Woman Chief that she could walk across their backs to the horizon without ever touching the ground.

By sundown, the vibrating ground began to settle down. The bison left behind were calves, old bulls, and those crippled or injured. Large packs of gray wolves snapped at the weakened animal's nostrils and hamstrings. A large section of the fire headed for the river, where it put itself out.

The hunting party camped on their high perch; by morning it began to rain. The drizzle cleared the air and settled the dust, but it also turned the prairie to mud. The remaining fire was reduced to smoldering clumps of timber in coulees and creek bottoms. After the rains subsided, Woman Chief gathered her party.

"From this day forward," she announced, "we will call these hills Crow Heart Buttes in order to remember this event."

Woman Chief led her drenched hunters down from their newly crowned landmark. Once down everyone began butchering and skinning the animals killed in the stampede. On the second day they packed all the meat and hides their animals could carry and headed back toward the Powder River junction. They passed flocks of buzzards, ravens, eagles, coyotes and wolves, all feeding on dead carcasses. Each coulee contained dead or injured animals, and the injured ones still fought against the wolves for survival. Woman Chief and her braves passed by. Some of the party members watching the forces of nature unfolding before them. They accepted this fight for survival as the natural order of life as they knew it.

In the grasslands of the Little Powder they passed several grazing herds; the animals had calmed down from their run. The rains had restored some order to the prairie. The hunting party finally located Yellow Belly's village camped on the Powder.

Woman Chief called out to Yellow Belly's lodge. "Oh, Great Chief! I drove the buffalo to you, as I promised. Did you catch any, or were they too swift for your hunters?"

Yellow Belly smiled. "I was not prepared for so many at once," he responded. "I had to send a messenger to invite our poor mountain relatives to assist us in butchering them because you sent too many. Next time try to keep them away from my lodge; I can't remember when I had to move so quickly."

By the time Woman Chief and her hunters unpacked their kills, they noticed that everyone in the happy village was already busy butchering, drying meat or staking out robes for tanning. For four days everyone worked, danced, and ate roasted tongues, ribs and humps to celebrate the end of a long, hard winter.

CHAPTER 41

When the rains came again, the rivers and streams began to rise. When the Powder overflowed its banks, Yellow Belly began to worry about the Mountain tribespeople who followed after Big Robber. The messengers he had sent out had not returned, and if Big Robber was trapped north of the Elk River, they might have trouble getting fresh meat. They would also be vulnerable to attacks by the starving Pecunis or Atsina; if they could get to the Assiniboine, they would have allies.

Woman Chief felt rested again and volunteered to lead a hundred warriors to extricate Big Robber from his precarious position. She told Yellow Belly, "I will take pack ponies to carry fresh meat to our people. If I can cross at Fort Alexander or Fort Sarpy, I will; if not, I may have to go to Fort Union. Where will I find your village upon my return?"

Yellow Belly pointed west. "You will find us on the Tongue. May the Great Spirit guide and protect you, but keep a close lookout for the Pecunis."

Woman Chief led her warriors due west, past Pyramid Butte. They then headed northwest to Deer Creek and followed it to the Rosebud, descending its west bank to its mouth. The Elk was swollen in all directions, and it was no use trying to cross at Fort Alexander. She started up the Elk, and at the Bighorn she decided to take only ten men. They swam their horses across the stream, while the remainder of the party made camp and waited for her word.

Woman Chief and ten young men continued on up the Elk, looking for some sign across the swollen stream of the Mountain Sparrow Hawks. When the sun reached its zenith, the small party reached Pompey's Pillar. While the men made a campfire, Woman Chief and Little Feather climbed the rock formation in order to search the countryside. They found strange marks carved into the side of the rock. These marks actually spelled out, W-I-L-L-I-A-M C-L-A-R-K J-U-L-Y 25, 1806, but neither of them had any idea what the etchings meant.

Straining her eyes across the water, Woman Chief spied smoke in the distance. "Little Feather," she said, "can you see who they are?"

Shading his sharp eyes, he studied the distant camp for several breaths before answering. "They are the lodges of the Whistling Water clan. Some are waving our way."

"Sign them, with your tunic," she ordered. "Tell them to travel east until they can find a crossing over the Elk. Tell them we will follow the river with them. Tell them we have meat, robes and skins to share." Little Feather waved back and forth until they responded that they understood. Then they allowed a small cloud of white smoke to rise to indicate that all was well.

After she and Little Feather descended the tower and returned to camp, they ate their fill of hump meat and turned into their robes early.

At dawn Woman Chief retraced her path to the Bighorn before stopping to camp for the evening. Gazing at their relatives' campfires glowing across the churning water, they went to sleep under a sky of stars and a full moon. Awaking early, she aroused her warriors, who swam with their horses back across the Bighorn, eager to report the good news to her main rescue party. They had made contact with their lost relatives.

The entire body of braves then packed their supplies, gathered their horses, and headed east, down the flooded valley of the Elk. They rode slowly, trying not to lose contact with Big Robber's scouts across the river. They forded Tulloch Creek and spent the night on Sarpy Creek before finally reaching the bluffs above the Rosebud. Here, they again sent smoke signals, and after receiving acknowledgment, moved on to ford the Rosebud.

It took two suns to reach the Tongue. After they crossed the river they built signal fires on the bluffs. Distant responses indicated that they were still in contact with Big Robber's band across the Elk. Two suns later they forded the Powder and camped on a high bluff. They had to wait one sleep before could renew contact with the Whistling Water scouts.

Woman Chief then led them across the O'Fallon and toward the Elk. When they arrived at the old earthen lodges of their ancestors, they established a camp to wait for a signal from Big Robber. Periodically they sent up a series of smokes to attract the Whistling Water scouts. Since they could also attract Cheyenne or Sioux, Woman Chief sent out wolf scouts to keep a sharp lookout for enemy warriors.

While Woman Chief waited, she wandered around the old ruins. These lodges appeared to be similar to those of the Mandan and the Sparrow Hawk relatives, the Hidatsa. She had heard Chief Long Hair say that the ancient Sparrow Hawk people once lived in those lodges and were farmers and hunters. She could not understand anyone choosing to be cooped up in an earthen lodge instead of being free to travel and live all over Absaroka. She liked corn, pumpkins and beans, but for her they could never replace elk, deer, sheep and buffalo.

At last Little Feather detected Big Robber's smoke signals. Woman Chief told him, "Signal the Whistling Waters to go on and meet us at Fort Union. Tell them they will not be able to cross the Elk until the spring floods have subsided."

As they traveled downstream, they rode past more of the buffalo that had been turned back by the swollen stream. Periodically, they saw the bloating carcass of an animal that had been pushed into the stream and drowned in the swift currents. Crows, ravens, coyotes and wolves were feasting on the carrion as it piled up in logjams and got caught on brush along the shoreline. The voracious animals hardly paid notice to Woman Chief's posse as they rode along the bluff overlooking the river.

When they neared the Big Muddy, Woman Chief gave new directions to her hunters. "Fill your pack animals with buffalo meat and robes so we can take fresh food, lodges and clothing to Big Robber's people when they arrive at Fort Union."

While they busied themselves butchering the meat and curing staked-down hides, Woman Chief had large signal fires built at the fort to attract attention. They signaled to one large group of warriors, but they moved on up stream without declaring themselves.

After three sleeps, a large wooden boat approached the shore from upriver. When they neared, Denig yelled, "I heard you were over here. I thought you Crow knew how to swim." When his boat reached the bank, he tossed the bowline to the waiting braves and jumped ashore.

"How did you know we were here," Woman Chief queried?

"My brother-in-law, First-to-Fly, and his Rock band of Assiniboines saw your signal fires and reported them to me," he answered. "However, I did not know for sure until I assisted Big Robber's bands across the Missouri. It took us two days to ferry his people across, and they sure were a sorry-looking lot. I was low on food myself, and now they have eaten everything I have. If it hadn't been for the Assiniboine, we would have all starved."

"We have plenty of food and robes," Woman Chief offered, "but we need your help transporting them to your post."

"Leave your warriors here in camp and load all the meat and robes you can spare," he replied. "You can go with me to deliver them to your Sparrow Hawks and the Assiniboine. If you can spare me some, I will allow you credit for any trade goods you need. Also, I hate to hurry you, but your people are camped near the Assiniboine. If we don't hurry back with food, they may kill and eat each other. You know that First-to-Fly and Big Robber hate each other."

Woman Chief and her men loaded the large flat-bottomed bateau, then boarded it with Denig and his French voyageurs.

"Little Feather," she said, "take charge of the camp until I return. Keep a sharp lookout for the Sioux and Cheyenne dog soldiers. Keep a fresh supply of meat in camp at all times in case we have to send the white man's boat for more. We will send up white smoke from across the water each day to indicate that everything is fine. If we send up black smoke, prepare for battle, and if you see two columns of black smoke, try to come to our assistance at once."

Denig and his men shoved the bateau into the current and began the long struggle of trying to cross the swollen Missouri, traveling the best way they knew how to get the goods upstream to Fort Union.

While his men struggled with their oars and tried to set a sail, Denig turned to Woman Chief. "I have talked to First-to-Fly and he wants to make peace with the Crow. You both have too many enemies to continue warring against each other. Since you are a reasonable and intelligent person, do you think you could get Big Robber and Yellow Belly to smoke the pipe of peace with the Assiniboine?"

She looked at the swollen river covered with floating logs and debris. "Life is like the muddy water," she said. "You can see the whirlpools and eddies but their cause seems to be a mystery." She did not care much for the Assiniboine, and she did not understand Denig's motives, but she liked and trusted her friend. If he wanted peace, then she would try to accomplish it.

She had to admit that Denig's words made sense. If First-to-Fly was indeed sincere, then his warriors would honor his pledge. Her biggest concern was Big Robber. Not only was he bellicose, but he resented any advice or suggestion she ever made. Besides being heavily influenced by Meldrum, he was jealous of Chief Yellow Belly's popularity. She knew that if she smoked the pipe of peace, Yellow Belly would honor her word, but she would have to deal with Big Robber and Two Face.

She finally turned toward Denig. "My friend, I will agree to peace with First-to-Fly, but if you wish to get a commitment from Big Robber and Two Face, you must first get Meldrum to agree."

Denig smiled and responded, "I know the River Crow don't like him, but Robert Meldrum works for me and the American Fur Company. He will do as I say, or I will run him out of this country."

Slowly the boatmen made their way upstream to Fort Union. As they approached, Two Face and his men stood at the shoreline to meet the boat. They caught the tossed lines and tied the laden craft to wooden stakes that had been driven into the soft earth.

Uncharacteristically, Two Face called out. "Welcome my sister. Once again you have come to the aid of your poor Mountain relatives. We have had a difficult time and have eaten nothing but plums and black cherries for many suns. We are in need of buffalo tongues and backfat to nourish our weak bodies. Please come to our humble council, so we can honor you for succoring us."

As Two Face took charge of hauling the food and robes back to his camp, Woman Chief turned to Denig. "Take my trade robes and whatever meat you need to your post," she said, "and you can set up a credit account for me. However, while I am in council with Two Face and Big Robber, you must talk with Meldrum. If Big Robber proposes peace, I will support him, but I cannot make the offer myself or he will reject it." She then turned and followed Two Face.

As she entered the council-lodge, Big Robber rose and motioned Woman Chief to sit at his left arm, while Two Face took the place at his right arm. Big Robber passed the pipe to her. After she took four sacred puffs, she passed it on to the left. The pipe was passed around the circle and finally back to Two Face, who sat to the right of Big Robber.

After smoking, Two Face spoke. "Woman Chief found us at the lookout tower and stayed with us all the way to Fort Union. She has brought us meat and robes for our worn-out bodies, and she has set up trade credits so we may replenish our depleted and lost supplies. I propose that we honor her by making her a voting member of our council, and that old Good Herald ride throughout the village and tell everyone of her many deeds."

Everyone nodded and grunted their approval as Big Robber studied the matter. Finally, he agreed. "Send out Good Herald to spread the greatness of Woman Chief to our people," he said. Everyone present seemed pleased with his decision. "Now we must make our plans for crossing the Big Muddy and returning to Absaroka and our hunting grounds," he continued. "The food we have will not last long, and we are in danger from the Assiniboine, Pecunis and Atsina. We are still in enemy territory."

At that moment, Meldrum entered the council lodge. Two Face moved over to allow Meldrum to sit next to Big Robber. Meldrum said, "My friends, I have just returned from the camp of First-to-Fly and Foolish Bear of the Assiniboine. They have proposed peace with the Sparrow Hawk Nation. They are still at war with the Blackfeet and Atsina, and they wish to have the Sparrow Hawks as allies. I urge this council to accept this offer of peace so we might strengthen our control along the Yellowstone and at the Fort Union crossing of the Missouri."

Though his announcement of support for the treaty surprised Woman Chief, she kept quiet. "Earlier in the green-grass season," he continued, "Frances Chardon and Alexander Harvey participated in the killing of many Blackfeet at Fort McKenzie. They had to burn the post and flee for their lives. Denig is now afraid that the Blackfeet will retaliate against Fort Union. The white men and the Sparrow Hawks now have a common enemy, and we all need an alliance with the Assiniboine."

Now Woman Chief understood some of Denig's motives in wanting to unite the Sparrow Hawks with the Assiniboines. He needed a buffer against the Pecunis and Atsina. Big Robber wished to stay in the good graces of Meldrum and Denig because they always allowed him credit at their forts. However, Big Robber was unhappy with Meldrum for getting him stranded on the north side of the Elk, and causing him to lose face. What was worse, he had to depend on a woman warrior for his rescue. After consideration, he decided to place the burden of peace, with First To Fly and Foolish Bear, on the shoulders of Woman Chief. If anything went wrong, she would be blamed instead of him.

"I will put the issue of peace in the hands of our honored councilor, Woman Chief," he finally stated. "If she and Yellow Belly will accept a treaty with the Assiniboine, then Two Face and I will honor it."

Everyone turned to Woman Chief for her reaction. "Thank you Great Chief," she responded. "We are a small tribe and we have many enemies. The Cheyenne and the Sioux are crowding into our hunting grounds on the Powder Valley. The Arapaho, Cheyenne and Utes have already taken over the Sweetwater and the Platte Valleys. The Snakes and the Bannocks have crowded into the Wind River Valley, and the Atsina and the Pecunis have pushed us from the valley of the Musselshell. We need the Assiniboine as allies, to hold back the Sioux and the Atsina, and to keep our trails to Fort Union open. I say we smoke the pipe of peace with the Assiniboine." Every councilor grunted in agreement with the wise words of Woman Chief. She often spoke with intelligence and experience that exceeded their own. Even though she was a woman, she was a wise warrior chief.

Big Robber tried to regain control of the council. "Meldrum, go and announce to the Assiniboine that we will smoke with them this day. Invite them to a peace feast and tell them we wish to give them many horses to show our friendship."

Meldrum's report delighted Denig, and he dashed into his stores for coffee, honey, molasses, corn, and pumpkins to add to the festivities. However, he locked the door to the cellar holding his whiskey and rum. After the massacre at Fort McKenzie, he did not want to take any more chances of an all-out war among drunk savages.

After four days of dancing, drum beating and singing, everyone was worn out. The Assiniboine said good-bye to their friends then they headed back toward the White Earth River and Souris River. It took the Sparrow Hawks four days to ferry their baggage and swim their horses across the subsiding river. Even though the water had gone down a great deal, they still lost several colts and mares as the animals panicked amid stream and tried to swim with the strong currents.

They found Little Feather and his hunters still waiting with fresh meat, new robes and lodgeskins. They feasted on humps and tongues for several days. They rested to regain their strength and searched for lost animals and baggage. For the first time in many seasons, the River clans and Mountain clans held warm feelings for each other.

CHAPTER 42

As the leaf-falling season approached, Woman Chief's Greasy Mouth Clan joined with Two Face's Piegan band to ascend the Powder River to its sources. They proceeded up South Fork and crossed over the hills to the sources of the Badwater. After following it to its mouth, they reached the Wind River, where they followed it southwest to the mouth of the Popo Agie.

They located a large village with many columns of smoke rising into the air above the valley. Two Face grew suspicious, but Woman Chief recognized the lodges of Washakie's Snake tribe. She rode forward to the village as dogs and children raced about in great excitement.

Woman Chief found Washakie talking with her old friend, Bill Williams. "Aiee! Scar Face. Aiee! Broken Arm," she called out. "It seems that each time the mountains freeze, you two seek my lodgefire. Be careful that you do not seek my robes. I sleep with one of Blanket Chief's beaver traps for protection."

Washakie and Williams both laughed at the painful thought of catching their manhood in a steel trap. "Welcome to my village dear old friend," Washakie said. "However, remind me to never invite you to sleep in my lodge."

They were all laughing as Two Face approached. Since he did not speak Shoshone, he did not understand their joke. Woman Chief introduced him. "Two Face, this is Chief Washakie of the Snakes and Broken Arm Williams, a free trapper. They are old friends of mine."

To Washakie she said, "Two Face is chief of the Piegan clan. Since these are the lands of his Mountain Sparrow Hawk, you should get to know each other. Two Face is allied with Chief Big Robber of the Whistling Water clan."

The three men nodded at each other and grunted. They were all self-important, strong and tall, but Washakie was more sociable and practical than the other two. However, he was older than Two Face and felt the younger man should show him more respect and follow proper protocol. Two Face had heard much of the famous Snake warrior and eyed him with envy. It also angered him that the Snakes were openly wintering in Absaroka without the approval of the Sparrow Hawks. He was polite, but cool, and excused himself to attend to his Piegan Clan.

Woman Chief stayed to visit with Williams and Washakie. Bill told them about his horse raids in California and about his visits to Fort Davey Crockett, Fort Hall and Bridger's Fort.

"Ole Gabe, he just left with thirty men fer Californi," he said. "I told him to watch out for them Meskin alcaldes. They'd as leave hold you for ransom as not, or ship you down to Mexican City. I had me several narrow escapes whilst I wuz out there tradin fer horses. When me and ole Peg Leg Smith hit that desert, we drove

190

them horses 'til they pert nigh dropped from thirst. Meskins shore don't like that desert and they liked our Hawkens even less. Har! Har!"

When Woman Chief finally returned to camp, she found an agitated Two Face. When she approached him, he spat out, "How dare the Snakes be so bold?" he yelled. "They act as if this land is theirs. Our fathers' fathers fought to keep this valley from our enemies. First the white men take our beaver and our game, and now the Snakes move in like they are our relatives. My father was killed by the Snakes, and I cannot stand to be among them."

Woman Chief tried to calm him. "Let me make my excuses and I will go with you," she responded. We can winter our bands at the Bighorn Hot Springs." Two Face scowled, but nodded in agreement, as Woman Chief left to inform Washakie that they were leaving.

But Bill Williams wanted to go with her. "Do you mind if me and my wife trail along with you?" he asked. "I can't stand her dadburn relatives and I know I'm gonna have some trouble. They done spent all my credit at Fort Hall and I need to get away from them rascals."

Woman Chief smiled as she answered, "Broken Arm is always welcome among the Sparrow Hawks." In a short time her Greasy Mouths were all packed and moving down the Wind River.

They spent one night on the Muskrat and another at the entrance to Wind River Canyon. Snow flurries began to fall as they entered the steep walls of the canyon. The trail was narrow and slow, but the rapid water and the high walls made a serene and very protective setting for their travel.

Woman Chief always felt secure from her enemies when she entered this canyon. She imagined that if she had enough warriors at each entrance, she could hold out against the entire world as she knew it. All they would need would be buffalo for food and sweet grass for the horses.

Winter at the hot springs proved much milder than previous winters. Hunting was good in the basin and Pecunis had not been seen for two seasons. As the river ice broke up and the initial floods subsided, Woman Chief and Two Face prepared their bands to join up with their relatives on the Horses River.

At last Williams packed his family to leave. "Well, Little Gal, I thankee fer yore hospitality," he told Woman Chief. "I'm a gonna head out toward Fort Laramie cuz I still don't wanna see Little Lamb's damned relatives. Her brothers take every horse I can steal, and I can't get no profit thataway. I'll be seein yee if'n the Utes or Blackfeet don't git me first."

"Good hunting, Broken Arm," she said. "Keep your eye on the horizon, your nose to the wind, your powder dry and I hope to see you again soon." Though she didn't look back as she hurried to catch up with her people, she nevertheless had a strange feeling she would never see Broken Arm again.

After the Sparrow Hawks reunited at the Horses River, they held four days of rejoicing and calling each other bawdy names. Fights, threats, wife-stealing and horse-swapping episodes abounded until everyone settled down to village life. Because elk, antelope, sheep and buffalo were abundant at this time, no one had to leave the valley for anything.

During the brown-grass season Yellow Belly wanted to take his Kicked-in-Their-Bellies band up the Elk River. Woman Chief approached him to say, "Chief, my people are sad, and they want to follow their relatives to the hot springs of the Elk."

Yellow Belly seemed pleased but yet aloof. "Woman Chief, you and the Greasy Mouths are welcome to come with us, but if you ever come to my lodge to see Doe Eyes, I cannot speak to you because you are my mother-in-law. You know that is tradition."

Woman Chief nodded. "I will follow our customs, my Chief," she said, and then she left to inform her band of the good news. Yellow Belly led the bands down the Horses River to the Elk before turning upstream toward the Shining Mountains. They traveled at a leisurely pace, crossing Clark's Fork, the Stillwater and finally reaching the prairie dog town. There were thousands of scurrying little animals all barking at the intrusion. Woman Chief always laughed at them when she was a young girl, she would watch them for hours at a time.

But now she had too many responsibilities to watch for long, responsibilities such as providing the rear guard and trying to keep her Greasy Mouths from lagging too far behind.

After spending a night on the Boulder River, the large party moved on up the Elk. As the group rode slowly up a draw, Little Feather raced up and called, "Mother, come quickly. There are many Pecunis at the mouth of the Shields, and Chief Yellow Belly will not back down from their challenge."

Woman Chief checked her weapons and mounted her favorite war horse, Thunderhead, in order to race after Little Feather. When they rode up they found Yellow Belly arguing with Tall Elk, a head chief of the Flatheads. The Sparrow Hawks had traded with his people for years and considered the Flatheads to be allies. She couldn't imagine why Yellow Belly was so angry, but he and his men appeared ready for war.

As Thunderhead slid to a stop, Woman Chief jumped out of her saddle and approached Yellow Belly. "What is it, my brother?" she asked breathlessly. Yellow Belly stared at Tall Elk but pointed across to the mouth of the Shields.

"Over there," he said, "is a camp of Pecunis with two black-robed white men. I know the Pecuni chief, Running Eagle; she was present when my brother, Rotten Belly, was killed. Now the black robes have ordered the Pierced Noses and Flatheads to defend the Pecunis."

Woman Chief knew the two religious men as Father de Smet and Father Point. She still did not like them, and now, not only were they siding with their old enemies, but they were turning their allies against them as well. The Pecuni camp was small, but the Pierced Noses and Flatheads outnumbered the Sparrow Hawks by more than two to one. Then she saw the female warrior called Running Eagle. Although she had never met or fought against her Pecuni counterpart, she had heard a great deal about the woman's prowess as a warrior.

"This is not a good day to die, my brother," she told Yellow Belly. "Let us move on to the hot springs and we will choose another day when the Pecunis are not so well protected." Yellow Belly ignored her pleas. With a crazed look on his face he lifted his gun and charged across the Elk, singing his death song. His warriors blindly followed their chief as Woman Chief quickly mounted Thunderhead to lead the women, children and older Sparrow Hawks to safety.

As bullets flew in every direction and the sounds of battle rapidly increased, she led the main body of Sparrow Hawks back to a wooded area, where they began building fortifications of logs and brush. She set up a line of defense with her own warriors and waited; though she prayed for the survival of Yellow Belly and his braves, she was angered by his foolishness in deciding to charge into such a superior force. After the gunfire subsided, all she could do was wait until Little Feather's sharp eyes detected movement.

"They come! They come!" he yelled. "Our warriors are returning."

"Hold your fire and positions until we can see if they are being pursued," she warned. Slowly the wounded and dying soldiers began to arrive, some falling from their mounts before they could reach the newly constructed fort. Some young men began running to retrieve their fallen comrades, but Woman Chief urged her warriors to stay put. "Quickly, retake your defensive positions," she yelled. As she suspected, Pecunis and Pierced Noses soon came into view; it seemed they were everywhere. Woman Chief was thankful that at least the Flatheads had remained neutral. "Take your time," she ordered, "and fire in lines while the next line reloads. Fight as Medicine Calf taught us."

When the enemy came within fifty horse strides of the fort, she yelled, "Greasy Mouths, fire!" Fifty rifles cracked almost in unison, and Pecunis and Pierced Nose warriors and horses went down in clouds of dust. Then she yelled, "Kicked-in-Their-Bellies, fire!" and twenty-five more rifles spewed lead and smoke as more soldiers and horses fell like a herd of buffalo falling over a buffalo jump. The superior attacking force fled in retreat from the deadly fire, as hundreds of arrows and volleys of bullets filled the air, until they were out of reach. When all was clear, young braves and women raced onto the battlefield to kill, rob and scalp the enemy warriors in bloody revenge.

Woman Chief began to taking a head count of her surviving forces. She had lost Chief Yellow Belly and twenty-seven of his finest men. Ten warriors had been severely wounded and had to be placed on litters, while another fifteen had sustained minor wounds. In spite of her protests, many women cut off joints of their fingers and scarred themselves in mourning. The crying and wailing began to unsettle her, but even worse, the group had no time to mourn their fallen chief because they were still in serious danger.

Reluctantly she directed Little Feather, "Take the point and lead our people back to the Horses River. I will guard our retreat. Move quickly!" The quicker they put distance between themselves and the Pecunis, the better.

CHAPTER 43

When Woman Chief noticed Bull's Horn had a red blanket lying across his saddle, she asked, "Where did you get the trade robe?"

He proudly responded, "I took it from the Pecuni woman warrior who shot Yellow Belly. Before she could reload, I counted coup and pulled her gun and blanket from her, but as I rode away, she reloaded and shot me in the shoulder. I will keep her blanket as my secret medicine power."

Woman Chief took his lead rope and led his horse down the trail. As they traveled, she repeatedly looked over her shoulder watch for any returning enemy forces. When the Sparrow Hawks reached the mouth of Rock Creek, she decided to stop the group until the wounded could be stabilized. They had already lost two more warriors due to their deep wounds and the people were exhausted. Since she felt they should be safe by now, she sent out hunters to obtain fresh meat.

They camped for ten sleeps, long enough for most of the wounded to recover except for Bull's Horn. He had seemed fine, but now he was feverish and small blisters covered his face and neck. Woman Chief knew about these signs from Deer Little Woman's description of Denig, who had these symptoms when he suffered from the white man's pox. She wondered how Bull's Horn could have contacted the pox when no one else in their camp was ill from the disease. Then she remembered the Pecuni red blanket and remembered that the Pecunis had suffered terribly from smallpox for several seasons.

She queried Bull's Horn. "Who have you touched since the battle?"

Struggling against delirium, he named nine people to whom he had shown his trophy blanket. Woman Chief rounded up all of the people he named and gave them the bad news. "You have been exposed to the white man's pox by the Pecuni blanket. We cannot take you with us until you are well. You must leave with your families and go to the rock cave until you have recovered. We will set up camp and wait for you for fifteen sleeps. This will allow the illness to run its course while we will remain near to protect you and send you food."

Woman Chief sent fifty exposed Sparrow Hawks upstream to wait out the painful and frightening ordeal. Her hunters kept them in camp meat, but made no attempt to come in contact with them. When she found five more of her people suffering from fevers and nausea, she quickly sent them upstream to join those already in quarantine.

Meanwhile, she named the survivors of Yellow Belly's clan *Bad War Honors*, in his memory. Yellow Bell had died in battle like his brother, Rotten Belly, by leading a mad charge against superior forces of Pecunis. Once more she would follow custom and adopt Doe Eyes and her children into her lodge.

After fifteen sleeps, a few scarred Sparrow Hawk survivors began returning to the main camp from their isolation camp to the south. They told horrible tales of mutilations, suicides and painful deaths of loved ones. Only twelve of the fifty-five survived. Bull's Horn was buried with his famous red trophy blanket.

The disease took a heavy toll from the Bad War Honors clan, so Woman Chief adopted the remaining members into her Greasy Mouth band. The village dried meat in preparation of their return to the Horses River. Woman Chief vowed to seek revenge against the Pecunis, for the life of Yellow Belly, and for giving the pox to her people.

As the survivors of the Battle of Elk River dragged back to the heart of Absaroka in mourning, Woman Chief calmed her sorrow by chewing her favorite sedative, tobacco root. When they reached the Horses River, she rode up Porcupine Creek to the Medicine Wheel to pray.

Big Robber, also known as Big Shadow, became the head chief of the Sparrow Hawk Nation. Because Woman Chief had few relatives, she could never become a head chief. Although Big Robber exhibited strong leadership in most areas, he was still heavily influenced by Robert Meldrum. Bear's Head, Rottentail and Woman Chief became more independent of the main body, while Two Face remained loyal to Big Robber.

After a moderate snow-falling season, the Sparrow Hawks moved into the Greasy Grass Valley. The hills were covered in antelope, elk, and buffalo. Occasionally, they still found a case of smallpox and when they did, the ill person was quickly removed from the village; many times he or she was never seen again.

Woman Chief continued to brood over the death of Yellow Belly. Besides being angry with the Flatheads and Pierced Noses for defending the Pecunis, she was also angry at the black-robed white men for their interference in the affair. She resented the implication that the white man's great spirit was more powerful than the Great Spirit of the Sparrow Hawks. She knew that Yellow Belly had just been stubborn, proud and foolish in his charge against superior forces. She vowed to never be so foolish, and to always wait until she had warrior superiority before attacking her enemies.

Woman Chief finally sent out scouting wolves to try to locate the Small Robes band of the Piegans, while she rode up the east fork of the Greasy Grass to the plains of the Tongue. When she found the spiritual rock column where her brother, Cracked-Ice, was buried, she camped and prayed for four sleeps. She faced the fact that she was getting older and Yellow Belly's revenge would probably be her last battle. Perhaps she should retire and become a shaman, or just remain a councilor and advisor to her people. She no longer desired to be a civil chief, and she was getting too old to lead war parties.

On the fourth day the sound of a horse approaching at great speed interrupted Woman Chief's meditation. She grabbed her rifle and stood behind her medicine rock. Because she had difficulty seeing anything in the distance, the rider was already within rifle shot before she recognized her adopted son, Little Feather.

As he glided off his lathered, snorting horse, he announced, "Mother, we have found the Pecuni camp! We have found Running Eagle and her Small Robes!"

Woman Chief soared out of her depression. She seemed to gain ten seasons of youth. "Where are they, my son?" she asked. "Where are they?"

As Little Feather fought to regain his breath, he calmed his exhausted pony. "She is on what the white men call the Sacagawea River. Her group has forty-five lodges."

Woman Chief stared at what she could see of the horizon, and envisaged the total destruction of the Small Robes, in atonement for the death of Yellow Belly. She broke her small camp, saddled her horse and hurried back to her village on the Greasy Grass. She had to leave Little Feather behind until his horse could recover sufficiently to follow.

As the Sparrow Hawk council smoked, Woman Chief spoke. "Chief Big Robber, allow me to take two hundred brave men and I will avenge the death of Yellow Belly and our people, who died at the hands of the Pecuni. My medicine is strong and my dream is true. The Small Robes are led by the woman war chief, Running Eagle. If any of you defeat her, it will be said that she was only a woman. If I defeat her, it will be called a great Sparrow Hawk victory. I have spoken."

Each councilor grunted in agreement with Woman Chief's words. Big Robber studied the matter and also saw that she was correct. He certainly did not want to take the chance of being defeated by a woman, who had already killed their famed chief, Yellow Belly.

Then Meldrum spoke up. "Chief, do not attack the Piegans or their entire nation will invade Absaroka. Woman Chief has been a fine warrior, but she is getting too old. She may lose all of your young men in battle. Also, this retaliation will anger the white traders at Fort Union."

Woman Chief rose to respond. "If I lose this battle, I pledge to die at the hands of the Pecunis. I have a battle plan and I do not act foolishly. My defenses on the Elk River saved the rest of our people from superior enemy forces. If Meldrum is a braver and better warrior than I, let him lead our revenge party. Denig is my friend, and he understands that we must avenge the death of our beloved chief, and he will support me."

She looked around at her audience before continuing, "I can remember when Meldrum used to be brave and fight by our side. He fought with Medicine Calf, Yellow Belly and I at the Pecuni rock fortress many seasons ago and we had one of our greatest victories. Perhaps it is Meldrum who is getting too old."

The white trader turned red-faced and clammed up in anger, as the councilors grunted in agreement, with Woman Chief's eloquent words.

Then it was Big Robber's turn to rise. "It is so. We must seek revenge and teach the Pecunis that they cannot attack us on our own lands without suffering severe consequences. If we do not retaliate, they will take Absaroka from us. Woman Chief is correct, in stating that only she can claim full war honors against the Pecuni devil-woman. Go my sister, gather your braves." Woman Chief rose and exited the lodge before Big Robber could reconsider. She knew she must pick only the best two hundred men available and went immediately to seek Little Feather.

"My son," she began, "you have been a loyal soldier, you are brave, quick and have the eyes of an eagle. However, you were born a Pecuni, and I captured you and adopted you when you were a young boy. Can you go into battle against your old relatives? I have had to fight my White Clay people many times, but I never stopped to consider if I was fighting friends or relatives."

Little Feather gazed into her eyes before answering. "Mother, I am a Sparrow Hawk and I am your son. I no longer belong to the Pecunis, and I wish to avenge the death of Yellow Belly. I will follow you with forty of my best Big Dog soldiers."

Woman Chief hugged him, as she gushed, "Thank you, my son. I want you to be by my side, to be my eyes. Get your men ready."

She then selected over sixty warriors from the Greasy Mouths and what was left of the Bad War Honors. Rottentail and Bear's Head came forward with fifty warriors each from their bands. Two Face and Big Robber declined to participate, because they were needed to guard the village in case of a counterattack.

Woman Chief led her army west across the Bighorn, and by the second sun, the group had reached the Horses River, which they followed to its mouth before crossing the Elk. They spent their third camp at Bull Mountain, and Woman Chief sent hunters ahead for fresh camp meat.

When they reached their temporary camp on the Musselshell, roasted fat buffalo humps and buffalo tongues awaited their voracious appetites. Spirits among the group were high, revelry and singing lasted long into the night. Woman Chief laughed as she listened to the war-path secrets of the young men. They told how many times they had made love and named the girl or wife involved. After such meetings and discussions, no one was allowed to retaliate or reveal their secrets to outsiders for fear their war-medicine would be destroyed.

As a young warrior, Woman Chief had never been allowed to participate in the rite of war-path confessions. She believed many of the young braves used the ceremony as a forum to vent their fantasies and to exaggerate about their exploits, for if all the stories told were true, every man in camp was sleeping with every woman.

She herself still had no secrets to confess, since she had only slept with Medicine Calf, and even then, only after they were married. She wanted this to be her last battle; in truth, she no longer found participating in these raids rewarding. Battles and raids seemed more like duty now; for her, they carried a great deal of responsibility and pressure. She wanted to chew some tobacco root this evening, but she would have to wait until after the battle. Success required a clear mind.

The next day she moved her large group due north across the North Willow and the Flat Willow to War Horse Lake, then on to Box Elder Creek. Here they ascended to the creek's elbow curve and stopped long enough to prepare for war. The Sparrow Hawks made sweat lodges, drank great quantities of water, and fasted in preparation for battle. They checked their weapons, stripped to their breechcloths, and mounted their best war-horses.

As the moon rose high in the shimmering sky, she led her men north across the headwater of the Sacagawea, descending along its north shore. She sent out scouts to keep the enemy under observation, while she and her large party moved slowly and quietly down river, hoping they would not be detected. Before dawn her wolf scouts returned and reported, "We have found the Pecuni village. It is unguarded, a short ride below the bend of the river."

Woman Chief called her chiefs into council. "Little Feather will take his band and cross the river, cutting off any avenue of escape. Bear's Head, you will attack from the west. Rottentail, your men will attack from the east. I will lead the main attack from the north. The signal to begin will be four rapid rifle shots at daybreak. Now prepare your men and take your positions. We go at first light."

Each group separated as Woman Chief placed her warriors into position. She had to be very alert to prevent even the most experienced warriors from charging prematurely in their patriotic ardor.

The lodgefires sent up thin wisps of white smoke as the sky opened its eyes to a new sun. Like most of her people, Woman Chief worshipped the sun, but she could not wait for its face on this day. It would be there to illuminate her victory. As she climbed aboard Thunderhead, she signed to her followers to mount. When she was satisfied that they were ready, she signaled to four braves to fire their weapons. As the loud reports echoed across the valley, smoke and the acrid odor of gunpowder filled the air.

With a glorious roar of "Aieeee!," everyone raced down the hill toward the enemy camp. By now, panicked Pecunis ran for their weapons or ran for cover. Women and children fled across the river as men tried to form a line of defense in the middle of the village. Woman Chief believed Running Eagle had been careless in protecting her camp. The female leader had no night guards and her position seemed indefensible.

As Bear's Head and Rottentail pinched in from the west and east, the Pecunis fell back toward the riverbank. Woman Chief could hardly see through the rifle smoke as she rode right through their lines until she came to the stream. Then she whirled Thunderhead around to lead a charge back into the village, but it was all over quickly.

All that remained for the Sparrow Hawks was killing the wounded and robbing the dead. Not a male Pecuni warrior was left alive. The silence in the camp made her feel as though she'd gone deaf, and her nose burned from the odor of gunpowder and death. As she rode slowly around the camp, she counted over one hundred bodies, but she did not locate Running Eagle. She rode across the river to locate Little Feather who had captured the horses, women and children.

"Have you seen Running Eagle?" she asked him.

He consulted with some of his war leaders and after a moments he responded. "We killed a few fleeing men and even some women who resisted with weapons, but we have not seen Running Eagle. We have over one hundred fifty women and children, and we will examine them."

Woman Chief had a sick feeling in the pit of her stomach. This was one of her greatest victories, and yet she had allowed Yellow Belly's killer to escape. She thought, "How can I ever prove I am the greatest woman warrior in the Shining Mountains? Who is this woman who tries to imitate me? Running Eagle may be a fine soldier, but I do not think she is a good war chief."

After Woman Chief regrouped her warriors, she announced, "When we return to Absaroka, I will sing the praises of each of you for your victory this day. We have fifteen wounded, but we have lost no one. Today we completely destroyed the Small Robes and have chased their chief back to the Marias River. I am placing all of their women and children into the Bad War Honors band, to replace those killed in the battle of Elk River."

She paused and looked at her adopted son. Proudly she proclaimed, "Little Feather shall now be known now as Eagle Feather, and he shall be the new chief of the Bad War Honors." Little Feather, now Eagle Feather, beamed. Woman Chief continued, "Each chief will divide the captured horses and camp equipage. We will need all of the food we have confiscated just to get us back to Absaroka. Now let us paint our faces black, so all will see that we have attained a great victory this day."

The warriors fired their weapons into the air, yelled war cries and broke into victory songs. They sang as they prepared for their triumphant return.

CHAPTER 44

In 1846 Denig sent word to the Crow that their new allies, the Assiniboine, were starving. The people had been forced to start eating their dogs and horses. There were rumors that some had even eaten a few children. Big Robber sent Eagle Feather and fifty hunters to the Powder River Valley to obtain meat and hides for the Assiniboine. Sparrow Hawk women began making bags of pemmican and drying jerked meat, so their friends would have food for the snow-falling season.

As the days grew colder, Woman Chief chose to keep her Greasy Mouth band in the Bighorn Basin at the hot springs. She knew the Pecunis and Running Eagle would seek revenge and she did not want to be surprised in open country. At the hot springs she spent much of her time meditating with the spirit of Long Hair, who had been entombed just above the spring.

Trying to get in touch with his spirit, she thought, "Oh, how I miss our great leaders and comrades Yellow Belly, Rotten Belly, Medicine Calf and Five Scalps. I am also concerned about the absence of Broken Arm Williams. I fear I will never see him again. It seems that most of the people I have loved are dead."

"What is the real meaning of life," she wondered. "Why are we really here? I have lived some glorious years, but I have also suffered a great deal of sorrow. What has it all meant; what will it matter to those who follow me?"

Once again she chewed tobacco roots to help her escape the depression and mental anguish that tormented her.

As snow melted in the mountains of Absaroka, the Sparrow Hawks learned that more white wagon trains had been spotted ascending the Platte and crossing over South Pass. As they traveled, they hunted. The Sparrow Hawks found hunting to be poor south and west of the Wind River Mountains. It was also poor along the Platte River because the Cheyenne and the Sioux were also encroaching on hunting grounds claimed by the Sparrow Hawks. Sadly, Powder River Valley had become a battle ground between the Cheyenne, Sioux, Crow, Blackfeet, Shoshone and Bannocks.

Woman Chief learned that Broken Hand Fitzpatrick had been appointed Indian Agent for the Platte and Arkansas River areas and was trying to reach peace among the tribes of the plains. She thought that she could talk to Broken Hand, because he had always been fair and respectful to her. After all, he had just concluded a peace meeting between the Cheyenne and Comanche at Bent's Fort. She believed he could stop the warring over Sparrow Hawk hunting grounds.

She and Eagle Feather moved the Greasy Mouths and Bad War Honors up to Seedskadee Creek on the Sweetwater. In the distance, they saw wagon after wagon of white pioneers heading for South Pass. Soon Eagle Feather and two scouts rode their lathered horses into camp from Split Rock.

They called to Woman Chief, "Mother, we saw Broken Arm Williams. He and Blanket Chief Bridger are guiding the white-eyes up the river."

Woman Chief became excited. "Hunters make meat!" she called. "Bring in fat humps, tongues, mutton and elk. We will throw a feast for our old friends." She put on her finest dress and saddled her best young stallion, Dancer. She and Eagle Feather rode down the stream to greet Williams and Bridger.

"Aiee, Blanket Chief! Aiee, Broken Arm!" she called. "Welcome to my lodge."

Williams and Bridger rode up and greeted her warmly. "Damn if'n I didn't take you for an Arapaho," snorted Bridger. "I thought I was in fer a fight fer shur." Then he roared with laughter. Williams' squeaky voice chimed in, "Hell, he's gettin so blind he fell in love with a buffler cow. He couldn't even see yee till I pointed yee out to im."

Woman Chief smiled at their banter, but she did not carry the matter further. Because her own eyes were failing, she wasn't about to tease Bridger about his eyesight. Instead, she asked, "Who are these people you are guiding?"

"These here people ain't goin to Oregon or to Californi," Bridger answered. We're a'guidin em to Salt Lake Valley. They calls themselves Latter Day Saints, but we calls em Mormons, and that there feller in that fancy carriage is the high muckety-muck. He calls hisself Brigham Young. This group's got seventy-three wagons and one hundred forty-three folks. Me and old Bill is a'tryin to save ther long-haired scalps from the Cheyenne and Arapaho."

He smiled at Williams, then continued. "Even if we can get 'em all to Salt Lake, old Walkara and his Utes ain't goin' to take kindly to permanent settlers in his valley."

Williams nodded. "Yeah, Walkara is a mean sonofabitch," he said. "He still ain't forgiven me for drinkin up his fur money that time over in Taos. I can only take these folks as fer as Gabe's fort, where I'm a'holin up fer the winter."

Woman Chief invited the group to camp. "Why don't you bring your wagon train to our village for a feast of fresh meat?" she offered. "My hunters are already gathering tongues and humps for roasting."

"Hot damn!" answered Bridger. "I would dearly love to chaw on a fresh buffler tongue. I'll see if Mr. Fancy Pants and his followers will jine us." Bridger rode back to find Brigham Young, while Williams rode on to camp with Eagle Feather and Woman Chief.

"Mr. Young," Bridger drawled, "the Crow are camped just ahead yonder, and ther chiefs invited us to have a feast with 'em. Yore folks could shore use some of their fresh red meat."

Young glared out from under the wide brim of his black hat. "We will not dine with savages," he retorted. "We aim to tame this country and save their heathen souls, and we will not allow them to think they are equal to us. We will camp across the Sweetwater."

Bridger looked at the pompous leader. "Suit yerself, sir, but me and Williams is a'goin to eat hump and buffler tongue. We'll see y'all in the mornin."

Later, as they feasted, Woman Chief could see the Mormon camp across the river. She sent fresh game to their campfires but Young refused the gift. After that, she decided she did not like the black-clothed Mormons any better than the black-robed Catholic priests. She wondered why white religious leaders always dressed in black.

As they sat around the fire, Broken Arm filled her in on the latest news. "Old Charles Bent wuz kilt in Taos by Meskins last winter. We trapped them damn renegades in the mission and blew 'em all to hell. When me, St. Vrain and old Jim Beckwith got through with 'em, New Mexico was quiet as a mouse. Then ole Jim up and went to Californi." Woman Chief's heart jumped at the mention of Medicine Calf. Now that he had traveled even farther west, he would most likely never return to Absaroka.

Bridger interrupted her thoughts. "Me and old Joe Meek has got our younguns in a white man's school over at the Whitman Mission," he said. "It's on the Walla Walla River. Them kids is shore smart and they like Missus Whitman right well. I speck my wife and me will go visit 'em at Christmas time, and I'll probably see ole Meek. He's the new high sheriff of Oregon now. If'n that don't beat all I ever heared of. Har! Har! Har!"

Williams added, "Ole Caleb Greenwood and Jim Clyman is a'guidin parties to Californi now. They was with the Hastings party last summer, and last winter they led the relief party to rescue what wuz left of the Donner party. Them folks practically et each other up afore they wuz rescued. I reckon I have et about everything on this here God's earth, but I ain't never et another person. I'd as leave starve to death first. Hee! Hee!"

Woman Chief watched the skinny old man as she listened to his high-pitched cackle. She liked him, and she agreed with him about what she would and would not eat. She thought, "I have heard of lots of people eating their dogs and horses when they were starving, but the thought of eating a human makes me sick."

As the new sun began to break across the high sky, Bridger and Williams said their good-byes and rode across the river to join the Mormon caravan. Woman Chief watched them until they rode out of sight, then she returned to her civil duties. She handled complaints, affected arbitrations, sent out scouts and hunters, and began preparing her village for the snow-falling season. Life in the village continued uneventfully until one day Black Panther ran into her lodge.

"A white man comes down the river," he announced. "He is very tall and rides a big brown horse." Woman Chief quickly exited her tent flap, shielding her eyes in an attempt to recognize the rider. At last he called out to them.

"Hello, the Crow camp! I am Joe Walker, mountain man. Who is your chief?"

Rushing to greet him she yelled, "Aiee, Walker! It is I, Woman Chief. What brings such a wealthy man as you to our humble village? The last time I saw you was at the trade fair on the Popo Agie and you were rich with California horses. Have your enemies made you poor again?"

He laughed. "No, I sold them to the Army down at Bent's Fort. Right now I'm a'carryin mail to St. Louie fer the white emigrants at Bridger's Fort. But I'm agoin back to Californi after this trip and I'm gonna get me some of the most beautiful yeller horses you've ever seen. I'm gonna sell 'em to them damn fancy Mormons over at Salt Lake. They need horses and cows in the worst way possible."

They spoke a few more minutes, then Walker asked, "What are the Crow doin' here on the Sweetwater?"

She laughed. "We are watching the strange white people ride up and down our streams, trying to find the best valley. They never seem to be satisfied. In fact, they act like migrating buffalo which return every season, searching for greener grass."

Walker stayed to eat, then said his goodbyes and mounted his big bay. He rode on down the Sweetwater toward the Platte. Woman Chief watched until he rode out of her line of sight, then she returned to her lodge. Her friend's departure brought a lump to her throat. It seemed as though the people she knew and trusted were constantly leaving her life, and new, often untrustworthy ones, were showing up more often.

The more things changed, the more her anxiety grew. She relied more on meditation and tobacco roots for solace.

CHAPTER 45

When the first cold winds hit Seedskadee Creek, Woman Chief and Eagle Feather decamped their bands and crossed over the Rattlesnake Mountains to the headwaters of the Powder River. They traveled at a leisurely pace until they reached the mouth of Mizpah Creek, but no sooner had they dug in among the cottonwoods than the first heavy snowstorm hit. For days they could not tell the sun from the moon.

When the storm finally cleared, Woman Chief sent Eagle Feather and some of his young hunters to chase buffalo through the deep snow. They brought back plenty of meat, but several braves received injuries when mad bulls charged their horses, which had been struggling against the deep snow.

After the hunt, Broken Arm Williams rode in to the Sparrow Hawk camp, heading straight for Woman Chief's lodge. "Here," he said, "I brung yee some fresh American tobacci. I reckoned that yee had been frozen for so long, yee was probably out of smoke. I had to get out of thet damned stinkin fort. It was full of belchin Assiniboine and fartin Frenchies."

"Thank you Broken Arm," she said. "I am in need of tobacco and I like the white man's leaves better than ours." Carefully, she took her red-stoned calumet from its ornate sheath. She tamped the cut leaves into the pipe, firmed them with her index finger, lit the pipe with a firebrand, and slowly drew in four times. The pipe lit up and warmed her hand as its smoke filtered through her lungs before exiting her cold nostrils. She then passed the pipe to Broken Arm, who squatted cross-legged before the lodgefire. He also took only four sacred puffs, as was the custom of the Sparrow Hawks.

They talked as they continued the slow ritual of sharing their tobacco. At first the white man's smoke made Woman Chief dizzy because she had grown accustomed to her own kinnikinnick mixed with bark.

"Well," Williams said, "I seen old Joe Walker at Bridger's Fort this winter. He brung a thousand ponies back from Californi and sold most of 'em to the Mormons. Old Gabe sold the rest to the Oregon emigrants. Walker sez they done discovered gold down at Sutter's Fort, and folks has gone crazy diggin' up the whole damned countryside. Gabe had to take off fer the Walla Walla, cause them damn Cayuse done kilt Mr. and Mrs. Whitman, and even Bridger's and Meek's kids. Gabe is all tore up, and I wouldn't want to be no damned Cayuse Indian right now."

Woman Chief was saddened at hearing of the loss her friends had suffered. She responded the only way she knew how. "I have never met the Cayuse," she said, "but if I ever do, I pledge total revenge upon them for what they've done."

They sat in silence for a few moments, then Williams changed the subject. He chuckled as he said, "Them damn Mormons was attacked by grasshoppers last spring, and they wuz pert nigh eaten up. If it hadn't been fer the seagulls and the Digger Indians, they'd have lost everythin'. Hee! Hee! I think them Diggers ate more hoppers than the gulls. It were the fust time I ever seen the Diggers fattened up. Hot damn, they do love their parched bugs."

Woman Chief grimaced at the thought of eating insects. This too she had heard of, but she had not needed to use bugs for food yet, and didn't relish the thought.

When the weather cleared and the thaws began, Williams saddled his horse and squeaked, "Thankee fer allowin' me the use of yore winter lodge agin. I'm off to Taos to get me some lightnin'. I ain't had a drink of whiskey fer so long my blood's got thick, and I aim to thin it down a mite. I'll see yee next winter."

After Williams rode off toward Fort Laramie, Woman Chief directed her people to decamp.

She and Eagle Feather led their bands to a camp at Devil's Gate. From here they could easily see the continuous flood of white people's wagons, cattle and horses. Her white friends later told her that over 30,000 emigrants and 60,000 head of livestock had crossed over South Pass. Trying to envision the numbers, Woman Chief figured it must have been as many as the northern buffalo herd in the Elk River Valley.

When they tired of watching wagons, Woman Chief directed, "Let us visit our relatives on the Big Horn." They crossed over Granite Ridge and descended Wind River, where they located some Sparrow Hawks with Big Robber and Meldrum. After a short visit and some minor trading, Woman Chief and Eagle Feather moved their bands down the Wind River to the hot springs of Bighorn Basin. Since Rottentail and Bear's Head had already camped their bands at the springs, Woman Chief decided they should move on down to Shell Creek.

She always liked the Shell Creek area because of the large cottonwoods and the cool stream. In the cold season, the timber shielded their lodges from fierce storms and provided abundant firewood to keep them warm. Shell Canyon also provided a verdant pathway to the Bighorn Mountains where sheep were plentiful. Occasionally, she even caught a big brown fish, which she would bake in a fire pit until it could be easily stripped from its bones. Good as the fish was, she still preferred buffalo hump.

She and Eagle Feather maintained their camp at Shell Creek well into the snow-falling season. They had to cut a great deal of hay to feed their numerous horses. After they ran out of hay, they had to strip the sweet inner lining from cottonwood bark to feed the animals.

At last, she had to send out a hunting party. "Eagle Feather," she said, "take some hunters over Granite Pass and get some fresh meat for our larders." His men found the meadows of the Goose and Little Goose loaded with fat buffalo cows. They brought back plenty of meat and hides for their people.

The Sparrow Hawks continued to spend an uneventful snow-season and at times, when the weather cleared, they even visited the Thick Lodges and the Without-Shooting-They-Bring-Game bands on Owl Creek. Woman Chief loved bathing in the river below the hot springs. She could always find a water temperature to match her mood. She made several visits to the tomb of Long Hair. The large white flows of the mineral deposits reminded her of fields of ice, and sometimes the clouds of steam reminded her of a large earthen lodge, like the one to the east where mother earth belched smoke, fire and hot rocks.

After the mountain passes cleared, Woman Chief and Eagle Feather moved their bands up the Nowood to Ten Sleep Creek. They then crossed over Powder River Pass, and after traveling for five sleeps, arrived at Fort Laramie.

When Woman Chief recognized her old friend, Andrew Drips, she yelled, "Aiee! Drips, why are you here?"

He took her hand as she dismounted. "I am in charge of this here post," he said. "It's owned by old Pierre Chouteau's son, but he's a 'tryin to sell it to the Army. If'n he would send me and Mr. Husband some damn supplies, we could make a fortune tradin' with them emigrants."

After Woman Chief looked around the fort. "We have more goods in our lodges than you have in your fort," she said. Drips smiled at her comment, but then he turned serious.

"Gal, you got to be careful out here," he said. "The last train that came through said them Cheyenne has got cholera, and I heard old Black Harris died from it down in St. Louie." The news about Harris saddened Woman Chief. He had been a great mountain man and a true friend of the Sparrow Hawks. He would have made a great warrior.

Drips continued giving her the latest news. "Oh, by the way, I just heard that Walkara and his Utes done kilt ole Bill Williams. We hear the Mormons promoted it in order to get him and old Gabe Bridger out of their country." That news dealt such a blow to Woman Chief that she cried out loud for the first time in many seasons. Broken Arm had been a good friend, hunter, fighter and trapper. When he had just wintered with her people one year ago, she had felt a foreboding about him. Now she would never again hear his squeaky voice nor witness his quick wit and his strange sense of humor.

The news Woman Chief received at the fort saddened her then made her angry. She led her people back toward the Platte River. As they planned their trip across the river, three men approached, yelling for them to get out of the way.

"Clear the crossing!" they demanded. "Stand clear there!" The well-dressed strangers were all dressed in black. They wore wide-brimmed black hats and rode four large, good-blooded horses. As Woman Chief's ill mood grew darker, she lost her normal poise.

"Eagle Feather," she shouted, "take the horses from these dung heaps and leave them four of our worst ponies. That is the price they'll pay for their insults."

When the Mormons saw the rifles of the Crow warriors, they dismounted. Reluctantly they mounted the worn-out Crow horses and rode as fast as they could to the safety of Fort Laramie. Woman Chief smiled. Watching her warriors prance around on their new, fat mounts helped ease her frustration.

In the months that followed, her warriors told and retold the story of the time when their great chief humbled the arrogant white men. The remainder of the brown-grass season proved uneventful and the Sparrow Hawks located their winter camp at the mouth of Horses River.

Word came up the river that First-to-Fly had battled with the Atsina on Porcupine Creek above the Milk River. The Assiniboine had lost fifty-two warriors while the White Clay people had lost twenty. This news made Woman Chief angry with her old tribe and she pledged to seek vengeance upon the White Clay People as soon as their horses regained their fat and their warriors were well rested.

But as the snows began to fall again, she found old people and children becoming ill at an unusual rate. They had chills, fever, aching muscles, coughs, sore throats, headaches and total debilitation. As more of the sick people died, fear accompanied the mourning throughout Absaroka. At first, she and the Sparrow Hawk Council feared they had again contracted smallpox, but these symptoms were not like those of the pox. They tried the Bear Medicine plant, Bayberry, Elder, Squaw Tea, Sage Willow, and Tobacco Root, but the deaths continued right on through the cold season.

The endemic did not subside until the green-grass season arrived. That winter the Sparrow Hawks lost over 400 people; hardly a family remained unaffected. Woman Chief mourned as much as anyone else, for she lost her beloved Sparrow and Blossom. This had truly been a bad year in her life—she lost too many old friends and loved ones—and the wounds to her heart became heavy indeed. Reflexively, she puzzled about the meaning of life.

"What is my purpose?" she asked herself. "Why did I try so hard? Why should I continue such struggle?" As was her habit, she chewed on her tobacco roots, and then cried herself to sleep.

During the brown-grass season of 1851, the Sparrow Hawks dwelt in the Greasy Grass Valley. Big Robber and Two Face commanded the village while Woman Chief, Rottentail, Bear's Head and Eagle Feather supervised the camp police, defense and hunting activities. Woman Chief hated camp police duties, but it was her turn. The position entailed listening to a steady stream of complaints and stories of family feuds, horse thieves, wife thieves, unauthorized hunts, and unauthorized raids.

Woman Chief knew the Sparrow Hawks to be socially undisciplined; they had always been an independent and rebellious people. When Sharp Nose stole Angry Bear's horses, Woman Chief fined him all of his horses and left him afoot. He then stole Angry Bear's third wife, Goose Down. She then fined his relatives fifty horses and ordered him to return Goose Down or face banishment. Then Sharp Nose raided the Sioux for one hundred horses, paid his fine and again stole Goose Down. The frustrated Angry Bear allowed him to keep Goose Down, but required an additional twenty-five horses.

When Woman Chief ended the moon of her duties she turned the policing over to Two Face, while she went in search of her other chiefs. She found Bear's Head and Rottentail at the junction of the Tongue and the Pumpkin. As they readied to break camp, Meldrum rode in.

"Where is Big Robber's main village?" he demanded. His urgency surprised Woman Chief. "I just left them on the Greasy Grass, but they are moving to the valley of the Rosebud at the mouth of Deer Creek. What is so urgent?"

"A great peace conference is going to be held in two moons at Fort Laramie," he answered. "All of the Missouri tribes and Yellowstone tribes are sending their chiefs to sign the talking papers. We need all of our leading chiefs. I will go to Big Robber and Two Face; you, Bear's Head, Rottentail and Eagle Feather need to meet Denig at Fort Union. He will direct you from there." Meldrum hoped to keep Woman Chief and the others out of the way so he could better control Big Robber. He intended to lead the main village of the Sparrow Hawks directly to Fort Laramie as soon as possible.

When Woman Chief's party reached the mouth of the Powder, they met Eagle Feather and his braves.

"I just met a party of chiefs coming from Fort Union," he said. "They were with the black-robed white medicine man, De Smet, and the Indian Agent named Culbertson. They say they are going to Fort Laramie for a big smoke, so they can sign talking papers with Broken Hand Fitzpatrick."

Woman Chief thought on this. What Eagle Feather had discovered was similar to what Meldrum had told her, but why had he tried to send her to Fort Union? Then she realized that Meldrum was trying to get the rest of the chiefs out of the way so he could control the peace negotiations for the Sparrow Hawks. He probably did not know that Father De Smet and Agent Culbertson were bringing the chiefs from Fort Union to the treaty meeting.

She turned to her chiefs and said, "My brothers, send your hunters back to the Rosebud. We must attend this peace talk so we can speak for all of the Sparrow Hawk people. Broken Hand will listen to me, and I know Agent Culbertson also. We will wait here until they arrive."

CHAPTER 46

Early on the second sunrise, the Sparrow Hawk scouts detected a party approaching from the northeast. Woman Chief recognized Agent Culbertson riding a chestnut gelding, Robert Campbell riding in a horse-drawn carriage, and Father de Smet astride a black mule.

She still did not like the spiritual man in black robes, but he appeared to be loved by the Flatheads, Pierced Noses, Pecunis, Assiniboines, Atsina, Hidatsa and Arikara. However, she did know and respect Campbell and Culbertson. Campbell had been a mountain man and trader for many years, and she knew his word was true. As she studied the delegation of twenty-eight chiefs following the white men, she realized that she knew many of them. She had already made peace with Foolish Bear, Mad Bear, Blue Thunder and First-to-Fly of the Assiniboine.

She greeted Culbertson. "Oh, Great White Chief, we wish to travel with you to the paper talk at Fort Laramie. You know my chiefs, Bear's Head and Rottentail, but let me introduce Eagle Feather, the new chief of the Bad War Honors band."

Culbertson nodded to each of them and then turned to de Smet. "Father, this is Woman Chief of the Crow. She has been a war leader and chief among her tribe for many years, and her words can be honored. She is one of the few Indians I have ever allowed trade credit at Fort Union and Fort Cass."

He then turned back to Woman Chief. "You are welcome to travel with us to the treaty grounds. I am a commissioner, and I would like to see all of my children at peace with one another. Major Fitzpatrick and Superintendent Mitchell have ordered many trade goods and supplies to be distributed to those who sign the new treaty."

Woman Chief became defensive and responded crisply. "Chief, we are no longer children. The Sparrow Hawks do not care for foofooraw. We want peace so we can retain our hunting grounds. Absaroka is our mother earth, and we do not wish to lose her."

Culbertson realized that he had sounded patronizing. Quickly he replied, "I will assist the Sparrow Hawk Nation in any way I can."

The peace-seeking party ascended the Powder to the Salt Fork and followed it across to the big bend of the North Platte. They slowly descended the Platte for five suns. Their progress was slowed by Campbell's carriage.

When they finally arrived at Fort Laramie, they found it almost empty. Lieutenant Hastings rode out to meet them on a big bay gelding. When he found Culbertson, he said, "Colonel, yore party is runnin' a little late. Proceedins are already under way down on Horse Creek. Some of these tribes has been here for almost two weeks, and us with less than three hundred soldiers to police over ten thousand Indians."

He glanced at Woman Chief and the others, then continued. "If yore party will just follow me, I'll escort you to the treaty grounds."

"Thank you most kindly, Lieutenant," Culbertson replied. He signed to the Crows, Hidatsa, Arikara and Assiniboine to follow Hastings down the Platte River.

When they reached camp in late afternoon, they discovered that they had missed the council with the Sparrow Hawk delegation. Now, more than ever, Woman Chief was absolutely furious with Meldrum and Big Robber. Meldrum knew that they were coming, and he purposefully did not wait.

But she was pleased to learn that at least the chiefs had not yet marked the talking papers.

After setting up camp, Woman Chief visited Broken Hand's tent. Fitzpatrick introduced his family. "Woman Chief, I want you to meet my wife, Margaret, and my son, Andrew Jackson Fitzpatrick."

Woman Chief studied Margaret, trying to determine from which tribe she came. She could tell the woman was of mixed blood, but she dressed as a white woman, and spoke the white man's tongue. She had light brown skin and sharp attractive features. The little boy was about one season old, and though he could not yet walk, he held tightly to his mother's long dress. Woman Chief nodded to Margaret, but the woman surprised her by signing that she had heard a great deal about the Sparrow Hawk warrior. She also signed that she was Arapaho.

Fitzpatrick interrupted in Crow. "Margaret is the daughter of Snake Woman and the old French trapper, John Poisal. Her uncle is Chief Left Hand, a close friend of my adopted son, Chief Friday."

Woman Chief had seen Poisal at various trade fairs and fur forts, and she knew Friday, the young Arapaho boy that Broken Hand had saved and adopted many years ago. Broken Hand had even sent Friday to St. Louis to be educated, and now Friday was here at the peace conference as a minor chief. She had also heard of Chief Left Hand and knew of his reputation as a fine warrior.

With the introductions over, Woman Chief turned the conversation to business. "Chief Broken Hand," she pleaded, "please do not allow Big Robber and Meldrum to give away the Sparrow Hawk hunting grounds. We seek peace among the other nations, but we cannot sacrifice food for our children and old people."

He touched her shoulder gently as he spoke. "I have always been fond of the Crow. They have always been receptive to the white man, and many times they have succored me and my men. I have lost a few horses and a few plews of beaver to your overzealous young men, but your chiefs have always been honorable. I will do the best I can, but I must make peace with all of the tribes in order to prevent all-out warfare. My primary motive, however, is to protect the white wagon trains passing through this country. I am under the orders of our great white father in Washington to protect them."

Woman Chief did not know where Washington was, but all Indians knew about the mystical Great White Father. He was considered the Supreme Chief over all the people, but this concept often left her confused. "How can he be more powerful than the gods of the Sparrow Hawk people?" she wondered. "Is he superior to the gods of the Mormons and the black-robed priest?"

At last she drew her puzzled mind back to the present. She signed to Margaret in friendship, and bade Broken Hand good-by, before returning to her own camp.

At daybreak, she arose for a walk and bathed in Spring Creek. She spent a great deal of time dressing and painting vermilion into the middle part of her long, shiny hair. Since she was graying, she oiled her hair regularly with a mixture of charcoal and sunflower seed oil. Her skin was holding up well and she was still muscular and trim, but she was fifty-one winters of age now. Since her eyes could no longer see distant objects, she was vulnerable to hostile forces and had trouble locating landmarks. On her way back from taking her morning toilet, she passed by the Shoshone camp.

"Aiee! Scar Face," she called at her old friend Washakie. He immediately came toward her and grasped her arm with his, almost lifting her off the ground.

"Well," he sparked, "I see they have sent for the high chief of the Crow, to try and make peace with her before she annihilates the entire plains."

She laughed. "They asked me to have mercy on the great Snake chief. They said he is aging and I must allow him to fill out his retirement in peace." They bantered back and forth for several minutes, until they both realized that they must get ready for the peace talks.

As she arrived at her encampment, Woman Chief heard the explosion of a large gun. This meant the paper talks were beginning again, and she hurried to take her place.

The white commissioners and white witnesses sat in the center of the meadow with the head chiefs lined up in front of them. Behind each chief were his subchiefs, and in back of them stood the tribal members. Sitting beside the head chiefs were the interpreters. In all there were over ten thousand people present.

Woman Chief knew Broken Hand, Colonel Culbertson, Superintendent Mitchell, Colonel Cooper, Colonel Chambers, Robert Campbell, Gratz Brown, Father de Smet and Major Chilton.

Robert Meldrum spoke for the Sparrow Hawks, Blanket Chief Bridger for the Snakes, Gray Blanket Smith for the Cheyenne and John Poisal for the Arapaho. In addition to the interpreters, Campbell, Friday, Culbertson and Father de Smet spoke English and several Indian dialects as well as sign language. The Assiniboine head chief was Foolish Bear, and his minor chiefs were Mad Bear, Blue Thunder, First-to-Fly, Grey Eyes, Wind Blanket and The Knife.

Big Robber represented the Sparrow Hawks and behind him were Two Face, Woman Chief, Bear's Head, Rottentail and Eagle Feather. Washakie spoke for the Shoshone and was backed up by Old Basil (son of Sacagawea), Pocatello, and Bear Hunter. The latter two were hotheads.

The Cheyenne were represented by White Antelope, Red Skin, High-Backed Wolf, Black Kettle, and Rides-on-the-Clouds. Medicine Man headed up the Arapaho along with Cut Nose, Tempest, Owl, Eagle's Head, Bull, Black Coal, Left Hand, Sharp Nose and Friday, who was Fitzpatrick's adopted son.

The powerful Sioux had One Horn, Little Chief, Shellman, Goose, Watchful Elk, Swan, Ioway, Crow Necklace, Red Leaf and Painted Bear. The Arikara only had Bloody Hand and Pachtuwa-Chta to speak for them, while the Hidatsa were represented by Two Crows, Red Thunder and Pointed Horn.

The discussions proceeded toward tribal boundaries, which caused a great deal of tension among the listeners. Fitzpatrick, Bridger and Campbell were the most knowledgeable white men regarding the geography and history of the tribal claims. At last, their proposed boundaries were agreeable to all tribes. The proposal left the hunting grounds of the Powder, Platte, Yellowstone and Missouri open to all to use equally. The treaty also allowed the white men to build roads and military posts on Indian lands. It further provided for an annual delivery of $50,000 in goods to all those who kept the treaty.

Big Robber and Washakie argued over the rights to the Wind River Valley and both became angry. Meldrum finally counseled Big Robber. "Let us agree to give up the valley above the mouth of the Popo Agie, and that way the Sparrow Hawks can still have the eastern lands along the Wind River, as well as the Bighorn."

Big Robber finally agreed, but pledged, "I will never allow the Snakes to exercise their rights. I do not like Washakie and I vow to someday put him in his proper place."

Two suns later, Woman Chief watched as the Father de Smet sought to baptize everyone at the peace conference; he even baptized Broken Hand's young son, Andrew. Woman Chief carefully avoided the priest for fear of adulterating her own medicine.

After three suns, the talking papers were marked by the commissioners, witnesses, and by all of the tribal chiefs. In child-like belief, many attendees felt they were all now at peace, but Woman Chief had been lied to too many times to place much faith in a piece of white men's paper.

During the conference she stayed clear of her enemies; she even stayed clear of Washakie, whom she noticed seemed different. He seemed to be playing up to the white men in order to get his way. She thought she detected an air of power and greed in his arguments for tribal boundaries. She thought he was taking advantage of her years of Sparrow Hawk hospitality, and that left her feeling used.

Although the treaty conference had concluded, the promised trade goods had not yet arrived. People became restless and impatient, but Fitzpatrick continued to assure them that the goods would indeed come. The Arapaho, Assiniboine, Cheyenne and Sioux began holding dog feasts, but the Snakes, Hidatsa and Sparrow Hawks refused to partake in the festivities. Woman Chief and Eagle Feather took their hunters north to Thunder Basin to locate some buffalo. Although some of the Snakes followed them, the two groups avoided contact with each other. The Sparrow Hawk party hunted for two suns and returned to their camp laden with buffalo.

After feasting through the moon and another sun, word spread along the Platte River and Horse Creek. The runners announced, "They come! They come!" Everyone raced to the treaty grounds to greet the arrival of the wagons, which were pulled into a corral to control the eager recipients. Fitzpatrick began yelling orders and signing to various tribe leaders. "Big Robber, place your Sparrow Hawks over here. Washakie, take your Shoshone over there by the creek. Foolish Bear, move your Assiniboine to that grove of cottonwood. Two Crows, I want your Hidatsa by the plum thicket, next to the Crow." Colonel Culbertson took care of assigning areas to the Sioux, Cheyenne, Arikara and Arapaho.

Fitzpatrick then stood on top of a wagon to give directions. "Now, I want each head chief to come forward and receive an army uniform and a saber. In this manner, you will be recognized as the leader of your tribe. Next, I want you to assist in handing out the goods to your people, to show that the chief will provide for them. When you are dressed, you may all begin."

As the interpreters finished their explanations, each head chief moved forward. Everyone giggled and snickered as the chiefs put on the white man's uniforms. They strutted around in their new clothing, still wearing their moccasins and headdresses. They were most proud of their long knives, and began to poke at everything with them. They were also given sealed certificates of peaceful references and peace medallions. At last, the chiefs handed out merchandise to their respective tribes; it took two suns to complete the distribution of goods. After its conclusion, each tribe began drifting back toward their sacred homelands. Some were suspicious, but most were basking in a sense of false security.

Fitzpatrick decided to take Friday, Eagle's Head, Tempest, Goose, Watchful Elk, Shellman, Little Chief, One Horn, Rides the Clouds, Red Skin and White Antelope back to St. Louis with him. No one else would go. "I will take you with me on the steam dragon," he promised. "We will visit our Great White Father in Washington."

Though invited, Woman Chief had no desire to visit the white men's towns. As the entourage started downriver, she noticed that Father de Smet was also going. Quietly, she slipped upstream, away from the busy treaty grounds.

Big Robber and Two Face decided to take their bands up the Sweetwater and over the Wind River Mountains to the Wind River Valley. Washakie and his Snakes had moved out ahead of the Sparrow Hawks, and Big Robber wanted to make sure they went on to the Seedskadee instead of stopping on the Wind River.

Washakie declared. "If the Snakes stop in our valley, there will be war, treaty or no treaty."

CHAPTER 47

Woman Chief, Bear's Head, Rottentail and Eagle Feather took their bands back down the Powder. She wanted no part of Big Robber or Meldrum. The bands rested for a full moon, then started down the Elk with Eagle Feather and a small party of hunters.

At the crossing of the O'Fallon, they detected sign of a small hunting party. Since there were no other Sparrow Hawks in the region, Woman Chief concluded that they must be Pecuni or Cheyenne.

After setting up an early camp, Woman Chief spoke to the other leaders. "Brothers, we must keep a guard posted and remain alert at all times. Our enemies are near, and we are few in numbers. I'm going to keep my horse tied to my wrist while I sleep."

They kept their fire low and built it where it would be shielded by a bluff. That way the flame could only be seen across the river; they knew danger would not come from that direction. Woman Chief rode up toward the high ground of the Blue Mountains and scanned the horizon for the sign of a campfire. Maybe it was due to her failing eyes, but she did not detect anything and soon returned to her tent. But before dawn someone roughly roused her from sleep.

Eagle Feather grabbed her and whispered, "Sister, we have detected enemy wolves trying to approach our horses." She leapt to her feet and quickly checked her tethers. Dancer was standing close, legs stiff and ears straight up, his large eyes rolling around in nervous anticipation.

"Quietly," she told Eagle Feather, "get everyone armed and mounted. At first light we will charge the wolves. If they are not too many, we can surprise and demoralize them. If they are too many, we can confuse them long enough to break through their lines."

Soon all twelve of them were armed to their teeth with rifles, bows, lances and knives. As they readied to ride out, Woman Chief thought again, "I am getting too old for this. I no longer create fear in the hearts of my enemies. It is probably a good day to die." After composing herself, she raised her arm and commanded her followers, "Follow me, brave friends; follow me to victory!"

As they raced toward the high ground, a warrior rode out of the brush and raced away, but Eagle Feather quickly overtook and scalped the interloper. Suddenly, ten mounted riders raced out of a coulee and headed east into the gray dawn. The Sparrow Hawks began yelling and firing at the fleeing horsemen. They fought a running gun and bow battle until midday, when the enemy forces reached the banks of Beaver Creek.

Woman Chief left five men to keep the horsemen penned down while she and Eagle Feather led the other five in a circular route across the creek. As they came up from the rear, they charged down the bank and crossed the creek, flanking the trapped Pecuni warriors.

She recognized their leader, Iron Horn, and immediately bore down on him. She jerked his empty gun from his hands, and Dancer's broad chest knocked him down the bank. Before Iron Horn could recover, she drove her lance through his body and quickly dismounted to slit his throat. As the creek sand absorbed his life's juices, she lifted his uniquely coiffured scalp. After tying the hairpiece to her lance, she took his rifle as a trophy, then mounted the lathered-up Dancer and rejoined her men.

As she rode around, she could see that all of the Pecunis had been killed, while her men only suffered minor wounds. She had been lucky this day, but she felt very tired, so she decided to camp right there on the Beaver instead of trying to return to the Elk.

It took Woman Chief's party three more suns to reach Fort Union. By that time, she was totally exhausted and decided to rest and repair her clothing before visiting Denig and Deer Little Woman. The cold wind blowing from the Shining Mountains down the Big Muddy told her that the snow would come early this year.

Woman Chief slept late, and then went for her bath. She took her time combing her hair, painting her part with vermilion and rubbing a mixture of charcoal and sunflower seed oil into her hair. She believed that if she did not hide her gray hair, the young men would not want to follow her. When she felt presentable, she took her lance and strolled into the trading post.

She found Denig in his funny grass hat talking to a young white man. When he spotted her, he called, "Woman Chief. I want you to meet a new friend of mine. I have been telling him a great deal about you. This is Rudolph Kurz, an artist from across the great water to the east. He wants to paint you in your war dress."

She glanced at the young man and said (through Denig's translation), "I am flattered by your request, but I believe the talking pictures will rob me of my medicine. I saw it happen to Chief Light of the Assiniboine, and to Buffalo's Back Fat of the Pecunis. Perhaps it is not so, but at my age, I do not want to take chances."

Then to Denig she said, "I have just returned from a victory over the Pecuni. I will present you with the lance and the scalp of Chief Iron Horn."

Denig translated as he examined the shells and beaded bangs of his former customer, Iron Horn, chief of the Small Robes band of Blackfeet. Denig wondered if there were any Small Robe warriors left alive, but he didn't ask. "Thank you, Woman Chief," Denig said. "May I give Iron Horn's scalp to Mr. Kurz? He is collecting trophies to take back to his country and it will replace the loss of your talking picture."

She smiled, removed the scalp, and handed it to the nervous young man. She visited for several days, and talked with Kurz through Denig and Deer Little Woman. The artist made many inquiries regarding her way of life, and his eyes bulged as he heard of some of her battles. She showed him several battle wounds she had received, along with the loss of two of her finger joints.

As the snows began to fall, she bid farewell, and led her party back up the Elk. During the trip, she felt lonely. Telling Kurz of her childhood and her life with the Crow had created in her a strange longing to visit the White Clay people.

Although she did not particularly believe their peace overtures, she still wished to see them again. During her slow ride back to Absaroka, she chewed on tobacco roots and wondered how she could go back to visit her true relatives.

CHAPTER 48

When Woman Chief's trading party rejoined the Sparrow Hawk Nation, she learned the Whistling Water Clan had contracted smallpox from their contact with white emigrants on the Sweetwater River. Woman Chief knew the clan members had robbed the emigrants, but when they contracted smallpox, they received more than they had bargained for.

Big Robber had fallen into disfavor and had been banned from Absaroka by consensus of the Sparrow Hawk Council. Even Meldrum and Two Face had abandoned him. Eagle Feather and Woman Chief agreed with the decision of the Council and honored the ban. As the snow-falling season of 1853 proceeded, she learned that over one hundred fifty of the Whistling Water Clan members had succumbed to the white man's plague. Most Sparrow Hawks believed that the Great Spirit was punishing the Whistling Waters.

"My children, hear my words," preached Woman Chief. "We have always been taught to honor the white man. Whenever our people have broken that tenet, they have been punished. May you forever remember my words, as I have learned them from the legendary warriors Rotten Belly, Five Scalps, Long hair and Medicine Calf."

When the green-grass season returned to the land, the Sparrow Hawks moved from the Bighorn Basin to Horses River to get further away from the Whistling Water Clan. Two Face and Bear's Head were considered joint chiefs of the two main bodies of the Nation. Even though Woman Chief had a large lodge and her own clan, she could not become a head chief because her mother was not a Sparrow Hawk, and she lacked relatives.

Woman Chief spent the next three seasons training Black Panther, Badger and Coyote. The boys were now full-fledged Hammer Owners and eager to become warriors, even though peace had now come to the plains. The Cheyenne, Sioux, Assiniboine, Arikara, Crow, Hidatsa, Snakes and Arapaho had signed Broken Hand's peace treaty at Horse Creek. For the time being, these tribes were honoring the treaty in order to receive the government annuities.

Because the Blackfeet, Bloods, Piegans and Atsinas had been devastated by smallpox, they were afraid to come in contact with their old enemies. Many of them would not even go to the white man's trading posts for supplies out of fear of the disease.

By 1854 even the Atsina were pledging peace with the Sparrow Hawks and Assiniboines. While Woman Chief visited Fort Union, First-to-Fly spoke to her. "The Atsina people treated us to a great feast and gave us many horses as tokens of their friendship. They cry because the Crow will not visit with them. Several of their young braves are here at the trading post, and if you will allow me, I will make peace between you."

Woman Chief considered his words. "The Assiniboine have been honorable, and have kept their pledge of peace with me and my people," she said. "I trust you, my brother, and I will meet with these young White Clay braves."

First-to-Fly took her to smoke with the young men and introduced her as a war chief and councilor of the Crow Nation. They were very nervous at first, as if they were meeting a legendary goddess, but as they studied her, they realized she was an old woman in an elk-toothed dress with graying hair and failing eyesight.

Woman Chief spoke in Atsina. "Brothers, I am of the White Clay people, as you are. I was captured by the Sparrow Hawks when I was only ten winters of age. I was trained as a warrior, because I was the daughter of the great White Clay war chief, One Ear. It is true that I have fought against your fathers many times, but now I am old, and I wish for peace between our peoples. Before I die, I wish to visit my old friends and relatives among you. Come, let us be friends."

The leader of the young band was called Shining Mountain. He said, "I am the son of a great chief, and I pledge that there will be peace between our people and the Crow. In good faith, you may come with us and visit our people. We would be honored to have the great Woman Chief as our guest. We can leave in two suns."

After the parley concluded, Woman Chief informed the Greasy Mouths and Denig of her planned visit to the Atsina village on the Milk River. Denig scolded her. "No, Woman Chief! You can't do this! It is too soon and I still don't trust the Atsina."

Woman Chief retorted, "Deer Little Woman's brother, First-to-Fly, has visited them, and they gave him horses and many gifts."

Denig continued, "But they had much to gain by making peace with the Assiniboines, and they hate the Crow too much to honor a treaty. You and your warriors have humiliated them too many times. Your name is known and cursed by all their braves. He who kills you, will become a legend on the Missouri."

Woman Chief's fatigue and depression showed as she said, "I am getting very old. I can no longer wage war, and my vision is failing me. I desire to visit the friends of my childhood before I die. I also want to see peace come between our nations. This will be my legacy to my two peoples."

Denig could see she would not budge from her position, and said, "Then please take some of your best warriors with you as guards. If you show strength, the Atsina will respect you and honor their pledge."

Fatigued, she responded, "No. Eagle Feather is off hunting with his band, and the Big Dogs do not follow me anymore. I will take a few of my young warriors for their experience." She smiled and Denig shook his head, as she clasped his hands in affection, then she hugged the tearful Deer Little Woman and returned to her camp.

When she announced her intentions to her village, she could only get four young Hammer Owner apprentices to agree to travel with her. They had never seen combat, so they were eager to seek honors. They dressed in their finest clothes and gathered their weapons. Woman Chief put on her white doeskin dress, adorned with seventy-five elks' teeth. It was one of the richest dresses ever seen at Fort

Union. She took only her rifle, to obtain food, and left all of her war weapons behind.

She hugged Doe Eyes and Little Wife, and said to her boys, "Black Panther, you will become the man of my lodge in my absence. You will continue to train with the hammer and the spear until you have mastered them. Help Badger and Coyote with their shooting until they can bring down an elk or a buffalo cow. When I return, I will take all of you on a horse raid against the Pecunis. I will bring each of you a fine pony from the White Clay people." Children yelled, women cried and dogs howled as Woman Chief and her four young braves rode off to meet the Atsina warriors.

Shining Mountain waved to Woman Chief as her party approached. "Welcome to our camp, my sister," he said. "You are just in time. We are eager to return to our home on Porcupine Creek."

Woman Chief vaguely remembered that creek. She could hardly wait to see her childhood home. She wondered how Little Feather had done. Since his father had been a head chief, surely Little Feather must be a chief by now. He probably had sons and grandsons, and he too, must be getting old like her.

For four suns, everything went well on the trip. The Sparrow Hawks relaxed. Then the leader of the group, Shining Mountain, turned up a creek before they reached the Milk River. Woman Chief questioned him. "Why do we turn up this stream? We have not yet come to the Milk River."

Shining Mountain smiled disarmingly and answered quickly. "This is the Little Porcupine. By ascending here, we can cut across to our village on the Porcupine and save half a sun's travel." Woman Chief studied the sun and horizon, deciding that his words seemed to make sense. For a time she was alert, but as they progressed to the west fork of the stream, she relaxed. Shining Mountain led them west across the plain, toward Porcupine Creek.

As dusk fell, Shining Mountain called for a halt and set up camp in the open prairie. Woman Chief did not like being in open ground like this, but since they were so close to the main village of the White Clay people, she again relaxed and joked with her young braves.

They hobbled their horses and left their rifles in their saddle scabbards. After much talk and laughter, they slept in their robes near the open campfire. The moon was full and the stars were as numerous as the buffalo during the green-grass season.

In the middle of the night, Woman Chief felt sharp pains in her back and sides. She realized that someone was repeatedly stabbing her. Because her arms were pinned to the ground, she could not reach her own knife. She felt her body becoming soaked by its own fluids, and she began losing consciousness. Her mind screamed, "Little Feather! Help me! I love you, Little Feather."

As her world became fuzzy, she had visions of Five Scalps, Rotten Belly, Long Hair, Medicine Calf, Eagle Feather, Badger, Coyote and Black Panther. Her last thought was, "Oh, Great Chiefs and friends, all our spirits will meet again in the happy hunting ground in the sun." Then she went to sleep.

Jerry A. Matney with D. A. Gordon

220

EPILOGUE

Shining Mountain was ecstatic. He trembled in the aftermath of his treacherous deed. The young men scalped the fallen Crows, and he and his young braves raced their horses into the White Clay village. They excitedly dismounted in front of the grand chief's lodge.

"Father!" Shining Mountain exclaimed. "I have just killed the great Crow warrior, Woman Chief. We have killed her entire party, where they had camped in order to spy upon our village. They must have been scouts for their main war party. I give you, my father, my very first Crow scalp to remind you of my deeds on behalf of our people."

Chief Little Feather handled the long graying hair and noticed that charcoal came off on his fingers. "If this old warrior was truly Woman Chief," he thought, "she had been trying to hide her age." He figured she must have been older than he because it seemed he had been hearing of her exploits all his life. He wondered if she had known his childhood sweetheart, Shining Sun, in whose memory he had named his son.

His heart felt pained as he remembered his friend's capture by the Crow about forty-five winters ago. He still felt guilty about her capture, and he wondered if she still lived, maybe as a slave, among the Crow. "Perhaps the young bucks raped her and used her up before she reached adulthood," he pondered. "I guess I will never know."

The old Atsina chief sighed and placed his hand on the shoulder of his only son. "Shining Mountain," he offered sadly, "I am proud of you for defending our village. However, we have been trying to secure a peace with the Crow for many snows, and now we have lost all chance for peace. You have killed their beloved Woman Chief, and now they will hunt you for the rest of your life in order to exact revenge. I am sending you to live with the Cree on the Saskatchewan. Think on your actions, and make reason of your judgments. Make your heart pure, and when it is safe, I will send for you."

Shining Mountain walked away bewildered. He thought, "My Father is old and has strange ways. When you find an opportunity to kill an enemy, you must act," he reasoned. "I do not fear the Crow. After all, I have just killed their greatest warrior with my own hands. My legend will live among the White Clay people forever, and I will become a greater chief than my father has been."

His mind soared irrationally as he prepared for his long trek to live with the Cree. What he still did not know was that he had been banished from the White Clay People for life.

For years the Crow attacked and raided the Atsina to avenge the loss of their beloved warrior, Woman Chief.

THE END

GLOSSARY

A'caraho

In Crow the word means the Mountain Crow or "where the many lodges are."

A-ra-poo-ash

Chief Rotten Belly of the River Crow.

Absaroka

The Crow called their home Absaroka and were sometimes called the Absaroke or Absaruke people. They referred to themselves as the Sparrow Hawk people. The French word and the English translation erred by interpreting their name as "Crow."

Alcaldes

This name is Spanish for the mayor or civilian head of a Spanish or Mexican mission district in the New World. Sacagawea's son, Jean Baptiste Charbonneau, served as a guide for the Mormon Battalion in 1846-47 and was appointed the Alcalde of San Luis Rey Mission in Oceanside, California in 1847.

Algonquin language

The language of the Arapaho, Blackfeet, Cheyenne, Atsina, and Plains Cree.

American Fur Company

Company created by John Jacob Astor, the most powerful fur company in the United States.

Astorians

Wilson Price Hunt led an American Fur Company overland expedition to the Pacific Coast in 1811-12 to establish trade with the Far East. The trading post was named Astoria and the members of the expedition were called the "Astorians." The project failed due mainly to the War of 1812 with the British.

Apache

This tribe was composed of the Chiricahua, Jicarilla, Mescalero, San Carlos, White Mountain, and Kiowa-Apache tribes. They lived in the Southwest plains and spoke an Athapaskan dialect.

Arapaho
Speaking an Alogonquin dialect, the Arapaho lived in the Upper Platte River country. They were closely allied with the Cheyenne tribe.

Arikara
A war-like tribe which lived in earthen lodges along the Missouri River. They spoke a Caddoan dialect and were related to the Pawnee tribe.

Atsina
This tribe lived on or near the Milk and Saskatchewan Rivers in northern Montana and Alberta, Canada. They were also called the Gros Ventre of the Prairies as well as the White Clay People. They spoke an Algonquian dialect, were an offshoot of the Arapaho, and at times were allied with the Blackfoot Confederacy.

Bannock
A branch of the Northern Paiute tribe, these people dwelled in southeastern Idaho. They spoke a Uto-Aztecan dialect and were usually allied with the Snake River and Mountain Shoshone.

Bateau
A light boat with a flat bottom, tapered at both ends.

Big Horn Hot Springs
This famous spring is now called "Thermopolis" and is located in northern Wyoming on the Bighorn River. Its temperature ranges between 128 and 130 degrees Fahrenheit and it flows at three million gallons per day. As the heated water evaporates, it leaves large mounds of travertine deposits that resemble ice floes. Where the hot water enters the Bighorn River, temperatures vary from very hot to cold the farther you get from the flow. Today several commercial bathhouses and a state park are located at the spring.

Big Muddy River
Many Indians and early mountain men referred to the Missouri River as the "Big Muddy."

Blackfeet
The Algonquian-speaking Blackfoot Confederacy consisted of the Piegan, Blood and Northern Blackfeet or Siksika tribes. They controlled the upper reaches of the Missouri River, its tributaries, and the Saskatchewan River region of Alberta, Canada. They were friendly with the British but hostile to Americans and were constantly at war with the Crow.

Bois d' arc
> This wood is also called Osage orangewood. The Plains Indians favored it for bow-making. The tree has a white, sticky sap and is easily identified by its large green apples.

Calumet
> The long, ornamental smoking pipe of the Plains Indians was usually made from a red stone quarried in Minnesota. The pipestone was named "Catlinite" after the painter of North American Indians, George Catlin.

Cayuse
> A tribe that resided in the northwest and spoke a Penutian dialect. They were related to and allied with their neighbors, the Nez Perce. Like the Nez Perce, the Cayuse were excellent horse breeders.

Columbia Fur Company
> This fur company was founded and administered by Kenneth Mackenzie for trade in the Rocky Mountains. In 1828 the firm was taken over by John Jacob Astor's American Fur Company.

Comanche
> Allied with the Kiowa, this tribe also spoke a Uto-Aztecan dialect and lived on the south plains. Excellent horsemen, they were very warlike.

Corps of Discovery
> President Jefferson set forth the secret Lewis and Clark Expedition in 1803 and called the project "The Corps of Discovery." He led his enemies to believe that Lewis and Clark were sent to explore the Mississippi River. Instead they were to explore and map the new Louisiana Purchase and to find an overland route to the Pacific Ocean.

Coulee
> A deep ravine or gulch.

Delaware
> A northeastern tribe who spoke an Algonquian dialect. They scattered after their defeat by General Anthony Wayne in 1795. Many joined the Rocky Mountain fur trade companies as "free trappers."

Diggers
> This was a derogatory term applied to the horseless, desert Shoshone tribes who dwelled in the area of Nevada and California. They spoke a Uto-Aztecan dialect.

Elk River
> The Crow Indians called the Yellowstone the "Elk River."

Erarapi'o
> The Crow name for the "Kicked-in-their-bellies," a branch of the Mountain Crow. They generally lived in the Wind River region of Wyoming.

Foofooraw
> The mountain men used this term to refer to gaudy trade items desired by the Native American women.

French Fur Company
> Founded in the Upper Missouri country in 1829, it consisted of the French families known as Papin, Chenie, Cerr'es, Delaurier, Picotte, Guion, and Bonfort. The firm had assets of $16,000.

Gewgaws
> A mountain man term for gaudy trade items preferred by Native American women. A gewgaw is usually an ornament.

Hidatsa
> Relatives and most often allies of the Crow and Mandan. They spoke a Siouan dialect and lived near the Mandan in earthen Lodges on the Missouri River in North Dakota. They were also called the Gros Ventre of the Missouri and Minitari (or Minetaree).

Horses River
> The Crow used this name to refer to the present day Pryor Creek.

Kinnikinnick
> Term used for Native American tobacco mixed with sumac leaves and the dried inner bark of red alder, dogwood, or red willow.

Latter-Day Saints
> These people were also referred to as Mormons. They lived in the Utah Territory. They kept good relations with most of the Indian tribes of Utah, Idaho and Wyoming.

Leaf-falling season
> Fall of the year.

Mackinaw boat
> A large, flat-bottomed boat with a stern rudder-sweep. Some had masts for sails and a superstructure for passengers.

Mandan
> A tribe of Siouan-speaking people who lived in earthen lodges on the Missouri River in North Dakota. They traded agricultural products to the Crow for horses, clothing, furs and robes.

Medicine Wheel
> Built by unknown, prehistoric people, the wheel lies prone in the northern portion of the Bighorn Mountains of Wyoming. The wheel has 28 spokes and is about 250 feet in diameter. Some Crow believed the wheel had mystical powers.

Missouri Fur Company
> Following on the heels of the Lewis and Clark Expedition, Manuel Lisa, William Morrison, and Pierre Menard founded the Missouri Fur Company in 1807. They built Fort Raymond (or Fort Manuel) at the mouth of the Bighorn River in order to trade with the Crow. Later they expanded and called the firm the St. Louis Missouri Fur Company. Lisa died in 1820 and the firm ceased operations in 1825.

Mohave
> This tribe spoke a Yuman dialect and dwelled on the Colorado River area of Arizona, California and Nevada.

Mormons
> Also known as Latter-Day Saints, these people settled and established the Utah Territory in the middle 1800s.

Muddy River
> Another name for the Missouri River.

Nez Perce'
> This Penutian-speaking tribe lived in Idaho, Oregon and Washington. They excelled in horse breeding and horse trading. They were credited with developing the Appaloosa horse and were allied with the Cayuse, who were also excellent horsemen. Nez Perce' in French means "pierced noses."

North West Company
> Founded in 1784 to rival the Hudson's Bay Company, the British government forced the two firms to merge in 1821.

Obsidian
> This is a black, hard lava glass that the Indians flaked or chipped to create arrow and spear points. It would not rust and tests have shown it to be sharper than steel points. Obsidian points penetrated animal flesh deeper than steel. The great Obsidian Cliff is located at the headwaters of the Yellowstone River in Yellowstone National Park.

Osage Orangewood
This wood is also known as *bois d' arc* and proved excellent for making bows. It was well used by the Plains Indians.

Parfleche
This is a Canuck-French word meaning "rawhide." Native Americans and mountain men used animal skins laced together to hold food, clothing, and personal effects. They folded the skins or hides like an envelope and many were elaborately decorated.

Pawnee
A Caddoan-speaking tribe, the Pawnee lived in the area of Kansas and Nebraska. They were housed in dome-shaped earthen lodges with an outer covering of grass and leaves.

Pecuni
The Crow used this name to refer to the Piegan tribe of the Blackfoot Confederacy.

Pemmican
Buffalo or other game meat cut into long, thin strips and dried. The hardened jerky is then pounded into powder and mixed with pulverized, fresh berries. Suet is poured over the mixture, which is then stored or sealed in parfleches or rawhide casings. The product could be traded as a commodity or kept as a nutritious food during the hard, cold winter.

Piegan
An Algonquin-speaking branch of the Blackfoot Confederacy. They lived in northwestern Montana and southern Alberta, Canada.

Pierced Nose
The French meaning of the name for the Nez Perce' tribe.

Plains Cree
A branch of the Kristinaux tribe who speak an Algonquian dialect. They dwelled in large areas of central Canada.

Pompey's Pillar
A stone tower located on the Yellowstone River approximately 25 miles northeast of Billings, Montana. William Clark named the tower in honor of Sacagawea's son, who was nicknamed "Pomp" This name meant "first born" in Shoshone.

Possibles
A mountain man term referring to personal effects.

Pine Leaf
The Crow name given to Woman Chief when she was captured from the Atsina at age 10. In 1856, Jim Beckwith documented her exploits in his book, *The Life and Adventures of James P. Beckwourth.*

Pox
A slang term referring to the dreaded smallpox disease.

Rocky Mountain Fur Company
Firm established in 1822 by General William H. Ashley. He made a fortune and sold out to his men, Smith, Jackson and Sublette. In 1830 they sold the company to Fitzpatrick, Bridger, Sublette, Fraeb and Gervais. The firm went out of business in 1834.

Seminole
This tribe originated from the Muskogean speaking Oconee of Georgia. They relocated to Florida about 1750. They were at war with the U. S. Army from 1817 to 1818 and from 1835 to 1842. Jim Beckwith fought in the Seminole War around 1838 and 1839.

Shining Mountains
Several tribes referred to the Rocky Mountains as the Shining Mountains.

Shoshone
A Uto-Aztecan-speaking tribe, the Shoshone were allied with the Bannock and at times with the Crow. They were also called the "Snake Indians" and various bands roamed from the Yellowstone National Park region, Wind River Valley, Green River and Bear River. They were usually friendly with the white trappers.

Shining Sun
This is the birth name given by the author to Woman Chief when she lived with her native tribe, the Atsina.

Snake
Because sign language for Shoshone resembled the movement of a snake, they were referred to as the Snake Indians. The river that the main tribe lived on is still called the Snake River. They spoke a Uto-Aztecan dialect.

Snow-falling season
This refers to the winter season.

Sparrow Hawk
This is the true name of the Crow Indians. The French name and English translation misinterpreted the name as "Crow."

Throwing bones
An Indian gambling game of tossing marked bones with a basket or with sticks.

White Clay People
The name the Atsina called themselves. They were also known as the Gros Ventres of the Prairies.

Woman Chief
The adult war chief name given to Pine Leaf as reported by Edwin T. Denig in his 1856 book, *Five Indian Tribes of the Upper Missouri.*

INDEX

St. Louis, 51, 115, 139, 152, 206
St. Vrain, 202
Stillwater, 95
Stillwater River, 77
Stinking Creek, 21
Stinking Water River, 109
Sun, 49
Sun Dance Ceremony, 56
Sun Dance lodge, 57
Sun River, 50, 96, 123
Sutter's Fort, 204
sweatlodge, 39, 44
Sweetwater River, 42, 133, 144
Taos, 174, 202
Ten Sleep Canyon, 68, 157
Ten Sleep Creek, 206
Teton, 49
Teton Dakota, 80
Teton Sioux, 48, 51
Three Forks, 65
throwing bones, 21
Thunder Basin, 80, 137
Timpas Creek, 133
tobacco, 204
Togwotee Pass, 109, 160
Tom Fitzpatrick, 97
Tongue River, 12, 48, 50, 138
Toussaint Charbonneau, 45
trade fair, 170
Tulloch Creek, 185

Union Pass, 108, 109, 146, 153, 173
Utes, 102, 103, 144, 174, 201
Walkara, 174, 201
Walla Walla River, 202
War Horse Lake, 27, 42, 197
Warm Springs, 169
Washakie, 148, 151, 211, 212
White Clay, 197, 218, 221
White Clay People, 3, 36
White Earth River, 188
Whitman Mission, 202
William Clark, 44, 51, 110
William Henry Harrison, 127
William Sublette, 71
Wilson Price Hunt, 38
Wind River, 12, 42, 133, 140, 205
Wind River Canyon, 44, 127
Wind River Mountains, 42
Wind River Valley, 41, 174
Wind Rivers, 102
winter trading, 132
Wolf Creek, 161
Woman Chief, 117, 157, 170, 218
Yaquis, 174
Yellow Belly, 33, 48
yellow-grass season, 17
Yellowstone River, 12, 39, 137
Yellowstone tribes, 208
Yellowstone Valley, 146
Zenas Leonard, 108, 123

About the Authors

Jerry A. Matney spent over a decade researching the life of Woman Chief, including interviewing members of the Crow tribe. Jerry's paternal great-grandmother, from North Carolina, was Cherokee. For 34 years Jerry served the Orange County, California school district as an educator and school principal. He also served a term as Mayor of Huntington Beach.

Jerry is now working on *Five Scalps*, a historical novel about a famous black mountain man who also became a chief with the Crow tribe. Jerry now lives in Arizona with his wife, Nedra.

D. A. Gordon is a computer consultant, instructional designer, teacher, writer, editor and Webmaster. She has taught on the Navajo reservation in both Utah and Arizona. She started helping Jerry with *Woman War Chief* after teaching at his school in Orange County.

Ms. Gordon plans to publish two of her books early next year. Born and raised in northern Utah, she currently lives near Moab in southern Utah.

For more information about the historical novels, *Woman War Chief* and *Five Scalps*, you can visit these Internet sites:
http://womanwarchief.com and http://fivescalps.com

Printed in the United States
828200004B